Pretty

Picture

"Elizabeth Little is part of an exciting new generation of crime writers who have been bending this sturdy genre into new, unexpected shapes. *Pretty as a Picture* is a glorious buffet – a twisty story, a cinephile's delight, a knockout of a heroine. I loved it"

Laura Lippman, author of *Sunburn*

"Funny, fast-paced, and a pleasure to read"

The Wall Street Journal

"A valentine to the intoxications of filmmaking and film-viewing"

The New York Times Book Review

"Elizabeth Little's fantastic new book is part parable of the film industry, part feminist thriller, and part ode to the rise of the true crime podcast"

CrimeReads

"Elizabeth Little has an impeccable ear for dialogue and a sharp eye for detail, and she's created a page-turner that is as well written as it is captivating. I enjoyed every scene and sentence of this glorious book"

Steph Cha, author of *Your House Will Pay*

"One of the year's most anticipated thrillers"

Bustle

Elizabeth Little is the author of *Dear Daughter*, which won the Strand Critics Award for Best First Novel, and two works of nonfiction, *Biting the Wax Tadpole* and *Trip of the Tongue*. She lives in Los Angeles with her family.

ELIZABETH LITTLE

Pretty as a Picture

PUSHKIN VERTIGO

Pushkin Press
71–75 Shelton Street
London WC2H 9JQ

© Elizabeth Little, 2020

Originally published in North America in 2020 by Viking,
an imprint of Penguin Random House LLC

First published by Pushkin Press in 2021

1 3 5 7 9 8 6 4 2

ISBN 13: 978-1-78227-701-9

Epigraph © David Mamet, 1989, *Speed-The-Plow*, Methuen
Drama, an imprint of Bloomsbury Publishing Plc.

Designed by Gretchen Achilles

Offset by Tetragon, London
Printed and bound by CPI Group (UK) Ltd, Croydon, CRO 4YY

www.pushkinpress.com

For Annabel and Robyn

Life in the movie business is like the . . . beginning of a new love affair: it's full of surprises, and you're constantly getting fucked.

—*David Mamet*

They say a picture's worth a thousand words.

That's not what I'd say.

I'd say it depends on the picture. I'd say it depends on the size and the color and the subject and the print and the framing and the focus and the composition. I'd say it depends on what you were doing the hour before, the day before, the year before, the life before. I'd say it depends on whether you're looking at it on a wall or scrolling past it on a screen or cutting it carefully out of a book, digging your knuckle into the gutter of the spine because the margins are so small and the blades are so long and it's impossible to get a straight line, but you don't want to dig up a guide and an X-Acto knife because you aren't willing to wait, you have to have it, you have to have this picture, right now, and your kitchen scissors are close enough and good enough—yes, *good enough*—and Jesus Christ, Marissa, when will you get it through your thick head: Imperfection is a price happy people pay to cradle the weight of something they love.

That's what I'd say.

But I understand some people prefer the cozy imprecision of "nice round numbers," so I'm willing to pretend, for the moment, for the sake of argument, that a single picture is indeed worth one thousand point zero zero words exactly.

It would follow, then, that two pictures are worth two thousand words.

A hundred pictures, a hundred thousand words.

At that rate it wouldn't take too many pictures before you'd have in front of you all the words there ever were in all the world and more besides, more words than anyone could thread together into anything resembling sense.

Think about that the next time you go to the movies.

If you want to trick the human eye into believing a series of pictures represents continuous motion—what first-semester film school students learn to call "persistence of vision"—you're going to need to present your audience with about sixteen frames per second. More, if you'd like, but no fewer.

Sixteen. Not round, but still a number people like to hang on to. It's often said that 16 FPS was the standard frame rate in the silent film era, but that's wrong—there was no standard. Those cameras were hand-cranked, and directors varied the frame rate from scene to scene depending on the rhythm that suited their story. But once talkies came along, picture had to sync to sound, and since then, the frame rate used in movie production and projection has been 24 FPS, with a few exceptions I won't let myself go into, because according to Amy no one wants to hear what anyone thinks about *Billy Lynn's Long Halftime Walk*.

By this reckoning, at eighty-five minutes, your average movie is made up of 122,400 frames. So if a picture's worth a thousand words—well, that average movie must be worth 122,400,000 words.

One hundred twenty-two million.

In the wrong hands, that's too much. Too much information, too much possibility. No one can find a signal in all that noise. You might as well eat a library. You might as well drink a dictionary. You might as well ask an actor how they're feeling.

That's why they come to me. The editor.

Give me enough time. Give me enough space. Give me a dark room and a roll of film, a Steenbeck, a Moviola, an Avid NLE, a director with a vision and an actor with some craft.

Give me an X-Acto knife and a guide.

Give me this, and I'll do all the things with pictures I can never do with words. I'll slice and stitch and lace and weave and cut and wipe and fade. I'll crack open the body of the beast and slip my hands beneath its beating heart.

Give me a movie and I'll find the meaning; I'll find the truth; I'll find the story.

Sometimes, if I'm very lucky, I'll find all three.

ONE

Not that I manage to say any of that out loud.

Of course I don't.

Sometimes I think everything wrong with my life can be located in the space between what I should have said and what actually came out of my mouth. No matter how hard I try, no matter how well I prepare, the right words are, for me, forever out of reach. Not because they catch in my throat. A cat hasn't got my tongue. None of the usual phrases apply. It's a more comprehensive kind of collapse. When faced with any real conversational pressure, my personality just goes offline, AWOL, and no matter how hard I try, it doesn't respond. Catastrophic system failure.

Speak, I tell myself in those moments. *Speak*.

Like I'm Uma Thurman in *Kill Bill*, lying barefoot in the back of that truck, gritting my teeth and trying to force my insubordinate body to bend to my iron will.

Speak.

But I'm not Uma Thurman in *Kill Bill*. I didn't train with Gordon Liu. I don't know the Five Point Palm Exploding Heart Technique, and I don't have the body to pull off a yellow leather motorcycle suit. So I never get my toe to move. I never drive that truck to Vivica A.

Fox's house. I never get revenge and I never find my daughter. I just starve to death in a hospital parking lot.

And in real life, when asked to explain to a potential employer why I'm the best candidate for a job I desperately need, I don't deliver a rousing monologue about the exhilarating, all-encompassing, soul-shifting, life-shaking power of cinema. Instead I just comb my fingers through my ponytail for the seventeenth time while mumbling something about my work ethic.

Then, to top it off, I shrug—I *shrug*—and I say:

"I just really like movies, I guess."

My agent makes a sound so pained I'm genuinely worried I might have killed her.

I don't know what else Nell expected, it's been six years since I've had to look for work. Six years since Amy hit it just big enough that we could coast from feature to feature to feature without having to hustle for work we hated in the interim. It took some doing—the plumbing in the Mid-City two-bedroom we shared was more vague promise than functional reality, and six nights a week we ate rice and beans we bought in bulk—but eventually she was able to stop taking AD gigs; I was able to stop doing TV. We found a rhythm that worked for us, postproduction bleeding into preproduction and back again, and if I didn't have time for a social life, I wasn't particularly bothered: I got to live and work with my very best friend.

But last month I decided it was time to start thinking about getting my own place, and Amy and I put the new movie on hold so we could figure things out.

It didn't take long to realize that blowing up my personal and professional lives all at once wasn't exactly the smartest thing I could have done. For about three days it felt freeing. But then I ran out of new-release movies to see.

And so, this afternoon, I found myself pacing the inadequate length of my short-term rental in Burbank, restless, anxious, fingers fluttering at my sides. I had finally managed to work up the nerve to send a few emails to old colleagues, hoping I could pick up an episode or two of I truly didn't even care what, but either they didn't remember me or they were all out to lunch or Gmail was down for everyone but me.

By two p.m., my nerves—already frayed by the arrival of my credit card statement—drove me to a desperate act: I made a phone call. I left a message for my agent explaining that Amy and I were taking a break, that I needed a job, and, therefore, that I might actually be willing to take her advice for once.

I should have known something was fishy when she called me back right away.

"You have a meeting," she said.

"Who with?" I asked.

"Don't worry about that. Get here by six, I'll take care of the rest."

"Today? At rush hour?"

"You want a job or not?"

"*Nell.* Have they even seen my reel?"

"Don't worry about that, either."

"The more you say that the more I worry."

She sniffed. "Worry, don't worry, either way this is the only open assignment that isn't scraping memory cards for *Transformers 7.* So if you want it, be here at six." She paused. "And maybe do something with your hair."

She hung up without saying good-bye, and I wished, not for the first time, that I were an agent, too.

Imagine being able to end a conversation whenever you want.

When I arrived at Nell's office—ten minutes early, despite a slow-down at Coldwater and Mulholland—I still didn't have a clue what I was walking into. Nell hadn't mentioned a script or a story or even a logline, so my best guess was that she'd arranged for a late-day meet-and-greet with a producer too green to know this was a below-the-line agency. As a strategy, it didn't make much sense: Nell knew my personality wasn't my strongest selling point. I figured she was planning to keep the meeting short.

Nell gave my ponytail a tug when she saw me. "You got this," she said, all historical evidence to the contrary.

And that's how I found myself sitting here, across the table from two agents, three lawyers, and an important studio executive, interviewing for a job I know absolutely nothing about.

I obviously forgot the important executive's name immediately. I think it has a "y" in it, maybe? He's wearing chunky statement glasses and a plain black T-shirt that probably cost more than my car payment. He's the picture of bland, reflexive courtesy, steepling his fingers and leaning forward in his chair, nodding at every third word no matter what that word is.

After more than a decade in the film industry, I can confidently assert that this particular demeanor indicates one of the following:

1. measured enthusiasm
2. catatonic boredom
3. a recent corporate-mandated webinar on best listening practices

I suppose it could be worse.

I blink his face back into focus. I think he's finally saying something relevant.

"—coming in this late in the game is somewhat less than ideal, obviously, so what we need here is a quick study."

My eyebrows go up. "And you called *me*?"

"Well," he says, "we've been told there's no one better at watching footage and knowing exactly what the director's trying to say."

"It helps that they usually give me a script."

The executive beckons to one of the assistants stationed along the back wall. She pulls out a folder and hands it to him. He slides it across the table toward me.

Inside is a photo. Glossy, eight by ten.

"That's not a script," I point out.

"No," he agrees. "It's a still. And I want you to tell us what you see."

I draw a breath, preparing to explain to the room at large why this is a terrible way to gauge an editor's skills (for a start, my job is putting pictures together, not picking them apart), but then I catch a glimpse of the photo, and because at heart I'm just a dog who happens to be into a very particular type of squirrel, this is all it takes to send my thoughts racing off in a new direction.

It's a medium close-up of a young woman asleep on a beach, and the first thing worth noting is that she's being played by Liza May, Oscar-anointed ingenue and the reigning, relatable queen of the "Stars, They're Just Like Us!" social media sphere. Last time I saw her, I think she was waxing her mustache on Facebook Live.

So this is a big-time job. For a big-time director. No wonder Nell was so responsive.

The second thing worth noting is that the woman is dead.

Her body occupies the left half of the frame, visible from the shoulders up, the straps of her neon orange swimsuit the only discordant shade in an otherwise tranquil palette. Her hair is silky, taupe and raw umber and dark blond, streaked by the sun. It falls in layers over her cheek; one strand teases at the corner of her mouth. Her eyebrows have been thinned out, which makes her look older than she is, but she's barely wearing any foundation, which makes her look younger than she is. Her skin is smooth and very clear.

She's lying on a weathered wooden beach chair with a white canvas cover. Her arm is stretched out over her head, her cheek pillowed against her right biceps, her profile radiant in the golden light of a late summer afternoon, that time of day when the angle of the sun and the particles in the atmosphere do what a reflector or bounce board can never quite match, what color grading can't quite pull off.

"Well?" the executive asks. "What do you think?"

"I think magic hour's a nice time to die."

The executive adjusts his glasses. "How do you know she's dead?"

"Well—" I draw out the word as long as I can, buying time to reverse engineer my own thinking. It's been a while since I've had to deconstruct the gut certainties that make me good at my job.

I stare at the picture until my eyes start to water, searching for something, anything that might help me stand out. Eventually my finger lands on a faint line that slices vertically through the frame, just past the edge of Liza's chair.

"The split diopter," I say.

"Explain," he says.

"It's a half lens you stick on the end of the camera if you want to keep two different planes in focus at the same time—like bifocals, but for the movies. So we have Liza here, in the foreground, and then all these beachgoers, there, way far away in the background— but they're both in focus, right? That wouldn't be possible without a split diopter. I wish people used it more often, but I guess De Palma kind of beat it to death back in the seventies and eighties, and now it's not—"

The executive holds up a hand. "Yes, I know what a diopter is, thank you."

My mouth snaps shut.

"What I'm wondering is how that tells you she's *dead*."

I sneak a glance at the door. "You know, I'm not the best at putting this stuff into words. Maybe I could just show you my reel?"

Nell wraps her hand around my wrist and whispers in my ear.

"Robots, Marissa. *In disguise.*"

"I get it," I say, and even I can tell my voice is tight and unfriendly. I edge my chair away from the table until I have enough room to jiggle my foot without accidentally kicking anyone. After a few seconds of this, I'm able to explain myself. "Since this is a studio movie, it's a safe assumption the crowd's being kept in focus because they're an important part of the scene. Because we're waiting for one of them to notice Liza—to find her. The prospect of discovery, that's what's driving the tension here. It wouldn't be dramatic if she were just taking a nap."

The executive props his elbow on the back of his chair and pushes his hair back from his forehead. "You're certain of that?"

I consider the shot again. "I guess it's possible the director just thinks it looks cool—"

Nell kicks my chair.

"—but either way, she's definitely dead."

The executive studies me over the rims of his glasses. "You're the first person to bring that up. Everyone else said the white lips were the giveaway."

"No, I wouldn't trust this makeup department."

"Why not?"

I point to Liza's face. "In the summer, someone with her coloring would freckle. They gave Liza a spray tan, obviously, but the cosmetician adjusted the color, washed it out—probably because her blood would already be pooling in her lower extremities, so she'd be paler than normal. Livor mortis, right? But dying doesn't make your freckles disappear. They should have painted some in." I brush my fingertip along her cheekbones. "Right now she looks too much like a movie star, and you don't want that, not when you're doing true crime."

The executive is frowning now, two small lines etched between his eyebrows, and it occurs to me that dragging their makeup department was not, perhaps, the best way to win this job.

Well, at least Nell won't be able to say I didn't try.

I open my mouth to thank them for their time—

"What makes you say it's *true* crime?" the executive asks.

I glance back down at the photo. Why *did* I say that?

"Judging by the costume design, it's a period piece—midnineties, probably? And I figure it's based on a true story because—yeah, the color hasn't been corrected or graded, I know, but the overall palette is so deliberate and carefully curated. Meanwhile, that swimsuit she's wearing is just . . . unbelievably orange." The answer comes to me the second before I say it. "So I'm thinking, probably, it's the same suit the real girl was murdered in."

"Hold on," he says, "I never said she was murdered."

"That just stands to reason. Why else would you make a movie about it?"

Now, I may not be a crackerjack conversationalist, but I'm something of a connoisseur of silences. You can, roughly, separate them into two groups: the kind of silence where everyone's looking at each other and the kind of silence where everyone's *not* looking at each other. Personally, I prefer the latter. If there's going to be cruel laughter, I'd rather it be out of earshot.

The silence that just settled over this room, however, is an extremely undesirable third variety:

Everyone's looking at something *else*. Namely, the speakerphone in the center of the table.

Which means they're scared.

Then there's a crackle of static, and a voice comes over the line, sealing my fate.

"She'll do."

Note: Dead Ringer *is produced for the ear and designed to be heard, not read. We strongly encourage you to listen to the audio, which includes emotion and emphasis that's not on the page. Transcripts are generated using a combination of speech recognition software and Suzy's little brother and may contain errors because lollll, guys, this is not* This American Life. *Cut us some slack.*

SUZY KOH: Hi, everyone, I'm Suzy Koh—

GRACE PORTILLO: And I'm Grace Portillo.

SUZY KOH:—and welcome to this week's episode of *Dead Ringer*, the true crime podcast for people who hate true crime podcasts.

GRACE PORTILLO: Seriously?

SUZY KOH: What?

GRACE PORTILLO: I don't know, that just seems, like, unnecessarily divisive.

SUZY KOH: Fine. It's also the true crime podcast for people who love true crime podcasts.

GRACE PORTILLO: Okay—

SUZY KOH: And for people who only kinda like them. And for people who don't even know what podcasts are—but that's okay, Grandma, I still love you. [*pause*] Did I miss anyone? Or is that inclusive enough for you?

GRACE PORTILLO: Oh my God.

SUZY KOH: Right, so when we left off last week, Tony Rees's big-deal dead-girl drama had just hit a snag, losing its highest-profile crew member to date—

13

GRACE PORTILLO: Not that anyone on the production staff would admit what had happened.

SUZY KOH: The excuse the producer gave at the time was that Tony and his editor had parted ways—

GRACE PORTILLO: Right—"creative differences." Which doesn't even make sense! They weren't even editing the movie yet!

SUZY KOH: Yeah, but we didn't realize that then. We'd never been on a film set before.

GRACE PORTILLO: What was the crew's excuse?

SUZY KOH: Probably something to do with not wanting to be fired?

GRACE PORTILLO: Oh. Yeah, I guess that makes sense.

SUZY KOH: So we begin today's episode with the arrival of Marissa Dahl.

> **GRACE PORTILLO:** Marissa, thanks so much for agreeing to speak with us.
>
> **MARISSA DAHL:** And thank *you* for agreeing to stop leaving me voice mails if I came on.

SUZY KOH: Marissa's a film and TV editor best known for her work with Amy Evans, the award-winning director of *Mary Queen of the Universe* and *All My Pretty Ones*.

GRACE PORTILLO: Best known until *recently*.

SUZY KOH: Well, right. *You* probably know her as the woman who cracked two of the biggest murder cases of the year.

ollywood has just two speeds, "We'll get back to you" and "We need this yesterday," and as soon as the speakerphone clicks off, we skip straight past the slow torture of the former and into the unforgiving maw of the latter. The lawyers and agents are all talking rapidly, all at once, about all the things I pay them to think about for me.

"I assume our previous deal memo stands."

"I'm happy to reopen the discussion of residuals."

"I'm happy to reopen the discussion of her quote."

"Her quote's her quote, Steve."

There's an assistant—who can say whose—at my side, tapping on two phones simultaneously, peppering me with questions I barely manage to register, much less respond to.

"Burbank or LAX? Nonstop on American or a layover in Chicago on United? Aisle or window? Six o'clock or seven twenty?"

"There's nothing tonight?" the executive asks.

I frown. *"Tonight-*tonight?"

The assistant chews her lip and flicks furiously at her screens. "No—last flight's at nine forty-five. She won't make it."

"Excuse me, I'm sorry, but are you talking about me right now?"

The executive peers at my agent. "Nell, you sure we can't send her coach?"

She shrugs. "If you think you can find a better candidate, go right on ahead."

The executive sighs and nods to the assistant. "Book the six a.m. We'll have our guy meet her there."

What is happening? Where am I going? Why is everyone acting like we're launching a military campaign? I glance around the room, but no one appears to be treating this as anything unusual. "Hello? Is anyone going to explain any of this to me?"

The executive spares me the briefest glance. "You're going to set."

I make a face like I've smelled something sour. "Why? Let the assistant editors handle the memory cards; I'll get everything set up here for post."

He waves a hand dismissively. "There are no assistant editors. Tony doesn't trust them."

One of the lawyers drops a pile of contracts on the table in front of me and tries to hand me a pen.

I swat the pen away. "I'm sorry, did you say . . . *Tony*?"

The executive freezes. He swallows, his Adam's apple dipping behind the crew neck of his overpriced tee. Then he lifts his head and looks somewhere past my left shoulder.

"Oh, didn't we mention that? Tony Rees—he's the director on this picture."

Live in LA long enough and you're bound to lose your sense of wonder.

I didn't grow up in a backwater—not by any reasonable standards—but even so, for a kid in Champaign-Urbana, seeing a celebrity was a big deal. I can still remember the envy and astonishment that rippled through me when I heard that one of my class-mates had seen Jennie Garth at the supermarket with her mother.

And Jennie Garth's *from* Champaign-Urbana.

After nearly fifteen years here, though, celebrities are just part of the scenery, another thing to not notice on the drive home, and I don't know what I hate more about my indifferent attitude, the cynicism or the way it sidles right up next to Hollywood cliché. But even so, very occasionally I'll cross paths with someone so special that those endless, breathless dissections of a five-second glimpse of the back of Jennie Garth's head make perfect sense again, and for a moment I'll remember how obscenely lucky I am to be in this business.

Like when Dede Allen smiled in my general direction. Or Agnès Varda shook the hand of someone standing next to me. Once I was introduced to Thelma Schoonmaker, and it turned out she already knew my name.

Then there's the time I fell into a fountain with Tony Rees.

I didn't feel so lucky then. It was two years ago, and I was at the Venice Film Festival with Amy. She was accepting an award, and she'd insisted I come with her. *We're a team*, she said. *You deserve this, too.* And I was too much of a coward to say no, so there I was, hiding out in the hotel courtyard, enjoying the symmetry of the colonnade, the palm trees that reminded me of LA, the sky. There was a bench in one corner, but I was walking the outline of the fountain: three sides of a rectangle, two sides of a triangle, three sides of a rectangle, two sides of a triangle.

It was a particularly good pattern. Sometimes, if I walk just the right way—at just the right speed, with just the right gait, in just the right direction—I can lull my worst thoughts into submission.

I was warm, I remember. And relaxed. Happy, maybe.

Then someone cleared his throat.

I recognized Tony immediately, but I know not everyone would. He's an average, inconspicuous white man in most respects, mid-forties, neither tall nor short nor fat nor thin. His hair isn't mousy or mahogany or sun-streaked or whiskey-colored. It's just brown. He has no visible scars, moles, or birthmarks, and only one tattoo: his daughter's name, on his forearm, in blue script.

Two things set him apart, though.

First, his eyes, which everyone says are strikingly green ("bottle-glass green" is the usual descriptor, though this seems uselessly expansive to me). They're vivid enough you can guess their color even in the solemn, black-and-white portraiture glossy magazines are forever commissioning of him.

Second, he never speaks louder than a low, intimate murmur. Not ever. Not in interviews, not on commentary tracks, not at awards shows, not even—as anyone who has ever worked with him will tell you, in vaguely stunned tones—on set. No matter the situation, Tony talks to you like he's inside you.

That's how Amy once described it, anyway. I'd just say he's kind of hard to hear.

How the most exacting director in Hollywood manages to make his movies without raising his voice is one of the great mysteries of show business.

We were separated that day by the reflecting pool, a comfortable enough distance that I didn't mind looking directly at him. He was dressed in jeans and a chambray shirt, the cuffs rolled back, three buttons undone. His tan stopped at his neck, tracing a line where a T-shirt would normally lie; below that, settled into the hollow of his throat, was the silver disc of a St. Christopher medal.

He was watching me, tapping his chin absently with one long finger, his right elbow propped on his left fist, and I can still taste the bile that burst on the back of my tongue when I realized what was happening. This wasn't the second lead on a network sitcom or the star of a new Verizon campaign. He wasn't waiting for fro-yo or prodding figs at the farmers' market or blocking the pasta aisle at Von's. This was one of America's most celebrated directors, a man whose work I admired deeply.

And he wanted to talk.

Or at least he looked like he wanted to talk. He wasn't showing any of the usual signs of impatience: His feet weren't shuffling; his gaze wasn't skipping around. But he wasn't saying anything, either.

Then, I felt it. A growing pressure behind my breastbone, a sensation I knew all too well. I sent up a last-second prayer: *Please God, whatever I'm about to blurt out, let it be sophisticated. Clever. Astute. About one of his earlier, lesser-known films. About a technical detail that would give me the chance to demonstrate my own expertise. About, at the very least, the weather.*

But God apparently had other things on His plate.

"Did you want to talk to me or did I just happen to wander into your line of sight?" I asked.

His finger stilled. His mouth moved. And his next question was so patronizing it took me a moment to register what he was asking.

"Did you just ask if I'm here for the *festival?*"

He nodded.

Dammit, I thought, *I knew* I was too short to wear this jumpsuit. Amy had been very clear that I needed to make an effort, an impression, that I couldn't just wear comfy pants and a tank top—"This is *Italy,* Mar"—so I'd gone shopping in Silver Lake before we left. I don't know much about fashion, but the girl who sold me on the jumpsuit was wearing oversized sneakers and jeans up to her armpits, so I thought I could trust her.

Just how ridiculous did I look? Did I need to worry that he was going to call security? Did I need to show ID? Pull up my IMDb page?

Ultimately, I did the only thing I could think to do under the circumstances—I didn't like doing it, but I didn't see any other way to establish my credibility.

I dropped a name.

"I work with Amy Evans," I said.

Sure enough, Tony's shoulders drew back and his gaze glittered with new interest.

Might've just been the sun, though.

"I'm a fan," he said, lightly.

I wasn't sure what to say to this. Obviously he was a fan. He was the president of the jury that had just awarded Amy the Silver Lion.

"She's very talented," he went on.

I guess I couldn't quite hide my disbelief, because he let out a low grunt of surprise.

"You don't agree?" he asked.

"I'm just not sure why you're telling me things I already know." My eyes caught sight of a single gull crossing the sky. I had to wait for it to disappear from view before I could return my attention to Tony. "But I guess you can't help being a director."

One of his eyebrows lifted, and an image of Joaquin Phoenix in Roman regalia, his thumb just tipping toward the ground, flashed before my eyes. Tony Rees, I remembered then, could destroy a career with a single phone call—with a single look.

Could and would and had.

But that day, for reasons I still don't understand, he chose instead to be amused.

His laughter was softer than his speech, softer even than the silky burble of the courtyard fountain, and I took a step closer, listening for the hard, tight tone that would mean he was laughing at me, not with me. When I didn't hear it, I caught myself wishing—fiercely enough that my pulse skipped at the thought—that he would be called away on some urgent matter so I could count the conversation a marginal success. The laws of probability were not on my side.

"Who are you?"

"Amy's editor."

"That's not what I asked."

"Then you should have been more specific."

"Oh?"

I explained it as delicately as I could. "Given the context, it stands to reason that the most useful and telling personal detail I could provide would be my area of expertise. You don't want to know my life story or who my favorite bands are."

"And if I do?"

"Then you're out of luck, because I mostly listen to white noise."

"*Anton*—"

We turned toward the sound. A few feet to Tony's left, framed perfectly by the doorway, stood a bird-boned woman in a crisp white dress, her arms akimbo, honeyed hair billowing in a breeze that appeared to blow just for her.

Annemieke Janssen, the hugely popular star of several of Tony's movies, and also his wife.

She's extraordinarily beautiful. Delicate. Ethereal. I'm guessing when she gave birth to their daughter, the only sound she made was a single, exquisite gasp.

Tony's lips pressed together. "Just a second," he said.

I plucked at the waistline of my jumpsuit and tried not to stare as he made his way to Annemieke.

I couldn't hear what they were saying, but even I could tell Tony wasn't pleased—his expression hadn't changed, but a muscle in his jaw was twitching. Annemieke, however, seemed unconcerned. She kept admiring the toe of her navy stiletto then looking back up at Tony from under her lashes. When she swept her bangs off her face, she used her pinky finger.

I peered down at my own hand, twisting it, palm out, extending my pinky. I lifted it halfway to my forehead before deciding I couldn't pull it off. I would just look like I didn't know how a normal human female pushed back her hair.

With each passing moment, I grew increasingly antsy, ever more certain I'd misunderstood him. He'd said, "Just a second," but maybe "just a second" didn't actually mean "wait a second" or "hold on a second" or "I know this sounds crazy, but would you please stay here while I get rid of my gorgeous wife, one of the great actresses of her generation, as I find myself oddly intrigued by your inability to apply eyeliner or track a conversation, and I'd like to know more."

Maybe "just a second" was the new "good-bye," but the *New York Times* Style section hadn't gotten around to telling me.

Was I wrong? Was he watching me out of the corner of his eye, wondering what I was still doing there? Were they talking about the awkward girl in the ridiculous outfit? Were they laughing at me?

And if they were, did I care?

Part of the calculus of being me: weighing discomfort against opportunity.

I decided to risk it. A small measure of humiliation was nothing if it meant Tony Rees might remember me the next time he was hiring. In this business, I can't afford pride. Not with my social skills.

So I waited. Soon, my feet led me back to the path around the fountain.

Three sides of a rectangle, two sides of a triangle, three sides of a rectangle, two sides of a triangle.

After two laps, my heartbeat slowed. My shoulders settled. And then—*there*—that twist of relief just behind my breastbone, like I'd unfolded a kink in a line, and my niggling sense of not-quite-rightness fell away. When I came back around to Tony's side of the pool, I walked directly into a cloud of Annemieke's perfume, and I was so relaxed I paused to catalog the notes: peach, violet, something that reminded me of Amy's favorite Moroccan restaurant. In that moment, not even synthetic fragrance could bother me.

I was so lost in my thoughts when Tony tapped me on the shoulder that there was really only one way for it to go: I startled, tripped, and threw out my arms to catch myself. But the only purchase available was the slender metal chain around Tony's neck.

And that's how I literally dragged the director *Film Comment* called "the first great filmmaker of the twenty-first century" down with me.

Into a fountain.

This is a disaster.

That last part I do manage to say out loud.

Nell's head whips around, and her face falls for a split second before she recovers. She levels a bland smile at the room. "Can I speak privately with my client, please?"

The suits and their assistants jump up, clearly happy to have an excuse to leave the room. As soon as they're gone, Nell leans back in her chair and crosses her legs. She does me the favor of not pretending not to know why I'm concerned.

"You did say *any* job," she points out.

"I meant any reasonable job."

"Editing a two-time Best Director seems pretty reasonable to me."

I pull my feet up on the chair and wrap my arms around my shins. "He's going to hate me."

She shrugs. "So?"

"Who am I replacing?"

Nell checks her notes. "Paul Collins."

"Do we even know what happened to him?"

"Death, destruction, Scientology—who knows, who cares. It didn't work out. And now they're desperate. They've been interviewing every unemployed feature editor in town." Her lips thin with annoyance. "I would've brought you in earlier if I'd known you were available. Could've saved me a hell of a lot of time, Marissa."

"I don't want to be somebody's rebound girl," I mutter.

"But wouldn't he be your rebound guy?"

I glare at her over my knees. "Amy and I didn't *break up.*"

She puts up her hands. "Of course not."

"And don't take everything I say and parrot it back to me in a cute, pointed tone. That's annoying. This isn't a script."

Nell uncrosses her legs and reaches forward, tugging my hands into hers.

I'm feeling bad about my behavior, so I let her.

"Marissa, listen. This is the perfect job for you right now. Setting aside the fact that it's a classy fucking gig, no one on earth will blame you if it goes badly. This is *Tony Rees* we're talking about."

"You're saying it's a *good* thing he's impossible to work with?"

"It's only, what, three months of your life?" She squeezes my fingers. "What's the worst that could happen?"

"I honestly don't even know where to begin with that."

Her grip tightens. "And anyway, it's too late to turn back now."

I look up. "What do you mean?"

When she smiles, it's even blander than before. "These people really don't like it when you say no."

GRACE PORTILLO: What's your process, generally, when you take on a new movie?

MARISSA DAHL: Well, on a big feature like this, typically I'd spend a few weeks working with the script, meeting with the director and the script supervisor and the rest of the editorial department. Then my assistants and I would be on hand during production, compiling a rough assembly cut as we went, and we'd be ready to hit the ground running once we got to post.

GRACE PORTILLO: But you came into this job knowing absolutely nothing about Caitlyn Kelly?

MARISSA DAHL: I'd never heard of her.

SUZY KOH: And you didn't think to google it?

MARISSA DAHL: With the information I had?

SUZY KOH: I'm just saying, if I were making a movie about a real-life murder, I'd kind of want to know a little bit about what happened.

MARISSA DAHL: Of course I *tried*. But I didn't have any details. At that point, I didn't even know her name. And looking up "dead girl movie" doesn't exactly narrow it down.

THREE

You don't even know what it's about?"

"They wouldn't give me a script. They made me sign a sixteen-page NDA before they'd tell me the *title*."

"Which is?"

I take a beat. "'Untitled Anton Rees Project.'"

Amy laughs, and satisfaction fizzes through me. I'd been thinking through the rhythm of that remark all morning. Sometimes when I try to tell a joke, it's like I'm pedaling a bike with a broken chain—but I got it this time.

It's nice to have one thing go according to plan.

I've been on the road for nearly three hours now. I was met in Philadelphia by my driver, a strikingly handsome black man with a shaved head and an impeccably tailored suit. His name's Isaiah, and he has legs for arms. He's the kind of guy Amy likes to call a brick shithouse, which I suppose must be accurate, because Manohla Dargis once wrote that Amy has a "gimlet eye for the vagaries of the human condition," but now that I'm saying this I realize I don't know for sure if it's meant to be an insult or a compliment because yes, brick shithouses are almost certainly more expensive and impressive than wooden shithouses, but still: They're *shithouses*.

He's big is what I'm saying.

"Let's roll," he said when he saw me, and that was it for conversation, which was fine by me.

At first.

But about ninety minutes in, my nerves took over. I wondered, is Isaiah not a casual talker? Or can he tell that *I'm* not a casual talker? Or maybe he was just waiting for me to say something first, and now he thinks *I* think I'm too good to casual-talk to him, and yeah, yeah, I know what *you're* thinking, there she goes again, that Marissa, always making mountains out of molehills. But, see, once the mountain's there, I can't simply *undo* it. Either I have to give it the respect a mountain deserves or wait eight to ten years for it to shrink back down to size.

And anyway, what was I supposed to do? Say hi? Ask him how his day was going? After almost *two hours*? No can do. He'd know I was only talking to him because I'd *realized* I was being weird. At least this way I have some plausible deniability on my side.

It wasn't until I could no longer trust that I wouldn't start saying this to him directly that I pulled out my phone and waved it in his direction.

"I'm so sorry," I said. "I have to make a quick call."

Then I smiled what I hoped was the smile of someone who really doesn't think they're any better than anyone at all, and I dialed the only person other than my mother who always answers my calls.

"Where are you shooting?" Amy asks.

"A *sixteen*-page nondisclosure," I remind her.

I guess this is still funny, because she laughs again.

"Ballpark, then."

I turn to the window and squint into the distance. There isn't much to see. A little grass, a few trees, a gas station every ten minutes or so. Nothing with a recognizable name. Still, I can make an educated guess: It's a quarter past seven, so it's been about two and a half hours since we left the Philadelphia metro area. And we're traveling at exactly 55 miles per hour, heading south, which means—

"I think I'm in Delaware?"

There's a pause.

"Well—at least you'll be spending most of your time in a windowless room."

"It's only six weeks," I say. "We'll be done by Labor Day."

"Did they tell you that before or after you signed the contract?"

"Before. But Nell—"

"And Tony's last film took how long to finish?"

I make a face. "That was a three-hour Balkan war drama."

"How do you know this one isn't?"

"I don't think you can shoot Dover for the Dardanelles."

"You sure about that?"

I don't need Amy to reiterate the concerns that have been running through my mind since I boarded the plane early this morning, so I try to find a way to wave her off.

"It's a good gig," I say.

"Of course it is."

A seemingly straightforward answer, but I've wrecked my ship on these particular shoals before. So I play her words back a few times, running them through my very precisely calibrated Marissa You Might Be Missing Something detector.

Did she say, "Of course it is."

Or maybe, "Of course it is!"

Or, God help me, "Of *course* it is."

Is she being sarcastic? Patronizing? Does she not want me to take this job? Is she mad about something else? All of the above?

Nothing throws me for a loop quite like a simple sentence followed by a pregnant pause.

On the other end of the line, Amy is packing her books. I can make out the hollow slide and scrape as Amy folds a cardboard flap into place. The rippled croak of tape pulling away from the roll. A rhythmless *thump . . . thump thump . . . thump . . . thump*.

I pick at the stitching of the car's leather upholstery. I really should have shown her how to pack them properly (line the box with crushed paper; sort the books by size; stack them spine to spine), but I can't say anything. Not now. Not after the text messages her boyfriend's been sending me. Because I refuse to give Josh the satisfaction of knowing that he's right, that I *am* holding Amy back, that I *am* selfish, that I *am*—in this one tiny but frankly pretty benign way—trying to keep them apart, and yes, it's true, I *do* think he's an only slightly better than average director of photography.

Maybe that's what she's angry about. Maybe Josh finally told Amy what she should've realized years ago: that I'm a pretty terrible person to be friends with.

I draw my lower lip between my teeth and bite down until I taste blood.

I met Josh at a Wong Kar-Wai retrospective—at a screening of *In the Mood for Love*—and at the time I thought it was one heck of a meet-cute. Just imagine: finding the love of your life at the most romantic movie ever made—even though, okay, Tony Leung and Maggie Cheung don't actually get together in the end, but that makes it even more romantic, right? Regardless, taste that good goes a long way.

It wasn't until much later that I discovered he wasn't a real fan at all; he was probably only there to pick up women. But I didn't know that then. I just knew a man with eyelashes so long they cast shadows on his cheeks was smiling at me like I was a girl who knew what she was about.

It did occur to me that if you viewed it from a certain angle, our conversation looked an awful lot like a general meeting: a mostly uninspired interaction between very loosely affiliated people that ultimately comes to nothing. I talked about what I was working on, he talked about what he was working on; I talked about my favorite movies, he talked about his favorite movies. But Amy always said generals were just first dates with an only slightly smaller chance of getting laid, so I thought: *Maybe.*

For someone like me, maybe's more than enough to build on.

A week later, I saw him at *Happy Together.* He was scanning the crowd, and his eyes stopped when they landed on me, and I thought: *Maybe.*

At *2046*, we sat together, his forearm whispering against mine, and I thought: *Maybe.*

And when he even showed up to *My Blueberry Nights*, I thought: *Okay, more than maybe.*

I was the one who introduced him to Amy, and isn't that a way-homer. But I was reckless with something warm and unfamiliar, so I invited him to Amy's birthday party, a party I wouldn't have even gone to except it happened to be at our apartment. It didn't occur to me to label him anything other than "a friend." Before I knew it, they were on the other side of the room, sitting on the blue velveteen couch she'd scavenged off a side street in West Hollywood, their heads bent together.

I'd always hated that couch.

I could see pretty quickly where things were headed, and I thought I was more or less resigned to it. But then I went into the kitchen for a Coke, and Josh was there, mixing drinks. And when he turned around, smiling, a red plastic cup in each hand, I thought, wildly, *What if I just haven't been clear about this? What if he just doesn't know?* So I plucked up my courage and leaned forward and pressed my mouth against his. His lips were warm and dry, and he was still smiling when I pulled away, but before I could say anything, Amy was poking her head through the door, asking where her drink was.

The next night, I went to see *Chungking Express*.

Josh wasn't there.

And I thought: *Maybe not.*

Why haven't I told Amy? A few reasons. First, I was embarrassed. I'm *still* embarrassed.

Second, I owe her. She's put up with me for years, and if she'd known I had a crush on him, she never would have gone out with him, no matter how she felt. And look! I was right! He *is* the one for her. They're moving in together. He's happy, she's happy, they're happy.

Third—

(I'm not proud of this one.)

I like having Josh around. Any affection that might have sprung up between us went rotten as soon as we realized we were competing for Amy's attention, but then the strangest thing: hating Josh was even better than liking him. He made me so mad I forgot to overthink things. For the first time in my life, I found myself able to bat back a text with something that looked like spirit, no matter that he was usually asking me to give him and Amy some fucking space already, *Jesus.* So what if his responses dripped with disdain? At least they were prompt. At least they weren't indifferent. I was so accustomed to nothing, I was ravenous for absolutely anything.

I knew that, even then. I just couldn't stop myself.

It's possible to be so lonely you'll latch on to the littlest thing, and yes, maybe that's sad, maybe that's pathetic and desperate, but isn't that better than forgetting how to latch on to anything at all?

That's not a rhetorical question. I really wish I knew the answer.

By the time I figured out what I was secretly hoping for—when I looked back at my browser history and realized I'd been reading exclusively enemies-to-lovers fanfic for *months*—it was too late to do the sensible, mature thing and tell Amy the truth. I announced instead that I'd finally saved up enough for a down payment on a place of my own, and I floated the idea that it might be time for her to consider moving in with Josh.

I'm so lucky I got out of there before she guessed what was going on.

But maybe that luck's run out. Maybe she finally heard something in my voice that gave it away, that unlocked it all, the corkboard in *The Usual Suspects*, the perm in *Legally Blonde*, the inconsequential everyday object that proves to be the key to the whole goddamn mystery—

No. This isn't a movie. Amy's a grown-up who goes to therapy twice a week. She talks about her feelings *all* the time, and she loves me, she says so, she squeezes my shoulders until I say I believe it. She would tell me herself if something is wrong. She promised she would tell me herself if something is wrong.

Plus, she laughed at my joke.

She must be upset about the job.

"Is there something you want to tell me?" I venture, hesitantly.

She doesn't answer immediately. I put my hand over my left ear and press the phone hard against my right. It's nearly impossible to figure out what Amy's feeling just by looking at her. She has a face like a cat's: You can tell if she's sleepy or surprised, but that's about it. The language of her features is limited.

When we first met in film school, when I couldn't tell if she wanted a friend or just someone to help with her thesis project, I tried to gauge her mood using everything I'd taught myself about facial features, about body language, seeking out clues in the angle of her elbows, the slope of her smile, the cardinal orientation of her feet.

"Is there something on me?" is a question she asked a lot back then.

After several months of trial and error—mostly error—I finally realized Amy's secrets are in her sounds.

When she's anxious, her jaw clicks.

When she's excited, her voice dips, counterintuitively, into a low rasp of a register.

When she's annoyed, her breath hisses through her teeth.

When she needs to tell you something, something sad, something bad, when she can't fully commit to the direction she wants the words to go, you can hear a soft flutter: the back of her tongue flapping against her epiglottis.

When she's absolutely outraged—well, then she'll stop breathing entirely.

Which is a real problem, because that's a hard thing to listen for.

Right now I can't hear her at all. Just the hum of the engine and the whir of the fan and the slight crackle that's been on every call since I dropped my phone in a snowbank in Park City. This might be it. She might be as angry at me as she was at that manager who told his teenage clients he needed to supervise wardrobe fittings, and she's going to banish me from her orbit as fast as she did him, and—

Her exhalation is rough and open-throated, from deep in her chest, and when I register the sound, I let out a great, gasping breath of my own. Thank God: This is the sound Amy makes when she's angry *for* somebody.

"I'm worried Nell's not telling you everything," she says.

"Why would she? She's my agent."

A pause. "Just—it's a lot, what you're walking into. That's all. It's been a long time since you've done a feature with anyone but me, and big changes are, well—"

I finish the thought so she won't have to. "Aren't really my thing."

Another pause. My fingers tighten around the phone.

"Well," she says brightly, "No point second-guessing now. You'll just have to call when you get in, let me know how it's going."

"Of course—"

"Promise?"

"*Yes.*"

"Even if you get your hands on dailies?"

I know better than to agree to that. "I'm hanging up now."

"Knock 'em dead, babe."

"Gosh, I hope not."

A last pop of static and she's gone.

FOUR

rub my nose a few times and turn to look out the window. We've left the highway and are now passing through the mixed business and residential district of a smallish town. On the left is a filling station, a firehouse, a Presbyterian church. On the right, a series of neat two-story houses, some blue, some a pale dusky green, their front gardens filled out with phlox or hostas, depending on their orientation. Nearly every house has a porch-mounted pole and an American flag. They're not so different from the house I grew up in, except our flag hangs from a pole in the front yard.

Just like this project won't be so different from my last one, no matter what Amy might think. A few things might be moved around, that's all.

A windowless room's a windowless room's a windowless room.

Which reminds me: I need all the vitamin D I can get. I let my body list a little to the left so I can catch the last rays of sunlight slanting through the rear window. I soak up the warmth for a few happy minutes, but then my smile settles into a sour crook, and an emotion I can't immediately identify needles at my cheeks, at my feet.

I close my eyes and try to figure out what movie I'm thinking of. Josh accused me once of having *The Film Encyclopedia* instead of a heart, and he would have been right if *The Film Encyclopedia* hadn't been four years out of date at the time. Ever since my family got our first VCR, movies have been all I can remember—and I mean that more literally than you might imagine. For years we only owned two movies: *The Right Stuff*, which my parents saw on their first date, and *Herbie Goes Bananas*, because my mother figured a preschooler wouldn't be interested in a 192-minute historical epic about the space program.

She was incorrect.

If you do the math (and I have), you'll find that between the ages of four and seven, I spent about the same amount of time watching *The Right Stuff* as I did going to school, and sometimes I wonder if all that repetition crossed my wires. To this day there are times I'll see a random photo, and I'll feel a flash of recognition—a happy sunburst of *hey, I've been there!*—only to realize seconds or even minutes later that no, I haven't been there at all, it's just Edwards Air Force Base. It's like if Proust bit into that madeleine, but instead of flashing back to his childhood, he saw Sam Shepard breaking the sound barrier.

It's possible I've spent so much time watching movies that the language of film has infiltrated some primal, necessary part of my brain. I catch myself processing my own emotions in scenes, in shots, in dialogue. Like when there's a burn in my sinuses and a sick clench in the back of my throat, but my brain doesn't supply a single word (*sadness*). Instead, it offers up a two-second clip from *Terms of Endearment*: *Huckleberry Fox, inconsolable, at Debra Winger's bedside*.

It isn't easy, or efficient, or necessarily clear. It would be much simpler, certainly, if I'd only seen a handful of movies, and if those movies had been directed by Steven Spielberg. Maybe then my emotions would be more manageable, more straightforward, a line instead of a scatter plot. But like Josh said, I have a whole encyclopedia up in there, and Huckleberry Fox at Debra Winger's bedside is very different from Troy Bishop at Debra Winger's bedside is very different from Shirley MacLaine at Debra Winger's bedside.

I press my ring fingers into the corners of my eyes and try, once again, to figure myself out.

Eventually, it comes to me:

A man in a bathroom. He's sitting on the counter next to the sink, one knee pulled up to his chest so he can fit his foot under the faucet. He's barefoot, bleeding, shirtless.

His walkie-talkie crackles.

"I'm here, John."

He lifts the radio to his face.

"Look," Bruce Willis says, "I'm starting to get a bad feeling up here."

So that's what this is.

Foreboding.

My eyelids snap open.

"Isaiah."

His head tips in my direction. "Hmm?"

"Where are we going?"

A rumble of something that might be laughter. "I was wondering if you were ever going to ask."

My ears heat. I knew it. I *knew* he'd notice. "I'm sorry—I'm not so good at talking to strangers."

"Well, not much point asking now." He lifts his index finger from the steering wheel and angles it in the direction of the horizon. "We're almost there."

My stomach tries to crawl out my mouth.

"That," I say, "is the ocean."

"What gave it away? We're booked on a seven forty-five ferry."

"You didn't say anything about a boat."

He shrugs. "You didn't say anything about hating boats."

My right foot flexes upward. I press it back down.

"Is there any other way to get where we're going? A long way around, maybe?"

"Depends—did you pack a swimsuit?"

I slump in my seat. "An island. Even better."

His gaze snags mine in the rearview mirror. "If it's a problem, I'm happy to call Tony directly. I'm sure he'd love to hear all about it."

His eyes are crinkled at the corners—is he laughing at me? Does he think this is funny? Is he really that kind of person? Or does he think *I'm* kidding. That this is a bit. That maybe I make a habit of playing at neurosis or clumsiness or hysteria to ease the discomfort of men in the presence of a more accomplished woman, and *God*, that might actually be worse. I'm not playing at anything—and I *don't* think I'm more accomplished than he is. *No one* should be intimidated by me, I'm a disaster. Not that I can tell him that. Because if I say I'm a disaster, it will seem like false humility, like I don't think he can handle—

When Isaiah pulls into the ferry terminal parking lot, my thoughts are still stuck in the same loop, and in my haste to get out and into the fresh air and maybe to run in the opposite direction, I shove at the door of the SUV—which slams straight into Isaiah, who I hadn't realized would be coming around to help me. I lean toward him without thinking, so when the door rebounds off his whiskey-barrel chest, it wallops me in the face. If there's a metaphor in there, I'm in too much pain to put my finger on it.

A phrase I haven't used in years pops out.

"Mothersmucker."

I fumble around for my nose to make sure it's still intact and wipe a tear out of the corner of my eye.

Isaiah kneels down and nudges my hands away from my face. He takes my chin between his thumb and forefinger and turns my head this way and that in a manner that makes me think he knows what he's doing. It occurs to me that it's very nice of him to look after me when I just tried to kill him with a car door, so I force myself not to pull away.

I do close my eyes, though. I wouldn't be able to cheat by looking at the tip of his ear or at his eyebrows. Not at this distance.

After a moment, he pinches my nose and gives it a wiggle. I open my eyes. He's taken a few steps back, giving me space.

"You'll be fine," he says.

"I'm sorry," I mutter.

The corners of Isaiah's eyes crinkle again, even though this time I *know* I didn't say anything funny. I check my clothes again out of habit, but they're all in the right place, and I haven't had the chance to spill anything on them, so what is it? Did I pull a face? Did I make a noise? Did I do something weird with my hands?

What off-putting thing did Marissa do this time? The perpetual riddle of my days.

I rub at my sternum, no less aggrieved by the knowledge I'm being irrational. "You could apologize, too."

He crosses his arms and looks down the bridge of his nose. "What do I have to apologize for?"

I tip up my chin. "For being a brick shithouse."

His laughter this time is rich and full-throated, and I'm so struck by the sound, it takes me a full thirty seconds longer than it should to remember what we're doing here.

I look past Isaiah, out to the water.

Mothersmucker.

Even as a child, even back when I could still stand swimming, I never liked the ocean. All the water did was chap my lips and tangle my hair, and the sand never stayed where it was supposed to.

I don't like chapped lips.

I don't like tangled hair.

I don't like things that don't—

"Is it boats you've got a problem with or water?"

I make myself turn back to Isaiah. "Water," I say.

"You don't swim?"

I slip my hands into my pockets to still them.

"Sometimes swimming's not enough."

"Stick close," he says. "You'll be fine."

It's more than likely I'm just desperate for a distraction, but his words—slow and certain and not too loud—set me thinking, and before I know it I'm taking a step back to get a better look at him, ignoring the way his eyebrow quirks at the inspection. At the airport I hadn't had much reason to make a study of his face or posture or frame, but now I see how he holds himself: His shoulders are back, his knees are slightly bent, and he's keeping all his weight on the balls of his feet.

A few years back, I cut a mob drama that used off-duty cops as extras, so I think I know what's going on here.

"Are you ex–law enforcement or ex-military or ex-something you can't even tell me about?"

He thinks this over. "The second one—and a little of the third."

I chew on the inside of my cheek. I've figured out over the years that a response like this—quippy, vague, delivered with pursed lips and an indifferent shrug—is more often than not a polite way of saying "I don't want to talk about this." I know I should respect that. I should move on. But my mind has a way of latching on to questions, like a dog with a bone. A wagon with a star. A Kardashian with a revenue stream. The only thing that'll work it loose is an answer.

Admittedly, it doesn't have to be the *right* answer—

Harrison Ford considers the golden idol in front of him, weighing the bag of sand in his hand.

—just a plausible one.

"Are you a security guard?" I ask.

Isaiah sighs. "Something like that."

"And now you're a driver?"

"Among other things."

"Do you carry a gun?"

"When I need to."

"Are you *paid* to be evasive?"

"No—I just like it."

Inside my pockets, my fingers curl against my thighs.

"Why would a mid-budget feature employ an ex-"—I squint at his neck—"Marine?"

He shakes his head very slightly.

"Ranger?"

He rolls his eyes.

"SEAL."

His smile is slow to come on, like he's enjoying the feel of his mouth moving into place. Like it's more about the journey than the destination.

A SEAL. Good lord. I can't believe I thought he was just a driver.

I can't believe he *knows* I thought he was just a driver.

Not that there's anything wrong with being just a driver! *Jesus.*

My hands scrabble for my ponytail; I comb my fingers through the ends.

"So what *have* you been hired to do?" I ask into my shoulder.

"You know that sixteen-page NDA you signed?"

I look up. "Yeah?"

He cups a hand around one side of his mouth and stage-whispers, "Mine was twenty."

SUZY KOH: Marissa, I'm curious—

MARISSA DAHL: I've noticed that, yes.

SUZY KOH:—do you often find yourself working with Navy SEALs?

MARISSA DAHL: I guess, yeah. Ex-military get hired all the time in Hollywood—consultants, security, stunt men, what have you.

GRACE PORTILLO: So you didn't think it was strange that Isaiah was working on the movie?

MARISSA DAHL: I didn't say that, exactly. But given what I knew at the time, I wasn't expecting the kind of action sequences that might require military expertise. [*pause*] That said, this *is* Tony Rees we're talking about.

GRACE PORTILLO: What do you mean?

MARISSA DAHL: I mean, I could easily imagine a man like Tony thinking he needed a Navy SEAL on hand for—for any number of things. He's an extraordinarily successful director. He gets to do stuff like that.

SUZY KOH: Ask for dumb-ass shit?

MARISSA DAHL: I'm not sure that's precisely the term I'd use, but . . . yes.

SUZY KOH: And let me guess, the more dumb-ass the shit, the more powerful he is if he gets it?

GRACE PORTILLO: Right, 'cause, like, any normal could get a *regular* driver.

SUZY KOH: Ugh, totally.

MARISSA DAHL: Have you seen *Fitzcarraldo*?

SUZY KOH: Fitzcarr-what-now?

SUZY KOH: Marissa does this a lot—references random movies from eight million years ago.

GRACE PORTILLO: It's not *that* old.

SUZY KOH: Oh yeah, I know, I just said that because I know it'll annoy Marissa.

MARISSA DAHL: You've never heard of it?

GRACE PORTILLO: No.

SUZY KOH: It's probably black-and-white, huh?

MARISSA DAHL: [*extremely audible sigh*]

SUZY KOH: I mean, let's be honest, I say a lot of things because I know it'll annoy Marissa.

MARISSA DAHL: It's a Werner Herzog film—from all the way back in 1982. Klaus Kinski plays a guy trying to drag a 320-ton steamship over a muddy hill so he can build an opera house in the Amazon rain forest. And instead of mocking it up or using a model, Herzog ordered his extras to *actually* drag a 320-ton steamship over a muddy hill, even though his engineer told him there was a 70 percent chance the cables would snap. He put lives at risk. Hundreds of them. Just to get a shot he wanted. And to this day people still praise him for that decision.

SUZY KOH: But here's the thing about Marissa's extremely niche references: They always have a point.

MARISSA DAHL: So, honestly, I don't know if there's anything Tony could have requested that would have struck me as "strange." He's the director. If you'd told me before I arrived that he'd Amazon Prime'd a grizzly bear bell choir for the opening credits, I probably would've shrugged and said I looked forward to seeing the dailies.

regret to inform you the ferry won't be repaired until tomorrow morning at the earliest."

We're in the terminal gift shop, where Isaiah's rapidly losing his patience with the elderly cashier. According to her badge, her name is Georgia, and her skin looks like my fingers after a long bath. She's garish, a rainbow: blue hair, orange lipstick, splotchy pink cheeks. I fiddle with the straps of my backpack and try not to let my eyes linger inappropriately on any one color.

She speaks entirely in monotone.

"If you'd like to reserve space on tomorrow's ferry," she says, "we will, of course, give you a discounted fare."

"I'm afraid that won't work," Isaiah says.

Georgia lifts her chin so she can look down at Isaiah through her green half-glasses.

"Nevertheless," she says.

"Another boat, then."

A twitch of a heavily penciled eyebrow. "At this time of night?"

"We need to get there ASAP." He ratchets his mouth into a smile. "*Ma'am.*"

She studies Isaiah, then reaches under the cash register to her left.

She pulls out a small spray bottle and a gray cloth that's been folded into quarters. She removes her glasses. She unfolds the cloth.

A muscle flexes in Isaiah's jaw.

Georgia sprays each side of each lens exactly three times. Polishes the front, the back. She settles the glasses on her nose and sighs.

"If only there were something I could do to help."

Next to me, Isaiah reaches for the small of his back, the tail of his suit jacket flipping up over his forearm as he goes for his back pocket, and there, on his belt—

Is that a gun?

He pulls out his wallet, flips it open, digs out a twenty.

"How's that schedule look now?" he asks.

Georgia narrows her eyes. "Could look better."

He takes out another twenty.

She plucks the bills from his fingers and stuffs them into her bra. "There's one private ferry that runs to Kickout. It's small. You wouldn't be able to take your vehicle."

Isaiah nods. "That's fine."

"That's *fine?*"

Georgia and Isaiah turn to look at me.

I moisten my lips. "Just—you know. Small boat. *Big* ocean. Seems like there have been better ideas, historically speaking." I draw Isaiah near, lower my voice. "Are you sure we can't wait until tomorrow?"

"Not an option."

"It's just a movie," I'm compelled to point out, "not an attack on Abbottabad."

For the first time since I met him, Isaiah's features arrange themselves into something less than jovial, and my heart sinks straight through the chipped laminate floor.

"I'm sorry, I didn't mean—"

He turns back to Georgia. "We'll take the boat."

She hands him a business card. "Captain's easy enough to find. Just head over to the floating docks—out the door, down and to the right. He'll be the only one out there."

Isaiah glances down at the card, and if I weren't used to listening so closely to Amy, I probably wouldn't have caught the hitch in his breath.

Georgia doesn't miss it, either. She tilts her head to the side. "Is there a problem?"

"This is our *only* option?" Isaiah asks.

The corners of her mouth tip up. "'Fraid so."

Isaiah turns on his heel and heads for the door. It takes me a second to realize I should follow.

"Hey," I call after him. "What was that all about?"

Isaiah grunts and lengthens his stride, heading for the car.

"I'm just going to keep asking until you explain," I say.

Isaiah pops the trunk and grabs my suitcase. "Most of the people around here seem to consider this production their own personal ATM. As soon as they find out you're working on the movie, prices double."

"But we didn't *tell* her we're working on the movie."

He slams the trunk closed. "Didn't have to. It's the only reason anyone has to go to that damn island."

At the end of the final floating dock, we find a small, faded sign that reads "Charters Available. Service to Lewes, Rehoboth, Cape May, Kickout Island." To our right is a weathered vessel—a trawler. Two decks, no more than thirty feet long, and not much to look at.

"It was an ad-lib," I say after a moment. "Did you know that?"

"What was?" Isaiah asks.

"*'You're gonna need a bigger boat.'*"

He bumps me with his elbow. "I promise we won't get eaten by a shark."

"Famous last words."

He takes a step toward the stern; my hand shoots out to stop him.

"You can't board someone's boat without their permission."

He gives me a long look. "Please, tell me more about maritime law."

My hand falls away. Fair enough. He's an ex-SEAL; I was extrapolating from *Star Trek*.

"You wait here," he says.

He steps on board, the boat dipping under his weight, and disappears inside.

I press a hand to my stomach and picture my therapist's most recent superbill. Much better to be on the water than in the water, I remind myself.

Isaiah reappears above me, on the bridge, where he looks to be conferring with the captain. They shake hands, clearly coming to an agreement, and soon thereafter I can see the outline of a spindly figure descending a ladder. The captain emerges on the swimming dock.

I steel myself for small talk.

But when he hops off the boat, he doesn't even look at me. He just walks past, chin tucked to his chest, and heads for the dock lines.

I take a moment to catalog what I can see: a fluff of white-blond hair, a sunburned neck, restless hands, a stick figure in a loose-fitting T-shirt and shorts. He's so tall and skinny I want to ask his height and weight out of pure, scientific curiosity. Can a BMI be negative?

He moves from cleat to cleat along the length of the boat, from bow to stern, his movements sure and steady and syncopated, like he's counting out a tempo as he goes, and I feel my head bobbing along, too. I am immediately and absolutely certain that he does this the same way every single time, no matter the weather, no matter the dock, no matter his mood. This isn't just a man who appreciates routine. He lives and dies by it.

If only his efficiency weren't in service of shipping me out to sea.

A slight movement catches my eye. I realize Isaiah's watching the captain from the upper deck. He's leaning his hip against the railing, his arms crossed, his expression inscrutable. His focus unwavering.

I glance back at the captain. What am I missing? Why is Isaiah staring at him like that? Is it his appearance? I guess he has kind of a funny face for such a scrawny guy. It's round and soft and well-fed and makes him look twenty-five instead of forty-five, and I wonder if that's why he hides it when he walks past—because it's the most vulnerable part of him. His hairline's a little strange, too, like maybe he had something tweaked. I wouldn't expect a small-fry ferryman operating out of Lewes, Delaware, to be the kind of guy to get plastic surgery, but these are the times we live in, I guess.

The captain's shoulders stiffen a second before I hear it myself: a chorus of sloppy voices from the other end of the dock. I turn to find three white men in shorts, sandals, and pastel shirts stumbling our way, two of them swigging cans of Bud Light, the third carrying what looks like a bottle of Jack Daniel's. It hangs between his index and middle fingers, swinging at his side.

When they catch sight of me, they fall silent. A look passes between them.

I shift, uneasy, far too many high school movies flitting through my mind for any single one to come into focus.

The one in the salmon button-down clears his throat. "Evening, ma'am. Uh—any chance Billy's around?"

"Do you mean the captain?" I check back over my shoulder—that's strange. Where did he go? He still has lines left to untie.

The sight that greets me when I turn back to the men only confuses me further. Pink Button-Down and Pale Blue Polo are going up on their toes, trying to see inside the tinted windows on the main cabin while the third man watches from afar. Something about him in particular unsettles my stomach. He's in his late forties or early fifties, fit and conventionally attractive if you ignore the red hair.

His forearms are corded with the kind of visible muscle you can only get from working hard with your hands or buying those grip trainers they sell on late-night TV. There are no obvious red flags—again, if you ignore the hair—but even so, there's something about his mouth I just don't like.

"For fuck's sake," he says, "I don't have all night."

He caps the Jack and sets the bottle to the side. He shoves his friends out of the way, plants his foot on the boat's hull, and boosts himself up. He leans against the window, hands cupped around his eyes.

A moment passes. Then—

"There you are," he says, mildly.

Blue Polo—his voice high and reedy and deliberately affectless in a way I haven't heard since elementary school—snickers and sings out, *"Billy Lyyyyle."*

Pink Button-Down joins in. *"Come out, come out, wherever you are."*

I take a step back.

The captain comes out then, dragging his feet behind him as he makes his way up from the stern. He stops in front of the third man, his eyes cast down at the dock's wood planking. One of his hands twists at his side; the other hangs loose and empty.

The men have gone quiet, and there's no one else around, so there's no laughter or conversation to lighten the mood—just the low, steady hum of the boat's engine and the gentle sound of the water lapping against the hull, like a cat attending lazily to a bowl of cream. Even in that soft, relative silence, I still struggle to hear what the captain says to the third man.

"I already have passengers, Nick."

Nick's head swings in my direction. "Where're you headed?" he asks. "Maybe we could split the cost."

"Um—" I glance up toward the bridge. "An island. We're headed to some island."

Nick strolls over, reaches out—

I take another step back.

He grabs the handle of my suitcase, twists the airline luggage sticker around—and bursts out laughing. He peels it off and shows it to his friends, and after a moment, they laugh, too.

"What's so funny?" I hear myself asking.

Nick ignores me, his lips zipping up into a sharp, knowing curve. He holds the sticker up in front of the captain's face and swings it from side to side, like a hypnotist's pocket watch.

"You see where they're from, Billy? *Los Angeles*. And you're taking them to Kickout."

The captain looks off to the side and mumbles something, angling his face in such a way that the light falls on a fading yellow bruise along the side of his jaw.

Nick, smiling now, advances on the captain, crowding him right up to the edge of the dock. "You know what they're here for, don't you, Billy? They're working on the *movie*. And you"—he presses a finger into the captain's chest—"are helping them."

Behind him, Blue Polo's shaking his head. "Man, that's fucked up."

Nick leans even closer, so close the captain must be able to feel his breath against his cheek—so close I imagine *I* can feel his breath against my cheek.

"Is it because you're ready?" Nick asks him. "Are you finally ready, Billy—to tell them what you've done?"

The captain scrambles out from behind him and stumbles forward. He lands heavily on the dock, rubbing his chest where Nick's finger had been. "I'm not helping them," he says. "They're passengers. They're paying me."

"Not anymore, they're not. This trip's my treat." Nick retrieves the bottle of Jack and waves it in my direction. "What do you think— can I get a credit? Transportation coördinator? Executive producer?" He tips his chin at the captain. "Animal wrangler?"

"There a problem here?" Isaiah asks, appearing—as far as I can tell—out of nowhere.

Nick's jaw works just a little at the sight of him, but his smile's back a split second later. It's a good smile. A believable smile. A smile I wouldn't be able to pick out of a lineup: not too big, not too tight, not too small. He's even remembered to carry it through to his eyes.

I wrap my arms around my middle.

"No problem," Nick says easily. "We were just hoping we could hitch a ride with you folks."

"This," Isaiah says, with exquisite care, "is a private charter."

Against his hip, Pink Button-Down's free hand curls into a fist. "Don't you know who we are?"

Isaiah doesn't respond—nor does Nick, to his credit. They both let Pink Button-Down register the absurdity of his statement on his own.

"But Nicky," he says, "how else are we going to get back?"

Nick eyes Isaiah speculatively. "He's right. They were here first. And a deal's a deal."

Blue Polo winces. "My wife's gonna be pissed, we're supposed to be meeting her parents for dinner."

Nick punches him in the arm affectionately. "Relax, we'll just take the ferry. We still got twenty minutes."

"That means I gotta *pay*," Blue Polo grumbles.

"But the ferry's not running," I say for some godforsaken reason.

Nick turns, lifts an eyebrow. "Yeah? Who told you that?"

"The woman at the terminal. Georgia?"

He barks out a laugh. "Well, shit. I owe that woman a drink."

He gives us one last toothy smile before hooking his elbows around his friends' necks and leading them down the dock like a couple of kids.

"Good luck," he calls back over his shoulder. "Sure hope you make it there in one piece!"

MARISSA DAHL: Right, so, obviously, looking back, that's when I should have known something was wrong.

GRACE PORTILLO: Why didn't you, though? What made you ignore your own instincts?

MARISSA DAHL: Oh, you know, the usual—just a lifetime of being told I have terrible instincts.

SIX

The captain offers no explanations and makes no excuses. He wipes his hands on his shorts, unties the last mooring line, and hurries us on board, all efficiency.

"Should take us twenty-seven minutes," he says before climbing the ladder to the bridge.

I find a seat with my back to the water, within reach of a life preserver. A moment later, the engine revs and the boat pulls away from the dock.

"Funny kid," Isaiah murmurs.

I slide my hands under my legs and press my feet against the deck. "What do you think that Nick guy was on about?"

Isaiah rubs the back of his neck. "If I had to guess? Some dredged-up high school shit."

"But what would that have to do with us?"

"What does high school have to do with anything? Doesn't keep guys like that from bringing it up every chance they get."

I squint up at him. "Are you being deliberately obtuse?"

His eyebrows draw together. "Excuse me?"

I nod in the direction of the docks. "Whatever just happened is obviously related to the movie. So either, like me, you don't know much about what we're doing here—or you're trying to change the subject."

He studies me for a moment. "I'm trying to change the subject."

"Oh. Okay. I'm sorry."

"I'm trying to change the subject," he says again, "because I'm not sure what I'm allowed to tell you. Tony has very particular ideas about the dissemination of information."

"You mean like news—or gossip?"

"I mean anything. It's a very 'loose lips sink ships' sort of situation."

I stifle a groan. "Can we please not discuss our imminent demise?"

His expression resolves into something somber and serious, a firm jaw and straight lips and a sure, steady gaze that has me drawing my fingernails into my palms. It's a kind of scrutiny I've always wished I could kick off but never quite can, like tangled sheets on a hot summer night.

"No one's demise is imminent," he says. "Not on this set."

I pull up my knees and hug them to my chest. "So confident. Have you worked on a lot of movies?"

"This is my first."

My eyes go wide. "Oh God."

He ducks his head. "Yeah, baptism by fire. I know."

"Do you . . . like it?"

"Still getting the lay of the land. Any words of wisdom?"

I press my cheek into my knee, trying to think of something useful to say. It's not often that people come to me for advice, and I imagine he's already picked up on the basics. It may be his first movie, but I bet he's seen more than a few hostage situations, and that's close enough. I'm also guessing he doesn't need some midwestern white girl lecturing him about institutional racism, so that's out, too. He certainly doesn't need to hear my opinion about the comparative advantages of Avid vs. Adobe Premiere. I could tell him about craft services, maybe?

No, even my parents know about craft services.

What's something that took me a long time to learn? What's something I wish I'd known sooner—

"Oh," I say. "You should steer clear of the DP."

He looks up. "The what now?"

"Director of photography."

"Why? What's their deal?"

I tap out a little beat against my kneecap as I consider this. *One-two-three. One-two-three.* The steps of a waltz; the beginning of a race—the rhythm of a joke.

"Alright, so, stop me if you've heard this, but: What's the difference between God and a DP?"

"I don't know," Isaiah says, playing along. "What?"

One . . .

Two . . .

"God doesn't think he's a DP."

The corner of his mouth moves. "Okay, I see what you're doing. What else you got?"

I settle back into my seat. "Um—what does an assistant director use for birth control?"

"Couldn't say."

"His personality."

He settles his elbow on his knee and rests his face against his hand. "Any others?"

The boat shudders beneath us, and only then do I realize we're half a mile out at sea. I narrow my eyes at Isaiah. "You're trying to distract me, aren't you?"

He hums. "Is it working? Tell me one more."

I shake my head. "Fine. What's the difference between a producer and a coconut?"

"No idea."

I smile. This one's my favorite.

"You can get a drink out of a coconut."

I steal a look at his lips, and my fingers go still. He's smiling, too—and here's a rare sensation, a current that zips along the top of my cheekbones, right where Amy tells me I'm supposed to put highlighter. An image of Humphrey Bogart and Claude Rains shimmers behind my eyes.

I reach up and rub the feeling away.

"And what about editors?" Isaiah asks. "What do people say about them?"

I glance at him, startled. "Honestly? Not much."

"There must be something."

"Most of the jokes about editors come from *other* editors, which means they don't meet what I'm given to understand is the technical definition of a joke." I pause. "In that they're not actually funny."

"Oh, come on. Try me."

"Fine. But don't say I didn't warn you." I rearrange myself in my chair, tucking my legs up under me. "How many editors does it take to change a lightbulb?"

"How many?" Isaiah asks.

"None, it's fine like that! Move on!"

I can tell right away: It doesn't land. Isaiah's still smiling with his mouth, but his eyes have uncrinkled at the corners. As usual, I should have quit while I was ahead.

Except then he surprises me.

"I know we only just met," he says. "But that doesn't sound like you at all."

I draw my ponytail back over my shoulder and wrap it around my palm.

"No," I say. "I guess it doesn't."

SUZY KOH: Okay, so, Isaiah, the 64,000-dollar question: Why didn't you tell Marissa that she might be in danger?

ISAIAH GREENING: As long as she was with me, she wasn't.

GRACE PORTILLO: But don't you think she had a right to know what she was getting herself into?

ISAIAH GREENING: You have to understand, my job is to manage fear. And that requires as much psychological finesse as operational expertise. Making sure that a client is safe and that a client *feels* safe are often two very different things. For most of my clients, particularly a certain kind of businessman, that means bells and whistles. The best tech, the biggest guys—over-the-top black-ops bullshit, you know? Even if I'm just escorting them to a forty-grand-a-plate charity function in the Hamptons. [*pause*] Marissa, though—she's not like my regular clients.

SUZY KOH: Well, yeah. For one thing, she didn't even know she *was* a client.

ISAIAH GREENING: But I would've lost my job if I'd told her. And I knew I was absolutely the best person for that job. I really didn't have a choice.

SUZY KOH: Are you trying to argue that you were doing her a favor by keeping her in the dark?

ISAIAH GREENING: If I'd told her the truth, she never would've gotten on that boat. And then where would we be?

SEVEN

The island sneaks up on me.

Bet you didn't know an island could do that. But this one does, and not just because I've been doing my best not to look at the water.

It sits just barely above sea level, broad and flat, skimming across the water like an oil slick, the two-story buildings along the shoreline concealing the bulk of the island from view. There's not much else to look at: A modest lighthouse sits atop a crumble of rock just south of the docks; to the north, a roller coaster and Ferris wheel peek out from behind a cluster of trees. In the distance, on the far eastern end of the island, is a rambling, hulking structure—a hotel, if I'm lucky. A hospital, if I'm not. It's too dark to trace the specifics of its outline, but I'd guess every light in the place is turned on: I count forty-seven visible windows in three higgledy-piggledy clusters. This has to be our destination.

Only a film crew would waste that much electricity.

"What's this place called again?" I ask Isaiah.

"Kickout Island."

I eye the building in the distance. "It's not a penal colony, is it?"

"It was *kijkuit*, originally. From the Dutch." The captain's standing at the top of the ladder. His gaze lands briefly on me before skittering away. "It means 'look out.' You might want to find something to hold on to, we'll be docking shortly."

"*Look out?*" I say. "What for?"

But the captain doesn't answer. I turn to ask Isaiah, but for the first time, he's studiously avoiding me.

The marina, a sprawling network of floating docks bookended by the lighthouse and the commercial jetty, runs the length of the western edge of the island. As we approach, I can see a lone worker scrambling up and down the jetty, prepping for the ferry's arrival. I guess Georgia really did lie to us.

Something doesn't sit quite right with me about that. I don't doubt Isaiah. I know it's not unusual for local businesses to try to make a few extra bucks off a production—not for nothing are contingencies built into the budget. But it feels like there's more to Georgia's trick. The guys on the boat—they'd laughed about it. Like it was a joke.

Then again, guys like that will laugh at anything.

I scratch absently at my forearm. I'm probably just imagining things. This is why I need a movie to work on. If you don't give me a story to tell, I'll make one up.

The captain guides the boat into an open slip. He hops down to the deck and moves quickly to secure the lines, displaying the same rote efficiency he used to release them back in Lewes.

I check my watch. Twenty-seven minutes travel time exactly.

When I look up, I spot a trim figure hurrying toward us. A woman, I think—probably a PA coming to pick us up.

Not that PAs have to be women, I'm not saying that. I just mean that, generally, this kind of job would be given to one of the less skilled members of the crew.

Not that PAs are generally unskilled—I'm not saying that either!

Well, no, that's not true. They are. But there's nothing *wrong* with that. Everyone has to start somewhere, right?

Anyway, the woman—whatever her title is—is rushing toward us, her hands waving, her mouth moving. It takes me a second to register what she's saying.

"Are you fucking *kidding* me, Isaiah?"

Next to me, so quietly I'm not certain I'm not imagining it, Isaiah lets slip the slightest huff of irritation.

On the dock, the captain checks the last line and heads back toward the stern. When he passes the woman, she shies away like he's made of spiders or scorpions or something that crawls down from your scalp to lay eggs in your ears. I glance at the captain, curious, wondering what she finds so offensive about him—and if he's offended by her offense—but his chin is tucked to his chest, as usual, and he's showing no signs of distress.

I study the woman with fresh eyes. If she's yelling at Isaiah like that, she's definitely not a PA. So what is she? If this movie had a different director, I might peg her for an actress. She's certainly pretty enough, with golden brown skin and dark, lustrous hair that falls to her shoulders in an enviably can-you-*believe*-I-just-woke-up-like-this wave. She's not wearing any makeup that I can see, but why would she, her brows are perfect, and according to Amy that's really all you need. She appears to be younger than me, but I know better than to assume that tells me anything about her actual age. Still, when it comes to leading ladies, Tony has very predictable type, and South Asian—stunning though this woman may be—is not it.

Maybe she has a supporting role?

"You said you were chartering a *boat*," she says, her tone arctic.

Isaiah nods stiffly. "Which I did. As you can see."

"You didn't say you were chartering *this* boat."

"I don't know what to tell you," he says, rubbing the back of his neck, a gesture I'm beginning to suspect is a sign of consternation. "It was the only one available."

"Don't you know how much trouble we could get into?"

"A lot less than if I hadn't gotten her to the island tonight."

"*Seriously*, Isaiah?"

He grabs my suitcase and starts down the dock. The woman stomps after him. After a brief moment of indecision—*shouldn't I say something to the captain before I go?*—I shoulder my backpack and follow.

That said, I don't exactly make an effort to catch up with them. I find, generally, that it's best not to pay too much attention when people are yelling at each other. They're just going to say things they don't mean, and that's a hard thing to keep in mind if they start yelling about you. Better not to listen in the first place.

As I walk, I slip my hands behind me and rub my fingertips against each other, just a little, running my thumb from index to pinky finger and back again, a quick *one-two-three-four, one-two-three-four*. I let the rest of my senses go soft. Soon, their angry voices are swallowed up by the soundscape, until their words aren't even words anymore, just noise, no more meaningful or necessary than bird chatter, dripping water, the grind and slosh of a dishwasher.

I tip my face up to the sky. A few stars are out.

I think I can see Jupiter.

It's the silence that snaps me out of it.

I turn around, disoriented. Isaiah and the woman are twenty feet behind me, staring at me with wide eyes. I check the front of my shirt, again, reflexively, just to be sure.

"What?" I ask.

They exchange a look, then close the distance between us with startling speed, picking up their argument where they left off.

"Did you pay with a card?" the woman asks.

"No," Isaiah says.

"Did you get a receipt?"

"No."

"Does he have a log?"

"I tore out the page."

"Well that's something, I guess." Apparently satisfied, she sticks a hand in my direction. "You must be Marissa. I'm Anjali. We spoke on the phone."

The name rings a bell, but Nell knows better than to let me get on the phone with anyone. "I think that was probably my agent," I say.

She shrugs. "Same diff. We're thrilled you're here, et cetera, et cetera. Is this really all your stuff?"

"Yes?"

She squints at my compact rollaboard. Next to Isaiah, it looks like children's luggage. "Which are you, hopelessly optimistic or hopelessly pessimistic?"

"I don't understand the question."

"It doesn't look like you intend to be here for long."

"I'm just really good at folding things."

She gives me the insubstantial smile I often get when I accidentally sound like a smart-ass.

"Let's hope that's not all you're—"

Her voice is drowned out by the brassy wail of a marine horn. We turn toward the jetty and watch as the main ferry comes into view.

"Isaiah," Anjali says after a moment. "What the *fuck* is that?"

"What do you know," he says, evenly. "I guess it's running after all."

Anjali's shoulders slump. "Do I even want to know?"

"Wouldn't tell you either way."

She shakes her head. "Whatever. Let's go."

She makes a sharp, irritable gesture with her right hand and changes course, heading for the tidy commercial stretch that runs the length of the marina. It's populated by all the tourist-oriented businesses you'd expect from a vacation destination: a visitor center, an ice cream parlor, an antique shop, a high-end consignment store. Even though it must be almost eight thirty, everything's still open.

The Italian restaurant is the busiest of the bunch. Il Tavolo, it's called, which I find faintly annoying—I count at least four tables in the alfresco dining area alone. There, three women, all dressed for a night out, are splitting a straw-wrapped bottle of wine. We're too far away to hear what they're saying, but the topic must be an easy one: Their conversation is bright and lively and unceasing, punctuated not, as mine are, by awkward pauses and stammered apologies, but by crystalline peals of laughter.

I remind myself that if I were editing a movie, a scene like this would be a pain in the ass. All that overlapping dialogue—more trouble than it's worth, really.

It's probably no less annoying in real life.

Probably.

The women pretend to ignore us as we pass, but I don't miss the way their eyes flick in our direction and back again.

Anjali stops in front of the nail salon, where a black Escalade has been parked diagonally across two and a half spots. She tosses Isaiah the keys; he snatches them out of the air without looking.

I barely have time to strap myself in before we're pulling out of the marina and onto what Anjali informs me is the island's sole road.

"It runs along the island's perimeter," she explains, sourly. "So you can't go across the island—you have to go all the way around." She stabs her finger in the air and sketches an exaggerated circle. "Like a fucking rotary phone."

I glance out the window. There's just five feet of shoulder and a battered metal guardrail between us and what appears to be a fairly abrupt drop-off. If Isaiah's attention slips for just a second—

I crack my window open, just a bit. Just in case.

I peer down at the water.

I open the window a little more.

"I'm not going to drive into the ocean," Isaiah says, his voice a low rumble.

"I was just getting some air," I say.

"You were establishing an escape route."

"A fringe benefit."

I drag my eyes away from the rearview mirror and realize Anjali has twisted around in the front seat. She's watching me intently.

I pretend to be very interested in the big building that looms in the distance. "Is that where we're going?" I ask.

Anjali follows my gaze, nods. "It's the only place *to* go, really."

"What is it?"

"A hotel."

"Is it where we're staying or where we're shooting?"

"Both."

The tension I've been carrying in my neck and shoulders drops by about 5 percent. Hotels are good. I know what to expect from them. High-end, low-end, they're all basically the same: a bed, a TV, a Bible. Spaghetti and meatballs on the kids menu. I can work with a hotel.

Bed and breakfasts, that's another story.

Something up ahead flashes white. A sign. *Hingham House. One mile.*

"Why is that name familiar?" I ask.

"Because it sounds like something out of Shirley Jackson?" Isaiah says.

Anjali stares at him for a moment, then looks back at me. "No one uses its real name," she says. "They just call it 'The Shack.'"

"Why?"

She throws up her hands. "Rich people."

I still don't follow, but I don't ask for clarification because something about this place is definitely pinging at my memory—but how? I've never been here before. Something from a movie, maybe?

"The Shack," I say, slowly, feeling my way around the words. "On Kickout Island."

"Yeah," Isaiah says, "the brochure really writes itself."

Anjali groans. "Enough. I didn't hire you for your commentary."

He says something sharp in return, and then she's smirking back, and I tune them out again, automatically, wondering—not *quite* idly—if they really don't like each other or if they really *do* like each other. I've always had trouble with that particular distinction. Whoever decided flirting should look like fighting has an awful lot to answer for.

They're still squabbling twenty minutes later, as Isaiah steers the car through two low pillars of stacked stone and onto a cobblestone driveway that just barely rumbles the Escalade's suspension. We pass a parking lot packed full of trucks and trailers, a copse of trees, a boathouse, a hedgerow. Finally, the hotel comes into view.

I press my face against the window to get a better look.

At first, I can't quite make out if I'm looking at one building or several: The hotel appears to consist of six or seven architecturally distinct structures all smooshed together. In the center is a grand, soaring portico supported by four scrolled white columns; behind that, a perfectly symmetrical four-story clapboard box with dormer windows; behind *that*, a six-story Victorian cupola with a widow's walk and two round windows set in a gray slate roof.

I wonder how far back it goes. Who knows what else might be behind there. A medieval guardhouse, maybe, or a Taco Bell.

Isaiah pulls the car up to the portico, and this time I remember to let him open the door for me.

"I'm only letting you do this because I don't want to take another door to the face," I say, ducking under his arm.

When I let myself look up at him, I'm hoping to catch a glimpse of one of his smiles. They're so straightforward, so undemanding. But his expression is so blank it puts me in mind of a prototype android or pathologically fastidious villain. Just like that, his face has been wiped clean of any and all incriminating signs of life.

But that's how it is, I guess. Now that he's delivered me to the hotel, his job's done. He was probably just pretending to put up with me.

"You should hurry," he says, nodding at Anjali, who's already halfway up the steps.

I swallow past a tightness in my throat that I choose to attribute to nerves or confusion or dismay or maybe just my body's realization that it's been eleven hours since I've had anything to eat.

"So that's good-bye, then?"

Isaiah draws back. "What gave you that impression?"

"You just got really serious all of a sudden."

"That's my job."

"Your job is to be serious?"

He hesitates. "My job is to keep an eye on things."

"Do you think something's going to happen to me on the stairs?"

His shoulders rise, fall. "Marissa—"

I tilt my head to the side and try for a joke. "It's okay, you can tell me. Are you afraid of stairs?"

He sighs. "Just go inside already, would you?"

I mean to obey, really I do, but my body's slow to respond, and before I know it, his fingers are at the small of my back, urging me forward.

I—don't hate it.

Something else I don't hate: the hotel. It's better than I could have hoped for. Even on a hot summer night, the lobby feels bright and airy and open, an impressive display of elegant furnishings and tasteful architectural detail. Along the southern wall, a series of French doors lead out to the sundeck; they've been left open to let in the breeze, their cream-colored curtains fluttering in the evening air. To my left, a wicker seating area is set amidst a collection of lush potted ferns; just past that is a grand mahogany bar. Overhead, polished brass chandeliers shine down on the high-gloss checkerboard marble floors.

Prestige drama has its perks, I suppose.

Isaiah makes some vague noises about needing to check his messages and points me toward the far end of the lobby. Anjali's waiting for me there—past the elevators, the dining room, and three more seating areas—leaning against the front desk as if she's been there for hours, when in reality it can't have been more than three minutes. Her fingernails tap out an indistinct rhythm on the gleaming wood surface.

"You're awfully small, aren't you?" she remarks once I'm in earshot.

I draw a breath, open my mouth—

She blinks, her attention drawn to something behind me. "Hold that thought."

I turn to follow her gaze. A man in tortoiseshell aviators has just pushed through the lobby door, flanked by two bright-eyed teenage girls in shorts and flip-flops. Anjali mutters an exceptionally rude comment about actors and crosses the room in a flash.

I revise all my earlier assessments. She's clearly a producer.

The man says something that makes Anjali clench her jaw so hard I can see her muscles tense from all the way across the room. She jabs a finger at a nearby chair; the man lifts his hands in surrender. But as soon as Anjali turns to talk to the girls, he executes a neat pirouette and heads in the opposite direction—to the bar. He signals to the bartender and slips off his glasses.

As soon as I see his face, my hand goes to knead my forehead of its own accord.

It's Gavin Davies, former teen idol, current adult misery. I've tried on at least six separate occasions to get a plausible explanation for his enduring appeal, but so far I've come up empty. He was the star of a billion-dollar trilogy ten years ago, but it's been ages since he's done anything that isn't obscure, demented, or disgusting. For some reason, though, the studio guys still love him. My best guess is he runs a poker game or flips houses or dabbles in a little light human trafficking. Or maybe he's just moderately talented and has an English accent. Who knows. Forget it, Jake, it's Hollywood.

We've never met, but we've worked together on three projects, so I know him fairly well. I'm not concerned about his acting. With the right material, he can be great. A little fluky, maybe. Out of every ten takes, three will be completely unusable because he forgot when he was supposed to sip his drink or stub out his cigarette or deliver his lines. But five will be fine and two will be brilliant, which is more than most actors give me. And anyway, it's not my place to complain.

What worries me is I know the kind of parts he picks.

What am I going to get stuck with this time: A sadistic enforcer for a coastal meth ring? A racist small-town cop? A deadbeat dad with a penchant for revenge porn? A racist big-town cop?

I scan his appearance for some hint of what I'm in for. He's lost the muscle he usually carries in his back and shoulders, and the cheekbones teen girls swooned over in 2010 are too sharp now to make me think about anything other than feeding him a sandwich. His hair, traditionally the cornerstone of his artistic process, is bleached and badly styled.

Best-case scenario, his character's an ordinary awful person. But that's what he played in Amy's last movie—and I know he doesn't like to play similar roles in back-to-back projects—so I'm guessing he's trying to switch things up. Probably by playing an *extraordinary* awful person.

Like a pedophile.

A white supremacist.

A pedophile white supremacist.

Although maybe that's not so extraordinary these days?

I rub the bridge of my nose, ignoring the lingering ache.

Even if nothing else comes of this job—even if Tony fires me the second he places my face—at least I can say I've learned my lesson: I'm never taking a job again without reading the script.

EIGHT

At the other end of the lobby, Anjali has just spotted Gavin at the bar. She storms over, and I'm leaning forward, my eyes glued to the scene, when I feel something nudge my shoulder. I look down. It's a scraggly calico.

"Hello, there," I say.

She turns two tight circles and flops down in front of me, tucking one paw under the wattle of her belly. I reach out to rub a knuckle along her jaw, and she stretches her neck to give me better access. Her throat vibrates with an intense, immediate purr.

I scratch under her chin and along her spine. Her fur's dry and slightly dusty; I suspect this is the most attention she's gotten all day. It's not that she's not soft, per se. She's just not as soft as she looks. So even though she satisfies a cat's basic requirements, she still doesn't meet the unspoken expectations, and now she's stuck out here on the front desk waiting for new arrivals because the only people she still has a chance with are the ones she hasn't already let down.

"Who's a good girl?" I murmur.

"Are you new?"

The cat leaps off the desk and scurries away. I look up. Standing in front of me is an older white man who must have just emerged from a back room. His face is friendly but oddly immobile, as if it's been permanently carved into a shape that's open and welcoming.

"Uh, yes," I say. "I'm the editor."

I was wrong. His face *can* move: from smiling to *really* smiling.

Clearly a civilian. I've never seen such a glowing response to that particular statement.

"—so worried about the delay," he's saying. "Not that it ever made much sense, mind you, making such a fuss about just one crew member—especially the editor. Seems to me editing's something you wait till the end to do anyway, right? But what do I know, I'm just a humble innkeeper." He sticks out his hand. "Wade Metcalf. Nice to meet you."

I give his fingertips a squeeze. "Marissa Dahl. Lovely hotel you have here."

"Can't take much of the credit, I'm afraid, but I'll be sure to pass that on to the wife. Will you be needing a room? Or will you be bunking down in the projection room like the last guy?"

I may be wedded to my job, but even I have limits. "I'll take my own room."

"Sure thing," he says. "Just give me a second to run to the office—computers are on the fritz, wouldn't you know. Don't go running off before I'm back!"

His laugh is a sudden roar, like the blast of heat you get when you open an oven door, and before I can recover, he's gone.

I check back in on Anjali. She's sitting at the bar next to Gavin now. Still arguing. Meanwhile, the bartender's polishing glasses and pretending not to listen, and the staff in the dining room is cleaning up after service and pretending not to listen, and a housekeeper's sweeping crumbs into a pile and pretending not to listen. None of them are any good at it. But give it a few more weeks, and I'm sure they'll figure out what the rest of us have: that no one in this business is actually worth listening to.

The lobby is largely empty, which strikes me as odd. I'd expect more activity on location, especially in the bar. But I suppose the crew's probably prepping for tomorrow and the cast is—I don't know. Doing whatever it is actors do when no one's around to look at them. Becoming one with the void, probably.

I dig my cardigan out of my backpack and wrap my arms around my middle. I must have worked up a sweat while I was chasing after Anjali, and I realize now how cold it is.

I've just stopped shivering when, over in the dining room, a busboy apparently decides stacking plates isn't nearly as much fun as dropping them onto each other from a great height. Wincing, I take a few steps in the opposite direction—which puts me in range of an air freshener. And not even a nice air freshener, it's one of those cones my grandmother kept behind the toilet. Less Alpine Meadow than Astringent Jell-O. And now that I've started noticing it, I can't stop. I press the back of my hand against my nose, but it's not enough.

On the reception desk is a vase filled with five perfect white chrysanthemums. I slide it toward me and bury my face in the flowers, breathing them in.

Damp soil. Cold metal. Radishes.

Not much of a perfume flower, I'll grant, but they're good for gardens—or at least that's what my mom says. She has a huge patch out back, mixed in with her vegetables. Apparently, they repel aphids.

I breathe in again, slowly this time.

A bit unfair of the aphids, really. The scent's not *that* bad.

The unpleasant buzz in my body is just beginning to fade when I'm confronted with one final sensory intrusion: the bell rings.

And rings.

And *rings*.

I lift my eyes over the top of the flowers. It's Gavin, of course, pounding his fist on the service bell at the other end of the counter.

"Wade'll be right back," I say, my voice more tremulous than I would like.

His hand freezes, hovering a bare inch above the bell. He turns to me and raises an eyebrow in a precise, controlled fashion that screams formal training.

"I *beg* your pardon."

With most anyone else I wouldn't know how to respond, unsure whether he was saying he genuinely didn't hear me or asking me to repeat myself or apologizing for disturbing me or just telling me, in exceedingly British terms, to fuck right off. But I've spent hundreds of hours alone in a dark room with Gavin, scrutinizing his face, his movements, his diction. I know what he looks like when he's irritated or excited or exhausted or triumphant or reluctantly aroused. I know which of his costars he liked and which he loathed. I have cataloged his every careless word. I know him better than he'll ever know me—not that he realizes it.

Which is how I know I need to apologize.

I sigh—

—and something tickles my nose. A chrysanthemum.

The relief is so strong it nearly knocks my knees out from under me. I still have my face stuck in the flowers, and I must have been mumbling into them. I was wrong: Gavin's not *mad*. He simply couldn't hear me.

"I said, 'Wade'll be right out.'"

"Yes," Gavin drawls. "I heard you the first time."

I shift my weight to the balls of my feet and gauge the shortest route to the front door.

Gavin comes around the corner of the reception desk, stopping a good six inches closer than I'm comfortable with. When he stretches a hand out in my direction, I can't help but recoil.

He draws back. "My reputation precedes me."

I shake my head. "Oh, no, I'm just being weird."

"What?"

"I mean, I'm sorry."

His face crumples a little. "Do I seem upset?"

"Kind of?"

He presses a palm to his cheek and wrinkles his nose. "I was aiming for rueful. Amazing what people will forgive if they think you have a sense of humor."

"Oh, I would never think that."

"Yes, darling, I can see that. I only wanted to tell you—you've got a petal."

I brush at my face—

"No," he says, pointing to his temple. "Here."

My hands fly up to pick out the petal before he can offer to do it himself, because that would be *intolerable*. This, however, creates a new problem. I don't see a trash can nearby, and I can't leave the petal at reception—the desk is too shiny, too clean, someone would have to pick up and polish after me. But I don't want to put it in my pocket either because I can only stand having two very particular things in my pockets: my phone and my lip balm. I make an exception for a walkie from time to time, but only begrudgingly. Having anything else in there would feel like a splinter or a kidney stone or a LEGO in my shoe.

I settle for rolling the petal into a ball and dropping it back in the vase.

There.

When I finish, Gavin has a funny look on his face.

"You're the new editor, aren't you?"

Three projects. We've worked together on *three* projects. I could probably hand him my passport and he still wouldn't be able to place me.

I nod, weary, the day catching up with me all at once.

"Why didn't you say so from the start?"

"I've found it's generally not the best thing to lead with."

Anjali materializes at my side.

"Jesus *Christ*, Gavin."

I turn to her, desperately. "Please tell me what I'm supposed to be doing."

"I thought I told you to go to your room."

"But I don't have a—"

She shoots me an impatient look. "I'm not talking to *you*."

"Come the fuck *on*," Gavin groans. "You can't confine me to quarters. You're not *Napoleon*."

"Would you rather take it up with Tony?"

"I'd rather take it up with my agent."

Their voices rise, clashing with the clatter of the dining room, the whine of an air handler that needs to be replaced, the intermittent clinking of glass at the bar, and a piercing, high-pitched tone that probably has something to do with the fluorescent light I can see shining from behind the office door. Beneath it all, faint but inescapable, is the sound of the ocean.

I wonder if they'd notice if I got my earplugs out.

I realize Gavin's looking at me expectantly.

"What?"

He tilts his head to the side. "I asked if you're having second thoughts yet."

Anjali steps between us. "Yeah, you're not supposed to talk to her, either."

This time Gavin's eyebrows actually seem to move spontaneously. "What? She's *crew*."

"Like you said, I'm not Napoleon. I don't make the laws—I just enforce them."

Gavin's lips twist. "Javert, then."

"Totally different time periods, pal. And don't pretend you didn't know what you were getting into."

"He's overreaching. Even for him."

"Well, luckily, you can leave whenever you want to. You'd be doing me a favor, really. I've got Dan Radcliffe on speed dial, and I bet he'd love an excuse to do something awful to his hair." She strides over to the reception desk, boosts herself up, and speaks in loud, crisp tones that stop the dining room servers in their tracks. "Wade! Mr. Davies would like to leave as soon as possible!"

She slides back onto her feet and puts her hands on her hips. Wade comes bolting out of the back office, his mouth slack.

"Mr. Davies is leaving? But he can't—"

"He can and he will," Anjali interjects. "Right, Gavin?"

She and Gavin stare at each other so long I half expect an Ennio Morricone music cue.

After what must be nearly a minute, Gavin relents. "No," he says, scrubbing a hand through his hair. "I'm not leaving."

Wade lets out a breath. "Oh, good. I mean, I'm glad to hear that. I was just telling Francie about Marissa here, and she was so happy you'd finally found a new editor because, you know, this movie means a lot to her, and—"

"Yes, thank you, Wade, that will be all."

I open my mouth to add my thanks, but Anjali drags me down the hall before I can say anything.

She already knows me so well.

GRACE PORTILLO: So, Gavin, why were you so eager to work with Tony?

GAVIN DAVIES: Because, Grace, mainstream critical validation is my love language.

SUZY KOH: At least you're honest, I guess.

GAVIN DAVIES: Plus, that *part*. An unattractive outcast unfairly accused of a crime he almost certainly didn't commit? Delicious.

SUZY KOH: I'm not sure that's how Tony saw it.

GAVIN DAVIES: Yes, well, to Tony's eternal displeasure, he can't *actually* control his actors' minds.

SUZY KOH: Yeah, what's that about?

GAVIN DAVIES: His penchant for psychological manipulation is well-known in the industry.

GRACE PORTILLO: Can you give us another example?

GAVIN DAVIES: He was an absolute nightmare to Annemieke, of course. On *Persephone*, rumor was he'd doctored a pregnancy test so for the first two days of the shoot she thought they were going to have a baby. She was, naturally, devastated when that turned out not to be the case.

GRACE PORTILLO: Are you kidding? And she stayed married to him?

GAVIN DAVIES: She won Best Actress, didn't she?

NINE

Would you please slow down?"

"No," Anjali says, her hand tightening around my wrist. "We're late enough as it is."

"And where is it we're going again?"

She glances back, a frown working its way between her eyebrows. "If I tell you, it will ruin the surprise."

For the past fifteen minutes, Anjali has been guiding me through the seemingly identical carpeted hallways that crisscross the hotel's lower level. I have long since lost my bearings, not to mention my breath. I'm also not sure if she's just fucking with me.

I knew I was in trouble the moment we stepped out of the elevator and were confronted with a sign detailing the litany of amenities to be found on the lower level: salon, spa, pool, squash courts, yoga studio, gallery, theater, wine cellar, cigar lounge, and others I forgot immediately. The list put me in mind of an apology that goes on too long, the kind that gets you into more trouble than you were ever in to begin with.

The deeper we descend into the hotel, the more completely I'm convinced that I am never going to find my way out—which is a problem. Because there's a non-zero chance I'll be fired as soon as Tony sees my face, and if that happens, I'll want to know the quickest way out of this place. If I'm going to be humiliated, I'm going to do it as God intended: alone, sitting in my shower. I do not want to spend the rest of my life in a broom closet or a laundry room or a service elevator, and, yes, I'm catastrophizing, I know—I *know*. But panic isn't Rumpelstiltskin. Simply naming it doesn't make it go away.

I make a fist and dig it hard into my hip.

We take a right, a left, another right and come, at long last, to a door. It's glass, diamond-paned, opaque, with big bronze handles shaped like crescent moons. Anjali hefts it open.

On the other side is a vast room, longer than it is wide, with a two-story ceiling tiled in lapis and burnished gold. Centered on the far wall, flanked by crimson curtains, is a small concession stand.

I rub my eyes with the heels of my hands and wait for my vision to clear.

Yes, Virginia, it really *is* a movie theater.

"Told you," Anjali says, smugly.

Unlike the lobby, it isn't in mint condition. The lingering scent of cheap chocolate and butter-flavored topping isn't enough to mask the faint, wet-sock smell of developing mold. The crimson and gold scallop-patterned carpet is so threadbare I can feel the subfloor through the soles of my shoes. Part of me wants nothing more than to take a bottle of Windex and some newspaper to the mirrors that line the wall.

Even so, I would've killed to work in a place like this. Of all the old movie theaters in my hometown, only two are still operating, and one of those didn't reopen until it was time for me to leave for college. So when I set out to get a job as an assistant projectionist, I didn't get to work at the Orpheum or the Lyric or the Rialto. I had to settle for the Carmike Beverly 18.

"It's beautiful," I say.

Anjali looks up and around, blinking a little, as if she's still sur-prised to find herself there. "Yeah," she says, "it doesn't suck. I guess the original owner of the hotel married an actress back in the day. He built this so she could screen her movies."

"Would I have heard of her?"

"Doubt it. She had a bit part in *Rebecca*, but that's about it." She points to a black-and-white headshot hanging above the nacho cheese warmer. "That's her. Violet *fake-French-name-I-can-never-remember*. She's ninety-seven and still kicking—maybe you'll get to meet her. Here we are. Keep it down, okay? They're rolling."

"Wait—what?"

She opens the door to the auditorium and pushes me through.

I lurch forward, grabbing the back of a chair to keep from falling over. As soon as my legs remember how to move, I dart to the side and flatten myself against the wall, unable to keep a curse from hiss-ing out between my teeth.

Some editors insist on isolating themselves from the vagaries of daily production. I'm not one of them. I don't have a problem seeing actors out of character or knowing a particular shot was a pain in the ass. I'm not precious. Still, I try to avoid physically being on set. Like I said, sometimes I mix up movies and memory—but it can go in the other direction, too. I'll see something in real life and then, later, in the editing room, I'll think I'm remembering coverage and will dig around in my files for the footage only to realize it's not there. It's inefficient, and it makes me feel silly. I don't like it.

Also, if people know I'm on set, they might try to give me notes.

But I can't do anything about it now, so I grab a seat, house left, as far from the crowd at Video Village as I can get.

In an art form dependent on the smooth coordination of a thou-sand different moving parts, the mosh-pit chaos of Video Village—which in this case consists of three monitors bungee-tied to a hotel room service cart—really stands out. There are a dozen people there even now, jockeying for position, pushing up against one another for a better view of the screens even though, really, the only people who need to see real-time footage are the director and the DP. Not the PAs. Not the grips. Certainly not the man in crisp jeans and pristine sneakers that everyone seems to be ignoring—the executive who interviewed me, I realize.

Amy always says that one of the hardest parts of her job is finding a way to focus on the footage when she's at Video Village, surrounded by gawkers angling for a better look. I heard once that Oliver Stone cloaks his monitor in Duvetyn, that he disappears beneath it like an old-time photographer ducking under a heavy black focusing cloth. So when the camera's rolling, no one's watching the feed, no one's watching him. It's just him and the rectangle.

Amy insists she'd never be able to get away with something like that. Because that is the *actual* hardest part of her job, she says: having to appear to be endlessly accommodating without actually accommodating anyone at all.

I crane my neck forward, trying to see through the scrum. Where's Tony?

"*Liza*, focus."

I whip around and there he is, down in front, stepping back from behind the camera, an ARRI Alexa on a carbon-fiber tripod. The sight sends a shiver through me. Of *course* he's operating the camera himself. Why would he relinquish control of anything to anyone? He's going to fight me over every single cut—assuming I make it that far.

He hops up on the small stage, joining Liza and another actress I don't immediately recognize. Liza's wearing jean shorts over the orange swimsuit from the beach scene, along with black, T-strap character heels, a style I haven't seen since I spot-opped my tenth-grade production of *Anything Goes*.

The other actress, an older white woman, is dressed in a bobbed platinum wig and a beaded silver dress. She's probably pushing seventy, but she has the calves of a twenty-year-old dancer. Eileen Fox, that's her name. She's a stage actress—she won the Tony last year for *Mother Courage*. Or maybe I mean *Hedda Gabler*?

A Broadway import's a mixed blessing. She'll hit her marks perfectly but forget which line she sipped her drink on. Hopefully Tony doesn't give her too many close-ups. Too often stage actors new to film overdo it on camera and end up looking less like real faces than state-fair gourds that eerily *resemble* faces.

I realize then that they're projecting a movie onto the screen behind Liza and Eileen.

Judith Anderson, Joan Fontaine.

Rebecca.

I reevaluate the tableau in front of me, slotting in the new variables and recomputing. Eileen must be playing Violet, the actress-wife of the hotel magnate. And I guess in this scene they're rehearsing?—but for what?

Something dreadful occurs to me then, and I come up on my feet, scanning the room for any elaborate sound equipment. But I don't see any floor mics. No one's setting up playback.

I put my hand to my heart. I think I'm safe.

If this had turned out to be a musical, I really think I would have had to fire Nell.

On stage, Tony shoos away the makeup artist who's trying to blot Liza's nose and stares down at his lead actress.

"I'd *love* to know what you think you're doing."

Liza smooths her hair behind her ear. "I'm doing what you told me."

He leans in, but his words carry all the way back to the cheap seats.

"And here I thought I told you to act."

Tony steps away, and the makeup artist hurries back in, fussing with Liza's lip color and murmuring words of encouragement until Liza's shoulders detach themselves from her ears. By the time the hairstylist joins them, Liza looks almost confident.

Eileen has retreated stage left, where she's leaning against the proscenium, arms crossed, head tilted back, one elegant ankle crossed over the other. The makeup artist makes a half-hearted move to touch up her foundation, too, but Eileen waves her off.

Tony ducks back behind the camera, and a hush falls over the room.

"Places," he says.

A flurry of movement: Eileen and Liza get into position, finding their light, tipping their chins and twisting their hips, hitting their angles. The sound guy presses one hand against his headphones; his other hand hovers over his mixing board. A man with long black hair and an intense expression—he must be the DP—makes a complicated series of hand gestures. A moment later, an electrician adjusts a bounce card. The DP shakes his head and motions to them to lower it back down. At Video Village, the executive low-key hip-checks a PA.

And—again—we wait.

The silence lasts no more than thirty seconds, but the suspense is unbearable.

"Liza," Tony says then, and I'm amazed she doesn't start at the sound. "Your left foot needs to come an inch stage left."

Liza slides her foot to the side.

"An inch, not a centimeter."

She moves it a bit more.

"Acceptable. Eileen, you're perfect, as always. Roll sound."

The sound guy nods. "Sound speed."

Tony settles in behind the camera. "Petra, mark it."

An assistant camerawoman slides into frame with a timecode

slate. She calls out the shot number and the take—39, *yikes*—and claps the slate. Then, a collective indrawn breath.

I find myself leaning forward.

"Action."

When I'm reviewing footage, working on an early cut, I hear these words a thousand times a day—more, maybe. *Action, cut, action, cut, action, cut, action, cut.* These aren't commands, not for me. They're more like everyday punctuation. A capital letter. A period. An indication that I should pay attention to what's going on in the middle. Actors and on-set crew, though, they have a more visceral, Pavlovian response. I'm pretty sure if you went to any coffee shop in Santa Monica and shouted "Places!" half the customers would freeze.

I'd really forgotten how different it is to be here in person.

Action.

Breathe in.

Cut.

Breathe out.

It's almost biological.

Maybe I'm too used to thinking of myself as the one who brings a movie to life. Too in love with the idea that, until it gets to me, a scene's just a play that someone happened to record. Maybe I've forgotten what an audacious act of creation this is—how exhilarating it can be to share this moment with a group of my peers, fellow film lovers all, each of us so passionate about our craft and our art and our—

The boom mic wobbles as the operator tries to hide a yawn with his elbow.

Three rows ahead of me, the makeup artist is texting on her phone. Two women from the art department sit slumped against a wall, whispering to each other behind their hands. I think one of the sound guys is literally asleep.

Well—it was a nice moment for a second there.

The image behind Liza and Eileen starts to flicker, then goes dark. Half the room turns to look at the projection booth; the other half turns to look at Tony.

"Exactly how often is this going to keep happening?" he asks.

"I'm doing the best I can!" the projectionist shouts down. "This thing has a mind of its own!"

"I'm delighted to hear that one of you does."

After a moment, the projector whirs back to life with a metallic screech that I feel in the back of my teeth. Tony circles a finger in the air. Everyone resets.

I tug at my earlobe. My ear's itching.

"Action."

Finally, Liza and Eileen get to run their scene. It's a cute shot: the two of them, dwarfed and doubled by the images of Joan Fontaine and Judith Anderson. A little on the nose, maybe, but I'm willing to give Tony the benefit of the doubt. The lighting helps. The tungsten bulbs the DP's using are slightly out of fashion, but the quality of the light sure is something. This guy has chops.

Not that he'll ever hear that from me.

Liza misses another cue. I don't catch what Tony says to her this time, but we all hear what she snaps in response.

"Well, maybe if I could get a decent night's sleep, I'd be able to remember my blocking."

Tony tilts his head to the side, considering. "Eileen seems to be doing just fine."

Eileen nods sagely. "Earplugs and Ativan."

Tony presses his eye to the viewfinder and lifts his hand.

I tug on my ear again.

"And act—"

"Wait."

The voice comes from the rear of the theater. It's a white woman, about fifty years old, tall and solid and strong. She reminds me

85

powerfully of my mother. I wonder if her forearms, too, are lean and freckled from a lifetime of being the first one to roll up her sleeves and get things done. She's standing just inside the door, lips pinched into oblivion.

Tony steps out from behind the camera, and I shrink back, sure he's going to unload on this nice normal woman.

"Francie," he says, warmly. "What did we get wrong?"

She nods in Eileen's direction. "Her makeup," she says. "My grandmother has worn bright red lipstick every day of her life since she was thirteen. She says no one should have to face the world without it—she even wears it in bed. She taught herself to sleep on her back so it wouldn't smudge during the night."

I catch myself reaching for my ear for the third time.

Tony turns, clears his throat. "Carmen? This is your area of expertise, I think."

The makeup artist drags her eyes up from her phone. She looks at Tony, then turns to Francie. "You know what brand she used?"

"Elizabeth Arden. Victory Red."

"Do you have that in your kit?" Tony asks.

Carmen props her chin on the heel of her hand. "I don't carry vintage stuff. You know who did, though? Penelope." She takes a beat. "Too bad you fired her."

Any good humor in Tony's expression vanishes in an instant. His lips shape a smile that's the stuff of nightmares. "Now there's an interesting idea."

Carmen sighs, stands up. "Yeah, fine, I can replicate it. Give me ten."

There it is again. That itch in my ear—except it's not an itch. It's a high-pitched whine. Faint, but definitely there. I glance over at the sound guy. He's clutching his headphones and frowning. I wave at him, trying to get his attention, but he's too focused to see me.

I think it's getting louder.

I pull myself to my feet. "Tony?"

Tony turns, blinks. "Who's this?"

The whine is definitely higher now. Like it's about to—

I swallow. "I think there might be something wrong with the genny."

His eyebrow lifts. "I wasn't aware we'd hired a new electrician—"

Pop.

I glance up; Tony does the same. We just lost a light.

Out of the corner of my eye, I see the DP take a tentative step forward.

Pop.

Two lights now. A small band of crew members rush the stage, but they're not quick enough, because—

Pop pop pop pop pop.

A series of small explosions, one after the other, like a strip of cheap firecrackers.

We lose all the lights.

And then, the projector goes out.

Darkness.

—followed by the clatter of forty-odd phones switching on, bathing the room in a pale glow.

"Everyone okay?" someone asks.

"I don't know," Eileen says. She's drawing on her stage voice now, and its round, rolling tones fill the room. "Does 'covered in fucking *glass*' count as 'okay'?"

A few seconds later someone finds a light switch, and then we're blinking into the amber murk thrown off by the theater's ancient house lights.

We all readjust—

And the room explodes into motion. Most of the crew members hustle over to the stage, where Liza and Eileen are still crouched down, their hands protecting their faces.

Anjali bursts through the door, shouting something into her phone and motioning urgently to a nearby PA. She stalks over to the DP, who immediately puts his hands up in a defensive gesture.

"Don't look at me like that," he says. "I triple-checked the setup—*personally*. It was perfect."

"*Perfect*," she says, shaking her head in disbelief.

A burst of static behind me; I glance back over my shoulder. A broad-chested man in khaki pants and a sports coat is standing just inside the lobby door, speaking into a radio, his hand shielding his lips from view. Next to him is Isaiah. He's sliding his gun back into its holster.

He catches me watching him. He has the grace to look a little sheepish.

"*Tony!*"

Onstage, Liza has pulled herself to her feet; two crew members are trying to help Eileen up, their hands cupped beneath her elbows, but they're thwarted by the slim cut of her dress. There's simply no way to lift her without risking indecent exposure.

Eileen swats their hands away and tugs her skirt higher on her hips, exposing the tops of her stockings. "For God's sake, I'm not precious. I did a twelve-week run of *The Graduate*."

Three members of the hair department race in. They comb their fingers carefully through the women's hair, picking out shards of glass.

"Are you okay?" Tony asks, coming over, shaking a few shards out of his own hair.

"I don't know," Liza says. "What do you think?"

"You're upset," Anjali says, joining them. "I get that. But please, don't worry. This was just a freak accident. We'll be back up and running in no time."

"A freak accident," Liza repeats, flatly.

Anjali nods. But for the first time since I've met her, the movement is tentative.

"I think we're starting to stretch the definition of freak," Liza mutters.

Tony reaches into Liza's hair and finds a piece of glass the hairdressers missed. "Are things really so terrible?" he asks.

Eileen snorts.

Tony's hand stills for a split second before continuing. "You have to trust me, Liza. Trust that I know what I'm doing—and trust that I'm doing it for a reason."

She sighs. "Okay, but—"

"I would never put you in danger," he continues. "I'm not a madman."

"But Tony—"

"And you don't think I'm a madman, do you, Liza?"

"No, of course not, but—"

Almost absently, he brushes a strand of hair off her face. A tendon in the side of her neck flexes. Her lower lip trembles.

Tony taps it with his thumb.

"There it is," he says, tender, soft. "You keep losing it." Then, without breaking eye contact, "Dice, can you rig something up, get us going?"

The DP looks up from his MacBook. His mouth opens and closes several times before he answers. "Give me twenty."

"Good. I want everyone ready to go once the lights are back up." He turns and finds me in the crowd, his expression grim. "Everyone but you, that is."

TEN

march out into the lobby, Tony and Anjali behind me, preparing to be fired for the second time in my life.

Under normal circumstances, it's pretty hard to fail at my job. By the time the footage makes its way to me, there's only so much that can go wrong, and most of that has to do with proprietary software. It's tough to fumble the basics. Cinematic grammar is so deeply engrained in the culture, you could probably pluck a six-year-old off the street and she'd be able to put together a half-decent assembly cut. There's a reason you rarely finish a movie and think, "Wow, that editing was *terrible*."

And, even then, it was probably the director's fault.

The only time I was fired, I was working on a high-profile, effects-heavy movie—a franchise reboot—and honestly, I never should have taken the job to begin with. But I was young and excited about the chance to assist an editor I admired, and cutting Amy's delicate, impressionistic short films wasn't exactly paying the rent. It wasn't even paying the water bill.

It became clear very quickly that even though I was green and totally new to that kind of big-budget workflow, the director was even more out of his depth.

But then, he was a franchise reboot, too: the son of an A-list director.

The night it happened, we had been cloistered together in the cutting room for ten hours along with the lead editor and three suits from the studio. We were trying to come up with a solution for I can't even remember what when the director barked at me to pull up coverage that I knew for a fact simply did not exist.

I looked to my boss for guidance, but he chose that moment to discover a sudden, all-consuming interest in a miniscule imperfection in the fabric of his jeans.

"I'm sorry," I finally said, "but I can't do that."

"Why not?" asked the director.

"Because you didn't get any close-ups for this scene."

"I absolutely did. It's on the shot list."

"No, you decided to skip them. And when I got the rushes and came and asked you about it, you said, 'Fuck close-ups, that wide shot is bomb.'"

My boss looked up from his jeans.

"I remember," I explained, "because you said 'bomb' and not '*the* bomb,' and it sort of stuck with me."

Later, my boss told me that if I'd just accepted responsibility, he would have been able to keep me on. Everyone in the room understood that the mistake was the director's, but we weren't allowed to openly acknowledge it. The fact that I'd done so could only mean one thing.

I was officially combative.

I related this all to Amy, hoping she could help me pinpoint where I'd gone wrong, but she rolled her eyes and said, "That's just Hollywood slang for a woman who uses declarative sentences."

"You were supposed to be here an hour ago" is the first thing Tony says to me. Not the most auspicious start.

"If you wanted me to come straight here," I say, carefully, "some-one should have told me."

"That one was actually my fault," Anjali puts in, brightly. "I had to stop to deal with Gavin."

"Do we have a problem there?" Tony asks.

"I mean, I caught him with those girls again, but I don't think it's anything to worry about." She pauses. "Those are two sentences that really shouldn't go together."

Tony hooks a finger behind his ear and rubs at the skin there. "Have Wade deal with it. I have too many girls to think about as it is."

On that note, he turns to me, and this is it, I guess. The moment of truth. I study his face as carefully as I dare. His eyebrows are in a neutral position, and the left side of his mouth looks to be a little higher than the right, which I think might be the start of a smile— unless it's the start of a frown.

I try not to twist my hands together.

"I'm sure you can appreciate that this is an unusual situation," Tony says. "I've never had to hire a new editor, sight unseen, halfway through a movie."

"As hard as that is to believe," Anjali adds.

Tony spreads his hands. "I'm trying to do something here."

She takes an exaggerated step back. "Okay, okay, you're the boss. I'll go—yell at some people or something. You okay on your own, Marissa?"

My brow furrows. "You mean with Tony?"

"Yeah—I can send in a PA if you'd like."

Oh. *Oh, right.* It's been a while since I've had to work closely with a man. Things are different now, aren't they? Or at least we're saying they are. I give myself a moment to think about it. While I'm not exactly comfortable with the idea of being alone with Tony, I'm even less comfortable *acknowledging* that I'm not comfortable, because that would make everyone else uncomfortable, too. Seems like kind of a glitch in the post-#MeToo matrix.

"I'm good," I say eventually.

"Cool, cool. I'll be back in a bit with your keys and phone."

"Phone?"

I wrench my gaze away from Anjali's departing figure to find that Tony's also moved on without me. I scramble to catch up.

"—by the time we get to set, I've typically had a few months' prep with my editor," he's saying. "But obviously I don't have that luxury now."

"Wait—you're not firing me?"

We stop next to the concession stand. He sweeps back a red velvet curtain to reveal a heavy wooden door, an open padlock hanging from the loop of a rusted hasp. He pulls the door open. "Sounds like someone's been listening to stories," he says, his expression bland.

I wince and step through the door, thankful beyond measure that it's dim enough to hide the embarrassed flush that's licking at my cheekbones like wildfire. There's barely any light back here—at the end of the hall, a single, flickering bulb hangs a few feet above the ground—but Tony's obviously familiar with the space. He leads us easily through the near-darkness, steering me around two separate spiderwebs. We stop at the foot of a steel spiral staircase, twenty feet high and very narrow. We ascend one at a time, the structure jolting and swaying with each step.

At the top, I squeeze through an opening so narrow I have to take a second on the other side to collect myself.

I'm still catching my breath when I feel the heat of Tony's body behind me.

"This is where you'll be working," he says, his mouth in line with my ear.

It's the theater's projection room—and it's set up for 35mm. I ignore the editing bay and rush over to the projector, a Philips DP70 with a three-deck Christie Autowind. Neither machine, I admit, is elegant to the modern eye. The DP70 is big and beige and boxy, and the Autowind is borderline ridiculous: three stacked aluminum platters, each about four feet wide, secured to a turquoise frame.

To me, however—

I have to resist the urge to spin in an awestruck circle.

The projectionist is busy scowling into the DP70's innards, and I catch myself craning my neck around, eager to see what he's doing.

"I haven't seen one of these since high school," I say.

Tony peers over my shoulder. "I'm old enough to remember when we still had to do changeovers."

I'm grateful my back is to him, because I feel myself pull the kind of face Amy always smacks me on the shoulder for. I could be 105 years old and working on my thirty-fifth feature, and some man would still find a way to imply he's been in the business longer than I have.

"The ST 200 came out in sixty-eight and the Autowind in seventy-one," I say. "If you remember changeovers, it's from your History of Projection elective at NYU."

I duck under Tony's arm and head over to inspect the front of the projector. It's not one I've worked with, but I've read about it—they have two at the Egyptian, and they used to have one at Grauman's—and when I run my fingers over it, the sprockets and stabilizers are as familiar to me as my own bones.

I go up on tiptoe and peer over the top of the lens. Next to it, positioned in the right-hand side of the projection window, is a small black box: an NEC digital projector. It's about 1/100th the size of the DP70 and of proportionate appeal.

"For the dailies," Tony says, unnecessarily.

"Shame we're not shooting on film," I say, just as uselessly.

"Not with these actors." His shoulder is so close to mine I can feel the space between us.

I move briskly to the opposite side of the room. There, along the wall, is a water-stained three-seater and an eight-foot-long melamine table. On top of the table are a microwave and a hotplate, a six-pack of single-serve Easy Mac, an unopened box of Constant Comment; beneath it is a stack of flattened pizza boxes. I pick up a mug that's been left next to the hotplate and glance inside. Whatever was in there has long since gone sticky and solid.

My gaze lands on a blue plaid blanket hanging over the arm of the sofa. I lift a corner and rub it between my fingers. I wonder if there's a pillow up here somewhere or if the last editor had to make do.

The question just gurgles up out of me, really.

"Why did you fire Paul?"

Tony presses his lips together, glances at the projectionist. "Gary?"

Gary tosses his wrench in his toolbox and scrambles to his feet. "I'm gone."

Tony watches him leave, waiting for the last clanging echoes of the man's descent down the metal staircase to fade away. Then he leans a shoulder against the wall and crosses his arms.

"Surely you've heard how I work."

"I have some idea." And then, because I simply can't help it, "And don't call me Shirley."

He clears his throat. "Yes, well, you know, then, that I require absolute dedication from my cast and crew."

I can't help but glance at the makeshift kitchen. "Are you telling me the guy who practically lived here wasn't committed enough?"

"If time was all that mattered to me, I'd hire insomniacs or buy a kilo of coke. I'm talking about dedication to your *role*. My editor needs to be my anchor—my *compass*. When I look at footage, I'm seeing the eight million or so decisions that went into each shot. You, however, can focus on the little picture: what's in the frame."

I scrunch up my nose. "I mean, of course. That's basically the textbook description of—"

He holds up a finger. "Which *also* means I don't want you spending time with the actors. So, I don't want to see you in the bar. I don't want to see you in the café. I don't want to see you at hair and makeup, gossiping with the stylists. Occasionally, like today, I will ask you to join me on set. Otherwise, I prefer that you spend your time here or in your room."

"I'm—"

"I understand that this may seem restrictive, but this is an unusual situation. Many of the people involved in this case are still on the island. In fact, some are in this hotel with us right now. And not all of them are as devoted to the notion of objectivity as we are."

I frown. "If you're so worried about outside influences, why didn't you just let me stay in LA?"

He shakes his head. "No, that wouldn't work at all. I like my toys where I can see them."

At this, my face does something indescribable.

He laughs, but not like you would at a joke. "Look at you. Less than an hour into the job, and already you're thinking about quitting."

My eyes narrow. "Why would you say that?"

"So you're *not* thinking about running back to California?"

"I was thinking about running back to California the second I landed," I admit.

He pushes off the wall and closes the distance between us. "We could make a great movie together, you and I. You may not be able to see the shape of it yet, but this isn't just some true crime cash grab. This story actually matters. You could really make a difference with this one. But you have to trust the process."

That easy drawl of his has gone even easier, so easy it makes me think of that cat from reception, of the way I massaged the spot just behind the hard ridge of her jaw, and I think maybe he wants me to roll over and go boneless and not notice that he's telling me—*gently, sweetly*—that he's going to keep me under house arrest for the next six weeks.

I stare down at my feet and do a quick calculation: It would take ten minutes to get back to the lobby, another ten to track down a car. Thirty minutes to the dock, five minutes to throw up, twenty-seven minutes to Lewes. Two and a half hours to Philly, five and a half hours to LAX, fifteen minutes to Ladera Heights. Factoring in a few delays and the time change, I could be at Pann's in time for breakfast.

But—then what? Find a new Airbnb? Beg Nell not to fire me?

How hard can six weeks of work be, anyway? It's not like he's asking for anything too difficult or outrageous. And I'm not exactly a social butterfly to begin with. It might even be nice. I won't have to come up with excuses for why I don't want to hang out with everybody on our nights off.

I make myself lift my chin.

"Yeah," I say. "I can do that."

He nods. "Good. Now, this is the last time we're going to talk about Paul, do you understand?"

"But—"

"The last time."

I hold up my hands. "Okay."

He takes the blanket, folds it into quarters, and tosses it to the other side of the sofa. "Come on—let's get you set up."

I follow him over to the editing bay in the near corner of the room. It's a standard setup: L-shaped desk, three HD screens, two nearfield studio monitors; a keyboard, mouse, and a Mackie compound mixer. An overpriced chair with six separate adjustment points. Tacked up on the wall to the right are several rows of reference stills, each one corresponding to a scene and shot number, a visual index of everything that's been filmed so far. I examine the stills, my gaze naturally landing on the photo of Liza they showed me at my interview.

"How long did it take them to find her?" I ask. "The real girl, I mean."

Tony rubs his hand over his mouth. "The coroner's estimate was sixteen to twenty hours postmortem, but no one's sure how long she was on the beach. She looked like she was sleeping. A hundred people probably walked by her that day and didn't realize she was dead."

I frown. "How do you get a body out onto a public beach without anyone seeing?"

"That's one of the things we're here to ask."

"So this is an *un*solved mystery?"

Tony slides his hands in his pockets. "Technically. No one was ever charged."

"And you're going to try to solve it?"

"Of course not." The corner of his mouth moves. "I'll leave that to the audience. An argument's more convincing if you let them think they've figured it out themselves."

I blink. "That's what my brother always says about his son."

"Does he?"

"His son's six."

A pause. "Ah."

I let out a shaky breath and turn back to the photos. I feel like there's something else I should be asking, but my brain's already allocating resources to the project in front of me, making lists, running through the narrative algorithms I've been compiling since the day my dad brought home that VCR. The possible storylines are unspooling in my head without any effort at all—there will be the victim, her family, her friends, a boyfriend (probably), the police, the perpetrator, the prosecution, a key witness or two—

"Marissa?"

I come back to myself with a start. A few feet away, Gary's at work on the projector; Tony is nowhere to be found.

How long have I been looking at these pictures?

I rub my eyes and turn to see who's at the door. It's Anjali and a woman I haven't yet met, a bare-faced almost-blonde in a cropped white T-shirt and baggy jeans. She has the mercurial, apple-cheeked beauty you sometimes see on Eastern European actresses: She'll look twenty years old her whole life so long as she stays thin, but the moment she gains five pounds, she'll look fifty.

"Sorry to interrupt," Anjali says. "I just wanted to introduce you to our line producer, Valentina."

Valentina grimaces around the silver Juul clamped between her lips. "Charmed."

She hefts a bulging messenger bag up onto the work table. She digs around inside for a few seconds before pulling out a badge on a royal blue lanyard. She tosses it in my direction; it bounces off my stomach and falls to the floor.

I pick it up gingerly, afraid of what I'm going to find. They didn't ask me for a headshot, so that means—yep, that they've used the only photo IMDb has of me. It's a Getty shot from an awards show a few years back. Just a third-rate critics circle, but it was my first nomination, so Amy dropped a dress in my lap and sent me to get my hair and makeup done. Afterward, my mother said I looked sophisticated; Amy said I looked hot; I said I looked like a kindergarten pageant queen.

I hold up the lanyard. "Do I really have to wear this?"

Valentina shrugs. "Depends. Do you *want* to be detained by security?"

I scowl down at the badge holder. I've never been on a set that required ID. Most productions I've worked on were content to outsource perimeter security to twentysomething PAs who may or may not have even known how to work a radio. It's a different story for a feature with big-name actors, I guess—but this is a shoot on a sparsely populated island. What are they so worried about?

Tony's words from before come back to me.

In fact, some are in this hotel with us right now.

That can't really be what this is about, can it? If it is, someone should really tell them a premium-cotton lanyard isn't going to provide much protection against a murderer.

Another object collides with my stomach; this one I manage to keep from falling.

"Your phone," Valentina says, with relish.

I pick up the gray flip phone between my finger and thumb. "What's wrong with my iPhone?"

"No smartphones. Nondisclosure agreement, page nine." She extends her hand, palm up. "Hand it over, please."

I shrink back. "You want me to give you my *phone*?"

"You know," Anjali says, "these days some people actually *pay* to have their phones taken away from them. Think of it as a media fast! It'll be good for you. God knows I wish I could stop looking at the news."

"How will people reach me?"

"You can always call your voicemail and check your messages."

I turn the flip phone over, examining the casing. "Can you even still do that?"

"No clue. I get to keep my phone."

I reach into my pocket and pull out my iPhone. Anjali snatches it out of my fingers, replacing it a second later with a set of keys. "These are for the front door to the theater and the padlock downstairs," she says. "Don't lose them. Anyone important enough to have a set of their own is too important to have time to let you in."

I curl my fingers around the metal until the edges of the keys press into my palm. "Okay, wait—wait. I have just a *couple* questions—"

Anjali nods sympathetically. "Of course you do. And don't worry, we'll set you up with Scripty first thing in the morning. She'll walk you through *everything*. Tony doesn't want you on set until noon, so you'll have plenty of time to catch up. Speaking of—" She looks at Valentina. "Has Brandon printed the call sheet?"

Valentina reaches for her Juul. "He is working on it now," she says.

"Yeah, well, it was supposed to be done an hour ago, so will you tell him to get a fucking move on?"

Valentina's left shoulder lifts an inch or two in the most desultory of shrugs. "I can only say the same thing so many ways."

"Then maybe you should say something new. You're Russian. Be creative."

Valentina takes a long, lazy drag, holds it, then releases the vapor from the corner of her mouth in a slow, steady stream.

"*Tak tochno.*"

Anjali snaps her fingers. "Yes, that's exactly what I'm talking about. I have no idea what that means, but it scared the shit out of me."

Valentina gives me a look like she's breaking the fourth wall.

Then she clamps her Juul between her lips, tosses her bag over her shoulder, and slinks out of the room.

Anjali gazes after her, shaking her head. "If she ever cracks, it's gonna be magnificent." She claps her hands and turns back to me. "We good here?"

Good? Are we *good*? No. We're not good. We're so far from good I don't even know what good is anymore.

"Like I said, I have some questions."

"And like *I* said: Scripty will handle that. Is there anything you need from *me*?"

Her smile is lethal, sweet and unforgiving—a fact I only register several seconds *after* barreling on ahead and saying, "So why did Tony fire Paul?"

That smile goes a little unsteady around the edges. "It's not my place to say."

"Are you sure about that?"

"Excuse me?"

"You're the producer, right? It's your responsibility to ensure that the movie gets made. Which means it's your responsibility to ensure that your new editor doesn't get fired immediately. So it seems logical that you would want to tell me what Paul did wrong so I can make sure not to do the same thing."

The smile has disappeared completely now. "You should really ask Tony."

"I tried. But he just responded with a slightly demented lecture about"—I wave an inarticulate hand—"*process.*"

She sighs, and for a moment she looks less than perfect—I can see faint circles under her eyes and a slight crease down the middle of her forehead. "Look, he wouldn't have hired you if he thought you were going to make the same mistakes."

"He can't know that. He barely knows me."

She laughs. "Since when did that stop anyone from making a snap judgment? You don't know anything about me, but you obviously have a theory or two."

I think back to the moment I met her. "Well—I was worried you might be an actress."

When she doesn't respond, I force myself to look at her face, and what I see there isn't understanding or impatience or even annoyance. Her eyebrows have drawn together, and the line of her mouth has gone very straight. It's an expression I've really grown to hate.

It's an expression that means she doesn't think I'm funny.

I'll be lucky if I last a day.

ANJALI BHATTACHARYA: I didn't think she'd last a day.

SUZY KOH: Why would you say that?

ANJALI BHATTACHARYA: You've met her.

SUZY KOH: Yeah, but our listeners haven't. So could you, you know—elaborate a little?

ANJALI BHATTACHARYA: I don't suppose I can deflect by questioning the validity of your metrics?

GRACE PORTILLO: Please don't be a jerk just because it's easier to be funny.

ANJALI BHATTACHARYA: Yikes. Out of the mouths of babes. Okay, then, honesty for honesty: When I met Marissa, I thought she was a little weird, but that didn't concern me. Most editors are.

SUZY KOH: But . . . ?

ANJALI BHATTACHARYA: *But* I didn't get the sense she'd be able to stand up to Tony—and since I know you gremlins are going to ask for specifics, no, I can't tell you exactly why I thought that. It was just a hunch. [*pause*] I mean, just goes to show, right?

ELEVEN

After Anjali leaves, I sit down at the editing bay, raise the chair, and pull the keyboard within reach. My eye catches on a yellow paper doll that's been taped to the corner of the center screen. It's an old trick: Some editors use a scale doll to remind them of the size of a theatrically projected film. It's cute, but not something I've ever bothered with. No piece of paper has ever been able to help me imagine my way into the feeling—or even into a decent memory of the feeling—of being physically dwarfed by a beautiful picture.

And these days most people stream their movies anyway.

I tap the doll—or what's left of it.

Someone's torn its head off.

I decide to start at the beginning, with the film's first scene: Liza, on the beach, dead but not yet discovered. The shot that started it all.

I find the file, adjust the volume, start playback.

In the background, the extras are already in motion, applying sunscreen and adjusting umbrellas and shaking out towels. Two children are hard at work burying their father's feet in the sand. A red-and-white beach ball has been abandoned in the water. It floats in and out of frame.

Liza, however, is just lying there. And Tony's letting the camera roll.

I jump forward. Five minutes, ten minutes—twenty minutes. Finally, at twenty-five minutes, Liza moves. It's not much, just a wiggle of her hips, and even though the editor in me cringes, I can't blame her. She must be incredibly uncomfortable. There's no way her arm hasn't fallen asleep.

Her chest shudders, a reaction familiar to anyone who's ever fought their natural breath, then stills.

Tony's voice, barely louder than a whisper, comes from off-screen: "Liza, we're still rolling."

Her nose twitches, but she doesn't respond. She's getting anxious now, I can tell; you can see her body working to hold itself in place. Her stillness is labored. And she's forgotten about her eyeballs—they're moving beneath their lids. She probably doesn't even realize she does that when she's concentrating on something.

"Stop thinking," Tony says, very calmly. "Dead girls don't think."

Behind me, unmistakably, someone giggles.

I pause playback.

"Gary?" I ask. "Is that you?"

Silence. Then—

"Uh—yeah, sorry about that, I didn't mean to interrupt you. I'm just wrapping up here."

Another pause.

"He's just such a pompous *dick*, you know?"

I spin my chair around. Gary's eyes are half closed and his hands raised in front of his chest. He looks like he's preparing to absorb a full-body blow.

"You're not gonna tell him I said that, are you?"

I blink. "I think maybe you can go now, Gary."

He nods. "Yes, ma'am."

I shake my head and turn back to the computer.

Following a hunch, I click through to the directory and sort the files by date. The footage I'm watching shoots straight to the top. So I was right, this isn't just the first scene in the script—it's also the first scene they shot. With most directors I wouldn't read too much into the production schedule. There are any number of reasons why they would start with this scene. Permits. Weather. The logistics of Liza's fake tan. But everyone knows Tony does nothing less than exactly what he wants.

What was he hoping to accomplish by picking this scene?

I restart the footage and scroll forward. The answer will be in here somewhere.

An hour and forty-six minutes in, it happens: Liza finally forgets her face is supposed to look good for the camera. Her lips part and her jaw softens and her eyes settle low in their sockets, and she releases a tension in her forehead I hadn't even realized she'd been holding. Her eyebrows aren't nearly as arched and symmetrical as she would have us believe.

This, I'm certain, is what Tony was waiting for.

For her to stop fighting.

For her to give in.

Sure enough, two seconds later, three background figures break away and head toward camera. Teenage boys, their swim trunks slightly different but complementary shades of blue. Tony has them miked even though they're talking about nothing at all.

Because of the split lens, the closer they get, the harder it is to see them, but then they cross into the foreground and come into such sudden, sharp focus I stiffen at the shock.

It's perfect timing: We're able to see them at the exact moment they should be able to see Liza.

My fingers curl around the mouse.

Any second now—

But they pass directly in front of the camera without stopping. They exit the frame. The screen goes black.

I push back from the desk and rub briskly at my arms.

He really did that. He really had her lie there in silence for nearly two hours, her eyes closed, sending the same signal to every part of her body: *Dead, dead, be dead, I am dead, this is dead, one day this will be me, dead.* The most important thing Tony wanted Liza to establish as part of her performance was what it would really feel like, in her body, to be dead.

A feeling I've spent thousands of dollars trying to forget, and here she is, conjuring it up by choice.

Something hot and sharp burns the back of my throat: a memory, but not the kind I'm expecting. A real one, from grad school. Second year, Amy and I took a class from this guy John Hale, an apparently well-respected critic with two acknowledged areas of expertise, Italian neorealism and hitting on his students. Unfortunately, only one of those was listed in his faculty bio.

The guy was fixated on *Stromboli* and *Umberto D*—so fixated, in fact, that he didn't deign to discuss anything made after 1951 until the very last lecture, at which point he glossed over the last seventy years of Italian cinema in three hours with the same sniffing disdain you'd expect from a society doyenne who'd just been served dinner from the right.

Over the course of that last three-hour class, Hale's commentary grew sharper and stiffer and terser until, finally, he hit some kind of limit two minutes into a clip from *Suspiria*. He paused playback, flipped on the lights, and turned to the class.

"This is garbage, of course. Real art deals with real emotion, with real life. None of *this*"—I can still picture the disdainful flick of his fingers at the screen—"is real."

There followed a lengthy, pained silence, and for once it wasn't my fault. At least half the guys in there had only signed up because Tarantino's an Argento fan. That's when Amy leaned back and stretched one arm along the back of the seat to her right, breathing out a luxurious sigh that had me edging toward the aisle.

Hale's shoulders rose and fell. "What is it now, Amy?"

"It's just bullshit, that's all."

He propped his elbow on the lectern and rested his chin in his hand. "I presume you're going to tell me that, thanks to the unparalleled expressive power of allegory, *Suspiria* helped you access some heretofore unknown corner of your heart—to learn something 'profound' about the human condition that you couldn't possibly have otherwise comprehended."

"No, of course not—but it helped *you* learn something, right?"

His eyebrows—white, wild, so low they sometimes tangled with his eyelashes; the only piece of his face my memory seems to have grasped on to—lifted a scant inch. He and Amy had been arguing all semester. Looking back, I wonder if he knew then that he was walking into a trap.

That he kept on walking tells me nothing. Men always do when Amy's involved.

"Oh?" he said.

Amy twisted her hand in a slow, counterclockwise circle. "Men make horror films about fantastic creatures and outlandish villains and beautiful victims. Women make horror films about what happens when the wrong guy gets into your car. You ever wonder why that is?"

Another flick of his fingers. "That's a grotesque mischaracterization."

I silently agreed with him. Sometimes women also make horror films about what happens when the wrong guy gets into your house.

"The answer, *John*, is that for you, fear is a fantasy." She paused and looked out at our classmates. "You can only conceptualize fear as an exception, when for women, it's the rule."

Hale rolled his eyes. "Oh, Amy. Did a *war* break out when I wasn't looking? Because last time I checked we were sitting in a very comfortable classroom at a school that your parents, presumably, are spending forty thousand dollars a year for you to attend. Come on. When's the last time you were really *scared?*"

Amy tilted her head to the side. Only pretending, I could tell, to think about this.

An inappropriate moment, perhaps, to picture Admiral Ackbar, but I just couldn't help myself.

"I'm fairly certain," she said, "it was two weeks ago—when you backed me up against a wall and asked if you were smelling my perfume or my pussy."

Hale ended class early that day, and I'd like to think he was ashamed of himself, but honestly he probably just couldn't bear to cover *Cannibal Holocaust*. Last I heard he was still teaching. Occasionally we'll run into someone who was in class with us that day, and they always try to bring up what happened, but Amy's embarrassed by it now.

"Never underestimate the intellectual arrogance a single women's studies course can give a girl," she always says.

("But seriously," she always adds, "fuck that guy.")

I drift back over to the wall of reference stills. Tony may be a slave to verisimilitude, but he can't resist tszujing the visuals: a little shimmer here, a little shine there, shapewear on everyone. Were the photos displayed in a more artful manner, it wouldn't be hard to mistake them for a series of curated vacation shots, the kind a tour company takes so you can populate your Instagram feed without having to pack a selfie stick. No regular human would look at these stills and confuse them for anything other than a carefully art-directed version of the real thing. And they haven't even been through post.

My hand kneads a knot of tension in my lower back. Normally I love Tony's aesthetic. In his movies, everything has its place and everything is *in* its place, and getting to live in a world like that for two hours is about as close as I can get to inner peace. But this is a story about a real person, a real murder. Shouldn't that demand a more rigorous commitment to realism? And still, Tony couldn't help himself. He just *had* to make it beautiful. Special. Exceptional.

This doesn't feel like fantasy. But it doesn't feel quite like reality, either.

"Already burning the midnight oil, huh?"

I turn. Isaiah's standing in the doorway, looking very powerful and matter-of-fact, like he's just about to announce the thesis statement of his TED Talk.

My shoulders curl in on themselves. "If you're going to be serious and stern, can it wait?"

He eases into the room. "The problem," he says, in a low, confidential tone, "is that they *pay* me to be serious and stern. See, you can't have a sense of humor *and* the ability to kill a man with your bare hands."

I feel myself relax just a little. He's bantering. This is banter.

"It's like they've never heard of The Rock," I venture.

"Right? It's 2019. A man can have layers."

After a moment, his face settles, his smile fading, but it doesn't quite revert all the way back to that bland professional mien. I can't help but feel mildly triumphant.

I look down at the work table, tracing the wood grain with my fingers. "Tell me—does everyone on the crew get their own personal armed escort?"

"That's just until you perform the blood loyalty oath."

A laugh sneaks out of me. "You sound like Amy."

He flops down onto the sofa. "Who's Amy?"

"A very good friend with a very bad habit of distracting me with jokes when she's sick of answering my questions."

"You do ask a lot of them."

I smile weakly. "My gift and my curse."

He picks up the afghan, turns it over in his hands. "I'm sure everything will make more sense after a good night's sleep."

"Now you sound like my mother."

He raises an eyebrow. "Careful. I might think you like me."

"Don't get too excited, those are basically the only two people I know."

He straightens abruptly and laughs, openly and easily, like it would never even occur to him that I wasn't funny on purpose, and I'm forced to admit that meeting this man might be one of the better things that's happened to me in a while.

I manage to make it back to my room without tripping or fumbling or otherwise embarrassing myself, and it's with no small measure of relief that I close the door behind me. I lean my forehead against it and count to a hundred. I find it helps me if I do this. I can't just switch myself on and off like a light. I have to give myself time to cool down.

Then I do a cursory survey of the room that's going to be my home for the next six weeks or so. High ceilings, crown molding, celadon walls. A four-poster bed, an antique brass lamp. On one wall, a historical map; on another, a vintage illustration of a horseshoe crab. Three plump needlepoint pillows are spaced along the length of the cream loveseat. It would be easy to imagine that this is exactly how the room looked back in 1948.

If it wasn't for the faint smell of fresh paint, that is. I press a fingertip lightly to the nearest wall, testing it. It's dry, but if I had to guess, it was painted within the last two months.

Once the initial spell is broken, the rest of the illusion falls apart. I realize the map's a reproduction—and now that I think about it, I'm pretty sure I saw that illustration at IKEA the last time I was there. That lamp definitely takes an LED bulb.

I wonder if they renovated for the movie or if I was just assigned to a refurbished wing. Tony doesn't skimp on his budgets, but even he might not be able to cover a historical restoration of an entire hotel.

Whoever paid for it, I'm grateful. They got the *good* hypoallergenic pillows.

I retrieve my suitcase from the closet, and I examine it carefully. I don't like to use bellhops if I can help it, but I still haven't figured out how to say that without offending them. It's not that I don't trust them. I just get anxious when someone else has my stuff. Even Amy doesn't know the full details of the way I like to keep my things. I'm very particular.

Which is why I can tell right away someone has been through my suitcase. Whoever it was did a pretty good job—they were careful to try to put everything back where they found it—but I notice right away that one pair of pants was rerolled with the wrong side out.

Is this another outlandish security precaution? Did I agree to that, too, when I signed my contract? Or is this island just some lawless netherworld where privacy rights and common courtesy no longer apply?

It occurs to me that I may just be describing Delaware.

I drag myself over to the chair and examine my new production phone. It's only a little smaller than my hand, a stubby rectangle with a display not much larger than a postage stamp. I flip it open—flip it closed. Flip it open. Flip it closed.

That's satisfying, at least.

I check the clock. It's only nine in LA. No wonder I'm not tired.

Oh *shit*. I forgot to call Amy.

She picks up immediately.

"Marissa?"

"How'd you know it was me?"

"Delaware area code—it was you or Joe Biden. You okay? I've called like five times."

For some reason, I hesitate. "Well—it kind of turns out we're not allowed to have our smartphones."

"*Excuse* me?"

"I know, you'd think it's a Marvel movie." An unpleasant thought occurs to me. "You don't think they'd bug the production phones, do you?"

"Seriously?"

"Are they allowed to do that? Is that legal? I've never had a company phone before."

"Look—"

I curl my ponytail around my finger. "Could you google whether Delaware's a two-party consent state? Probably not, right? Because it's Delaware."

"Marissa! Enough with the phones. Listen: We've been asking around—"

I wince.

We?

On cue, I hear a familiar voice in the background.

"Hold on," Amy says. "Josh wants to talk to you."

Hell's bells. I pull the phone an inch away from my ear.

"Marissa."

I pinch the bridge of my nose. How a person can manage to cram so much disapproval into three simple syllables, I'll never know.

"I didn't realize you were there," I say. "I'll keep it short, I promise. I'm not trying to interrupt."

"No, no, that's not it—I mean. *No.* Look. I asked around, and it doesn't sound good. My gaffer's buddies with a couple guys on your crew, and he told me your shoot's got some real bad mojo."

It's my absolute certainty that he thinks he's doing me a favor right now—that he thinks he's *such* a good guy—that makes me do it.

"I think you mean juju," I say.

He pauses. "No, I mean mojo."

"A mojo's a magic charm for protection or love or luck or power that you keep on your person. You can have it or you can lose it, but it can't be bad—otherwise, why would you keep carrying it around? You're thinking of juju."

"Does it really matter?"

"Or maybe you mean karma?"

"For fuck's sake, would you just—*ow*! Dammit, Amy! Yeah—yeah. I know, but—"

A flat silence settles over the line. He's hit mute. I wish I could blame Josh for not liking me, but his reasons are solid. I truly can't help myself.

That doesn't make him any less of a jerk, though.

"Marissa? You still there?" It's Amy.

"Yeah," I say.

"He's just trying to help."

"I'm sure he is."

"Just—listen to him, okay? For once. It sounds like something's off about that set. Shit keeps going wrong, people keep quitting."

Given everything I've seen so far, that's a more than fair description, but I'm not about to admit that Josh is right.

"You could say that about half the films in production right now."

Amy sighs. "Yeah, but apparently on this one, the authorities have had to get involved? There was a setup that went wrong or something, I don't know."

A pause that has me digging my thumbnail into the chair cushion.

"And Josh's friend doesn't think it was an accident," she goes on. "He claims Production's covering something up."

This is such a wild assertion that when I try to figure out how to respond, my brain sort of misfires, pulling up way too many memories all at once—old ones, new ones, clear ones, crummy ones—and I'm just not sure what I'm supposed to be paying attention to. *The captain's face. Isaiah's gun. My mother's garden. Anjali's keys. The door to the editing room. The entrance to the caves. Wade's laugh. Liza's lips. Whoopi Goldberg.*

Whoopi Goldberg?

Marissa. Focus.

I rub a hand over my face and let my feet move as much as they want to, and eventually, the signal fights its way through the noise.

A petty, tangential signal. But a signal nevertheless.

"Why is Josh suddenly so interested in my career?" I ask.

"He's worried, that's all."

"No, he isn't." *Amy's* the one who worries about me. Josh—Josh does whatever the opposite of worrying is. "He doesn't think I can handle myself."

"That's not true—Tony's just difficult, you know that."

"Amy, if I never worked with difficult directors, I'd never work."

I want to take it back immediately. "Difficult" isn't how Amy sees herself. She sees herself as the kind of director who creates safe, supportive spaces for her cast and crew. Who listens to every complaint. Who cares about every answer. Who pays out of her own pocket for hot sandwiches on rough days. Who squeezes her actresses' hands in sympathy, nodding with them, swaying with them, saying, "I hear you. I *hear* you."

But while all these things are true, it is also true that she's *incredibly* difficult, exacting and demanding and everything else you'd expect from an overachiever who truly believes she can bring the people around her up to her level. I tried to tell her once that as far as reputations go, "difficult" is way better than "weird," but even though I gave her an entire anthology on the subject for Christmas, this, apparently, isn't one of the things she can *hear*.

Great. Now I'm mad—so here's me saying more terrible things.

"And anyway, what does Josh know about having a hard time?"

"He's just trying—"

"To help. I know. But, like—you know I've worked on more movies than he has, right? Won more awards. Put up with more BS in a single day than he has in a *decade*. So—I don't need his help. I don't want his help. And I'm not going to quit my job—and breach my contract—just because some gaffer Josh worked with one time on some *web series* is spreading rumors."

She doesn't answer. But, over the line, I can just make it out. The very slightest noise: a flutter.

I wince. Shit.

"Marissa?" she says after a moment.

"Yes?"

"Why don't you like him?"

"It's not that—"

"Because if there's something I should know—"

"There isn't," I say, firmly.

TWELVE

y the time I get off the phone with Amy, it's been fourteen hours since I last ate. As soon as I realize this I'm up and on my feet. My hand is already reaching for the doorknob—I think I saw a vending machine in the lobby—when I remember Tony's instructions.

I'm not supposed to leave my room.

I hesitate.

But he can't want me to starve, can he? And it's too late to call anyone for help—not that I even *can* call anyone, because no one's given me a call sheet. Plus, it's late. Everyone else is probably in bed. No one will see me. I'll be fast. I'll just pop right down and back. Easy-peasy.

Maybe I'll take the stairs, though. Just in case.

I reach the ground floor and poke my head out into the lobby. As I'd suspected, it's empty, completely quiet. So quiet, I can only hear the ocean.

I pad past reception and head for the vending machines, walking on my toes and keeping to the carpet. Once I'm certain I'm alone, I let myself indulge in the happy little daydream that's coming on: that I'm the only person in the hotel—the only person on the *island.* Yes, that's better. Then I wouldn't even have to worry about someone coming to the door. Even the most distant prospect of intrusion—a neighbor, a solicitor, a package that's coming in five to seven days— can spoil the pleasures of solitude.

My smile fades when I find the vending machine. It's one of those *healthy* vending machines with KIND bars and kale chips and soy nuts and organic cotton socks. A waste of perfectly good pocket change.

I turn my back on the machine and consider my options, my hands on my hips.

I guess there's nothing for it. I'm going to have to find the kitchen.

I head for the darkened dining room, slipping between tables already set for tomorrow's breakfast. On the back wall, between a booth and the beverage station, I find a narrow hall that leads me past the restrooms to a pair of silver doors with porthole windows.

I peer inside. The overheads are off, but there's a faint blue light coming from somewhere, and it's just bright enough that I can make out the line of the countertops and a faucet and what I think is a range hood. The scent of bleach is strong enough to have me scratching at my nose.

I push through the doors and wait for my eyes to adjust.

Immediately to my left is a hand-washing station, and beyond that is some kind of storage, and then there's the—

The light goes out.

I pause only briefly. I spend my life moving from one poorly lit room to another: It's not the dark I'm afraid of.

But then, from the far corner of the room, comes an unmistakably human sound.

My mouth goes dry. I may not be scared of the dark—but people scare the shit out of me.

"Hello?"

As soon as I say it, I want to smack myself in the forehead. Like, sure, go ahead, Marissa, give away your position, announce your cluelessness, pull back that shower curtain so the killer can get a better look.

And what am I expecting to hear, anyway?

So happy you could make it!

I've been expecting you!

Is it me you're looking for?

When the lights come on, I scream.

"Dude, chill."

Behind me, one hand still on the light switch, is a young East Asian girl. Fourteen or fifteen, maybe a bit younger? Her black hair is tangled and tucked behind her ears, and her bangs could use a trim. She's dressed in cutoffs and a sleeveless gray hoodie; two black hair bands wrap around her left wrist.

I've seen her before, I realize: earlier, in the lobby, with Gavin.

"I'm Suzy," she says.

"And I'm Grace."

I twist around. It's the other girl from the lobby. She's perched on a countertop in the corner, partially obscured by the commercial refrigerator. She's smaller than Suzy, with light brown skin and a big dimple in her left cheek, and she's dyed her hair the color of a Flamin' Hot Cheeto. Her clear acrylic glasses are too big for her head; they're barely clinging to the tip of her nose.

I don't know what the right thing is to say in this situation, but it's certainly not what I land on:

"I'm not supposed to be here."

Suzy shrugs. "That's okay. Neither are we."

"What brings you to Kickemout Island?" Grace asks.

I blink. "I thought it was Kickout Island?"

Suzy hops up onto the counter next to Grace. "Not since Tony shitcanned the first AD," she says.

"You mean the 2nd AD," Grace says.

"No, Ryan was the first AD."

"*Phil* is the 1st AD."

"Oh, right, I see what you're saying." Suzy turns back to me. "Sorry. Not since Tony shitcanned the *first* 2nd AD."

I look back and forth between them. They don't look alike, but the way they're talking—

"Are you two sisters or something?"

Suzy shakes her head. "We've just been stuck on this island for weeks with no one else to talk to."

"A hundred percent possible we're going crazy," Grace says.

Suzy elbows her friend. "We talked about this."

Grace doesn't miss a beat. "A hundred percent possible we've become profoundly socially maladjusted."

My mouth, I realize, is hanging open. I ask a question just to give it something to do.

"Are you two from here?"

"No," Suzy says. "We're from New York."

Grace rolls her eyes. "She's from New Jersey."

"And"—God, why can't I stop blinking?—"I'm sorry, but who are you again?"

"My dad's the executive chef," Grace says.

"My mom's the pastry chef," Suzy says.

"We think it would be better if it were the other way around. But, you know"—Grace gives her fingers a wiggle—"the *patriarchy*."

And just like that, my spirits lift.

"That means you know where the food is."

"Oh!" Grace says. "You missed dinner."

"That sucks," Suzy says.

"It was lamb merguez—"

"With a warm carrot salad—"

"And an orange-basil granita—"

"There might be some leftovers?"

I scratch the back of my neck and look away. "That sounds lovely, but I was sort of hoping I could just make myself a peanut butter sandwich."

Grace slides down off the counter. "Don't be silly, I'll make you some pasta—what do you want? Puttanesca? Arrabbiata?"

I feel a frown coming on; I fight it back. "A sandwich is fine, really."

She adjusts her glasses and plants her hands on her hips. "My dad would seriously disown me if he knew I fed someone a peanut butter sandwich for dinner."

"But I don't want pasta. I want a peanut butter sandwich."

The girls exchange a look. "My mom did that peanut butter semifreddo a couple weeks ago," Suzy says. "We might have some Jif left over."

Grace wrinkles her nose. "She didn't make her own?"

"It's better with the cheap stuff."

"Gross. I'll check the pantry."

She disappears into a back room. Suzy, meanwhile, crosses to the other side of the room and crouches down behind the counter. Digging through a cabinet? Who knows. Who cares. At least she's not talking. I cast my eyes to the heavens and try to remember if there's a patron saint of comfortable silences.

"So what job will *you* be fired from in the next three to five weeks?" Suzy asks, her voice slightly muffled.

"I'm the new editor."

Her head pops up. "Really?"

"Is that surprising?"

She gives this some thought. "I guess not. We barely saw the last guy, that's all. Figured Tony had him locked away in a dungeon somewhere."

"Not a dungeon," I say. "Just the cutting room. But I understand the confusion."

"Yeah, we heard he was a crazy—I mean, an extreme worka—" She huffs. "An exceptionally diligent worker."

They knew Paul? Now that's interesting. Tony and Anjali weren't forthcoming, but maybe Suzy and Grace would have some useful information for me. Maybe they even know why Paul was fired.

"How do you know so much about the crew?" I ask.

Suzy shrugs. "We spend a lot of time at crafty. Or used to, anyway. But Anjali cracked down on that, and now we get in trouble if we go anywhere near the actors."

Her expression is so solemn and sincere, I have to wonder if I'm misremembering things.

"Didn't I see you two with Gavin just a few hours ago?"

"Oh, right." She breaks into a smile. "We probably should've snuck in through the sun deck, huh?"

"What are you doing with him?"

She shakes her head. "Sorry, that's our business."

The question that leaps immediately to mind isn't one I particularly want to ask, but Gavin's very famous and they're *very* young, and Amy would kill me if I didn't say something, so:

"Now, you're not—he isn't—"

I drum my fingers against the countertop. *How do I put this?*

Suzy laughs. "Molesting us? No way. If Gavin even *thought* about trying anything, there are like eight line cooks here who've known Grace since she was a baby—and they all have access to the meat grinder. We've made this clear to Gavin."

"Okay, well, that's very empowered."

She puffs out her chest. "Don't mess with a cook's kid."

"But then what are you—"

Suzy squeaks and ducks down behind the counter. I turn around just in time to see the man I met at the front desk come in.

He stops short when he sees me, his hand still on the door. "Oh. Marissa, right?"

I nudge my mouth into a smile. "That's right."

He's leaning to the right—Wade, that's his name—trying to see around the counter. I glance back over my shoulder, somehow not surprised to find no sign of Suzy.

Wade's frowning and rubbing the side of his face. "I don't suppose you've seen a couple of kids running around back here, have you?"

I hesitate. On the one hand, I like rules. Rules are good. They tell me where to go and what to say and how to not upset people. They're clear and they're comforting, and they make my life easier and happier. Grace and Suzy are clearly breaking the rules. They should face the appropriate consequences.

On the other hand, sometimes part of following the rules is knowing when *not* to follow the rules, even though it seems to me that they could have just included that in the rules from the start, as I told my eighth-grade English teacher on *several* occasions.

And it's not like I'm supposed to be in here, either.

I wonder if Wade knows that.

"Kids?" I murmur.

"Teenage girls. One's Hispanic and one's—I don't know, I think the other one's Chinese?" He flinches. "Sorry, sorry, I didn't mean that. Chinese American."

Thump.

Wade squeezes past me, the door flapping shut behind him.

"Did you hear that?" he asks.

He circles the room, moving carefully, quietly.

"Why are you looking for them?" I ask.

(Now, it's possible that I say this a little more loudly than I need to—and also that I try to direct my voice in the general direction of the pantry. Just, you know, in case anyone who might be in there needs a heads-up.)

"They've been bothering the actors," he says.

"Everything bothers actors," I point out.

"Yes, but Mr. Rees has very strict rules, and if I don't abide by them—"

He breaks off.

"You're the owner," I say. "He can't fire *you*."

"Pretty sure he could fire his own mother," he mutters. He looks at me then—really looks at me—and his brow furrows. "Why are you here?"

If I had a dime . . .

"I know," I say. "I'm not supposed to be. It's just that I missed dinner, and—"

Another of his *this-one-goes-to-11* smiles. "Well, we can't have that, can we? Our new editor going hungry on her first day? Let's just see what's in the pantry—"

"No!"

He pauses mid-turn, his smile dipping down to an 8. "No?"

"You don't have to go to all that trouble," I say. "Just—point me to the vending machines." I punctuate this with what is almost certainly the worst fake laugh of my life, and that includes the time I went to a friends-and-family screening of *Office Christmas Party*.

His eyebrows come together. "Why are you in the kitchen if you're looking for vending machines?"

Good point.

"I just—don't want to be a bother—"

"But you're our guest."

Think, Marissa. What can you ask for that isn't in the pantry?

"Eggs?" I say.

"Scrambled?"

"Perfect?"

He goes to the refrigerator and pulls out a carton of eggs, a big block of butter, some fancy milk in a glass jar.

I glance at the pantry door and pray Grace is smart enough to stay where she is.

Wade finds a whisk next to the grill. He takes a plate from the shelf and a pan down from the rack. He looks around, slapping the whisk absently against his palm.

"Bowls, bowls, bowls." He bends down to check the cabinet at his feet. "Nope."

He opens another cabinet. "Not there."

He reaches for the next one, and I realize then that if he makes it to the end of the row, he'll find—

I drop down and thrust my hands under the counter. I grab the first vaguely round shape I find and hold it up.

"Will this work?"

Wade straightens and looks at the object in my hands. So do I.

It's a colander.

"Just kidding," I manage. "Hold on, I know I saw one down here."

I check again and this time I get lucky: Just to my left is a stack of metal bowls. I hand one to Wade and he sets about whisking the eggs.

"The secret," he says, "is the heavy cream. Used to do a fair amount of cooking here myself, if you can believe it. I'm no chef, but I can hold my own."

"For some reason I assumed you were the owner," I say.

"Uh, no. That's Francie, my wife." He fiddles with the knobs for a few seconds before he gets the burners to light. "I pitch in wherever she needs me."

"Have you been here long?"

He pours the eggs into the pan. "Just over twenty years now."

I feel my expression brighten. "So you were here when that girl was murdered?"

His arm jerks; the egg mixture splashes up over the side of the pan, sizzling against the burners.

I wince. "I shouldn't have said that."

He cleans his hand with the hem of his shirt. "No, it's fine, I don't mind talking about it. It's kind of hard not to, these days. I guess it's just that word, you know? *Murder*. It's so—"

"Gruesome?"

"—bad for business."

"Huh," I say. "I would assume the opposite. But I guess it depends on the type of murder."

He doesn't respond, and I have to glance over at him. He's frozen—just standing there. Staring at me. Wondering if I was raised by wolves, probably.

I clear my throat. "I'm so sorry, I—did you know her?"

He runs a hand over the back of his neck a few times. "Caitlyn? Yeah, sure, everyone knew her. Her family had been coming to Kickout for years. She practically grew up here."

I take a moment to study his expression. He doesn't appear particularly sad—his face isn't drooping, his eyebrows aren't pinching upward—but he's a man, so that doesn't tell me all that much. I recite one of my stock expressions of sympathy just in case.

"That must have been very hard for you."

"Harder on Francie," he says. "Caitlyn was like her kid sister."

Caitlyn. Her name was *Caitlyn*.

I look down at my hands. Until this moment, it hadn't really sunk in for me how messed up this situation is. What is Tony *thinking*, filming this movie on location, in proximity to all the people who have been hurt the most? Surely he could've gotten a few establishing shots and done the rest on a sound stage. Authenticity is easy enough to fake.

I try to imagine having to watch a film crew reenact my worst memory. What would it feel like to be back at that campground? To watch an actress go into that cave? Would she wear the same navy blue Keds with the worn-soft soles? Would they wait for a rainy day?

For the creek to rise? Who would they cast as the other campers? Who would they cast as me?

"Does Liza look like her?" I ask. "Like Caitlyn?"

He scrapes the eggs out onto a plate and hands me a fork. "She's a dead ringer."

The words hang in the air, and I watch with grim fascination as Wade pales beneath his tan.

He recovers quickly, though, clearing his throat and wiping his hands on his pants. "Well, I guess I'll leave you to it. I'm sure Francie will be needing me."

"Thanks, Wade."

"Yeah, uh—*bon appétit.*"

I wait until his footsteps die away and then, just to be sure, I wait another minute more.

I push the plate away.

I hate scrambled eggs.

THIRTEEN

Wade's gone," I call out.

Suzy emerges from the cabinet with a clatter. She groans and goes up on tiptoe, stretching her arms over her head.

When she comes down, she turns to me and sighs.

"For the record, I'm *Korean* American."

The pantry door swings open. Grace's head pops out. She looks left, looks right. Then she tosses me a jar of peanut butter and a loaf of bread.

"On the house." She sidles up to Suzy and nudges her with her elbow. "Dude, I was *just* about to come out when I got your text."

All of a sudden, I'm able to place the blue light from before. "You guys are using your smartphones?"

"Don't tell anyone," Grace pleads. "I promise we're not using them to take pictures of the sets or anything."

"We just need them for research," Suzy says.

"What for? Aren't you guys on summer break?"

They're so in sync, they give themselves away by just how hard they're *not* looking at each other, and here I have to make a decision, because I have what I came for: this giant jar of perfect, processed, non-crunchy peanut butter. These girls are not my friends, their behavior is not my business, and these fluorescent lights are really beginning to get to me.

But—

I think this is one of those niggling questions that's going to worm away at me. Like when you're talking to someone who just got a haircut, but there's one strand that's longer than the rest, and you can't hear anything they're saying because all you can think about is how much you want to lunge forward and yank out that piece of mismatched hair. Sure, they might charge you with assault, but it would be worth it.

I set the peanut butter and bread on the counter.

"What are you up to?" I ask. "It has something to do with Gavin, doesn't it?"

Grace bites her lip.

"You can trust me," I say.

Suzy looks up at the ceiling.

"Did I or did I not get rid of Wade for you?"

"*Fine,*" Suzy says. "But if you rat us out? Remember those line cooks I mentioned."

"Hugely disproportionate physical threat duly noted."

"We're working for Gavin," she says.

"But we don't, like, get him lattes," Grace says.

"Or do his dry cleaning."

"Or pick all the green M&M's out of the bag because *real* artists don't—"

I hold up my hand. "I get it. You're not his assistants. So what's he paying you for, then?"

They look at each other and grin. And when they answer, they do so in unison.

"We're detectives."

My stomach turns over.

Grace goes on. "He wants us to exonerate him."

"Well, not *him*," Suzy says. "His character."

"I'm not sure he sees the distinction?"

I let my upper body slump against the counter. "So—Gavin's playing the killer."

Suzy makes a face. "I mean, obviously."

"But he doesn't think the guy really did it?"

"Right," Grace says.

It takes a moment for this to sink in—I'm honestly shocked Gavin would want to play an *innocent* man.

"And what do you two think?" I ask.

"We don't think," Suzy says. "We know. The evidence is circumstantial at best."

Saints preserve me.

"If you're going to be 'detectives,'" I say, slowly, "you should probably be aware that most evidence is circumstantial. Fingerprints are circumstantial. DNA is circumstantial. Blood spatter is circumstantial."

"Oh," Grace says. "Then I guess they don't have circumstantial evidence, either."

Suzy gives me a speculative look. "How do you know all that? You're not a lawyer."

"I cut three episodes of *Suits*."

Suzy leans over to whisper in Grace's ear. Grace nods, and they turn to face me, their arms linked.

"You should help us," they say.

I take a big step back. "They weren't very good episodes."

"Yeah, but you're way nicer than anyone else we've met, and I bet you know all sorts of useful stuff," Grace says. She pokes Suzy. "Google her."

Suzy pulls an iPhone out of her pocket. "What's your last name?"

I narrow my eyes. "None of your business."

She snorts. "Like that ever stopped me."

Approximately ten seconds later she hands the phone to Grace and points at something on the screen.

Grace lets out a breath. "Whoa."

"Right?" Suzy says.

"What?" I ask.

"You know Amy Evans?" Grace says. "We're *obsessed*. We saw her last movie, like, eight times."

"Now you *have* to help us," Suzy adds.

"Because I worked with Amy?"

"She wouldn't hire someone who sucked."

I rub my nose. "You'd be surprised."

Suzy slides her phone back into her pocket. "So you'll do it?"

I hesitate. "I have a job of my own, you know—"

Suzy leans forward and slaps her hands against the counter. "That's right—you're a part of this, too. Well, Gavin says Tony's one hundred percent certain Billy Lyle's guilty. Like, that's that. Case closed. Q-E-whatever. Do you really want your name on a movie that's going to ruin an innocent man's life—for the second time?"

Wait—*Billy Lyle*? How do I know that name? I don't think I would have read about the case, I was in middle school at the time. Was there a cast list lying around somewhere? Did I see something in the editing room?

Then it comes to me.

"The *boat captain*?"

Grace's eyebrows go up. "You know Billy?"

"He brought me out to the island."

She smiles. "Then you know what a nice guy he is."

"I'm not sure that's *exactly* the word I'd use."

"I know he's a little weird when you first meet him," Suzy says, worrying the bands around her wrist, "but once you get to know him—well, okay, he's still pretty weird, but I swear, he would never hurt anyone. He's a sweetheart. I've seen him drop everything to move a cockroach out of his way."

"I don't know," I say. "I bet plenty of murderers like bugs."

"Billy's *not* a murderer," Grace says.

"Then why is everyone else so sure he did it? You should've seen the way these guys were treating him tonight."

"Because he's different! Because he makes people uncomfortable. They just look at him and think he's, like, *wrong*."

Shit.

I grab the jar of peanut butter, twist off the top, and scoop out a generous fingerful. I suck it into my mouth and smash it between my tongue and my palate so that I can draw out as much sweetness as possible before the peanut butter melts. This was the only way my mom could get me to eat any protein as a kid. I preferred Skippy back then, but my tastes have broadened over the years. Now I'll eat Jif and Peter Pan, too.

Is this the worst idea in the world or the best idea in the world?

It's obviously the former, right? I'd be potentially putting my job at risk to help a couple of teenagers play Nancy Drew. Worst idea.

Then again, the whole point of Nancy Drew is that adults aren't very good at solving mysteries. What if these girls really do know something Tony doesn't? What if he's genuinely going down the wrong path here? And what if this is our one chance to stop him?

So—best idea?

I swallow the peanut butter and wipe my mouth with the back of my hand.

I turn to Grace and Suzy.

"Okay. Tell me everything you know."

————

"So it's a pretty classic setup," Suzy says, splaying her palms on the counter. "Caitlyn Kelly, a rich girl from Philadelphia, comes to Kickout Island every summer with her family. Somewhere along the line, she falls in love with a good-looking boy who works at the hotel. Very *Dirty Dancing*—but without the dancing."

"Or the illegal abortions," Grace points out.

"Or Patrick Swayze," Suzy allows.

I drop my face into my hands, feeling very tired all of a sudden. "So, not like *Dirty Dancing* at all, really."

Suzy ignores this and continues with her story. "But then, plot twist, one day—just, like, out of nowhere—Caitlyn's dead body shows up on the beach, and no one knows how she got there. No one knows exactly how she died. And no one has any idea why *anyone* would have wanted to kill her. Everyone loved this girl, right?"

I reach for the bag of bread. "They always do, once they're dead."

"But eventually word gets around that the weird loner kid who worked in the boathouse was totally obsessed with her. The cops raid his boat, find serial killer collages, creepshot photos, the whole nine yards. Everyone on Kickout is sure he did it." She pauses. "I'm talking about Billy here."

"I figured, but thanks for the clarification." I take a slice of bread and tear it in half. "Why wasn't he arrested?"

"He was," Grace says, "but they didn't prosecute. They didn't have enough evidence. Billy, like most loners, did not have an alibi."

I tear the bread in half again. "It's the only good reason to go to a party."

"But they also couldn't prove he was anywhere near Caitlyn at the time of her death. And, yes, she *might* have been killed with one of the oars from the boathouse, but, apparently, head trauma can be caused by *all sorts* of things. It also sounds like the police messed up pretty bad, procedurally speaking. So at the end of the day, they just weren't able to make a case against him. Not in court, anyway."

"Who do *you* think did it?" I ask. "Assuming it wasn't Billy, that is."

"Well," Grace says, "everyone in Caitlyn's family was cleared, so smart money's on the boyfriend."

I look up from my pile of bread. "Why's that?"

Suzy's eyebrows pinch together. "He's the *boyfriend*."

"And what happened to him?"

"We're still working on that. There are three hundred people on this island, and none of them will talk to us about anything but Billy."

"We actually started keeping track," Grace says. "Seeing how long it takes a local to tell us Billy did it. The average time is twelve seconds. We say 'Caitlyn,' they say 'Billy.' It's kind of like being a cheerleader, but, you know—for the miscarriage of justice."

"So do you know *anything* about this boyfriend?"

Grace shakes her head. "Just that his name was Tom."

"And there are no other suspects?"

Suzy makes an equivocating gesture. "I mean, kinda? There's Francie's grandma. She was some sort of movie star back in the day. Married the heir to the hotel."

"Oh right," I say. "*Rebecca*."

"No, Violet. She and Caitlyn were close—she was the last person to see Caitlyn alive. They were rehearsing in the movie theater the night Caitlyn was murdered. I guess Caitlyn wanted to be an actress or something. But according to Violet, Caitlyn went back to her room at the usual time. She was never considered a suspect."

"How do you know all this?"

Suzy reaches over and steals a scoop of peanut butter. "The inter- net. Also we stole a shooting script from Anjali's bag—God, this stuff is disgusting. How do you eat it?"

I frown down at the Suzy-shaped indentation in the peanut butter. "Anjali told me that everyone loved Violet. Could they have been covering for her? Like, a conspiracy?"

Grace and Suzy blink.

"Huh," Suzy says. "That's not bad."

"I don't know," Grace says. "You really think a grandma could have done it?"

I hold out my hand. "Suzy, give me your phone."

"You're not gonna call my grandma, are you?"

"Just—give it."

She unlocks it and passes it to me. I thumb three keywords into Google and hand it back.

She looks down and reads the first search result out loud. "'Seventeen little old ladies who were actually unspeakably brutal murderers.'"

"It still seems unlikely," Grace insists. "Violet's *tiny*. And the coroner was pretty clear there was no way a woman her size would have been able to inflict that kind of head trauma."

"What about the other hotel guests?"

"Also cleared."

I set my chin on the heel of my hand. "So that's it? There are no wild, outlandish theories? Like that the real killer was, I don't know—Santa Claus? An owl? Christopher Walken?"

"Nope," Suzy says. "There are really only two options. Either Billy killed her—because he was in love with her and she turned him down. Or the boyfriend killed her—because he was in love with her and she turned him down. Tale as old as time."

I scoop out another bite of peanut butter and swirl it around in my mouth. It seems so ordinary to me. Maybe Tony is, like the girls say, setting out to prove Billy's guilt. But what's the story there? Would a studio really invest millions of dollars in a movie that gives us an obvious answer? I sure wouldn't. But maybe I'm just naïve.

Maybe there's big money to be made in telling people they were right all along.

It would really help to have a script.

"Okay," I say. "What do you need from me?"

Grace's smile is so wide it nearly splits her face. "Well, right now we're trying to get our hands on the actual police report—"

I let my hands fall to the counter. "To be clear, I'm definitely not breaking into a police station for you."

"—but in the *meantime*, maybe you could, you know, find out if Tony has any research of his own? I mean, he probably hired detectives and fact-checkers and stuff, right?"

"Yeah, sure, I'll see what I can find." I cross my arms and consider the two of them. "I have one condition, though."

"Is it peanut butter?" Grace asks.

"From now on, stay away from Billy, would you? Just in case. Let's not be Janet Leigh in *Psycho*—let's be John Gavin in *Psycho*."

Suzy shakes her head. "I only understood half that reference."

I reach across the table and set my finger against the back of her hand. I want to make absolutely sure she's paying attention to what I say next.

"I mean it. Be careful, okay? The last thing this place needs is another dead girl."

SUZY KOH: So what made you think you could be a detective?

MARISSA DAHL: What made *you* think you could be a detective?

GRACE PORTILLO: Harsh. But fair.

SUZY KOH: You still have to answer.

MARISSA DAHL: [*sighs*] When you think about it, an editor—that is to say, a *film* editor—isn't really so different from a detective. We're both presented with an incomplete collection of imperfect information and tasked with piecing together a coherent narrative.

SUZY KOH: You could almost say—every film is a puzzle, really.

MARISSA DAHL: Suzy. Are you quoting Walter Murch at me?

GRACE PORTILLO: Walter Murch, for those of you who don't know, is an acclaimed editor and sound designer—

SUZY KOH: And beekeeper!

GRACE PORTILLO:—who has won three Academy Awards—

SUZY KOH:—for *Apocalypse Now* and *The English Patient*. Guy's got range.

SUZY KOH: Of course not, that's just something I found when I was googling memes for our Instagram.

MARISSA DAHL: [*inaudible*]

SUZY KOH: There's another one I liked . . . hold on . . . here it is. "The whole eloquence of cinema—

MARISSA DAHL: —is achieved in the editing room." Yeah. Same guy.

SUZY KOH: Cool. Has he worked on any movies I've heard of?

MARISSA DAHL: I think we're done for the day.

FOURTEEN

A s soon as I get back to my room, I turn off the overhead lights, yank back the bedspread, and fall face-first onto the mattress. I kick my legs out over the edge of the bed, and I bounce them up and down, my shins springing against the mattress in a steady rhythm, building up a bright, fizzy feeling in my bones that zips all the way up to the top of my skull.

I breathe in.

I breathe out.

And I keep doing that until my body releases the tension it has been holding on to for—rough estimate—the past thirty-six hours or so.

When I'm feeling like myself again, I grab my toiletries and pajamas and head for the bathroom. I shower, floss, brush my teeth, floss again. Wash my face, comb my hair, check under my nails to make sure I didn't miss anything, scrub them with a nail brush anyway. Put on pajamas. Climb into bed.

Then I tune the clock radio to static and close my eyes. Under the covers, I rub my feet together. Right over left, left over right.

I do all this every night, without exception.

It's cute when some people do it. Like—remember that speech in

High Fidelity? Not the one about what you like and what you *are* like—that one's awful—this is later, when John Cusack's finally realizing how badly he messed up with the Danish actress who was given so much more to do in *Mifune*.

"Top Five Things I Miss about Laura," it's called.

"Number five," John says, "She does this thing in bed when she can't get to sleep. She kinda half moans and then rubs her feet together an equal number of times. It just kills me."

What I wouldn't give to be granted one-tenth the behavioral leeway a man allows a leggy Scandinavian by default.

It's been a year since I last spent the night with someone and two years since I've really wanted to. The most recent guy was a barista who's trying to make it as a comedian. I didn't really like him, but he laughed at one of my jokes, and I was lonely enough to be flattered, so I talked myself into going through the motions.

He asked if he could stay over, and I said sure—because that's what Amy and my therapist and my mother are always telling me to do, to give people a chance, because who knows? They might surprise you.

But then I saw the way he looked at me as I went through my nighttime routine, so I wasn't surprised at all when his next questions were, *Do you have to listen to that horrible noise?* and *Does it have to be so cold?* and *Why do you have a sandbag for a comforter?* and *Do you really have to keep doing that thing with your feet?*

When I told him to leave, he announced he'd only come home with me because he was angling for an audition with Amy.

Then he told me I was the worst lay he'd ever had.

I bet five years from now he's a huge star.

I didn't exactly enjoy the experience myself. Touching the wrong person—well, it's hard for me to explain exactly how it feels. The best way I can think to describe it is that there's a beehive in my chest, and most people upset the bees. The nearer they get, the worse it is—and direct contact makes them swarm. I can feel them massing even now, in the knob of my clavicle, behind my triceps, along the tendon on the right side of my neck. Just the thought of being back in bed with that guy sets them scrabbling beneath my skin.

Love is a many-splendored thing. Anxiety, I suppose, is a many-legged creature.

I sigh and roll over onto my back. I should think about something else—something cheerful, something uplifting.

Murder works.

Cautiously, I invite in the thought I've been fighting back. Some-one killed Caitlyn Kelly. That someone was never caught. So there's a very real chance they're watching now as a bunch of Hollywood doofuses meticulously re-create what was either their greatest tri-umph or their worst mistake. They might even still work at this ho-tel. It's possible I've already met them without realizing it.

How often does that happen? How many times in our lives have we met a murderer? Greeted a murderer? Slept with a murderer?

I consider googling but think better of it.

I slide my hands under my thighs and adjust my shoulders. It isn't always easy to fall asleep in a new bed, but I think I'm tired enough to make it work.

It's been a such long day.

I'm so glad it's over.

Thump.

My eyelids fly open. I sit up.

Thump.

Is someone at the door? At this hour? But that's not a knock. It's more like a—

Thump.

Oh my God, is someone trying to get in?

I scramble out from under the covers. What do I do? Should I say something? Should I ask who's there? Is it smarter to let them know I'm here or to pretend I'm not? I mean—I guess the answer to that would depend on whether they're trying to kill me, right?

I give my hands a rough shake, then another. Then another.

It's probably just a crew member heading back to their room—drunk, maybe. And they just bumped into my door by accident.

Thump.

Bumped into my door by accident four successive times.

Shit. I creep over to the door and go up on my toes, craning my neck until I can look into the peephole. I don't see anything. Did they leave? I don't hear anything, either. Was I just imagining it?

I check that the security bar is engaged and ease the door open.

And I come face to face with the culprit.

"*You.*"

The cat blinks once, lazily, then returns her attention to the abandoned room service tray next to the door opposite mine. She's trying desperately to jimmy her nose underneath a stainless-steel cloche, but all she's managing to do is knock the tray into the wall.

Thump.

"If I lift the lid, will you stop making that noise?" I ask.

Thump.

I prop my door open and step out into the hall. I'm just reaching down when the door across the hall opens, too. I freeze, my hand hovering over someone else's leftovers, and look up into the face of one of the brightest young stars in Hollywood.

Like most white actresses, Liza May is startlingly narrow, her body a straight line from armpit to ankle. She's wearing a tank top and yoga pants, and her hair's bundled back into a messy ponytail, and if I feel any envy in this moment it isn't because she's prettier or sexier or more talented than I am. No. I hate her—just a little—because I know, deep in my heart, that she'll never get shit for walking around in yoga pants. She gets to wear whatever she wants. She's the kind of person who can only ever be dressed down, never underdressed.

"It wasn't me, it was the cat," I say, all eloquence.

"Oh," she says after a moment, equally nonplussed. "Is that—yours?"

"I think she lives here. I met her in the lobby this evening when I checked in."

She looks up. "You're the new editor?"

I take a step back, wiping my hand on my pajama pants. "Was there an all-hands about me or something?"

She pulls her door closed behind her and glances to either side. Then she leans in and says, "You should quit."

I draw back. "But I just got here."

Her hand curls around my shoulder, and I'm too shocked to shimmy free.

"Seriously," she says, "woman to woman, you want no part of this. I'd be out of here in a hot second if I thought I could." She pauses. "Did they have you sign anything?"

I nod, speechless.

Her hand falls to her side. "Shit. Well—whatever, that's why we have lawyers, right? Break the contract. Go back to LA. Thank me later."

"Wait, I don't—"

But it's too late. She's already slipped back into her room. I almost make a move to follow her, to ask her just what she's talking about—because come on, you can't just say something like that and *leave*—but there's no misinterpreting the sound of the deadbolt sliding into place.

After a moment, the cat pads over to weave figure-eights around my ankles. I look down at her.

"Well, that was disconcerting."

She lifts her chin and chirrups.

"No, I don't suppose Liza helped."

She meows again, insistent.

"Fine. But I'm going to have to insist that you gorge in private, like the rest of us."

I reach for the plate.

There's no way I'm going to be able to fall asleep now, so once we're back in my room, the cat tearing happily into her hunk of half-eaten steak, I pull out my computer.

I figure I'd feel pretty sheepish down the line if it turned out the internet had the answer all along, so I go to Google and type in, *Who killed Caitlyn Kelly?*

The first thing I learn is that Caitlyn was twice unlucky: Not only was she murdered, but she was murdered in 1994, just two weeks after Ron Goldman and Nicole Brown Simpson, and back then we weren't as practiced at holding multiple media-worthy murders in our collective consciousness at one time. Even the *Philadelphia Inquirer* could only find enough space for a near skeletal write-up:

CAITLYN KELLY, 19, DAUGHTER OF PHILADELPHIA
BUSINESSMAN MICHAEL KELLY, WAS FOUND DEAD LAST
FRIDAY ON THE GROUNDS OF A LUXURY HOTEL ON
KICKOUT ISLAND, A POPULAR SUMMER DESTINATION FIVE
MILES EAST OF LEWES, DELAWARE.

I guess you would have had to do something really special to break into the news that summer. But—I click on a few more links—all the details of Caitlyn's case are unremarkable. She was college-aged, which wasn't young enough to be truly shocking; she was majoring in drama, so the what-could-have-beens weren't particularly impressive; and she died from regular old everyday blunt force trauma.

She must have been beautiful—we are making a movie about her, after all. But maybe that didn't matter as much before social media.

Still, I can't quite believe there isn't more information online. Has the true crime crowd really not heard of this one? Maybe that's the reason for all the NDAs. This is probably the only murder that doesn't already have a podcast.

The cat jumps up on the bed and drags the corner of her mouth against the edge of my laptop.

I wonder—

I return to the search bar and type in two new words:

Anton Rees.

Generally, I try not to google people I work with. I prefer to pretend I'm not personally complicit in propping up the celebrity-industrial complex. But this is an unusual situation, and Tony has many fans of the Extremely Online persuasion. If his cult of followers is substantial enough to keep two competing subreddits going, I figure there should be *some* information about the film online.

I hit enter.

I regret the decision as soon as the results come in.

It's not just the fanboys who are talking about Tony—it's everybody. His very famous wife has just very publicly left him.

I scroll quickly through the first few stories that pop up. It's mostly the usual stuff: breathless, secondhand, hyperbolically punctuated. "Annie's heartbroken!" friends say. "Tony's devastated!" sources report. According to one outlet, they've already reconciled and are trying for a biologically improbable baby. According to another, Annemieke's hiding out at their summer home outside Amsterdam. Several gossip blogs claim that just yesterday, Tony was spotted French kissing a twenty-year-old plantfluencer in the parking lot outside Bristol Farms.

The least believable detail: Representatives for both parties are officially asking for "privacy during this challenging time."

I keep scrolling, skimming more or less the same story over and over again. At the bottom of the first page of search results is a provocatively titled link to a British paper I'm usually too embarrassed to read, but since I've already abandoned all my scruples, I don't see any reason why I shouldn't click on it, too.

I'm lucky I do—it's the only article to mention the movie:

"Tony's basically broke," an extended family member reveals. "He's always put money into his own films, and sure, that's fine when you're making cozy indies, but he's putting millions into this new project, and eventually Annemieke got fed up. She gave him an ultimatum: 'The movie or me.' He picked the movie."

I set my laptop to the side and reach for the cat. I settle her on my chest, right under my chin, so I can pretend it's just her weight I'm feeling pressing down on me.

It's one thing to work for a famously demanding director. It's very much another to work on his passion project. If he's willing to leave his wife for this movie, what else might he be willing to do?

FIFTEEN

When Isaiah knocks on my door, it feels like I've only just nodded off. I squint up at him through lashes still sticky with sleep.

"Not a morning person?" he guesses.

I glare at the windows, scowling at the light squeezing in between the louvers. "It doesn't feel like morning," I grumble.

"In LA it isn't. Anjali wants you downstairs to meet with someone she calls Scripty?"

I rub my eyes. "Yeah, that's the script supervisor."

"Can you be ready in a half hour?"

"I can be ready in half that."

He nods. "I'll be outside if you need me."

I pad into the bathroom. One of the many things I enjoy about being an editor is that no one expects me to come to work in full makeup, so my morning routine is basically my evening routine.

Shower, floss, brush my teeth, floss again, wash my face, comb my hair, check under my nails to make sure I didn't miss anything, scrub them with a nail brush anyway, put on clothes.

Today I finish by applying two coats of mascara because I read that's the easiest way to look "put together" (whatever that means) and swiping on the thirty-dollar organic lip balm Amy introduced me to. Apparently ChapStick dries out your lips? I don't know. I can't really tell the difference, but Amy always seems happy when she sees me using this stuff.

Fifteen minutes later, I step out into the hallway. Isaiah makes a grand show of checking his watch. "I thought you'd never be done."

I shrug, self-conscious. "All my work clothes match so I don't have to waste time worrying about what to wear."

His mouth moves like he wants to say something to that, but he changes his mind.

He takes me down to the lobby and deposits me in the hotel's business center, which Anjali appears to have appropriated as her command center. It's a substantial room, large enough for a warren of computer carrels, a twelve-foot conference table, a wet bar and kitchen area, and at least two dozen fake plants—not to mention the ten or so PAs milling about. It smells of carpet cleaner and hot ink.

Anjali catches my eye and waves me over. Next to her is a young black woman practically groaning under the weight of an armful of binders and folders and papers. As soon as she sees me, the woman staggers forward and dumps the materials on the conference table. A binder tumbles open, papers spilling out in a rainbow of colors.

She mutters something under her breath but makes no move to tidy them.

I twist my hand in the hem of my shirt.

Anjali points at each of us in turn. "Marissa, Scripty. Scripty, Marissa."

The woman—the script supervisor—gives me a tired smile.

"Scripty'll take you through what we've shot," Anjali says. "Tony wants you up to speed ASAP."

Scripty sighs. "Of course he does."

Anjali thrusts a hand behind her. A PA places a sheet of paper into it, which she passes on to me. It's a call sheet.

"He wants you *both* on set—"

I start. "What?"

"—call's at four."

I glance down. "Wouldn't my time be better spent looking at footage?"

"They're still repairing the projector," Anjali says. "You'd be in the way."

"I do have a laptop, you know. It has three whole USB ports."

She dimples. "You're funny." She presses something into my hand and spins me by the shoulders until I'm facing the conference table. I look down. She gave me a can of soda.

How did she know I drink regular Coke?

Scripty's waiting with her hands on her hips, gazing mournfully at the materials strewn across the tabletop. She's pretty—really pretty—built like a ballerina, long and lean and muscled and conspicuously graceful: All her body's boundaries seem to taper to a delicate point. Her eyelashes are so thick, I bet she could donate half their bulk to kids with cancer and still star in a Maybelline ad. I glance across the room, then realize with a rotten, sinking feeling I recognize from middle school that, like Scripty—and Liza and Anjali and Carmen and Valentina—the PAs could have stepped straight out of an aspirational Instagram feed.

Everyone on this crew is otherworldly beautiful.

I should've known it was a three-coats-of-mascara kind of morning.

But I should be *proud* to work on a production with so many female crew members. Unless maybe I should be concerned that they've only been hired to meet certain aesthetic standards? No, it's unfair to assume beautiful people are lacking in substance. Models are people, too. I read that somewhere.

This would be so much easier if Amy were here to tell me what I'm supposed to feel.

I slump into a seat and angle my body in Scripty's direction. I lift my chin and try not to be jealous of her cheekbones.

"My real name's Kim," she says after a moment.

"My real name's Marissa."

We both fall silent. I look off to the side and think, very hard.

"So have you worked with Tony before?"

She lets out a strange laugh that prickles the back of my neck. "No, this is my first time—and my last."

I sit up a little. "It's that bad?"

Her lips give the barest impression of a smile. "Tony never hires the same script supervisor twice. It's one of his 'things.'"

"Do all positions have the same level of turnover?"

Kim tilts her head, thinking. "No, not everyone's miserable. There's an inner circle. Like Daisuke and his guys—"

"That's the DP?"

"Yeah, they've been together forever. Same goes for Anjali."

"Wait—really?"

She nods. "She's produced his last five films, I think."

"But I've never heard of her before—and I spend half my life on IMDb."

"That's because she's only ever credited as his assistant."

"Oh."

We both look down at the table. After a moment, I reach for my soda.

Kim clears her throat. "Anyway, he and Paul had only done—what—three movies together, I think? So you may have big shoes to fill, but they're not, like, impossibly large."

I take a sip of soda to give myself time to formulate my next question. Normally, I work too closely with the director for the crew to risk taking me into their confidence. But since I'm new, maybe Kim would be willing to open up to me—

"I don't want to make you uncomfortable," I say, "but do you know what happened there? No one told me *why* Paul was fired."

Kim picks up a pen and twirls it in her fingers. "I'm not exactly sure. Paul's a bit of a character. Sleeps during the day, works all night, communicates mostly by Post-it." She points the pen at one of the items she dumped on the table, a bulging plastic pouch filled with fluorescent yellow squares. "But he was good at his job. I never heard Tony say anything bad about him."

She starts twirling the pen again, this time in the opposite direction.

"But I never heard him say anything good, either." She shrugs. "I don't think he was fired because of his job performance. Even for Tony, it's a little early in the process for a director and editor to disagree."

I drag my eyes up from the pen. "So you don't actually know what happened?"

"Well, Paul can't exactly tell me his side of the story—unless he wants to mail me a Post-it." She squares off her script and sets her hands on the table. "Now, the first thing we should—"

"But if you had to guess."

Kim relents. "There was *one* scene."

I let my heels bounce beneath the table while I wait for her to go on.

She tucks a curl behind her ear, two lines forming between her eyebrows. "So, at a certain point, I started ranking the scenes by how many Post-its Paul gave me. One to five Post-its, the footage was probably in good shape. Five to ten, I was going to have to go back to my notes. Any more than that, I'd just send Tony in to talk him through it—not that it ever helped."

When she doesn't continue, I glance up at her. "Are you waiting for me to ask how many Post-its he gave you for this one scene or are you just prolonging the suspense?"

The corners of her mouth drop. "Forty-seven," she says. "He gave me forty-seven Post-its."

She fishes a shooting script out of the pile and slides it over to me. I run my thumb across its edge, counting six different colors of paper, which means we're on our fifth revision. A familiar sight: Amy likes to run her writers ragged, too.

"Turn to page sixty," Kim says.

EXT. ENCHANTED WONDERS AMUSEMENT PARK — DAY

The sort of summer day that, years later, will make you question your own memory, because surely nothing real could ever feel so perfect, so vital, so rich with sensual promise, when the sea breeze is a hand running restlessly through your hair and all around you are sounds of pleasure and revelation, and the afternoon light limns the curve of a beautiful girl's neck and you can't help but wonder what it would feel like to put your mouth there, if her skin would taste like sunshine, if the world would taste like sunshine.

I look up at Kim.

She heaves a sigh. "I *know*."

"Who wrote this?"

"I've never heard of him. Unpublished novelist, probably."

I flip forward, scanning ahead, finding walls upon walls of text. Each scene is described in stultifying detail. The weather. The light. The blocking. The cut of Caitlyn's clothes. The tenor of Caitlyn's voice. The shape of Caitlyn's lips.

Description, description, description.

Caitlyn, Caitlyn, Caitlyn.

"Is it just me, or does this guy—"

"Have a fixation? Not just you."

"Did he know her or something?"

She shakes her head. "Men don't talk that way about women they actually know."

I turn back to the script, skimming, searching for the action.

> CAITLYN
> [wicked and shy and sweet all at once]
> Took you long enough.

Behind them, in the distance, the roller coaster begins its run, clambering to the top of the initial rise.

> TOM
> Well, that sort of thing takes planning.
> It takes time. You can't just ask a girl out
> like it's nothing.

The roller coaster is close to the top now . . . The first car is just beginning to round the peak . . .

> CAITLYN
> Are you trying to tell me I'm something?

> TOM
> Something else, maybe.

The roller coaster SCREAMS down the track, tearing through a 360-DEGREE VERTICAL LOOP, careening into a DEAD MAN'S CURVE. It rockets into frame behind Caitlyn and Tom—and it is here the eagle-eyed viewer sees him, staring at the glowing, happy couple:

BILLY LYLE.

"—a bitch of a scene," Kim's saying. "I guess Liza hasn't eaten sugar since like 2013. We had a spittoon under the table, but she could never find the right moment to duck down and hock out the cotton candy, so it was impossible to sync the coaster from take to take. Plus, they fired the 2nd AD halfway through the day, which means we didn't have anyone to direct the extras, and Anjali couldn't keep Tony from taking over and talking to them—so now half the island's SAG eligible."

She takes a breath.

"And I haven't even mentioned the derailment."

I look up. "The *what*?"

"Right? The roller coaster jumped the track. It wasn't really that big of a deal—no one was hurt—but still. The guy we brought in to get it back up and running told us the coaster had actually been closed in '94, and Tony flipped his *shit* because that sort of mistake does *not* fly with him, you know? Anyway, that night, after he watched the dailies, he fired Paul and half the art department."

I let the script fall to the table. "I'm amazed there's any crew left. Who else is gone?"

Kim digs a legal pad out of her bag, flips to the third or fourth page, and runs her finger down the margin. "An assistant props mistress, a wardrobe assistant, three sound guys."

"Don't forget makeup," a PA whispers as she breezes past.

"Right," Kim says, grimacing. "Penelope. That one hurt."

I wince. *Sorry, Freckles.*

Kim reaches for a pencil and scratches something out.

"What is that?" I ask.

"We're running a pool. Who's next to get the boot."

"Who's the odds-on favorite?"

She hesitates, then flips it around to face me. I lean forward to read the first name on the list.

The Unlucky Bastard Who Has to Cut This Fucker

I open my mouth. "That's—"

"Yeah, we kind of assumed it would be a dude. Our bad."

"Is that what you think? That I'm the next to go?"

Kim studies the list with a glum expression. "No, my money's on Gavin."

"You don't sound too happy about that."

She sighs and puts the pad back in her bag. "Anjali likes to make it seem like she has eight million other actors raring to go, but between you and me? Gavin's the only one the studio would get behind. If he goes—*poof!* So goes our greenlight."

"You're telling me *Liza May* can't get this movie made on her own?"

Kim shrugs. "It has something to do with China, I don't know."

"But she won an Oscar."

"And he played a hot wizard one time." She gives me an impatient look. "You work in Hollywood. I shouldn't have to explain this."

SIXTEEN

When I set the script aside two hours later, one thing is clear. In the universe of this movie, Billy Lyle was obsessed with Caitlyn Kelly, and he murdered her because she didn't return his affections.

It's not the most original story, but I can work with it.

Assuming I get the opportunity, that is. I'm no closer to understanding why Paul was fired, and I can't help but feel I'm doomed to repeat his mistakes.

I dump the Ziploc bag of Post-its out on the table in front of me. Kim, bless her, has already done the hard work of coding each Post-it to each shot, but the notes aren't in order—and there are several *hundred*—so it takes me a few minutes to pick out the forty-seven that refer to the amusement park scene.

Forty-four relate to an avalanche of continuity concerns: questions about eyelines, about hairstyles, about the prop department's baseline competence. There's a fair amount of bluster evident in Paul's wording and handwriting—a black Sharpie makes a strong point—but apart from the sheer volume of paper, there's nothing here that's really out of the ordinary. If Tony's going to insist on strict factual accuracy, there are necessarily going to be a huge number of details to keep track of.

The last three notes, however, are more interesting to me.

I tap each one in turn.

What are you looking at?

What are you seeing?

What are you missing?

These aren't questions you ask a script supervisor. These are questions you ask yourself—in the middle of the night, in the middle of a project, your stomach lurching like you've tried to take a step that isn't there, like you've realized you left the gas on, like you've just remembered that time in college you mixed up *The Last Emperor* and *Empire of the Sun*. These are questions born of stress and uncertainty.

Which is to say, they're questions I ask myself all the time. I just don't usually write them down.

I try to tell myself that it's only natural to worry so much—that, in fact, it's worrying so much that has made me good at what I do, that my biggest weakness really *is* my greatest strength, just like the self-help books keep trying to tell me.

Maybe one day I'll believe it.

I pick up my pen and try to give it a spin.

If this pile of yellow paper is anything to go by, Paul's a worrier, too. Okay, fine. But why is he focusing so much on *this* scene? It probably won't even make it into—

The pen flies across the room and ricochets off the side of a metal trash can.

This scene won't even make it into the movie.

Not as it stands. Not now that Tony knows the roller coaster wasn't functioning at the time of the murder. This is a man who's willing to fire a department head over freckles. No way would he let an anachronism make it into the final cut. And after three movies together, Paul would have known that.

So why was he tearing his hair out over unusable footage?

How do you get fired over unusable footage?

I look at the notes spread out in front of me and feel my shoulders slump. It's pictures I'm good at communicating with, not words.

If I want to have any chance of figuring this out, I'm going to have to call Paul.

I lay my forehead against the table. This is the sort of diplomatic back-channel stuff that I usually delegate to Amy. I don't even know where to begin. I can't exactly ask Tony for Paul's number. What would I say? *Hey, Tony, I was wondering if maybe you could put me in touch with your estranged collaborator, because I'm confused about this scene you're for sure going to cut and also I have some pretty indiscreet questions about just how much of a controlling jerk you are.*

No, not Tony. Amy won't be any help, either. She doesn't even know any other editors. And Josh—no. I'm not calling Josh.

Is it really possible? Is *Nell* my best option?

I grab her number off my laptop and move into the quietest corner of the room, squeezing between a fake philodendron and a fake fiddle-leaf fig.

"Tell me they haven't fired you" is the first thing she says to me, and I'm so shocked she answered her own phone it takes me a moment to respond.

"Give it a day," I manage.

"What do you need?"

I tuck the phone between my chin and my shoulder. "I was hoping you could help me track down the last guy who had this job—I need to talk to him."

I don't bother to elaborate, and I trust Nell not to push. One thing I've always appreciated about Nell is that she's allergic to anything that would slow the process down. The opposite of me.

"Sure, no problem. Paul Collins, right?"

"Yeah."

I hear her tapping away at her keyboard. Her door creaks open, and she shouts, "Hey Arnie, you know a guy Paul Collins? No—not the singer, that's *Phil* Collins, you banana tree. Why would I even be asking you that?" A pause. "Seriously? *Shit*." She comes back on the line. "Sorry, kid. Bad news. He's repped by Vera Madigan, which is a crying shame because a) she's fucking terrible at her job, and b) we are not speaking to each after a small incident at the Spirit Awards, which was entirely her fault. I'm sure I can get his number, but I'll have to ask around a bit, get back to you."

"That would be great," I say, "but if you find anything, don't call me. Just send an email."

"I wouldn't put it past Anjali to have your Gmail password, but okay, I guess."

"Thanks, Nell."

"Hey, Marissa—"

"Yeah?"

"Don't fuck this up. These people don't mess around."

"I promise, I'm trying really hard not to."

I snap the phone shut and stare at it for a moment. Then I open and shut it a few more times for good measure—ten times, because why not.

I scan the call sheet Anjali gave me, searching for someone I might be able to trust, but I don't recognize any of the names. Only an editor could work in Hollywood for nearly twelve years and know so few people.

So who can I ask? It has to be someone discreet. Someone who would hold on to old papers. Someone who wouldn't particularly care what Tony thinks of them—

The answer's so obvious, I'm angry at myself for not thinking of it sooner.

I flag down a PA.

"Do you know where Tony is?"

She taps at her iPad. "Looks like he's down in the squash courts with Daisuke, working the setup."

"The squash courts—those are on the other side of the hotel, right? Like, really far away?"

She blinks. "I guess."

"Could you do me a really big favor?"

She glances at Anjali, takes a step closer. "Maybe?"

"Could you have someone call me on my production phone to let me know if Tony's schedule for this afternoon changes?"

"Would you like me to try to set up a meeting?"

"No, just tell me if—you know. Things change."

She leans in. "Are you asking me to warn you if he shows up so you can make sure he doesn't catch you doing something you're not supposed to be doing?"

I lean in, too. "Is that okay?"

She rolls her eyes and makes a note on her iPad. "Honestly that's like ninety percent of my job."

I smile my thanks, grab my backpack, and slip out into the lobby. I try not to look like I'm running as I rush out the front entrance and down the driveway toward the parking lot.

To the teamsters.

Apart from the times I've caught a ride with Amy to set, I've never had much reason to interact with Transportation, so I know as much about teamsters as Isaiah knows about DPs.

Which is to say, a few jokes.

How can you tell which kid on the playground is the teamster's son?

He's the one sitting around watching all the other kids play.

There are about five hundred others, but they're all basically the same: Teamsters don't do anything, ha-ha!

Not that you'd ever hear me say anything like that out loud. Not on one of Amy's sets, oh *no*. She's intensely protective of her drivers. She prides herself on it, in fact. "They only have to do one thing, but they do it perfectly," she told me once, her expression fierce. "It's all fun and games until you get stuck in a non-union truck."

But when I clear the trees and step into the parking lot that's being used as base camp, my first thought is that maybe Amy was doing that thing where she overcompensates because she feels guilty about her upper-middle-class white privilege, because given what I'm seeing, the jokes don't seem too far off the mark. The crew is out by their trucks, lords of all they survey, and they have an impressive setup: A portable tent, a TV and a fan, two easy chairs, a couch, a *minifridge*.

They're also all on smartphones.

A man in cargo pants and a Dodgers shirt comes to his feet and shields his eyes with his hands, watching my approach.

"Howdy," he says.

I lift my hand hesitantly, realizing too late I should have prepared an opening gambit.

"Hi?"

I come to a stop a few feet away. The man eyes me.

"New editor?" he guesses.

I sigh.

"I'm Chuck," he says. Then, pointing to the other drivers in turn, "Tim, Big Bob, Little Bob, Mindy."

"Marissa," I say, pointing at my own chest for some reason.

Tim, leaning against the nearest truck, sips from a can of Diet Coke, a serene expression on his face. "Don't know that we've ever seen an editor in broad daylight," he says. "Kinda figured you guys slept in a coffin."

I fiddle with the straps of my backpack until I come up with a characteristic response: "Huh?"

Tim bares his canines, curls his free hand into a claw, and hisses.

I tilt my head. What is happening? Is he pretending to be a cat?

But before I can ask, Chuck holds out his hand, and someone—I don't even see who, it happens in such a swift, smooth manner—tosses him a can of soda. Regular Coke. He pops it open and takes a long draw. "What can we do you for? You need to go somewhere or did someone tell you we have the only DirecTV feed on the island?"

"I'm just trying to track down some contact information," I say. "I'm hoping I can ask the last editor a few questions about some of the material he left behind."

Chuck takes another sip of his soda. "Valentina should have all that on file."

Big Bob sticks his hand in the air. "I'll ask her for you."

Mindy swats his shoulder. "Don't be gross."

"I'd rather not trouble her," I say.

Chuck runs his thumb along the side of the soda can, looking thoughtful. "So you'd rather trouble *us*, is that it?"

Uh-oh. Not thoughtful. Pissed.

"No, that's not what I meant at all. I—"

"Oh, you just thought we'd be too dense to ask what you were up to?"

My eyebrows jump so high they nearly hit my hairline. "What? *No.* I asked you because you could drive your truck through the hotel lobby and Tony still wouldn't be able to fire you."

There's a pause—then a collective grunt of agreement.

"Okay," Chuck says. "We can help you—once you tell us why."

"I'm just asking for a phone number."

"In an incredibly suspicious, roundabout manner."

I throw up my hands. "Fine! I'm breaking the rules, okay? I'm not allowed to ask around about Paul. You could definitely get in trouble for helping me. But if I don't find a way to talk to him I'm worried I'll lose my job, and if I lose my job I have to go back to LA, and if I have to go back to LA I have to face the fact that my best friend is moving in with my mortal enemy-slash-shameful crush, which means I'm probably never going to see her again outside of work. Not to mention, it would be hugely professionally embarrassing."

Chuck gazes at me steadily while I catch my breath.

"That was a lot," he says.

I tuck my hands back down by my sides where I can see them. It *was* a lot. I hate when it comes out of nowhere. Like, one moment you're just trying to upgrade your cable modem, and then—*boom*. You're telling Myrtle at AT&T U-verse how hard it is to find cardboard-applicator super tampons, and you're painfully aware with each passing second that Myrtle is not happy, that this is *not* what Myrtle signed up for, but you can't help it, what's coming is coming, it's like the tide or gravity or the last stages of labor, because you haven't talked to anyone but your mother for a week.

"It's been a long couple of days," I manage.

Chuck angles his head toward the only man who hasn't yet spoken, a bearded giant in a Padres cap. "Little Bob," he says. "Binder."

Little Bob hauls himself to his feet and lumbers over to the trailer. He emerges a few moments later with a big purple binder, which he pushes into my hands.

I find a seat on the sofa and balance the binder on my knees. Inside, I find all the paperwork they've received from the production office, revisions *and* originals, exquisitely organized. They've even custom printed the tabs.

I glance at Chuck.

"Little Bob loves Staples," he says.

Little Bob shoves his hands in his pockets and rocks back on his heels. "There was a sale," he mutters.

The directory's in the back. I grab a notebook out of my bag and start to copy out Paul's number. "While I'm here," I say, "maybe you can help me with something else. The shoot at the amusement park—"

All five of them groan in unison.

My pencil stills. "So you know what I'm talking about?"

"We're lucky no one got hurt," Big Bob grumbles.

"Total clusterfuck," Mindy agrees.

Chuck crushes his soda can and tosses it into a nearby trash can. "That coaster never should've been turned on to begin with."

"So what happened?" I ask, stowing my notebook. "Was it an accident?"

Chuck gives me a funny look. "As opposed to . . . *not* an accident?"

His voice is so plainly incredulous that I don't know how to respond. Am I really so wrong to wonder whether something else might be going on here? Am I too inclined to see intention where there isn't any? Maybe I am. Maybe it's a defensive reflex—if I linger too long on the fact that so much of what we put onscreen is the product of frantic, last-second problem-solving, it really undercuts the notion that we know what we're doing.

I tug my ponytail loose and retie it, annoyed with myself.

On the other hand, maybe I'm not overreacting. Maybe *I'm* the sensible one. My first day on set, they had a major lighting malfunction, and now I'm finding out a roller coaster jumped the track? That's two more accidents than there have been on any other production I've ever worked on, and now that I think about it, it's incredibly weird that everyone on the crew seems to be A-OK with that.

"It wasn't anyone's fault," Chuck says, clearly following my train of thought. "The coaster'd been busted for years. Mechanic I talked to said some boy lost a leg on the thing back before the park closed."

I shake my head, confused. "So why did so many people get fired?"

Tim coughs into his sleeve. "Yeah, well—Mindy'd know more about that."

Mindy's hands go to her hips. "What're you trying to say, Tim?"

All four men cast their eyes up at the sky, their expressions uniformly bland.

"You *assholes*. You're worse than my brothers." She turns to me. "I had a crush. A tiny, little crush." She holds her thumb and forefinger ever so slightly apart. "Befitting a tiny, little man."

I frown. "I thought Paul was like six three."

"No—*Ryan*. The 2nd AD."

"And why was *he* fired?"

"'Cause he roots for the Angels?" Big Bob says.

"'Cause he smokes ultralights?" Tim says.

"'Cause he *sucked*?" Little Bob says, surprising everyone—myself included.

"We all know what he did," Mindy says, leveling another irritated look at her coworkers. "That day, one of the extras broke into a trailer, and instead of calling security or being a reasonable human being about it, Ryan went, like, full alpha douchebro and knocked the guy out."

My hand goes to my throat. "Oh God. Was the extra okay? Did he press charges?"

"I don't know—I don't think so? Anjali was pretty intent on keeping it quiet. I'm sure she paid him off."

"Probably double if he didn't tell Tony," Big Bob says, darkly.

"Tony doesn't know?" I ask.

Big Bob shrugs. "*We're* sure as shit not gonna tell him."

I hand the binder back to Little Bob. "Thanks for this."

He looks down at the ground. "Anytime," he mumbles.

Chuck saunters over. "Look, you need anything else, you come find us, okay? You ask me, this shoot's been rotten from the get-go. The sooner it's over, the better for everyone."

I nod gratefully. "I appreciate that."

Tim leans down and reaches for the Smokey Joe they've got set up between the easy chairs. He holds up a caveman-size kebab. "For the road? No garlic, I promise."

"How did you know I don't like garlic?" Then, "Oh, because I'm a vampire, you mean."

He grins. "Got it in two."

CHUCK KOSINSKI: In case anyone's wondering, this one's *my* personal favorite: What's the last thing Jesus said to the teamsters?

GRACE PORTILLO: I don't know, what?

CHUCK KOSINSKI: "Don't do anything till I come back."

SEVENTEEN

dial Paul's number with trembling fingers. Not because I'm afraid of what I'm going to find out. Because I hate making cold calls—no matter how badly I need an answer. When I hear the voice on the other end of the line, I nearly faint with relief.

Your call has been forwarded to an automated voice messaging system.

Poetry.

I leave a brief message.

"Hi, Paul, this is Marissa Dahl, and I'm the editor who took over for you on Tony Rees's new movie, and I was hoping you might have some time to talk about the cuts you've made so far and maybe about some of the footage I have here and also I was sort of wondering if you're okay because it seems like things were kind of rough there at the end? Also there's some stuff that I just really don't understand, so if you could call me back at this number, that would be great. I know you're super busy and don't have much time and probably want to wash your hands of this whole production, but I would just really appreciate it if you could be in touch. When you get the chance. If it's convenient. Thank you so much. Again, this is Marissa Dahl—that's Dahl as in Roald, not as in Barbie. Yeah. Okay. I hope you're well."

I hang up the phone and rub my temples. If I never talk to another person, it will be too soon.

A hand snakes around my wrist and yanks me into the hedgerow.

"What the—"

"*Shh*, Marissa, it's me."

I shove a branch away from my eyes and find myself scowling into the gaunt face of Gavin Davies. "You can't just grab people like that, Gavin. This isn't acting class, okay? What do you want?"

"Something that has been demonstrably absent on this set to date—"

He takes a beat.

"—*intelligence.*"

God. He probably times his bowel movements for dramatic effect, too.

"I'm not sure why you'd come to me for *that*," I say.

He shrugs. "You're the editor. Editors always know stuff."

"I got here *yesterday.*"

"Also, the girls told me they'd recruited you. So—I thought you might like to come with me to meet Billy."

"What—now?"

He checks his watch. "Yes, now. Down by the beach. It won't take long, I promise. I have to be in makeup in an hour."

"Are you afraid to go alone or something?"

"No, not at all. But I've been meeting with Billy for six weeks now, and he still won't tell me about the night Caitlyn died. I was wondering if maybe he might be more willing to talk to you."

"Me? Why?"

He takes another beat.

A deliberate beat.

A *very* deliberate beat.

Oh, for Pete's sake, he's not going to continue until I prompt him, is he?

I clench my fists and look into his eyes. They're a clear, brilliant blue, like a Texas wildflower or a lake in the Canadian Rockies or the poster for *Requiem for a Dream*, and because this is a man who's spent half his life holding for extreme close-ups, his gaze is unwavering.

"*What*, Gavin?"

"You remind me of him."

My own gaze falters, drawn to the nearest colorful object that's not his face. His shirt—red—a soccer jersey, I think.

Fly Emirates, it reads.

If only I could, I think.

"Why would you say that?"

"Well, you're both in your own little worlds, aren't you?" He sketches a vague loopy shape next to his temple—an attempt, I think, to illustrate his point. I find I'm not offended by the implication so much as the imprecision.

"It's the same world as yours. I just notice it differently."

"I didn't mean—"

"I know what you meant," I say, quietly.

He reaches for my elbow, thinks better of it. "Marissa—don't you want to know what happened?"

An absurd question. Of course I want to know. I want to know *everything*.

With the following exceptions:

1. What my brother did with the sports bra he stole from me when he was twelve.
2. How many times I've made my mother cry.
3. What people say about me behind my back.
4. About bugs you can feel but not see.
5. Where the first jet engine in *Donnie Darko* came from, because there's no way the answer is anything but infuriating.

A much better question is: How far am I willing to go for that knowledge? Sometimes, admittedly, it's a little *too* far. I won't just read one book, I'll read every book. I won't just click on one link, I'll click link after link after link after link until my eyes cross and my battery dies and I know I'm going to have to clear my cache in the morning because I ended up in some very, very dark places. I won't just send an email—I'll make a phone call.

Other times, I'm not even willing to wait for IMDb to load on a slow network.

"If anyone catches me with you," I tell Gavin, "I could lose my job."

"And doesn't that strike you as suspect? Have you ever worked on a film where the director asked something like that of you?"

"No, but I've also never worked on a film where the lead actor tried to spirit me away to some clandestine meeting with a suspected murderer. Did you do this to Paul, too?"

He gives me an incredulous look. "Paul? God, no. He didn't have time for me. He was too busy pissing into jars in the projection room."

The branch slips from my fingers and slaps me in the forehead.

"*That's* why he got fired?"

"No, of course not, I just made that up. You looked like you needed a laugh."

"There's nothing funny about pee jars."

His smile vanishes. "There's nothing funny about any of this. Did you know they almost beat Billy to death?"

"Don't you dare emotionally manipulate me."

He ignores this and takes a step closer. "When the DA declined to prosecute, a group of guys went down to the docks and confronted Billy. Demanded that he confess. When he wouldn't, they tried a more . . . physical means of persuasion."

I draw a breath. "How badly was he hurt?"

"He was in and out of the hospital for months. He had to have plastic surgery, dental reconstruction, everything. It was years before he walked properly again."

"Did they ever charge anyone with the assault?"

"Officially, no one knows who did it. No one talked. Not even Billy."

"Unofficially?"

"It was Caitlyn's boyfriend and a bunch of his friends."

It whispers out of me: "Goddammit, Gavin."

He moves closer, pressing his advantage. "Everyone on this island thinks he did it. Including Tony. They're not even interested in looking at alternatives." And then he makes his face do something I've never seen from it before, not once, not in three movies' worth of raw footage.

This is what he looks like when he's begging for help.

"*Please.*"

"Oh, fine," I say, pushing past him and stepping out of the hedge. "I'll do it."

"I changed my mind, I'm not doing it."

We're standing on the warped and weathered boardwalk that cuts through the deserted beach, facing a rocky outcropping that extends about forty feet out into the ocean. Unfortunately for me, the boardwalk doesn't go around the rock. It doesn't go over the rock.

It goes *through* the rock.

"What? Why not?" Gavin asks. "Are you scared of caves?"

"No, of course not. I just prefer not to swim, spelunk, or stream *The Descent.*"

I'm not scared of caves.

I'm *terrified* of caves.

The summer after fifth grade, my mom decided to send me to a sleepaway camp one of her church friends had recommended. Her thinking was sound. She thought it would be good for me to get some sunshine and exercise and maybe find a friend. That last part was wishful thinking, of course, but that's always been Mom's biggest failing: her perfect faith in us.

The camp was a couple of hours southwest of Urbana, not far from St. Louis, and it was probably a good camp, as camps go. When we weren't singing or swimming or telling stories, we were hiking or climbing or learning to groom horses. It wasn't fancy. The food was either chili on hot dogs or hot dogs on chili, and the window screens had so many holes you wondered why they even bothered. But I liked hot dogs even if I didn't much care for chili, and the mosquitos left me alone. I didn't make any friends, but the kids there weren't mean to me, either, and they could have been. I was grateful for that.

The trip to the caves had been planned well in advance, but they hadn't counted on the flash flood. And even then, it wouldn't have been such a big deal if I hadn't been alone.

But I was.

Like usual.

And I got trapped.

It was dark, and there was so much water, and I was alone. All alone. Alone as the water rose. Alone as I tried to escape. Alone as I failed.

Alone as I stretched toward the ceiling, frantic, searching for that one last pocket of air.

Alone, finally, as I lost consciousness.

It was a counselor, they tell me, who got me out. Gave me CPR. Kept my heart beating.

On the plus side, Mom never tried to make me go to camp again.

I bury my hands deep in my pockets. "Are you sure we can't meet Billy somewhere else?"

"It's too late for that," he says, pulling a flashlight out of his pocket. "But don't worry. I won't let the cannibals get you."

I gaze at the entrance to the cave, my hand on my chest, hating how I must look but unable to do anything about it.

Gavin sighs. "Look, how about this—if you come with me, I promise I'll try really hard not to look at the camera just to mess with the shot."

I bite my lip. Adolescent trauma aside, that's actually tempting.

"*And* I'll pay attention to continuity for once."

"You? Seriously?"

He presses his hand to his heart. "I'll take notes and everything."

My eyes narrow. "If you mess up, I'm not covering for you."

Gavin grins, clearly sensing victory. "Yes, fine, whatever you say." He turns and heads inside, the narrow beam of his flashlight bobbing along in front of him.

I wipe my mouth with the back of my hand and follow him through the archway. The cave is dark. The air is thick—but not in the way that fog is thick or that silence is thick, more like the way your head feels when you try to picture four-dimensional space. Like there's an answer you're never going to be able to get to.

"This place isn't prone to flash flooding or anything like that, is it?" I ask, my voice rising at least an octave.

"Of course not," Gavin calls back. "It just fills up with ocean water twice a day. But don't worry, that's hours away."

He leads us to an eight-foot-tall crevice that curves through the rock in the shape of a scimitar, narrowing to a sharp point halfway to the ceiling.

"We're going through there?" I ask, weakly.

"You'll be fine," he says, and if he's acting, it's some of the best work he's ever done. I almost believe it.

I grit my teeth and ease my way into the crevice. It's narrow, but I'm small enough to fit without much effort, and I only stall twice on the way through. The first time Gavin talks me forward; the second time he just gives me a sharp poke in the ribs.

After twenty feet or so, the passageway opens up into a grotto, cool and quiet and blue, reflected light shimmering across the ceiling. On the far wall, a narrow opening leads out to the ocean, and if I crouch down and crane my neck, I can just about see a sliver of sky. To my right is a wooden mooring pole; lashed to that is a two-man rowboat. My eyes travel from the boat to the long, low shelf that runs along the wall of the grotto. At the other end, sitting cross-legged on a wide rock, is Billy Lyle.

Gavin picks his way over and hunkers down next to Billy, the posture clearly familiar to him.

"Billy," he says, "this is the woman I told you about. The editor. We were hoping we might ask you a few more questions for the movie."

He looks at me, blinks. "I know you."

Gavin's eyebrows jump. "That's new information."

"I was his passenger the other night," I explain. "He brought me here from Lewes."

Billy's gaze flickers, drops to my shoulder. "I'm sorry you had to see that."

Gavin glances between us. "See what?"

"Three guys tried to bully their way on board." I look at Billy. "I'm sorry I didn't do more."

He gives his head a shake. "Nothing you could have done."

"So you know," Gavin says, his expression fierce. "You've seen it yourself. How everyone on this island has it out for Billy. And Tony's no different."

He sweeps out his arm for emphasis, inadvertently shining the flashlight across the rock we're sitting on, illuminating a scrawl of graffiti, equal parts snotty teenage commentary and the sorts of outlandish romantic sentiments I've never even felt compelled to say out loud, let alone commit to geologic history.

And also dick jokes.

You can't say happiness without penis

Carpe Dickem

Penis Penis Penis Penis LOL

But mostly it's names of couples. Joe and Stacy. Peter and Julie. Victor and Danielle. Victor and Katie. Victor and Lucy.

"Did you come here, too?" I hear myself asking. "With Caitlyn?"

A muscle twitches in Billy's jaw. "No. Caitlyn and I were just friends."

"But, like, just friends or *just friends?*"

His head comes up. "What?"

"You weren't in love with her?"

He scowls. "How many times do I have to say it? Being her friend was the best thing that ever happened to me. It wasn't some kind of consolation prize."

I hum in sympathy. "Yeah, I know, it's a really shitty trope."

"But I can't win either way," he says. "I'm not even sure which one's the taller tale. That Caitlyn could've loved me as a boyfriend— or that she could've loved me as a friend. Most days, I think it's that second one. And you know what? I think that scares them more. Because if someone like her could be friends with someone like me, then what's their excuse?"

I frown. "What do you mean, 'someone like you'?"

I don't know, someone who—" He looks down at his chest, holds out his hands. "Someone who just can't get it right."

If there's one thing I've heard over and over again in my life, from all the people I love, it's that there's nothing wrong with me.

From my mother, when no one came to the tenth birthday party I hadn't wanted anyway: "There's *nothing* wrong with you!"

From my second-grade teacher, after she moved me to a desk in the far corner of the room: "There's nothing *wrong* with you!"

From Amy, on the occasion of yet another failed first date: "There's nothing wrong with *you*!"

Increasingly counterproductive variations on a fundamentally disingenuous theme, the sort of statement that, when repeated, tends to communicate the exact opposite of its literal meaning.

Don't worry!

I'm fine!

She's just a work friend!

That sort of thing.

My dad's the only one who doesn't bother with the pretense. "Your brother's popular enough for the both of you," he told me after my equally unsuccessful eleventh birthday party. Then he rested his hand on the top of my head for a count of three—as much physical affection as he's ever shown me before or since—and went back to his lab.

Intellectually, I can appreciate what everyone's trying to tell me, and maybe sometimes I almost believe it, but the knowledge I hold in my heart is this: Even though I do everything the books and classes and columnists tell me to, even though I've trained myself so well there's a fair chance I'll luck into the right response—the right comeback, the right reference, the right animated gif—people can still tell something's a little bit off. A snow-white mosaic with a solitary cream-colored tile. A marquee with 0's in place of O's. A by-the-numbers Oscar speech, delivered by Anne Hathaway. You can't immediately figure what, exactly, is bugging you so much, but the longer you look at it, the more certain you are that you just don't like it.

The closer you are to right, the more unsettling it is for the people who are sure you're wrong.

But I don't think that's what Billy wants to hear right now, so I clear my throat, searching for something more comforting to say.

"You know—my friend Amy always says, 'If you're going to lose the game no matter what, why bother playing by their rules?'"

The corner of Billy's mouth twitches. "Caitlyn used to say something like that."

I smile. "Was she ripping off *War Games*, too?"

He ducks his head. "Do you—want to see a picture?"

"Of course."

He opens up his wallet and pulls out one of those school photos you used to get in sheets of eight and sixteen, supposedly so you could sign them and trade with friends. The picture itself is terrible. The lights are too yellow and the angle is too low; Caitlyn's skin looks sallow, and the camera position highlights the baby fat under her chin. But her smile's big and bright and happy enough that my brain can't help but supply the word "pretty."

Gavin peers over my shoulder. "Everyone says she looks like Liza, but I don't see it."

I turn the picture to the side, considering. "I don't know. I'd say she looks more like Annemieke Janssen."

Gavin hums. "Maybe a little Charlize Theron?"

I hand the photo back to Billy. "She was lovely," I say, honestly.

He tucks it into his wallet with care. "I didn't kill her."

I lean back against the wall, my fingers curling around a lip of rock. For some reason I'm inclined to take him at his word, but do I believe him because he's credible? Do I believe him because he's convincing? Or do I believe him because we happen to have something in common?

"Have you thought about bringing this to Tony?" I ask.

Gavin shakes his head. "Tony says it would taint the process. I begged—for weeks—but I got nowhere. Eventually I tried to sneak Billy into my trailer, thinking I could ambush Tony with a meeting—I just really believed that if he saw Billy's face, he'd rethink things, you know?"

I glance at Billy. He's looking off to the side, two fingers tapping his temple.

"But then," Gavin continues, "while I was on set, an AD found him, assumed he was a trespasser, and punched half his jaw in. That's when Anjali called in the Delta Force guys—to make sure Billy can't get anywhere near set again."

"I'm pretty sure they're ex-SEALs," I murmur.

"Meanwhile, the police aren't exactly forthcoming, so the only people on our side right now are the girls—and now you, I suppose. But unless something massive changes, we're at something of an impasse."

I draw my lip between my teeth, thinking. "You could quit."

"Which would accomplish—what, exactly?"

"The studio won't make the movie without you. So if you quit—all this goes away."

Gavin's shaking his head. "No, the people on the island will still think he did it."

"Yes, but at least things wouldn't get *worse*."

"And Tony would make it work without me, he'd find a way. He'd have effects build a Gavin Davies skin suit and make Anjali do the part."

I turn to Billy. "I haven't heard you say what *you* want to do."

Billy sets his cheek against his shoulder and gazes at the water, at the small rowboat rising and falling with the tide.

His answer is so familiar to me I find myself marveling at its sound on someone else's lips.

"I just want them to leave me alone."

EIGHTEEN

Gavin and I return to the hotel separately. He elects to make his usual grand entrance through the front door. While everyone's busy looking at him, I take the opportunity to slip in through the sun deck, ducking behind a column to hide from a PA. I feel my face split into a grin, and I nearly trip over my feet at the implication: that I'm beginning to enjoy the cloak-and-dagger of it all.

The pleasure is short-lived, replaced seconds later by a sick twist in the pit of my stomach.

I'm doing it again. Convincing myself that I'm important—that I matter. That I might have a key role to play in what's to come. That I'm Sarah Connor. Luke Skywalker. Kung-Fu Panda. That I may appear to be an inconsequential klutz *now*, but just you wait: There's a training montage in my future.

How easy it is to think I might be the hero of this story.

When in truth I probably don't even have a speaking part.

I dash back to my room to clean up, then I hurry down to today's location. I actually think I'm about to make it there on time, when—

"Out of my way!"

A hand shoots out in front of me; I flatten myself against the wall to avoid it, my script tumbling to the floor as Daisuke storms past, a light meter in his hand, a trail of grips and electricians in his wake. He proceeds to fling the doors to the squash court open with all the relish of an archvillain unveiling a doomsday device.

I gaze after him, rubbing at my nose.

He seems much nicer than most DPs.

I lean down to retrieve my script. When I lift it, a square of yellow paper flutters to the ground—a rogue Post-it.

I grab the note and flip it over. A string of numbers, scrawled in Paul's now-familiar handwriting.

Unlike the other notes Kim gave me, there's no neatly printed notation at the bottom indicating the scene it references. So this must be a note Paul left for himself.

I squeeze my way through to the squash court, heading for the empty chairs in the far back corner, opposite Video Village (which today only has *two* perilously mounted monitors). I sit down, studying the note in my hands.

A package wrapped in aluminum foil falls into my lap.

I look up to find Suzy and Grace settling into the seats behind me.

"Just the way you like it," Grace whispers. "Disgusting and over-processed."

I peel back a corner of foil and peek inside. A sandwich. I barely manage to say thank you before I'm tearing into it. This is the first food I've had all day.

The girls lean forward, settling their arms on the backs of the chairs on either side of me.

"I thought you aren't supposed to be around the actors," I say around a mouthful of peanut butter.

"We aren't," Suzy agrees.

"What's that?" Grace asks, pointing to the Post-it.

"No idea. You wouldn't happen to know what it means, do you?"

"I can look it up. Hold on." Suzy disappears into her hoodie—consulting her phone, no doubt. After a moment, her head pops back out. "It's an international phone number," she says.

I squint at the paper. "I don't recognize the country code."

"Google says the Netherlands."

I take a bite of my sandwich. Chew it. Swallow.

"Huh."

"Huh?" Grace asks.

"It's probably nothing," I say. "I mean, there are, what, twenty million people living in the Netherlands?"

Suzy ducks back under her hoodie. "Seventeen-point-three," she says, her voice muffled.

That's seventeen million two hundred thousand nine hundred ninety-nine people who *aren't* the soon-to-be ex-wife of Anton Rees. Plus, Paul's been in this business a long time. He probably knows tons of people from the Netherlands. Like Jan de Bont. Or Eddie Van Halen.

I'm probably jumping to conclusions.

What would Paul have wanted with Annemieke, anyway? She's not in the—

"We heard you met with Billy," Grace says.

"How'd you—nevermind, obviously you know everything. Yes, I did. You didn't tell me he and Caitlyn were friends."

"Well—that's *his* story."

I twist around in my seat. "You don't believe it?"

Suzy shrugs. "Isn't that what they always say?"

"Do people really lie about having friends?"

"They certainly lie to themselves about it."

I look at the two of them. They're pressed together from shoulder to knee, their affection so strong it practically shimmers around them, like a deflector shield or that pink goo from *Ghostbusters II*.

It's so easy for them. It occurs to me, not for the first time, that my childhood might have left me with a few gaps in my social understanding.

"You've only known each other for, what, four weeks?" I ask.

Suzy gives it some thought. "A little more than that. Since Memorial Day."

"But you seem like you've known each other for longer."

They glance at each other.

"It's just one of those things," Suzy says.

"*'Things'*?"

She waves a hand vaguely. "Yeah."

"So there was, what, a moment? When you knew? That you were destined to be together?"

"I mean, you know what it's like—having a best friend," Grace says. "Right?"

I hesitate. "Of course."

They exchange another endlessly expressive look.

Suzy leans forward, wrapping her hands around the chair in front of her. "So a few days after we got here, we were climbing around back behind the hotel, exploring some of the beaches and rocks and . . . stuff."

"You were looking for clues, weren't you?"

She scrunches up her nose. "Do you want to hear this story or not?"

I sigh and gesture at her to go on.

"Anyway, the sun was setting, and we knew Grace's dad would be pissed if we were out any later, so we decided to give up and go back inside. But by then the light was, like—you know in the early evening when it goes all soft and golden, like an Instagram filter?"

"Magic hour?"

"Yeah, that. And Grace had all this awesome music on her phone

I'd never heard of, so we just kind of sat down on a rock together, and I wore one earbud and she wore the other, and we looked out at the ocean and listened to this song and everything was so chill, time just sort of, I don't know. Stopped or something."

Grace gives me a look. "The song she's talking about is actually *super* long, so that probably added to the effect."

Suzy elbows her in the ribs. "I was being poetic, you dork. What I'm trying to say is that with Grace, I can just kind of—*be*."

Then she elbows Grace again for good measure.

I sit back, thinking hard. Amy and I have had moments I cherish, moments of connection, like when we've been stuck on something for hours and then she makes a suggestion that sparks something in me that sparks something in her and suddenly the ideas are coming fast and fierce, one after the other, a rapid-fire hand-stack building to a team cheer, and when we reach the top we're breathless, laughing, together.

But have we ever had that outside an editing room? If we have, I can't remember—and if I can't remember, it seems unlikely that we have.

That sort of thing would stay with you, right?

If I'd been alongside Grace and Suzy that day, I would've spent the afternoon grumbling about the smell of the ocean and the sand in my shoes. And I would've passed on the music because earbuds never fit quite right, and even if they had I still would've declined because I'm just generally opposed to sharing objects that are placed inside bodily orifices—not that we would have even gotten to that point to begin with, because Grace would have said something anodyne like, "Wow, what a nice sunset," and I wouldn't have been able to keep myself from informing them that, actually, the sun hasn't *set*, it's still about six degrees above the horizon, which reduces the lighting ratio and scatters the blue light in such a way that we're left with the diffuse, golden light so characteristic of that particular time of day, and, hey, you know what we should do instead of this? Rewatch *Days of Heaven*.

And that, as they say, would have been the ballgame.

No one wants to share earbuds with that girl.

"Sounds a lot like love at first sight," I say.

"I guess," Suzy says. "But, like, the friend kind."

"Maybe that's how it was for Billy and Caitlyn, too."

I turn back around, feeling unsettled—though I couldn't tell you why.

We're shooting today in the largest of the hotel's three squash courts, which is currently home to the sets for Billy's childhood bedroom and the Lewes PD interrogation room. Right now, the camera is trained on the latter, which consists of a metal table, two chairs, and plywood flats painted an industrial blue. Gavin's sitting at the table, wearing jeans and a dark T-shirt. They've done something to his foundation to make him look paler than usual. He delivers his lines directly to camera, over and over again, until I've heard them so many times the words begin to lose their meaning.

"I would never."

"I couldn't."

"I don't understand."

"I loved her."

At the end of each take, Tony doesn't make any changes or offer any feedback. He doesn't even come out from behind the camera.

He just says, "Again, from the top."

"Again, from the top."

"Again, from the top."

Maybe these words lose their meaning, too, because on take 32, Gavin places his palms on the table, gazes at his fingertips, and goes off script.

"Being her friend was the best thing that ever happened to me," he says. "It wasn't some kind of consolation prize."

Tony's head shoots up. "Cut! Gavin—what the fuck?"

Gavin's body doesn't move, but he lifts his eyes to meet Tony's. "I thought I'd give you a couple of options."

Tony's hand opens and closes at his side. "Scripty, if you would, please provide Gavin with the *correct* line."

Kim hurries over, script in hand. "'Don't you know what it's like to want something you know you can never have?'" she reads, mechanically.

Tony nods sharply. "Yes, thank you. Okay, everyone, let's reset, please."

Gavin rolls out his neck and adjusts the angle of his chair. A makeup artist steps in to blot his forehead.

Five minutes later, it happens again.

"You know what Caitlyn always tells me?" Gavin says, his eyes closed, his body moving, just a little, from side to side. "She says— she says, 'Billy? If you're gonna lose the game no matter what, don't bother playing by their rules.'"

"Is he quoting *War Games*?" Suzy whispers.

"Gavin," Tony murmurs. "That's two strikes."

"What?" Gavin says, eyes wide. "I'm just saying what feels right in the moment."

Tony lowers his voice further. "If I wanted to work at an improv theater, I would buy one. Now, if you please—we're still rolling."

Gavin nods. "Okay, okay. Just a second." He takes a sip of water and cracks his knuckles. Then he looks directly at me—and winks.

I blink and Gavin's gone, replaced by his character, a frightened, confused, and increasingly despondent young man. His nostrils flare and his chin comes up; his hands wrap around each other.

"It's the same world as yours," he says, gazing at the far corner of the table. "I just notice it differently."

A walkie-talkie crashes into the flat behind Gavin's head.

For several endless silent seconds, everyone in the room stares at the square-shaped divot it left behind. Then, as one, we trace its trajectory back to Tony's still-extended hand.

It's Gavin who breaks the silence. He stands up, lifts his shirt, and starts untaping his mic. "I'm not going to work under these conditions."

Anjali rushes over and wraps a hand around his wrist. "Gavin, stop."

He shakes her off. "I don't want your bullshit, Anjali. I know you see it. I know you *know*. And whatever magic you've pulled off in the past, it's not happening here. This is a fucking shitshow."

Anjali grimaces. "And yet, according to the terms of your contract, this shitshow must go on."

Tony comes up between them. He curls his hands around Anjali's shoulders and draws her away from Gavin.

"Forgive her," he says. "Someone once told her she's funny and she's never gotten over it."

"*You* told me that," Anjali says.

"And I've regretted it ever since." Tony turns to Gavin, his expression mild. "What do you think we're doing here, exactly? Do you think this is fantasy? Do you think this is make-believe? Do you think facts don't matter?"

Gavin laughs. "Since when do you care about *facts*?"

Tony runs a finger along the edge of the table then knocks it with his knuckle. "Did you know that this is the same model that was used in the police station here in 1994? Same design, same material, same finish. I made the art department scour the country until they found one *just* right. This one came from a yard sale outside Buffalo, almost five hundred miles away. Now, why do you think I did that, Gavin—because I'm sloppy? Because I'm careless? Because I don't care about the *facts*?" He leans forward. "Or did I do it because no one cares about this movie more than I do? Did I do it because no one knows more about this case than I do? Did I do it because no one else is capable of coming up with a vision even *half* as vital as mine—much less executing it?"

Gavin considers this for a long moment.

Then he shakes his head. "I think you did it because you're a controlling dick."

Tony drops his hands to his sides, all pretense of civility abandoned. "Fuck you, Gavin."

"Sorry, boss, some things even *I* won't do for money."

Never one to pass up an exit line, Gavin pushes past the camera and strides out the door.

NINETEEN

t's the sound guy who recovers first.

"So I guess that means we don't need to get room tone?"

Tony mutters something inarticulate and stalks over to Video Village.

Anjali turns and takes in the room, her eyes narrowed. "If any of this shows up on YouTube, I will hire Bob Mueller himself to find out who did it."

Grace leans forward. "Is that it, then? Is the movie canceled?"

I shake my head. "No, people on movies threaten to quit all the time."

"Like *that*?"

I look over at the cracked shell of the walkie-talkie. "Well—usually it's the actors who throw things. In my experience, anyway."

Suzy slumps against her seat. "I do *not* want to go back to New Jersey."

"I'm sure it won't come to that."

They make identical sounds of disbelief.

I pull my backpack into my lap and wrap my arms around it as I watch the crew break down their equipment.

"After all," I say, distantly, "since when did Hollywood ever let anybody down?"

Judging from the inebriated roar that greets me when I step into the lobby, Grace and Suzy aren't the only people worried about the fate of the film. I clap my hands over my ears and stare in astonishment at the overcrowded bar.

How did they all get here so fast?

I see Daisuke and Kim and Carmen the makeup artist; I see Chuck and Tim and Mindy and both Bobs; I see Kim and Eileen and Valentina. And they're all doing their level best to spend their per diems as God and Oliver Reed intended.

Even the hotel staff seems to be getting into the spirit of things. Over at reception, Wade's finishing off a pint of beer. Next to him, Francie sips a whiskey.

End-of-day drinking is par for the course, but this gathering has all the manic intensity of a pre-apocalypse bender. One look at these people, and you know: There's going to be unprotected sex in this hotel tonight.

Honestly, it would probably be better for me if Gavin follows through for once and actually quits. But I can't say that to the people here. For many of them, this film is their big break. Their first speaking role, their first union job, their first studio credit. Life is going to be *different* for them after this. But if the movie's canceled, it's back to square one. Their old apartment. Their old car. Their old life. They'll have to tell all their friends and family and the people they were trying to sleep with that no, actually, it didn't work out, they haven't actually made it, but it's okay, really, that's just the way it goes, the way things work, the way the cookie crumbles, don't worry—there will be another chance!

No matter that they know, deep down, there probably won't be.

That's what the stakes are in this business, if you really care about it. Not quite life or death, but not far off, either. We're like Damocles, but we have only ourselves to blame: This particular banquet has an open seating plan.

I try not to think too much about what would have happened to me if I hadn't made it—if I hadn't met Amy—if I'd had to go back to Illinois and find a job in the real world. If I even *could* have found a job in the real world. Movies are all I'm good at. All I've ever been good at. With my résumé, I probably would've ended up back at the Carmike Beverly 18. It's an AMC now. Digital only. The only thing they need people for is the popcorn.

That's what I'll have to look forward to if I screw up this job badly enough. Flavacol and butter-flavored topping.

I trudge over to the elevator. I hit the button for my floor and tuck myself into the far corner of the car, chewing on the inside of my lip, tapping my toes. Just as the doors are closing, the cat lopes in, easy as you please. She rubs her cheek against my jeans.

"You need a name," I tell her after a moment. "I'm not going to call you 'Cat.' I hate that movie."

An inquisitive, birdlike noise.

I look down my nose at her. "It didn't make sense that Audrey and George would end up together. And if the ending's rotten, you can't trust anything that came before."

She nudges her way between my calves and starts circling my ankles.

Amy always wanted a pet, but I argued that we didn't have the time, money, or sufficient cleaning subroutines. But maybe I was wrong. It could be nice to have a little creature like this to take care of. I bet I could train her to pee in Josh's shoes.

When we reach my floor, she follows, padding silently alongside me.

I'm fumbling for my room key, just about to round the corner, when I hear Anjali's voice.

"Come on, Liza, I know you're in there."

I stop short. Anjali has one hand fisted at her hip, the other braced against Liza's door. At her feet is another tray piled high with plates and napkins.

I take a hasty step back, out of view.

There's a pause, then Anjali's pounding on the door with the flat of her hand. "I'm not leaving until you come out and talk to me. I can't do anything if you don't talk to me."

I peek around the corner. I'm so close to my room—it's only, what, twenty feet away? Maybe if I'm very quiet and stay very close to the wall and move very, very slowly.

"If you don't open this door, Liza, I'm telling TMZ what happened to your chinchilla. Now let me *in*."

I take a step. Another.

Incredibly slowly. *Imperceptibly* slowly.

The cat zips past me and over to Anjali, chirping out a greeting. *Turncoat.*

Anjali looks over, her face tight, her lovely thick eyebrows drawn together. She blinks. "What are you doing here?"

I point at my door. "Just going to my room."

"You haven't seen Liza by any chance, have you?"

"Is something wrong?"

Her mouth falls open, and a laugh gurgles up out of her. "Oh, no, everything's perfect. Just *peachy*."

I take a step toward my door, then stop. I don't think Anjali likes me very much, but she's clearly upset, and the piece of my brain that's convinced I'm the root cause of all human suffering is screaming at me to do something to make her feel better.

"Gavin will come back," I say. "He quits all the time—he probably thinks it's part of his process."

Her lips twist into a rictus grin. "Process can go fuck itself."

Well, I tried.

I unlock my door, letting the cat in ahead of me. I drop my bag on the bed and toe off my shoes. I clear the throw pillows off the loveseat and stretch out along its length. The cat settles her hindquarters on my thighs and begins kneading my stomach, purring, her claws catching and snapping at the cotton of my shirt.

I nestle my head into the cushion and stare up at the ceiling. Somehow, I feel like I know less about this movie than I did when I arrived. I can't make heads or tails of anything; it's all elision and insinuation. And maybe Tony's right, maybe an answer means more if you figure it out yourself. But I really wouldn't mind a solid hint or two.

That cat's rumbling so loudly it takes me a moment to realize my phone's ringing.

I lift my hips and dig my phone out of my back pocket. "This is Marissa."

"Hi, it's Paul Collins, returning your call."

My eyelids flutter in relief. Finally.

"Yes, Paul, thank you so much for calling me back, I was just—"

"I can't tell you anything."

I shift the cat to the opposite end of the loveseat and sit up, swinging my feet to the floor. "I'm sorry?"

"I'm not allowed to talk to you. Legally, I mean."

"So you *called* me to tell me that?"

"Yes." A pause. "We can talk about other things, just not the movie."

I squeeze the bridge of my nose. "This is strictly between us, I promise. I'm not interested in secrets or gossip or drama or anything like that. I'm a very boring person who is just trying to do her job—and I was hoping you could help me."

"You should also know that I'm recording this conversation."

I stare at the phone in disbelief. "It's a pretty simple question."

"This is Tony Rees we're talking about. There are no simple questions."

"He's a man, not a philosophy midterm."

Paul laughs darkly. "Try telling him that."

My fingernails press into my palm. "Look, I'm not trying to be difficult. I would just really appreciate it if you could tell me why he fired you so I can make sure it doesn't happen to me."

"I wish I could, but their lawyers will *annihilate* me. Dragon fire, salted earth, the whole nine yards."

I slump back against the couch cushions. "Isn't there *anything* you can tell me? I'm desperate for information here."

He takes so long to respond I begin to worry he's disconnected.

Then he sighs. "Just—go look at the film, okay? Everything you need, it's all there. You just have to look for it."

"Th—"

The line goes dead.

"—at's annoyingly cryptic," I finish.

I roll onto my back and kick the air in frustration. *God.* Everything in this whole horrible world would be eight million times easier if we just said what we meant and meant what we said and sure, we would probably have to sacrifice drama and comedy and irony and suspense, but honestly, the time we saved might be worth it.

I push myself up on my elbows. The cat is perched on the arm of the loveseat, licking her front paw and smoothing it over her head.

"What do you think I should do I now?" I ask her.

She closes her eyes and scratches her left ear.

"Yeah. I like that better than my idea, too."

I sit up and reach for my sneakers. What was that line of bullshit Nell fed that executive again? That there's no one better at watching footage and knowing exactly what the director's trying to say?

I suppose I might as well find out if that's true.

Assuming I can find the footage, that is.

I'm standing on the hotel's lower level, green patterned carpeting stretching in all four directions, and I *think* I'm supposed to turn left, right, left.

But maybe it's a right, left, right.

I *knew* I was destined to get lost down here.

Taking a different elevator, that was my first mistake. But I didn't want to have to walk through the lobby—what if I had to *talk* to someone?—so I used the service elevator back by the ice machine instead, figuring it would take me to more or less the same place.

Which it did.

Which is the *problem*.

It's impossible to distinguish anything down here, and without a sign or PA to guide me, I can't tell which way I'm headed—or which way I've been.

There's only one thing for it, I guess.

I retie my ponytail, say a quick *eeny-meeny-miny-moe*, and turn decisively to the left.

Five minutes later, I come to a door at the end of a hallway, and I want to cheer. This has to be it: The doors are bronze and glass, with diamond-shaped panes. The handles—yes, I remember those very clearly. Crescent moons. This is definitely right.

I push through and step directly into a thick, pungent steam.

This is definitely wrong.

I clamp a hand over my nose, but it's too late, I've already smelled it: the fusty twang of sandalwood and, beneath that, a cloying, powdery rose. Eau de Grandmother's Undercarriage.

I'm in the *spa*.

I wave my hand in front of my face to clear the air even though I know it's pointless. Between my eyebrows, I can already feel the tell-tale pinch of an oncoming headache.

Since the damage has been done, I move tentatively into the center of the room. There, I find a small, circular fountain brimming with rose petals, lit by half a dozen floating tea candles. On the lip of the basin is a red lighter and a saucer with two stubbed-out cigarettes. A few feet away, a gleam of silver: an ice bucket whose contents have long since melted. An open champagne bottle lies next to it, abandoned on the floor.

I turn in a slow circle. Around the perimeter of the room are a series of alcoves, each furnished with teak lounge chairs, a stack of thick white towels, red velvet curtains on a scrolled bronze rod. The first five alcoves are empty, but the sixth, if the flicker of candlelight coming from beneath the curtain is any indication, is very much in use.

Balls.

I don't panic—not exactly. This wouldn't be the first time I've interrupted a couple in flagrante. On a shoot, just about everyone hooks up—particularly on the weekends, particularly near the pool—but as long as everyone's there by choice and no one tries to get me to join in, it doesn't bother me.

That said, I don't exactly want to barge in on someone I've never met.

Or, worse, someone I *have* met.

I back toward the entrance, minding my feet, trying not to do the obvious thing and knock over the ice bucket.

A low, masculine murmur is followed by what I fear very much is a giggle.

I pick up my pace.

The velvet curtain ripples, and a hand curls around its leading edge.

I'm closer to one of the alcoves than I am to the door, so I dart around a pillar seconds before the curtain sweeps open. I slap a hand over my eyes a moment too late: Our lead actress is apparently modest enough to want to wear a robe, but not enough to tie it closed.

The soles of her feet make a sucking sound as she makes her way across the wet tile floor. I press myself back against the wall. I don't think she'll be able to see me, but I can't risk it. I'm committed now. Once you go full French farce, there's no going back. Those are the rules. I have to hide from the naked people until they leave or I die, whichever comes first.

"Shit." Liza says. "We're out of champagne."

There's another low murmur in response.

"We're out of that, too," she says.

This time I can't hear anything at all, but he must say *something*, because she muffles a snort.

"Yes," she says, "I suppose *that's* a sustainable resource."

At this the curtain is thrown all the way open, its metal rings scraping along the rod, and I'll admit, part of me wants to look, to see who's in there with her, but I've already invaded her privacy enough as it is.

A moment later the curtain closes again, and I'm pretty sure I don't want to stick around to hear what happens next. I creep around the pillar, sidestep the length of the room, and slip out the door.

I have to pause in the hallway to clear my lungs. I've often envisioned hell as a series of scented candles; that room could have been the ninth circle.

I whisk a bead of moisture off my eyebrow and consider my options. I suspect most any other person would take the past twenty minutes as a sign and just call it a night. Go back to their room. Crack open a bottle of Stoli. Draw a bubble bath. Watch whatever prestige television the internet has deemed *necessary* today.

But I don't drink. Bubble bath gives me eczema. And you know what? It's time someone took a stand against all this good TV.

I'm going to find my way back to the theater if it kills me.

I march back down the hallway, retracing my steps.

Right, left, right—left, right.

Right.

The moment I unlock the door to the theater, I feel ten times calmer. Maybe this is why Paul never left the projection room.

Maybe this is the only place he felt like he belonged, too.

I lock the door behind me, giddy now at the prospect of having the place to myself. I shove my keys in a backpack pocket and hurry through the curtained door and down the back hall. At the base of the spiral stairs, I pause. I'm all alone, and no one's around to hear me—and there's no acoustic tiling in this part of the hall. And if I'm guessing correctly, each step will produce a very satisfying clang if I put enough weight on it.

I jump my way up the first steps to the opening of Beethoven's Fifth.

On the fourth note, the staircase shudders violently. I fling out my arms to catch my balance, tangling my left hand in the light-bulb's pull cord. I give it a sharp tug to shake myself free, and the bulb promptly sputters out.

This night just keeps getting better and better.

I glance back down the hall—or what I think is the hall, anyway. It's so dark now even my eyes have trouble making sense of it. I think my best bet is just to keep going. There's a task lamp up in the projection room. Maybe it has an extension cord. I grab on to the railing with both hands as I climb the remaining stairs.

Inside the projection room it's even darker, but I'm too impatient to wait for my eyes to adjust, so I pull out my phone. I just need a little light to help me find my way to the desk—

And then there's a hand wrapping around my wrist and wrenching it forward, a hand that's not my own, a hand that's strong and strange and cruel, and it's twisting my arm around and—

Jesus *Christ* that hurts.

The phone's ripped out of my grasp. The hand settles on my lower back for a split second before shoving me roughly forward. I make a quick calculation and heave my body to the right, altering my trajectory just enough to keep my chin from cracking against the Autowind. My arm catches the edge of the aluminum platter as I fall; it punches through my skin, chiseling out a strip of flesh.

I hit the floor hard, the impact knocking my teeth together, the noise they make like a walnut cracking open, and for a moment, I can't move, stunned as much by pain as indecision. I've never been in a situation like this before. I don't have a script. I don't have a plan. Why don't I have a plan? What should I do? Amy would know what to do. *Amy, what do I do?*

But it isn't Amy who gives me the answer.

It's Uma.

Uma Thurman stares down at her foot. She narrows her eyes. "Wiggle your big toe."

Translation: *Move your ass, Marissa.*

I come up on my knees and use my good arm to drag myself over to the far side of the projector.

For some reason the intruder has retreated to the corner of the room, over by the editing bay. Are they trying to steal something? Break something? Whatever they're doing, I shouldn't waste time thinking about it.

I crouch down and fumble with the zipper of my backpack. There must be something in here I can use as a weapon. Laptop, no. Mouse, no. Soda, headphones, battery, notepad—*no, no, no, no.* Come on, even Jimmy Stewart had a flash bulb. Then, at the very bottom of the bag, I find it. My only plausible option.

I press my back to the wall and hold it in front of my face.

Something crashes to the ground, and in the split second I take to wonder what it was—*please don't let it be the 4K ColorEdge*—I almost miss the sound: breathing, throaty and labored. Then, the scuff of shoes against carpet. The intruder is moving with awkward, shambling steps, like some sort of reanimated creature, and even though I can't tell how big they are, I know one thing with absolute certainty: They're bigger than me.

And they're getting closer.

I hold my breath and put my finger on the nozzle of my backup bottle of screen cleaner.

But the next thing I hear isn't a growl or a roar or a mouth mashing at my face. It's a bright, metallic clamor because—*oh, thank God*—they're leaving. Running down the stairs. Clumsily. The rhythm is weird, uneven. If I didn't know better, I'd think they had three feet.

It's certainly nothing like Beethoven.

They're long gone by the time the last echo dies away.

GRACE PORTILLO: Had you ever been in a situation like that before?

MARISSA DAHL: Um, no, that was the first time I ever found myself trapped in a small room with a potentially violent stranger.

GRACE PORTILLO: What was it like?

MARISSA DAHL: I've had better evenings.

SUZY KOH: But you've probably seen, like, eight million movies where that happens, right?

MARISSA DAHL: Yes, that number definitely sounds accurate.

SUZY KOH: You know what I'm getting at.

MARISSA DAHL: If you're asking whether my annual repeat viewings of *Die Hard*, *Toy Soldiers*, and *Under Siege* somehow prepared me mentally or physically for the experience of having to find a way out of an enclosed space because someone wanted to hurt me, let me assure you, the answer is no.

TWENTY

And then silence—of a sort.

Because even if I were able to regulate my breathing, the blood rushing through my head would still be louder than any ocean. But I *can't* regulate my breathing, so there's that, too, and it isn't exactly a smooth flow of air, like the wind through the trees. No, my breath's rough and far away, like I'm a scuba diver or a prank caller or Tom Hardy in *The Dark Knight Rises*.

Or Tom Hardy in *Fury Road*.

Or Tom Hardy in *Dunkirk*.

There's a rustling, too—my hair, rubbing back and forth against the acoustic tile—and, to my right, an unpleasant rasp. I look down. I'm scratching my fingernails against the carpet, over and over again.

After a moment or a minute or maybe an hour, I manage to get to my feet. Sure, I have to throw out a hand immediately to catch myself, but I'm fine. I'm fine! I'm going to be fine.

Pretty fine.

In parts.

My arm is definitely bleeding from the fall. I'm guessing it'll hurt pretty bad once the adrenaline wears off.

I reach down and dig my cardigan out of my backpack. It's one of my very favorite cardigans—long, black, soft, with sleeves that don't rub at my wrists—but it has a higher purpose now. I wrap it around my bleeding arm as best I can, tying it up with a granny knot and using my teeth to tighten it. I grab my backpack with my other arm and feel my way out of the room and over to the stairs.

I don't trust my legs or my luck, so I go down on my butt, my teeth clacking with each impact. When I reach the ground floor, I inch forward, stretching my fingertips out ahead of me until I make contact with the cool, concrete wall. I follow this along to the right, my hand skimming its surface. Soon I see the narrow sliver of light beneath the lobby door. I wrap a shaking hand around the doorknob, drop my shoulder, and shove.

It opens maybe half an inch.

I stare at the door in disbelief. My attacker used the padlock to trap me in here while they made their escape. So now I'm stuck here. Late at night. In a remote wing of the hotel. Bleeding. Without a phone.

I rub at the space between my collarbones. When an anxiety attack comes on, it starts in my throat, and I can feel it now. At the moment it's just a tickle, a tendril of dread, the mildest suggestion: *Oh, hey, by the way, no big deal, but I thought you might maybe like to know the world is ending.*

I won't be able to control it much longer. Not if I'm just sitting here.

I need to find another way out.

I scramble back up the stairs and into the projection room. I pick my way carefully over to the editing bay, stepping over boxes, cables, my feet crunching on hard plastic, shards of glass. My fingers find the edge of the desk and fumble for the task lamp. It's been knocked over, but I'm hoping the bulb's intact.

Please turn on please turn on please turn on.

It doesn't turn on.

Okay. That's okay. Surely that's not my only option. I let my hands feel their way across the desk. It seems like there are still two monitors up here. I can just turn on the computer. That should give me enough light to see by.

I reach under the desk for the PC tower—

And find nothing but cables, dangling into space.

I'd collapse into the fancy desk chair if I had any idea where it was.

It clicks, then. *That* was the dragging, thumping sound I heard. Whoever was here—whoever attacked me—they took the computer. They've stolen the movie.

The movie—

I jump up. *That's it.*

I stumble across the room and over to the projector. It may not be the model I'm used to, but I'm sure I can figure it out. I find the control panel and run my fingers over it. The start button is always bigger than the rest of them, so it should be right about—*there*. I press it. Nothing. I press it again, harder.

Again, nothing.

I close my eyes, grit my teeth, and run through my routine from the Carmike Beverly 18.

The third time through, it comes to me.

Of course: *the main power switches.*

I move my hand to the right. There they are. I hold my breath—and flip them up.

Inside the housing, the xenon lamp comes on, almost painfully bright. Power. I have power.

I press the start button again, and this time the projector whirs to life. A second later, the three giant platters of the Autowind go into motion. My eyes automatically check the threading, tracking the film from the reel to the projector, reflexively reciting the name of each mechanism, from the whimsical to the technical to the sublime. The brain, the dancer, the tree. The sound reader, the projection plate, the framing window.

And then—

I reach for the dowser switch and open the lens.

The picture.

Onscreen, *Rebecca* flickers to life.

For a moment, I forget what I'm doing.

My God, was Laurence Olivier pretty. Even with that mustache.

I gather what wits I have left and scan the floor of the projection room. I spot my phone lying against the wall, under the snack table. I crouch down and grab it, flipping it open, and—

There's no service. *Of course* there's no service. Why would there be service? Have I learned nothing from shitty low-budget thrillers?

I roll the digital projector out of the way and, with a grunt, manage to wedge open the right-hand projector port. I thrust my arm through, out into the theater, and squint at the phone's display. Still no service.

I start to pace the length of the projection room, but then I notice how badly my legs are wobbling, so I lower myself onto the couch instead. I cradle my arm against my chest; it's starting to hurt in a way I won't be able to ignore for much longer. I press my palm against the knotted cardigan. It's not soaked through—I'm not going to bleed out—but I don't think it would be wise to wait here the ten or so hours it will take for someone to find me.

If I'm lucky.

And what if the intruder's still out there? What if they run into someone else and hurt them worse than they hurt me—and what if I could have stopped them?

Or what if they change their mind? What if they come back, knowing I'm still here? Trapped. Hurt.

Helpless.

No, I have to get out of here.

There's only one viable exit I can think of: the projector port. I walk over to examine it, running my good hand around the frame. The opening isn't as big as I'd like, but I think if I scrunch my shoulders and suck in my stomach, I might be able to fit. I lean my head out and look down. It's an eight-foot drop to the ground. Doable, if I'm careful how I land.

I use the awful afghan from the couch to lower my backpack to the theater floor, then I boost myself up onto the lip of the port. I tuck my knees to my chest and twist around until I can stick my legs out on the other side. I scoot forward until I'm just barely clinging to the edge.

I draw a shuddering breath.

On screen, Judith Anderson is clutching Joan Fontaine's arm.

I think I know this scene—

"Go ahead. Jump. He never loved you, so why go on living?"

I close my eyes. Am I really doing this? I'm really doing this.

"Jump and it will all be over."

I let myself slide forward.

I land hard on my left ankle, but I don't have time to cry about it. I snatch up my backpack and limp over to the nearest set of lobby doors.

Wait—

I can't go out this way, I'm just going to get lost again. And the intruder would expect me to use that door. They might be watching.

I need another option. I squeeze my hand into a fist and pound it against my thigh.

Marissa—think!

A fire escape—there has to be one. Surely they have *some* building codes in this state. And if I can just get outside, I can circle around back to the lobby. I can't get lost if I can see the sky.

I hobble down to the front of the theater, shining my phone's light along the curtains. One has an extra seam down the middle, and I lift a shaking hand to push it back.

Behind it is a door.

I'm so relieved I don't think to check what's on the other side before I throw my body through, and just like that I'm standing on the edge of the ocean in the faint light of a crescent moon, the waves crashing against the rocks, misting me with their spray.

The door creaks behind me. I whirl around and lunge forward to catch it before it slams shut, but I'm not quick enough. I fumble with the keys Anjali gave me—my hands, I notice with near scientific detachment, are shaking—but none of them fit the lock. There's no going back.

I turn and take stock of my surroundings. I'm standing at the top of a rusted iron staircase—not a spiral one this time, but a real, proper fire escape like you'd see in *Serpico* or *West Side Story*. It leads down to a metal walkway, which—I try to picture the hotel's layout—I *think* should take me around to the beach. But I'm not entirely sure. The architecture of this place defies inductive reasoning.

Not that it matters what I think. Unless I want to go for a swim, this walkway's the only way forward.

I descend the stairs cautiously, gripping the phone in my bad hand, using the light from the display as best I can. I keep my good hand on the waist-high railing on my right—the walkway is slippery with God only knows what, sea slime and fish poop and several decades of shoddy upkeep. The railing on the left is useless. It rattles if I move too close, one solid push away from tumbling into the ocean.

I let myself risk a glance at the water, about twenty feet below. A fall from this height, onto those rocks—

I force myself to keep my eyes on my feet.

Eventually, I come to a narrow, weathered boardwalk that just barely breaks the surface of the water. Each time a wave rushes in, the planks disappear beneath the dark, swirling tide. Then, slowly, they reemerge—only to be swallowed again.

It's fine. It's fine. It's all fine.

Before I can think too hard about what I'm doing, I stuff my shoes and socks in my backpack and roll up the cuffs of my jeans. I dip one foot into the water, flinching at the feel of it—at all of it. The water, the wood, the salt, the seaweed, the absurdity.

There's no railing at all here (*it's fine!*), so when the next wave comes in, I widen my stance, bracing myself with my hands on my knees. Then I wait until the foam clears and I can see the path again. It's slow going.

Step, step, *hold*. Step, step, *hold*.

That's when I see what's ahead, what I missed because I was too busy thinking about my feet and the water and my arm, and I stop dead in my tracks—and isn't that an appropriate turn of phrase. Because if I'm not mistaken, I've just found the back entrance to the cave Gavin brought me to earlier today. And this time I'm alone.

All alone.

I take a halting step forward and peer inside. Darkness upon darkness.

I double over and barf up a half cup of watery bile.

Cognitive behavioral therapy can really only get you so far, I guess.

I sweep my phone out in front of me, trying to use the light to get a better look around. Some people might not want to look into the corners of a cave, afraid of what they'll find, preferring instead to pretend nothing's there. Me, I want to know what to avoid. The next time death comes for me, I'd like to see it coming.

Right now, though, I can only see a foot in front of me, if that.

(It's *fine*.)

I square my shoulders, steady my breathing, and reach out. The cave wall is smooth to the touch. I walk my fingers up until I find the rough edge that marks the waterline.

It's an inch above my head.

And if something happens to me in here, no one's coming to find me.

I swallow back another kick of bile and start forward, sliding my foot out in front of me as I go to make sure I don't topple off the edge of the boardwalk. About ten yards in, the wall falls away. I inch forward, fingers spread wide, palm out, feeling for signs of a breeze. Maybe this is the way out.

Wait—

I go very still and listen very hard—as hard as I listened on my first day of film school, as hard as I listened when Amy told me about Josh, as hard as I listened when my mom told me how to make friends—but all I hear are the waves outside, lashing the rocks.

But for a second, I could have sworn—

On the next step, my toe catches an uneven board, and I topple forward, landing on my hands and knees. My head hangs low as I absorb the pain. My arm is screaming; my ankle's throbbing. My jeans, soaked with saltwater, stick to my freshly scraped knees. But I have to get up. I have to keep going. Because the water's getting deeper and the ocean's getting louder, and am I really *so* certain someone's not behind me?

A breeze riffles through my hair.

At least I think it's a breeze.

Oh, forget this.

I scramble to my feet and run.

I burst out into the night air, but I don't stop to savor it. I keep moving, running, legs and elbows and heart pumping. I drag myself over a dune, away from the water, toward the hotel. The stars are just barely visible through a haze of light cloud cover, but after the darkness of the cave, they seem almost shockingly bright. My vision is astonishing. It's like I'm an owl or a mutant or a serial killer in night-vision goggles, trailing Jodie Foster in a basement.

I think it's possible I need a doctor.

I hurry past the lifeguard station, skirting a pile of rolled-up umbrellas and a lounge chair someone forgot to put away. The sight of the chair sparks a memory so sharp and clear I can almost see it in front of me: the strap of an orange swimsuit, a wisp of blond hair, the pale length of an outstretched arm.

I stumble; my knees hit the sand.

It wasn't a memory.

I lift my head. In the chair in front of me is a slender ankle attached to a slim calf.

I know that leg.

"Liza?" I whisper.

She doesn't move. Maybe she's sleeping—or sleeping something off.

"Liza," I try again.

Still nothing. I pull myself up and brush the sand off my jeans. I reach for her shoulder—

And that's when I see her face.

I know immediately that this time she's dead for real.

She's just not that good an actress.

SUZY KOH: What was it like, finding a dead body?

MARISSA DAHL: Not an experience I would care to repeat.

GRACE PORTILLO: Was it scary?

MARISSA DAHL: It was a dead body. A dead human body. Someone who had, hours earlier, been walking and talking and laughing and, I don't know, probably complaining about something totally mundane. Someone with a mother and a father and sisters and dozens of friends. A person, Grace. She was a real person. And she died. And I was right there. Scary isn't the right word for what it was. Scary's something you seek out. Scary's fun. Nothing about this was fun.

've spent a lifetime imagining worst-case scenarios. Every time I stand on a subway platform, I think about how easy it would be for someone to push me in front of a train. When I see a child's ball rolling toward a curb, I can't help but picture a tiny body being zipped into a black bag. Once, Amy and I were sitting out on our old patio, and she tipped her face up to the sun and smiled and said, I don't know, something about how great it is to get to live in Southern California, probably, and I followed her gaze and thought: *Just five billion years until that sucker burns this planet to a crisp.*

Overanxious mothers, people who browse WebMD, guys with signs that read THE END IS NIGH, those who consider *Final Destination* service journalism. These are my people.

Still—

I am not prepared for this.

My hands hover over Liza's face, trembling, unsure. Useless. I don't— I really don't know what to do. Do I look for a pulse? No—she's clearly dead. This is a body. A dead body. She's not coming back. This is done. This can't be undone.

I swallow past the panic that's filling my throat like rushing, brackish water, and I force myself to look back over my shoulder, to scan the length of the beach for someone, anyone, but everyone's inside, aren't they? They're all still inside, drinking and gossiping and flirting and thinking the worst thing in the world is losing a *job*.

Jesus Christ, what do I do?

I put my hand to my chest. It's heaving. So why does it feel like I'm not getting any air?

I should go inside. I should get help. But I can't leave her alone, not like this. What if there's—what if there's something I can do? What if there's someone coming for her?

What the *fuck* do I do?

I've always thought it seemed over the top when people screamed in movies, but now I understand. Sometimes there's just nothing else for it.

If only someone could hear me.

The only other thing I can think of is to call someone—but who? I only have three numbers memorized, and none of them would be able to—

I almost laugh when I realize what I've overlooked. And maybe I actually do laugh, I don't know, nothing in my body feels like it's in my body anymore, it's all just floating along behind me, like a balloon tied to a child's wrist. If I'd read this scene in a script, I would've rolled my eyes. I would've sent a screenshot to Amy. I would've said this is what a hundred years of skewed representation has wrought, because what actual human woman would forget something like *that*?

I punch in the fourth number I know.

"Nine-one-one, what is your emergency?"

It's at this precise moment that I realize Liza isn't just dead.

"Hello? Is anyone there?"

She's also in costume.

"Hello?"

Someone's dressed her in Caitlyn's clothes.

For the second time that night, I throw up.

The dispatcher tells me not to move, they'll be there right away, but I've decided this is a terrible idea. Liza isn't just dead—she was murdered. I need to get to the lobby. To the lights. To *witnesses*. I wipe my face on my sleeve and start across the sand.

It's much harder to walk than it should be. I have to fight for every last bit of sensory input: I have to squint to keep the hotel in focus; I have to strain to hear through the rushing in my ears; I have to stomp my feet to feel the ground beneath them, and even that doesn't do much.

Maybe the dispatcher had a point.

I use my good hand to grab on to any surface in reach, to keep my balance, to move me forward, and still I fall twice before I manage to reach the hotel driveway.

I plant myself there, on the steps, against a column. It's the best I can do.

This is where things start to get fuzzy.

Two police cruisers pull up in front of me, along with a boxy, silver-plated vehicle that's either a food truck or a fire truck.

Probably the latter.

Probably.

A blur of faces, a chorus of "ma'am"s.

I extend my arm in the direction of the beach, and the cops take off.

I slump back against the column.

I guess I'll just wait here, then.

I can still see the edge of Liza's chair.

Behind me, the door crashes open. Whoever it is runs for the beach, too.

After a moment, someone else screams.

At least, I think it's someone else.

A blue sedan with a crumpled front bumper rumbles up the drive. It has one of those magnetic sirens movie cops slap on the roof of their cars before doing something exceptionally dangerous at rush hour.

It also appears to have "24-Hour Locksmith" painted on the passenger door.

I rub my eyes. What exactly did I tell the dispatcher?

The driver's side door opens, and a pale giant of a man struggles to climb out, his limbs awkward and uncertain, like he's emerging from a chrysalis instead of a dented Corolla. I point him to the beach, too, but he ignores me.

He crouches in front of me instead and pulls something out of a black bag.

"It's an arm," I say.

He gives me a sharp look.

"Not a lock," I add, in case that wasn't clear.

He glances back at his car, then at me, and the line between his eyebrows smooths away. "I'm a paramedic," he says.

"Oh." I sit up a little straighter. "Ever seen *Bringing Out the Dead*?"

He searches my face, and I find I don't mind studying him back. He has a wide mouth and a crooked nose and lovely large ears. Good features. Trustworthy features. This guy definitely wasn't popular in high school.

"Can you look at me?" he asks.

"I *am* looking at you."

"No, I need to see your eyes."

I grit my teeth and lift my chin.

"Are you dizzy?" he asks. "Nauseous?"

I take a steadying breath. "I didn't hit my head, if that's what you're asking."

"Good. Is it okay if I touch your arm now?"

I nod.

He unwraps the cardigan and rotates my arm gently to get a better look. The wound isn't nearly as deep as I thought, but it extends the length of my forearm, from my wrist to my elbow. I almost find myself admiring the curve of it, knowing it would hug perfectly against the curve of the Autowind, a broken-heart pendant matching up with its mate.

He turns away to reach for his bag.

All of a sudden, an arm slides under my knees and another goes around my back, and before I know what's happening, I'm being scooped up off the ground.

The paramedic comes to his feet. "What the *hell*?"

I tilt my head back to see who's carrying me. Oh. It's Isaiah.

"You okay?" he murmurs.

This is such a spectacularly inane question, all I can do is shake my head in disbelief.

Anjali appears at the top of the stairs, alongside two stone-faced men I don't recognize.

"Take her inside," she says. "I've called a real doctor."

The paramedic runs a big hand through his shaggy hair. "Now, ma'am, I don't know who you—"

I don't hear the rest because I'm being carried up the stairs, inside, through the lobby, past the still crowded but now nearly silent bar. Isaiah takes me into the conference room and settles me in one of the soft, high-backed chairs.

Without thinking, I use my good hand to push the chair into a spin, and—*oh*—that's nice.

Isaiah catches the arm of the chair, stopping me. "The police are going to want to talk to you. You're going to have to get it together."

I slide my hand under my thigh and dig my fingertips into the fake leather. "Did you see her?"

A pause.

"I did."

"So I didn't imagine it, then?"

Another pause.

"You didn't."

The first thing Anjali's "real" doctor does is squeeze my jaw open and slip a narcotic under my tongue.

"Don't move," he says sternly.

I never would have imagined that a strange man sticking his gloved fingers in my mouth without my permission could be the least bad part of an evening, but you learn something new every day, I guess.

My head lolls to the side.

I'm dimly aware that someone's arguing out in the lobby. I think they're getting closer.

"I will not be ordered around by some small-town, shit-for-brains—"

The door flies open. Anjali stumbles through, an outraged look on her face. As soon as she recovers her balance, she turns and tries to head back out—

The door slams in her face.

"They took my phone," Anjali says, looking stunned. "They took my *phone*."

An inappropriate laugh knuckles up out of me. "Did they also make you sign an NDA?"

Before Anjali can respond, there's another flurry of voices from outside the door.

This time it's Valentina who barges in. She scans the room, mutters something in Russian, and bolts back out into the lobby.

The door slams shut again.

Anjali clears her throat. "Any chance either of you understood that?"

"The literal translation," Isaiah says, "is something like 'fuck-digging.'"

Anjali and I stare at him.

"It means 'goddammit.'"

"Of course you speak Russian," Anjali says, but there's no real heat to the accusation.

We fall silent. The only sound in the room is the rough draw of the black thread being laced through the flesh of my arm. Whatever pill the doctor gave me is doing the trick: I can feel the needle curving up through my skin, the thread pulling through the hole, the knot tugging it closed, but it doesn't bother me. On the contrary, the doctor's steady rhythm is sure, soothing.

In, through, out, closed. In, through, out, closed.

It's a good pattern.

Isaiah shrugs out of his coat and drapes it over my shoulders. "You're shivering," he says.

I look down, surprised to see that he's right. I'm disgusting, too—crusted in blood and sweat and seawater and who knows what else. I pinch my shirt between my thumb and forefinger, drawing it away from my skin. The fabric makes a damp sucking sound as it peels away.

Just like the sound of Liza's feet against that tile.

Liza.

Another gurgle of laughter threatens to escape, and I squeeze my lips shut, hoping I can hold it back.

What the hell are we doing, just sitting here?

Liza's *dead*.

This time I don't notice the door opening. It's as if Gavin's just appeared out of thin air, his hands shoved deep in his pockets, so pale and haggard you'd never imagine so many people are willing to pay to look at him. Tony and Valentina are right behind him, only marginally more prepossessing.

Anjali groans. "Gavin, get back to your room."

Gavin dredges up a smile. "Sorry, Mummy, you're not in charge anymore."

He flings himself into the nearest chair; Tony and Valentina sit next to Anjali.

"The police asked us all to wait here," Tony says, his voice so low I want to curl in on myself. His gaze drops to my arm. "Jesus, what happened?"

"She's fine," the doctor says.

"I believe I asked *her.*"

I open my mouth to answer—but where do I start? Do I open with the projection room, or do I begin earlier, in the hallway? In the spa? Do I just skip to the part with the dead body?

I know, I know. An editor who can't tell a story. *Ha-ha.*

But this is different. When I'm cutting a movie, I control the flow of input. I can skip ahead, rewind, zoom in. I can pause, leave the room, refill my Coke. I can take all the time I need to sift through everything I'm seeing, hearing, feeling, to find the clues, the turns, the heroes, the villains, and then—and only then—do I string it all together into a single narrative. When I have to do it on the fly, like now, when I have nothing to go on but a tidal wave of sense-memory—augmented by what I'm beginning to think were some fairly powerful psychostimulants—I'm not exactly able to massage the evening's events into a neat three-act structure.

Or five acts, if we're talking TV.

"Someone stole the movie," I say, eventually. "They attacked me, and they stole the movie, and then, while I was stuck in that theater and getting lost in a *cave*, they must have gone to find Liza and—"

I cut myself off, not wanting to say it out loud. But it's one of those thoughts everyone's going to hear whether you say it or not, so all I've really done is forced everyone else to think it through instead.

Imagine that. Me, making things worse.

It's Anjali who breaks the silence. "You saw who it was? Can you describe them? Was it a man?"

I open my mouth, ready to tell them that the lights were out, that I couldn't get to the lamp—and that if they weren't, or if I'd been able to, then maybe I wouldn't be here now, because what are the chances—*seriously*—what are the chances we're dealing with *two* separate perpetrators? And if he killed Liza, he could just as easily have killed me.

(Huh. I guess I do think it was a man.)

But before I can say any of that, Isaiah lays a hand on my shoulder. "You should wait to talk to the police," he says.

Anjali snorts. "Oh yeah? And what are they going to do?"

I open my mouth again; Isaiah's hand tightens around my shoulder.

I look up at him. "Why are you squeezing me?"

He snatches his hand away; it goes to rub at the back of his neck. "I just really think you should wait for the police."

I come up out of my seat. There's something he's not saying, and maybe I'll be able to figure out what he means if I can just get a better look at him. But he turns away before I get the chance.

"Isaiah?" I ask.

Across the room, Gavin heaves a sigh. "Darling, don't you see? He doesn't want you to reveal too much. He wants you to be quiet in case one of *us* is the killer."

No one seems to have anything else to say after that.

The doctor takes that opportunity to stick a second pill between my lips. This is a very different kind of drug, clearly, because by the time he's finished my dressing, I'm amped up and alert, and while I may not be pain-free, I'm more or less pain-indifferent—and thank God for that, because here's another miserable surprise: The guy who tried to barge his way onto Billy Lyle's boat is now barging his way into this room.

"Men at the docks, men at the doors," he snaps at someone just out of sight. "No one leaves this island, no one leaves this hotel. I see anyone with a camera, I'm throwing it in the *fucking* ocean."

Nick. His name is Nick. And he must have been *very* drunk that night on Billy's boat, because I can tell right away that, when sober, this is a man who worships at the altar of right angles and neat creases. His khakis are ironed; the sleeves of his green knit shirt are precisely sized; his part is so straight I wonder, for a second, if he's wearing a wig. If I saw this guy in a movie, I would assume his character was being set up to have a nervous breakdown.

"Ms. Dahl?" he says. "I'm Detective Decker, Lewes PD, and this is my—"

He looks up, pauses. If he's surprised or dismayed to see me and Isaiah there, I can't tell, and that makes something in me go hard and tight. Someone with his complexion shouldn't be so difficult to read, but I can't see even the slightest hint of color blooming beneath his freckles. The barest twitch to the corner of his mouth is the only other sign he gives that he's recognized us—and I might be imagining that.

It's a level of control that would be impressive in an actor. It's downright unnerving in a civilian.

"This is my partner, Detective Hanson," he says after a moment, indicating a brown-haired man I recognize as Blue Polo. (Tonight, said polo is purple.) Nick's eyes flick down to my arm, then back up to my face. "We have a few questions."

"Of course," I say. "I'll help however I can."

He sits down across the table from me. His partner pours a glass of water and slides it in my direction.

Nick takes out a notebook and flips it open. "You were the one who found Ms. May's body and called the police, correct?"

I nod.

"Can you describe the events that led up to that discovery?"

I look around the room. "What, *now*?"

Nick's mouth tightens. "I didn't realize I needed to make an appointment."

"No, I just meant I assumed you'd want to talk to me alone."

"This is just a preliminary interview, ma'am. If I think I'm close to cracking the case, I'll be sure to ask everyone to gather in the dining car for the denouement. Will that suffice?"

I nod, abashed.

I may be more alert, but I'm still not sure where to start, so I just tell him the same thing I told everyone else. Everyone perks up a little when I mention coming across Liza in the spa, but when Nick asks, everyone admits that they had no idea Liza was seeing anybody.

When I'm finished, Nick looks up from his notebook. "They *stole* the movie?"

"Not exactly," Anjali says. "The movie's backed up, obviously."

"But whoever it was has access to the raw footage," I point out. "For whatever that's worth."

Nick scratches the back of his neck, thinking hard. "And you say you didn't get a good look at the guy's face?"

"No. In fact, I'm not entirely sure it was a—"

"You're wasting your time," Anjali interjects. "I already know who you should be looking for."

If Anjali expected Nick to respond with enthusiasm or gratitude, she must be pretty disappointed right now. He looks like a waiter who's just been told the entire table is going to order off-menu. He slumps in his chair and holds his pen high over his notepad. "Yeah, okay. Who?"

"Our last AD," Anjali says. "He left under less than pleasant circumstances."

For the first time since she entered the room, Valentina removes her Juul from her lips. "Not *Chris*," she says.

"No," Anjali says, "The 2nd AD."

"Phil?"

"The *first* 2nd AD."

Gavin drops his face into his hands. "*Ryan*," he mutters. "She's talking about Ryan. *Fuck*. Even I know that."

Nick taps his pen against his notepad, looking distinctly unimpressed. "You got a last name for this guy?"

"Kassowitz," Anjali says. "He was mostly in charge of getting the actors where they needed to go. He was also responsible for communicating with the background players. The extras, I mean. But it wasn't a good fit, and a couple of weeks ago we had to let him go. He was pissed; it got ugly. I had to have him removed from the island."

"Problems?" Nick asks. "Could you be a little more specific than that?"

Anjali chews on her lip and glances sidelong at Tony. "Well—he kind of assaulted an extra."

Tony leans forward. "You didn't tell me about this."

Anjali nods, a pained expression on her face. "We've been having things go wrong on set ever since he left—it could be a coincidence, but I didn't want to take the chance. That's why I brought Isaiah and his team on board."

Nick looks at Isaiah. "You have a team?"

"I run a small private security firm," Isaiah says. "I have five employees here on the island with me."

Nick raises an eyebrow. "This probably isn't going to help your Yelp rating, you know."

"Murder wasn't exactly part of our brief."

"Indeed." Nick makes a note. "Do you happen to know the current whereabouts of Mr. Kassowitz?"

"As of yesterday at noon, he was with his mother outside Philadelphia."

"Do you consider him a threat?"

"I consider everyone a threat."

Nick blinks a few times. "I'll have my guys look into it. Is there anyone else we should know about?"

Anjali laughs, and it almost sounds genuine. "I mean, Tony's pissed off so many people, they probably have their own Facebook page."

Tony grimaces. "Thank you for that, Anjali."

"Has there been anyone else who's seemed at all suspicious?" Nick presses. "Anyone unfamiliar?"

Anjali shakes her head. "Not that I can think of."

"None? Not anyone?" Nick's gaze goes sharp. "Not even Billy Lyle?"

"Absolutely not," she says.

"So you've never seen him in or around the hotel?" Nick asks.

Anjali's jaw tightens. "Not as far as I am aware."

"Or on set?"

"Not that I can recall."

"But surely you've *seen* him."

Gavin slams his hand on the table. "For fuck's sake," he says. "Billy had nothing to do with this."

Nick turns to Gavin for the first time. The corner of his mouth twitches down, a glimmer of distaste. "And how do you know that?"

"Because he was with me. I was interviewing him. For research."

"Well, that's fascinating news." Nick turns to a new page in his notebook. "Were you on his boat?"

"No. We met—" Gavin's mouth goes soft all of a sudden, a divot forming in the middle of his chin. "We met down on the beach."

Nick nods. "And you were together until what time?"

Gavin sucks his lower lip between his teeth. "Well, I'm not *exactly* sure . . ."

"Why don't I rephrase that: Were you still with him at the time the body was found?"

Gavin looks down at his hands. "No."

"That's what I thought."

A uniformed officer pushes through the door. "Nick, you've got to see this."

Nick tosses his notebook aside and shoves a hand through his hair. "Yeah, what is it?"

The officer comes around the conference table and hands him a small plastic evidence bag. I'm close enough that I can see what's inside: Caitlyn's school photo. The same one Billy showed us earlier today.

Nick lets out a low whistle. "Where did you find this?"

"On his boat," the officer says. "No sign of him, though."

Nick looks over at Anjali. "I want all your people in their rooms, *now*. We need to start searching this hotel. This guy is still out there, and I'm not letting him get away with it again."

TWENTY-TWO

W hy are you doing this again?"

"They were rolled the wrong way."

"They look the same as your other pants."

"They look *nothing* like my other pants."

"Then why didn't you fix them before?"

"So I could prove someone had been in here!"

It's possible that right now any conversation would seem this absurd, this outlandish, this malapropos, the corporate Twitter feed that forgot to pause its automated queue after a national tragedy.

Still, I can't quite believe I'm talking about this. Folding really does feel like a bridge too far.

They held us in the conference room for another hour once the police started searching the grounds. When they told us that our rooms, at least, were clear and that we were dismissed for the night, Isaiah announced he was coming with me to mine.

"Out of an abundance of caution," he said.

In a truly shocking turn of events, Anjali agreed with him.

"You're the only eyewitness," she said, dimly. "You've seen enough movies to know how this goes."

Outrageous, I thought then.

Ridiculous, I think now.

You might imagine that seeing a corpse up close would make a person fear death in a real, immediate way—and three hours ago, I would have said that, too—but somehow, it's had the opposite effect on me. This has been the most dramatic evening of my life, and yet somehow I was still just incidental to it all. Death now seems even more like something that only happens to other people.

I guess that's why I still care about folding.

"Look," I say to Isaiah, pulling out my spare pair of jeans to show him. "First I fold my pants in half longways, and then I roll them from the waist down."

"I'm still not seeing the problem."

I point to the offending pair. "I always face the right side of the pants out. On these, the left side is out."

"Why do you roll them that way?"

"Because I'm right handed."

"What does that have to do with your pants?"

"I don't know, that's just how I like them! And if they're not, I can feel it. I know they're wrong. It's like a—" I wave a hand in the vicinity of my neck "—it's like a tightness, you know? A silent alarm sort of thing? Like when you're in the airport and you see an unattended bag, and, on one hand, 'see something, say something,' right? But what if you do say something and Homeland Security takes the bag, but it turns out to belong to some nice old lady who had to run to the bathroom because she has bladder control issues, and she was going to be right back, really, it was just going to take a second, but now she's being interrogated by the FBI and oh, look, you've ruined her trip—and, by the way, she has hypertension. So all the stress gives her a stroke and she dies and now she'll never get to hold her grandchild." I take a breath. "*Or* it really *is* a bomb, but you don't say anything because you're a maladjusted weirdo who worries too much about imaginary grandmothers, and as a result a hundred fifty people die, horribly. You're on all the national news, disgraced, forever."

Isaiah takes this in. "You think about all that when you look at a pair of pants?"

"I think about all that all the time," I say, rerolling the pants and tucking them back into my suitcase.

I lower myself into the chair with a grimace. I should have asked the doctor to take a look at my knees, but my jeans don't pull up past my calves, so I would have had to take them off, and I simply didn't have it in me. The blood has dried now, and I can tell the scabs will tear away when I change for bed.

Maybe I'll sleep in my clothes.

Maybe I'll sleep in my clothes for the rest of my life.

I smother a yawn with the back of my hand. "Why are we talking about this again?" I ask.

"Because I brought your suitcase up here myself. If someone's searched your suitcase, someone's been in your room."

"Oh. You're saying a murderer might have a key to my room." I give the thought a moment to sink in—but it doesn't. It floats instead on the surface of my thoughts, stubborn and undeniable, like that island of garbage in the Indian Ocean. A slow-moving indictment of all the ways we've gone so horribly wrong.

I wonder idly if my panic will be visible from space, too.

"Should I change rooms?" I ask, faintly.

Isaiah considers this. "You could."

"I'm also happy to change hotels."

"There's another option," he says, crossing to the door. "Because he can't come in while you're here—not through this door, anyway. Even if he has a key, he won't be able to get through this."

He turns the deadbolt and swings the security latch into position.

"I could also be convinced to leave the state," I point out.

"But let's say he does get in." He walks past me and goes over to the window. "I'll make sure he won't get very far."

He closes the curtains and flops down on the loveseat, sending two of the needlepoint pillows flying.

"Absolutely not," I say.

He stretches his arms out along the back of the loveseat. His fingers drape over the sides.

"Anjali's right," he says. "You need protection."

"Then you have to find another way to do that, because you're not keeping watch while I sleep. That's not a plan. That's a bad romantic comedy."

He pretends to think about this. "Who would they cast as me, do you think?"

"Depends on the budget. Probably Terry Crews. Stop distracting me. Why can't you post someone outside the door?"

"What if he doesn't come in through the door?"

"Who, Terry Crews?"

"The killer."

I suck in a breath. "Do we really have to call him that?"

He gives me a steady look. "It's what he is."

I press the heel of my hand against my forehead and let out a growl of frustration. How am I supposed to put this in a way that doesn't make me sound like a jerk? On a bad day, what I need—all I need—is to be left alone. My parents understood this. Amy understood this. Even my college housing office understood this. My freshman year I was one of eight students in the whole class to be given my own tiny room—what everyone called a "psycho single," and wasn't that a good joke to roll around in my mouth at night while I was lying between cool cotton sheets, blackout curtains drawn, white noise machine set to "Rainforest Harmony."

I don't care if I'm in literal mortal peril. I need a moment to my-self. I can only bear to be around others if I know the situation's temporary.

Isaiah's staring at something near my hip. I look down. My right hand is twisting furiously at my belt loop. I untangle my fingers and curl my arm around my stomach instead.

"I make you uncomfortable," he says after a moment.

"*Everyone* makes me uncomfortable."

I sit down on the bed and try not to look like I'm upset. I'm being managed. And I hate being managed. Because it means not only that I'm being belligerent and stubborn and unpleasant, but also that I'm going about it in such a sad, pathetic manner that people feel bad for me. I can't even lash out like a regular person.

I close my eyes and try to come up with a good get-out-of-jail-free phrase for when you've been an asshole but also really meant what you said.

I crack open an eyelid. "It's been a long day."

Isaiah laughs like he knows exactly how I got to that sentence, and there's no stopping my scowl now.

"Tomorrow will be even longer," he says. "Trust me."

"Because the shock will wear off, you mean? Is that when all this will finally start feeling real?"

"Oh, no, that's months and months away. I just meant we have a lot to do if we're going to catch Liza's killer."

My eyes fly all the way open. "What?"

His smile is faint. "You don't think I'm going to leave this investi-gation in the hands of Percy Weasley down there, do you? I don't have three and a half stars on Yelp for nothing, Marissa."

"But—me?"

"Yeah, you're going to be my sidekick. It'll be a—what do you guys call it? A 'two-hander'?"

"I really wish you would stop trying to distract me with inappropriate humor."

He leans down until his eyes are level with mine. "I'm serious. I want you to help me track this guy down."

"No," I say.

He goes on as if he didn't hear me. "I have my team, but they don't know much about movies."

"I've been here a day. Ask Tony or Anjali instead."

He shakes his head. "I'd rather not involve them until I absolutely have to."

It takes a moment for the implication to settle in. Then my mouth rounds into an O. "You think they might have had something to do with it?"

"I see no reason to rule them out."

"No loyalty whatsoever, huh? No wonder Anjali hates you."

"Hold on, I wouldn't say she *hates* me—"

"So she *does* want to sleep with you?"

Isaiah laughs. "Anjali? And *me*?"

"What? There was banter."

"That wasn't banter. That was two smart-asses talking over each other. Unless I'm very much mistaken, Anjali's interests lie elsewhere."

My lip curls. "You mean *Tony*?"

"No—Valentina."

"There you go. That's why I'm the wrong person for this. I can't read people, not in real life. And apparently I have some extremely heteronormative assumptions to work through."

Isaiah reaches out, the tips of his fingers grazing my injured arm. "Marissa, you're the only person I'm certain had nothing to do with this."

"I can think of wilder twists," I say. "Ever seen *Angel Heart*?"

His expression softens. "Let me put it this way," he says. "You're all I've got."

I sneak a glance at his face, and when I catch the shape of his lips, I stifle a groan. I can read the intention there.

"No," I say. "Don't do it."

He draws a breath.

"*Don't* say it."

He holds out his hands.

I clamp my palms over my ears.

"*Help me, Obi-Wan Kenobi. You're my only hope.*"

I grab a pillow and throw it at his head. "No more *jokes*. I mean it. I know that you've probably seen hundreds of dead bodies and that this is a coping mechanism—and maybe it's a good coping mechanism, I don't know, who am I to say. But I don't like it, okay? I've spent my whole life training myself to laugh at other people's jokes so they wouldn't realize I can't keep up with a conversation, and it's too late to change that now, even though I really, really, *really* don't feel like making myself laugh at the moment. It feels wrong. I feel wrong. Liza is *dead*. So quit asking it of me."

He draws back. "You're right. Force of habit."

I blink back an appalling wetness in my eyes. "I'll help you, okay? Obviously I'll help you. But I'm not sure what good it will do. I'm not exactly a natural detective."

He shrugs. "You're a movie lover. I'm sure you can come up with a role model or two."

I snort. "I'm no Nora Charles."

He squints at my face and tilts his head to the side. "No—I was thinking Marge Gunderson."

This shocks an honest laugh out of me, but I clamp my mouth shut almost immediately because, God, I was so obviously surprised, and what if he thinks *I* think he doesn't know much about movies, that I'm one of those people who's always like, *well, if you know so much about* cinema, *let's see you spell* Koyaanisqatsi *without googling it*, that I'm a snob, an officious gatekeeper, that I think *Fargo* is some kind of cult movie when in fact it's a pretty mainstream hit, when really the truth is I just can't quite believe someone's teasing me and not trying to be mean about it.

TWENTY-THREE

The compromise we hash out is this: Isaiah gets Wade to give him the key to the adjoining room, and I agree to leave the connecting door ajar. Even though the sight of an open door gnaws at me, I can't justify putting up a fight about something so small. It's a terrible line for an obituary.

Marissa Dahl, 36, died this week, murdered because she insisted on closing a door.

I'll just have to settle for closing the bathroom door an extra time or two.

I turn on the taps in the shower and wait for the water to get hot. Never have I been more grateful for my routine than I am tonight. One of my high school English teachers recommended we memorize poetry in case we ever find ourselves locked in a dungeon and needed something to keep ourselves sane, and though I suspect her tongue was firmly in her cheek—it can't have been easy to teach the Romantics to a bunch of engineering faculty brats—at the time I took it quite literally. To this day, a single line of Keats is enough to make me break into a cold sweat and map out a path to the nearest exit.

But now—now I get it. Because the only thing tethering me to the earth is the familiar rhythm my body's moving through all on its own, no matter how unfamiliar the accompanying thoughts may be:

Shower, floss, brush my teeth, floss again—*I don't understand*—wash my face, comb my hair, check under my nails to make sure I didn't miss anything—*why would someone steal the footage if it's backed up anyway?*—scrub them with a nail brush anyway, put on pajamas—*and if they killed Liza, why didn't they kill me?*—climb into bed.

I tune the clock radio to static, close my eyes, and rub my feet together.

John Cusack walks across the Chicago River. "Top five things I miss about—"

"Marissa—are you awake?"

I bolt upright, disoriented, arms flying out to catch myself, even though I'm incredibly safely ensconced in a California king. Before I can do anything but suck in a breath so sharp it burns the back of my throat, the lamp flicks on.

It's Grace and Suzy.

The words explode out of me: "What the *hell*?"

The girls exchange a look.

"We came to see how you're doing," Suzy says.

"We heard what happened," Grace adds.

"So you broke into my room—do you not—when it's the middle of the night—and there's a killer—I mean, this is just such a—who *are* you?"

I can't seem to stop yelling.

Grace winces. "Maybe we didn't think this one through."

"We just wanted to make sure you were okay," Suzy says.

"And maybe we got a little carried away—"

"But also, we were thinking—"

I hold up my hand. I reach over to turn off the radio, then I give myself a moment to collect my thoughts. There aren't many of them, so it doesn't take long.

"How did you get in here?" I ask.

Both girls look up at the ceiling.

"Well?" Grace says.

"We might have lifted a key from housekeeping," Suzy says.

I clench my jaw. "What about the deadbolt?"

"We lifted the key for that, too," Suzy says.

"And the security latch?"

Grace holds up a "Do Not Disturb" sign. She gives it a little shake. "We used this to, like, jiggle it open."

"Where'd you learn how to do that?"

"YouTube?"

I scratch at the back of my head where my ponytail has tangled against my scalp. "So much for security, I guess." I swing my legs over the side of the bed, hop off, and stalk over to the connecting door. Just as I lift my hand, Isaiah pulls it open.

"Everything okay?" he asks, casually.

For a moment all I can do is punch at the air in Grace and Suzy's general direction.

"They broke in," I eventually manage.

Isaiah gives the girls a narrow look. "How long did it take you?"

"About twenty seconds," Suzy says.

"Huh." He walks over to the door and pulls it open. Out in the hallway, flanking the door to Liza's room—now cordoned off with crime scene tape—are two uniformed police officers. "Too busy guarding that door to keep an eye on this one?" Isaiah asks them.

The shorter officer shrugs. "They said it was their mom's room."

"You didn't wonder why they were out and about in the middle of the night?"

The taller one points at Suzy. "She said she needed . . . girl stuff."

Suzy smirks. "It's pronounced *TAM-pon*, Greg."

Grace bites her thumbnail and stares intently at her toes.

Isaiah exchanges a few low words with the officers before closing the door behind him. "I'll have one of my guys out there from now on," he tells me, leaning close.

"You don't think the girls are in danger, do you?"

"Until we figure out what's going on, I think everyone's in danger."

His breath is warm against my skin, and I take an ungainly half step back, ducking awkwardly to my left, barely managing not to trip over my feet as I retreat to the other side of the room.

I glance at the girls, then at Isaiah, and I make a graceless back-and-forth gesture between them. "This is Isaiah," I say. "He's also pretending to be a detective."

Isaiah coughs. *"Pretending?"*

Suzy frowns. *"Also?"*

"They're investigating the Caitlyn Kelly murder," I explain. "They think Billy Lyle's innocent."

The girls are watching me closely, wearing expressions my own face is familiar with: They're trying to figure out if I'm making fun of them. I'm not—though it wouldn't be too hard, were I so inclined. They've changed clothes since I saw them last, both of them dressed now in mismatched black. Grace has tucked her hair under a Yankees cap; Suzy's socks are decorated with tiny skulls.

"What's so funny?" Grace asks.

"Nothing," I say, honestly. "You're running around without supervision in a hotel where someone was just *murdered*. That's not remotely funny. I truly have no idea what the appropriate response is in this moment, emotional or otherwise. Calling your parents, probably."

Grace takes a step forward, a piteous crinkle between her eyebrows. "Please don't."

My hand taps out a rhythm against my hip. "How old are you two?"

Grace swallows. "I'll be fourteen in August."

I look at Suzy.

"I'll be fourteen *next* August?"

This time I do laugh. At that age, I was busy saving up for a laser disc player and refusing to take showers after gym class because I'd seen *Carrie* too many times. What would it even feel like to be so assured, so daring, at such a young age? At any age. Were they born this way or did they learn it somehow? Who from? Is it generational? Can they can teach me, too?

"That's old enough to know not to break into someone's room," Isaiah's saying, which, yes, is also a really important point, and now that I think about it, I am *extremely* upset that they invaded my space, but—

"I'm sure they had a good reason," I hear myself saying.

They tear their eyes from Isaiah and turn toward me.

"We do," Grace says, slowly.

"We have a *really* good reason," Suzy says.

I scrub at my nose with the back of my hand.

"Go on," Isaiah says.

Suzy bounces up on her toes. "We know everyone's saying that Billy killed Liza."

"They are?" I say, unconvincingly.

Suzy rolls her eyes. "She was killed the same way Caitlyn was and left in the same place and dressed in the same outfit. Of course that's what they're saying."

"But you don't believe it," Isaiah guesses.

"It doesn't make sense," she says.

"I agree."

Both girls blink in surprise.

"Anjali thinks there's another likely suspect," Isaiah explains. "And it's not Billy."

I tug on Isaiah's sleeve. "Should you really be telling them this?"

He glances over. "It kind of seems like they're just going to find out anyway."

"We already know about Ryan," Suzy says, loudly.

"See?" he murmurs.

"—and anyway, he's obviously a red herring."

Isaiah's head comes up. He fixes the girls with a look that has them shuffling their feet and looking off to the side, and only when Grace's lip starts to wobble does he soften his expression. He sighs and wedges his body as best he can into the chintz armchair, resting his elbows on his knees.

"Okay," he says. "I'm listening. Tell me why this investigation I've dedicated dozens of valuable manhours to is pointless."

Suzy takes a deep breath. "For one thing, Ryan was just nine years old when Caitlyn was killed."

"And living in San Diego," Grace adds.

A pause.

"Just how bad at this do you think I am?" Isaiah asks, wonderingly.

Suzy clears her throat. "Yes, well, did you also know he hasn't left his mom's basement for three days?"

"What? How did you—"

"Our friend Quincy hacked into Ryan's T-Mobile account."

Isaiah blinks. "I have an entire team trying to get that information."

Grace reaches out and pats him on the shoulder. "I'm sure they'd be faster if they could break the law, too."

"But you still think we're talking about a single killer here, right?" I ask, settling myself awkwardly on the edge of the bed.

"No," Isaiah says. "If the person who killed Caitlyn is still around—which, in my opinion, is highly unlikely—why would they kill again? Especially now, with so many people around."

"A perfectly reasonable point," Grace says. "Unless there's a *really* compelling motive."

Isaiah raises an eyebrow. "Which is?"

"*The movie*," Suzy says. "We think there's something in there. A clue. A prop—or a line of dialogue, we don't know what. But it's something the police missed the first time around, and we bet it points to the identity of Caitlyn's killer. I mean—it fits, right? He broke into the projector room to destroy the evidence, and then he killed Liza to make sure the movie would never get made."

It's such a tidy solution—and so close to the plots of at least two movies I'm extremely fond of—that I feel a little bad pointing out the obvious.

"But they *didn't* destroy the footage," I say, gently. "They just destroyed one copy of it. There are probably at least three separate back-ups. This is a major Hollywood production; we have *millions* of dollars. We're not film students."

Suzy frowns. "Oh. Well, whoever killed Caitlyn has to be pretty old by now. Maybe they don't know about all that."

"About . . . computers?"

She sinks down onto the loveseat and pulls one of the pillows into her lap. "Fine, maybe the killer was just trying to get the production shut down, then."

"I suppose that's possible," Isaiah allows.

Her chin comes back up. "Because they know if the movie's released, the truth will come out!"

Isaiah rubs his neck with both hands and mumbles something to himself that sounds an awful lot like *the hell am I even doing.*

"In my experience," he says, "people are moved by simple greed or big feelings—not grand conspiracy. And then one small bad decision snowballs into a bunch of big ones."

Suzy and Grace object to this in tandem.

"But what evidence—"

"We're not babies—"

"I'm a *professional*—"

I look down at my feet. They're swinging, ankles together, my heels knocking against the bedframe in a steady, satisfying rhythm.

After a moment, something shifts in my mind, a slight but necessary adjustment, a nudge to a picture frame to make it level.

"Why did Anjali hire you?" I ask Isaiah.

Isaiah hesitates. "She told me there had been a number of disturbing incidents and inappropriate workplace interactions on set. There was one ex-employee in particular she wanted me to keep an eye on—Ryan Kassowitz. She said she had reason to believe some members of the production might be in physical danger."

"Like Liza?"

"Among others."

"Like me?" I ask, quietly.

"I know," he says. "I let you down tonight. I let Liza down tonight. But I can't do my job if my clients aren't honest with me—and I'm beginning to think Tony and Anjali have been holding out on me since day one. I'm done with their bullshit. Starting tomorrow, we're going to get some answers." He looks at Suzy, then Grace, then me. "The four of us, we're going to figure this thing out."

SUZY KOH: Okay, so a lot of our listeners have been asking us about this—and the answer is yes, we really did break into a hotel room with a "Do Not Disturb" tag.

GRACE PORTILLO: It was super easy.

SUZY KOH: For real. I'm never staying in a hotel room again. [*pause*] I mean, unless it's a really nice one.

TWENTY-FOUR

S o I've been thinking about the Bobbsey Twins," Isaiah announces as he strides through the connecting door.

I only managed to get a few, fitful hours of sleep after he took the girls back to their rooms late last night, so it's no surprise that I have no idea what this is supposed to mean. I cast my mind about for context until I realize he must be talking about Grace and Suzy.

"But they don't look anything alike."

"Yes," he says, "that's why it's a—"

"And weren't the Bobbsey Twins a boy and a girl?"

Isaiah sighs. "Forget I said that. My point is, I think they might be onto something."

I'm not sure if I'm still waking up or if he's just trying to inject some drama into the conversation, but either way, I'm out of patience.

"If we're going to do this," I say, "you should know that I really hate it when people talk like they're going to commercial. Please get to the point."

He rubs his neck. "I'm just trying to say that I'm willing to consider the possibility that Liza's death does, in fact, have something to do with Caitlyn's murder."

"Why didn't you just say that from the start?" I ask, swinging my backpack awkwardly up onto my shoulders. "Why'd you have to do that whole Bobbsey Twins bit—it didn't even make sense."

He looks down at my backpack. "Do you really need to bring that?"

"Be prepared—isn't that your motto?"

"That's the Boy Scouts."

"Are you really going to pretend you weren't a Boy Scout?"

"Just stay close. If anyone asks, you're going to the doctor for a follow-up."

"Wait, what—"

He ushers me out into the hallway, where I come face-to-solar-plexus with a huge stone slab of a man. He's nearly twice my height and three times my weight. When he crosses his arms, his pectorals strain at the fabric of his button-down shirt.

I blink up at him. "I'm going to the doctor for a follow-up."

Isaiah hooks two fingers around my elbow and draws me down the hallway, toward the stairs. "Relax, he's one of mine. You can tell by the general air of competence."

We're heading for the movie theater. We agreed last night that our first order of business today should be a walk-through of the attack. Isaiah hopes it might jog my memory. I'm not so optimistic—but I want to make sure the police turned off the projector correctly.

At the bottom of the stairs, Isaiah pulls me behind him. "Hold on." He cracks open the lobby door and glances out. He closes the door gently and presses a finger to the earpiece I hadn't noticed until just this second.

"Hey, Jonesy, wanna keep those guys busy for a second?"

He waits for acknowledgment, then beckons me forward. "Come on. Quietly."

The lobby is so deserted it feels as if it's been empty for years. The bar and restaurant are dark; every curtain is closed. None of the lamps are lit. The only sign of recent life is a vacuum cleaner that has been abandoned by one of the seating areas. It's still plugged into the wall.

I wonder, fleetingly, what happened to the cat.

Isaiah leads me through the lobby, keeping close to the wall. Standing at the other end of the room, just next to the entrance, are two uniformed cops. They're laughing with a sandy-haired man the size of a pickup truck.

"Another one of yours?" I whisper.

Isaiah's hand squeezes mine.

We make it to the end of the hall and round the corner. As soon as we're out of sight, Isaiah tugs on my hand, pulling me alongside him.

"How many employees do you have?" I ask.

"Those two and three more. I have a second team just outside Baltimore, but the cops aren't letting anyone on or off the island right now, no exceptions. Early this morning they turned away a fishing boat with two photographers stowed away on board." He pauses. "Unfortunately, they came back with helicopters."

I wince. "So the news is out?"

"The news is out."

I stop short, overcorrect, and stumble forward.

Isaiah grabs my shoulder to steady me. "You okay?"

"I just realized I should call my friend."

"It can't wait?"

"If she doesn't hear from me and has reason to believe something bad has happened, there's probably no one alive who'll be able to keep her off this island. Not even you."

He glances back toward the lobby. "Okay, but make it fast."

I reach for my back pocket—

"Actually, can I use your phone?"

He raises an eyebrow.

"If I call from my phone," I explain, "she's more likely to pick it up because she knows the number."

"You're calling your friend—your friend who would apparently fight through police and special forces to get to you if she thought you were in danger—and you're hoping it goes to voice mail?"

I nod. "Yes, exactly."

He gives me an exceptionally unimpressed look. "Use your own phone, Marissa."

"Fine." I flip open the production phone and cringe when I see the display. Twenty missed calls.

I dial her number—and brace myself.

"Amy?"

I'm greeted with a slurry of words and noises too complicated for me to even begin to parse, so I just keep repeating *I'm okay* until she quiets down.

"It's true, then?" she asks.

"That depends," I say, carefully.

"At first everyone was saying it was an overdose, but I just read that she was *murdered*? And that now there's some *manhunt*?"

I cover the phone with my hand and look at Isaiah. "The police haven't put out a statement yet?"

He shakes his head.

"Where are you getting all this?" I ask Amy.

"Twitter."

"I thought you deleted your account."

"I signed back up, okay?" She makes a strangled noise of frustration. "I called eight thousand times, and you didn't pick up. I didn't have any other options. There's so little credible information coming out, it's like . . . pre–internet era. Even Josh's sources have dried up, and you know he's like the gaffer-whisperer. Whoever's handling crisis PR at the studio deserves a raise."

"I bet I know who's in charge of it. She's terrifying—you'd love her." Isaiah taps my shoulder and makes a wrap-it-up gesture. "Amy, look, I have to go, but—but I'll call tonight, okay?"

"You're safe, right?"

"Of course I'm safe."

"You answered that way too quickly."

"I'm *saaaaaaaaafe.*"

The laugh this gets is tiny—very tiny—but I'll take it.

I unlock the door to the theater and duck under the police tape. I look back at Isaiah. "Stay close. Be careful on the stairs. And for God's sake, watch your head."

One side of his mouth kicks up. "The tables have turned."

"Yes, well—you're in my world now. We're smaller here. I hope you brought a flashlight."

Isaiah promptly produces one and clicks it on.

"There's no way you weren't a Boy Scout."

He shrugs. "Guess you'll never know."

The projector room is more or less in the same shape I left it in last night. Someone dragged a ghost light up from the theater and kicked the majority of the broken glass into one corner, but that's the only difference. They didn't even bother wiping down the Auto-wind: I can see the dark, bloody smear on the edge of the lowest platter. When I crouch down to examine it, I find a few crusty bits that can only be my own dried flesh.

Should I be bothered by that? I think maybe I should. A normal person would be.

A regular person, I mean.

A *typical* person.

But despite it all, I still feel at home here, calm and warm, surrounded by projection equipment and acoustic tiling, by the sharp, sweet smell of industrial carpet cleaner and, beneath that, the whiff of vinegar that tells me the film that's loaded is starting to deteriorate.

I pick my way across the floor, glancing briefly at the photos still tacked to the wall.

Liza, Liza, everywhere.

My eyes linger on that first shot, on the picture of a dead girl who was, for me, a game, a triviality, a neat little puzzle to figure out. I cringe at the memory now. How did I put it again?

That just stands to reason. Why else would you make a movie about it?

"What is it?" Isaiah asks.

I nod at the photo. "Liza's body was posed in an identical fashion."

He ducks under the doorframe and crosses the room in two giant strides. "You're saying her body was arranged to match the movie?"

"Well, either that, or she was arranged to match Caitlyn. There's no way to tell the difference. Tony probably based this shot off the crime scene photos."

Isaiah swings his head around to look at me. "For real?"

"Well, yeah, why wouldn't he?"

He lets out a long breath, then reaches over my head and plucks the still off the wall. He unzips my backpack and slides it inside.

"Hold on to that for me, would you?"

"Shouldn't we be worried we're contaminating the crime scene?"

"I'm sure the police did that well enough on their own." He steps back and surveys the room. "Now, the attacker was in that corner when you came in, right? About where you're standing?"

"The lights were out, so I can't be sure. But he came at me from this direction."

"Did he attack you as soon as you walked in?"

"Not really—not until I opened my phone."

He crouches down next to the Autowind and peers at the bloodstain. "So he pushed you, you fell—you made contact here. And you rolled to the side."

"Then I crawled over there," I say, pointing to the wall behind the projector.

He makes a noise in the back of his throat. "Next time maybe crawl somewhere with an escape route. Better yet, run."

I put my good hand on my hip. "Look, everything was moving very fast, okay?"

"So while you"—he makes air quotes—"'hid' here—"

"Seriously?"

"—your attacker presumably carried the computer down the stairs, and—"

"Dragged."

His chin comes up. "What?"

"They didn't carry it. They dragged it."

"You're sure?"

"Sure I'm sure. I could hear it. Those stairs are *loud*."

Isaiah strides out of the room, sliding the flashlight out of his back pocket and shining it across the ceiling, the walls, the length of the hallway. My eyes catch on the slow swirl of the dust motes caught in the light. *Brownian motion*, my mind supplies, dimly recalling one of my father's dinnertime lectures. Movement that only makes sense once you account for objects invisible to the naked eye.

Isaiah's asking me something.

"What was that?"

"Can you turn on the lights out here?" he repeats.

I shake my head before remembering he can't see it. "No, the light's broken. It goes out if you look at it sideways. This place probably predates modern building codes."

He glances over the edge of the walkway. "The way these stairs are built, I'd say it predates modern engineering."

He runs the flashlight back and forth across the top tread of the stairs and begins his descent. He moves slowly, methodically, checking each step in front of him before he moves on. But when I go to place my own foot on the stairs, he holds up a hand.

"I don't want to put any more weight on this thing. Pretty sure I already half broke it on my way up."

Two-thirds of the way down, he stops short—and the entire staircase starts, as if taken by surprise. He bends down to pick something up. "Looks like you're right," he says, holding it up. "A piece of the computer casing. Must've broken off."

"Of course I'm right, I told you—I heard it."

"Yeah, well, shock and blood loss don't make for the most reliable witnesses."

"I didn't lose *that* much blood."

He gestures vaguely at the stairs in front of him. "Splatter says otherwise."

My eyebrows knit together. I distinctly remember thinking the gash wasn't that serious, but I guess that's another symptom of shock. I lean forward as far as I dare. Sure enough, if I squint I can make out a few dark spots in the beam from Isaiah's flashlight. It's hard to tell against the steel tread, though.

"Are you sure that's not rust?"

"Could be," he allows. "It's fresh blood I'm familiar with. How heavy would you say that CPU tower was?"

"I don't know, pretty big. Forty pounds, maybe? Why?"

He hums in response, then turns and moves purposefully down the hallway. I clamber down the stairs after him.

"Why does it matter what the computer weighs?" I ask again.

He doesn't answer. He just stares at the lobby door and taps his toe.

"You were bleeding, badly," he says after a moment. "But those doors were locked when the cops came to investigate. Did you really take the time to lock the door behind you when you left?"

"No, I didn't think it was safe to go that way. I went out back, down the fire escape."

His eyes meet mine. "Show me."

To my great dismay, Isaiah isn't interested in examining the fire escape—the wind and water would have long since done away with any evidence, he says.

Nor is he particularly concerned about the boardwalk or the beach.

He does, however, want to see the cave.

I would have preferred to spend another twenty to twenty thousand minutes talking about the sea slime, but apparently my opinion on this particular subject holds little weight.

Admittedly, in the daylight, with Isaiah at my side, the cave isn't as intimidating. The water's higher than it was last night, but at least this time I can see it.

I still want to hurl, though.

"Where did you say you were from again?" Isaiah asks.

"Illinois." I pause. Then—"You?"

He slants me a faintly amused look. "I wasn't making conversation."

"I thought maybe you were trying to distract me."

"No, I was just trying to figure a few things out."

"Did you?"

"Yeah. That talking makes you *more* nervous."

My arms try to wrap themselves around my stomach, but I will them down to my sides.

"I'm going to go in, take a look around," he says. "Do you think you're up to it? Or would you rather wait here?"

My first inclination is to fashion a blithe expression—like this is the easiest thing in the world, like I'm just going to bed or to a movie or home to my mom. But then I change my mind.

"I'm really scared of caves," I say. "I almost drowned in one when I was a kid."

He nods. "Figured it was something like that. I've almost drowned a couple times myself. It's not great."

"No," I agree.

He extends a hand. "How about we not do it again?"

Is it just my imagination or is he looking the other way on purpose, like maybe he's giving me the chance to pretend he's just gesturing me forward? But his palm is up, and his fingers are curved in. There's something almost courtly about it, an ermine-trimmed cloak being tossed across an Elizabethan puddle, and I can't decide if I'm supposed to be annoyed at the presumption or grateful for the assistance.

Or maybe there's some third option I have yet to consider.

When my fingers brush against his, something hot and sharp rouses beneath my right shoulder blade. Something new. It's not necessarily unpleasant.

His hand curls around mine, and he leads us into the cave.

In the light, I recognize the passageway immediately.

"It was here," I say. "Last night, I stopped here—I thought I heard something."

"You didn't think to mention that?"

"I figured I was imagining things."

"Or maybe your attacker came this way, too." Isaiah shines the flashlight through the narrow opening. "Do you know what's back there?"

My mouth opens to tell him about my meeting with Gavin and Billy, but for some reason, I hesitate. "It's a grotto," I say instead, sticking to the bare minimum. "You can get a boat in that way— which means you could get a boat out."

He splays his hand out across the opening. "I'm not sure I'll fit."

"I'm sure you've been in tighter spaces."

"Only figuratively." The set of his jaw and his brow and his shoulders is all business, but his lips still press into something very nearly smile-adjacent. Like he can't quite help himself.

And I guess I can't quite help myself either, because the suggestion just bubbles up out of me. "I could go first?"

He looks over at me in surprise. "Really?"

"Sure," I say, turning my head so he can't see the way I'm screaming behind my eyes. I tuck my backpack into a secluded niche, grab the flashlight, and ease my way into the crevice. I did it before. I can do it again.

This time, through, I'm even more keenly aware of the physical dimensions of the space. There's plenty of room for *my* hips and shoulders, but if I were a foot taller—which Isaiah easily is—this would be a tight fit. Maybe if he turns to the side, though, and sort of scoots to the left—

I turn to say as much to Isaiah.

The ground disappears beneath me, and I pitch backward into the water.

I come up sputtering, confused, dimly aware that Isaiah is calling my name.

"Marissa? What's happening?"

I sweep the water out of my eyes and suck in a breath. "I'm—"

My mouth dips back below the surface. *Dammit*, I'm out of practice. I've forgotten how to tread water, and the cavern leads straight out to the ocean, so this water is *moving*.

(*Not rising*, I tell myself sternly. *Moving*.)

I kick my legs hard and sweep my arms out to my sides. There's nothing graceful about my movements, but I manage to stabilize myself just enough to take another deep breath before I sink back under.

The water's warm and gritty, like the liquid left in the bucket after you mop. I clench my jaw and arrow my arms out in front of me, trying to ignore the pain in my left arm, to pretend that salt water isn't seeping between my stitches, under my skin. I reach for the cave wall, desperate for something, anything, to hold on to, but my fingers find only sleek, smooth stone. The strain in my lungs and my diaphragm and my cheeks is becoming unbearable.

I'm not going to be able to hold my breath much longer.

I arch my back and stretch my neck and flail my legs and—*there*—I steal another sip of air, another burst of energy, and I cast wild eyes around the cavern. I see it just in time: the rock shelf. It's just five feet to my right.

I go under again, twisting myself into what I hope is the right direction—

Brad Pitt, in an awful jacket and an even worse shirt: "I want you to hit me as hard as you can."

—and I appreciate what my brain is trying to tell me, I really do, but I swear to God, if *Fight Club*'s the last movie I think of before I die. . . .

Still: I kick and I pull *as hard as I can*.

My forehead slams into the shelf. A second later, the water tries to pull me back.

I fling my good arm toward the rock, curling my fingers into claws to gain purchase. I catch the edge, but one hand's not going to be enough. The water's too strong.

My thumb slips off.

I clamp my lips shut against the pain and heave my bad arm up out of the water, slamming it into the rock. I give it everything I have—

The water rolls back toward me, and I have the presence of mind, just barely, to use the momentum to pull myself out of the water, up onto the shelf. I tumble onto my side and let my mouth fall open even though I'm not sure why I'm bothering. The oxygen doesn't seem to be doing much for my brain.

"Marissa!"

I lift my head, weakly. Isaiah's standing at the entrance to the passageway.

"You fit," I rasp.

"You weren't answering," he says, as if that explains how he managed to shrink his entire body down to half its size.

A noise shudders out of me, a noise I think is trying to be laughter, and it's followed by a splash that for a single, dazed second, I assume is the sound of my own body falling back into the water. But no, it's just Isaiah. He boosts himself up onto the shelf and peers down at me.

"Are you okay?"

I flop over onto my back and cover my face with my hands. "You ask so many questions, Isaiah."

Eventually, I manage to sit up. I scoot myself back until I'm up against the wall, as far from the water as it's possible to get. I breathe in, deeply. My shoulders start to settle.

Then Isaiah lunges toward the water, and my hand shoots out to save him, to pull him back, to stop him from going in, even though this man could probably swim the English Channel and back—he could probably swim the *Pacific Ocean* and back.

My face heats when I realize he isn't going anywhere. He's just fishing something out of the water. I sit up to see what it is.

Oh. Of course his flashlight floats.

He wrings a good two cups of water out of his Henley before wandering over to the far edge of the shelf. He turns on the flashlight and aims it at the mooring pole. "What is this place?"

"I'm not entirely sure," I say. "I think local kids like to come here. Make mischief. That sort of thing."

He begins to search the cavern, sweeping the beam of the flashlight back and forth across the rocks. When it hits the far corner, my eye catches on something new.

"Stop," I say.

I lean forward on my hands and knees to get a better look. There, caught in the cool light of the LED, is a spiral of iridescent green paint.

CAITLYN KELLY DIED HERE.

"Well, would you look at that," Isaiah says.

I glance back over my shoulder. "Is that true? Is this where she was killed?"

"No idea. Like I said, that's not the job I was hired for."

"Kind of a weird place to kill someone, don't you think?"

He shines the flashlight at the entrance to the grotto. "Well, you can get here by boat, so that's a plus. And it's private, dark enough that you could catch someone off guard. The acoustics aren't ideal, but with all the ocean noise, you probably wouldn't be able to hear anything out on the beach, no matter how loud the echo. How did she die, again?"

"Blunt force trauma."

"That could mean anything."

"We should probably talk to Grace and Suzy. I think they have the coroner's report."

"Of course they do."

I wrap my arms around my legs and prop my chin on my knees. "But why would you go to all the trouble to lure a girl to a secluded location, only to then go to all the trouble to drag her dead body out to an incredibly *unsecluded* location? Could you even get a corpse out through that narrow passageway? Wouldn't there have been abrasions? Debris? Something?"

Isaiah considers this. "You could take it out by boat?"

"In that case, why not dump it in the ocean?"

"Maybe the killer wanted her to be found."

"Why would you *want* a body to be found? For attention?"

"If you want attention so badly you'd kill for it, would you stop at one girl?"

"It's not a serial killer, cause of death doesn't fit. I mean, Jack the *Ripper*. The Boston *Strangler*. Hannibal the *Cannibal*."

"'Blunt Force Trauma Frank' doesn't have quite the same ring to it."

"Maybe he was just trying to send a message?" I suggest. "Maybe Caitlyn was caught up in something—drugs or prostitution. Or maybe her father—"

"We should get out of here," he says, abruptly. "You look like Baby Jessica after they pulled her out of the well." He swings his legs around and slips into the water with more grace than I would have expected. Like Esther Williams in a water ballet—if Esther Williams could deadlift a Camry.

"Something funny?"

"I'm just picturing you in a swimsuit."

His eyebrows jump up.

"No, not like that," I rush to explain. "A *woman's* suit."

"Oh, well, in *that* case."

I cover my face. "Also not what I meant."

"*Marissa.*"

I peek through my fingers. He's holding out his hand—again.

It's getting a little too easy to take it.

He cups his other hand under my elbow and guides me toward the passageway as I do my best doggy paddle.

"Almost there," he says.

"I'm not going to freak out," I say, surprised to discover I mean it.

We reach the entrance to the passageway, and I rest my forearm on the ledge, ready to push myself up and put this whole thing behind me, when—

What—the hell—is that?

—my toe grazes something I'm absolutely certain is not supposed to be there.

I snatch my foot back, nearly kneeing Isaiah in the stomach, but he catches my leg just in time.

"There's something under there," I manage.

Before I have a chance to object, Isaiah's hands wrap around my ribs. He tosses me up onto the ledge like I'm a sack of produce and disappears back under the water. I land awkwardly, on my hip, and I'm still smarting when his head and shoulders reemerge, his arms weighed down by some object he's apparently decided to drag up to the surface. I catch my breath.

Isaiah's neck tenses, and I can tell he's about to pull whatever it is out of the water—

My vision goes white around the edges.

Please don't let it be another body.

A metallic clang echoes through the cavern. I look down.

It's the stolen computer.

I blink the water out of my eyes. "Huh. So last night when I thought I heard someone—"

He tugs me to my feet before I can finish the thought. "Take me to whoever told you about this place."

TWENTY-FIVE

O h, it's you." Gavin leans his elbow against the doorframe, a greasy hank of hair falling over one eye.

"Were you expecting someone else?" I ask.

"There's a cat—I don't know if you've met her—but I made the mistake of feeding her one night, and she's been coming to my door ever since." He blinks; a frown puckers at his chin. "I thought we weren't allowed to leave our rooms. Does this mean they've found him?"

Next to me, Isaiah shakes his head. "No, not yet."

"Christ, what a fiasco." Gavin turns and walks into his room, leaving the door open. "Well, come on in before someone catches you."

We follow him into a room that looks exactly like mine except it's three times larger and has six times as many throw pillows. Gavin waves us over to the small seating area in front of the French doors and crosses the room to the minibar.

I sit down and squeeze the last of the water out of my ponytail. We stashed the computer in Isaiah's room and changed before coming here, but I was so focused on rebandaging my arm and knees, I forgot about the more socially relevant parts of my appearance. It didn't occur to me to do something with my hair.

Now the back of my shirt is soaked through and—I cast my gaze to the ceiling—yes, of *course*, I'm sitting directly under an air-conditioning vent.

Gavin returns a moment later, a martini glass in each hand.

"I don't drink," I say.

"*Please*. They're for me."

He sets the first glass down carelessly, half the cocktail sloshing across the table. He lifts the second glass to his lips. He swallows, shudders—coughs.

"Gilbey's," he explains when his eyes have stopped watering. "I tried to bribe the policemen to bring me a bottle of Tanqueray, but *apparently* they have more important things to be doing." He takes another sip—a much smaller one. "I never would have expected you to be out and about. Maybe I should have tried bribing you instead."

"Yes, well—"

He smiles, showing teeth. "Why are you here?"

"I would also like to know the answer to that question," Isaiah says, his voice a low rumble.

How do I explain this in a way that doesn't implicate Billy? Gavin and I might be willing to give Billy the benefit of the doubt, but Isaiah has no reason to do so. I have to make sure he has the right context. Otherwise he'll hear that Billy knew about the cave and immediately conclude that he was killer.

I wipe my hands on my jeans and turn to Gavin. "I was hoping you could talk to Isaiah a little bit about how you've been preparing for your role."

Gavin sets the cocktail aside. He leans back in his chair, clasping his hands over his stomach. He draws a deep breath. "Well, it all started when I studied at the Actor's Studio—"

"No," I say, sharply. "I mean tell him about your time with Billy Lyle. What you know about him. What he's *like*."

He cuts his eyes to Isaiah. "Over the past two months, I've spent a great deal of time with Billy Lyle. We'd meet every few days so I could work on my characterization—physicality, mannerisms, that type of thing. Just sitting with him, mostly—he doesn't talk much, I don't know if you were with him long enough to notice that. And while he may not be the most stimulating company—I can't say he'll be making the guest list for one of my dinner parties any time soon—he never once gave me the impression he was remotely capable of malice. Granted, I may not have studied forensics or medicine or psychology, but I like to think I know a thing or two about human behavior—and I don't believe Billy Lyle is capable of killing anyone."

Isaiah's frowning. "But what does this have to do with—"

I hold up my hand, keeping my gaze on Gavin. "Then why'd you take the part?"

His hesitation is so brief—infinitesimal, really. If I hadn't seen it a thousand times before, I would think it was just the natural rhythm of his speech.

"What do you mean?" he asks.

"Three of your last five parts have been murderers."

"Yes—and?"

"The other two were rapists."

"What's your *point*, Marissa?"

"That you even took the part is probably enough to convince people he's guilty."

Gavin casts his eyes up to the ceiling. "Can't I play anything but the baddie? I'm sick of it. Christ, even Christopher Lee got to play the hero a time or two."

"So why didn't you pass?"

"I was going to. When I read the script, it seemed so *cliché*— 'disturbed young man stalks beautiful young girl.' But then they told me Tony was going to be directing it, and I thought, well, if it's worth *Tony's* time, then perhaps there's something to it."

I try to maintain a neutral expression, but I'm not quite fast enough: Gavin catches it.

"You thought the same thing, too," he guesses.

I nod. "I signed on without even seeing a script."

Isaiah looks between the two of us but doesn't say anything.

"Things changed when I met Billy," Gavin says, leaning forward, resting his forearms on his knees. "I just thought—I don't know, that I could save him. God, that sounds arrogant now, doesn't it? But I honestly believed that even if he wouldn't tell me what happened that night, even if I couldn't outright prove his innocence, maybe I could still perform him in such a way that I could change some people's minds. Make his life a little easier." He looks down at his hands. "You know his boat is still vandalized at least twice a year? Last winter someone stuffed a half dozen dead rats inside his ceiling. He didn't know they were there until maggots started pouring out of the light fixtures."

"That's all very noble," Isaiah allows. "But do you have any actual evidence of his innocence?"

Gavin sighs and reaches for his glass. "Well, that's the problem, isn't it? There's just not much evidence on *either* side. It's intuition vs. intuition, which means Billy's at a disadvantage, because when people look at him, they just think he's—"

"Wrong?" I say.

"No—not quite. If that were the case, they'd want to keep him around just so they could feel smug about it. That's not it."

I blink. "Then why don't they like him?"

"Because he doesn't hide what's hard for him, and they take that personally. He makes *them* feel wrong. The tragedy is that he's desperate for a connection. Billy is both incredibly lonely and incredibly solitary, and everything that's gone poorly with his life is probably the result of a failed attempt to reconcile those two things." He peers into his glass. "God, what I'd do for a smoke."

I fall back against the chair, stricken.

"Last night you said you saw Billy just before the murder," Isaiah says.

"That's right. Normally we don't meet twice in one day, but I'd contacted him earlier because I wanted to tell him I was quitting. I had to do it in person—I couldn't have him thinking I was abandoning the cause. Or him."

"And where was this again?" Isaiah asks.

"The usual place—"

I try to sit up—I try to say something. I try to stop him.

Context. He needs context.

But my body's forgotten how to move.

"There's a cave just down by the beach," Gavin goes on, blithely. "It's the only place we could both manage to get to without anyone seeing."

Isaiah shoots a glance in my direction. "Did anyone else know about that cave?"

"Oh, sure, it's no secret," he says. "Marissa was there with us just yesterday."

"Please don't get mad. I wasn't going to keep this from you. That's why I brought you to Gavin! To tell you about the cave!"

Isaiah glances back at me only briefly as he strides down the hallway. "Not here, Marissa."

"But your face is doing that thing," I say, already out of breath—how are Isaiah's legs so damn long? "I just want a chance to explain."

He stops; I promptly collide with his back. At the other end of the hall, two police officers are shining flashlights through the window of the hotel's twenty-four-hour gym. Isaiah grabs my elbow and steers me through the door immediately to our right, pushing me in ahead of him.

On the other side is the wine cellar—but it's not a very good one. All the bottles are arranged in carefully color-coordinated tableaux atop elegantly aged oak barrels. There's no sense of organization or any sign of labeling system. You couldn't find anything in here.

"Isaiah—"

He holds up a finger and proceeds to conduct a swift search of the room, ducking down behind each set of bottles, checking for—I don't know. Police. Murderers. Cats.

When he's finished, he turns and looks at me, fifty feet of rustic wood flooring separating us. "Why didn't you tell me about Billy?"

"I did," I say. "You know everything I know."

"You're protecting him. That's information I could have used."

"If I'm protecting him, it's only because I think that maybe everyone's a little too quick to judge him. I mean, you say a name in low spooky tones often enough and eventually people are going to start thinking that person must *be* spooky. But Isaiah—it doesn't make any sense. Honestly, there's only one person I can think of who's *less* likely to have killed Liza."

"And who's that?"

"Tony. He would never kill his lead actress, it would jeopardize the project." I pause. "Although, he could always turn it into a documentary. That might actually make more money than a feature, especially now that someone else has died."

Isaiah squints at my face, and whatever he sees makes him laugh in a way I haven't heard before, a sound that's more like spitting up than spilling over.

It's awful. And for the first time it occurs to me to wonder how we look to him, to someone who has shouldered the weight of life and death. How silly we must seem—the wigs, the gossip, the special effects. We're all playing make-believe while he's busy in the real world, out there making a difference, risking his life and his team because he believes in truth and justice and kicking ass, and there's a counterargument here, I know there is. I know that what we do matters, too—*somehow*. But all I can think right now is that I once spent three months cutting a live-action feature about an ostrich who moves to New York City because she dreams of making it as a Rockette.

It's very possible that we're all terrible people.

I pick up the first wine bottle I see and pretend to examine it. Something safe for my hands to do. For my face to do.

"That came out wrong," I say. Meaning, I suppose, that it came out easy.

"*Marissa.*"

My shoulders tense. I hate when people say my name like that.

I turn my face to the side, peering at Isaiah through the half gloom. It's not that I want to look at him. I just know this is a thing people do when they need to make clear they're saying something they really mean: You reorient your body toward the listener, you flatten your lips into a solemn line, you take a beat.

"I'm just trying to think about this logically," I say.

"But you're *not*. You're trying to think about this *creatively*." He runs his hand over the back of his neck. "Marissa, I'm sorry, you're kind and interesting and fun to talk to, but you are just *the worst* at this. You may be great at coming up with wild ideas, at shoehorning plot points into the most entertaining narrative possible, but real life—it's just not that much fun."

"I think you're overstating things *slightly*."

"I bet you could come up with a perfectly plausible argument— right now—in favor of any one of us being the killer."

I draw back, stung. "That's ridiculous."

"Oh yeah?" He settles his shoulder against one of the rough-hewn wooden posts that line the length of the room. "So there's no way that—say—Grace and Suzy could've done it."

I don't know what my face does in that moment, but I know it does something. Maybe I flinch, maybe I wince, maybe my eyes go a little dreamy, just for a second, as I consider the possibilities. Whatever it is, I can tell from Isaiah's vaguely pitying expression that I've given myself away.

My shoulders slump. "Well, of course they *could* have done it. They think Billy Lyle's innocent. Killing Liza could have been their way to get someone to take them seriously, to look into it for real. Alternatively, maybe they arranged for this to happen because they expected that Billy would have an alibi, which they hoped would absolve him of *both* murders."

"There are easier ways to go about making a point," Isaiah says.

"They're children."

"You can't have it both ways. Either they're clever, or they're not."

I smile, just a little. "Amy always says, 'Shit creek's littered with the bodies of people who think they're smarter than the rest of us.'"

His gaze meets mine. "You don't say."

My hands have twisted themselves so tightly in the fabric of my shirt that the tips of my fingers are starting to go numb, but I need more than that, so I give in to the urge to pace the length of the room, setting my feet carefully to avoid the grout lines between the meticulously laid stone tiles, picking out a pattern as I go—*circle-circle-square, circle-circle-square.*

"What are you doing?" Isaiah asks.

I keep my eyes on the tiles. "In the business, we call this the dark moment."

Circle-circle-square, circle-circle-square.

Everything he just said was true. I've trained myself to look for the best story, the most interesting story, the most compelling story—it's what I do, every day. With my work. With my life. Of course I'd look at a photo or a phone or a pile of Post-its and see something sinister and shocking, something only I, with my hard-earned perspective and expertise, could recognize. Because that's *actually* my favorite story, isn't it? That I'm special, that I see things no one else can, that I have something valuable to offer the world.

Circle-circle-square, circle-circle-square.

But the truth is, the only useful thing I've done since coming to this island was falling in the fucking ocean.

My legs go still, but my hands keep moving. Opening, closing, opening, closing.

Two young women are dead, killed in what appears to be the same way. Whoever killed Liza was probably obsessed with Caitlyn. Whoever killed Caitlyn was definitely obsessed with Caitlyn. By all accounts, there's one man who fits that particular bill.

And if I weren't so insistent on finding myself in this story, I would have seen that from the start.

My hands fall to my sides. "Okay," I say. "So, *logically*—"

Isaiah makes a noise of encouragement.

"Logically," I continue, "all things being equal, the simplest explanation tends to be the right one."

"Are you quoting a movie or reciting Occam's razor?"

I sneak a look at him from under my lashes. "I'm quoting a movie about Occam's razor?"

He sighs. "Go on."

"So the simplest explanation—" I break off, clear my throat. Then I draw a shaky breath and begin again. "The simplest explanation—"

"Just *say* it, Marissa."

I curl my fingers into fists and push the words out through the tightness in my throat. "The simplest explanation is that Billy Lyle killed them both."

TWENTY-SIX

Nick paces the length of the conference room, his arms swinging wildly each time he changes direction. It's hard to believe that just last night, I thought him sharply dressed. He has to be on his third shirt of the day. He's sweating through the arms of his cream-colored button-down in front of our very eyes.

Gavin, Isaiah, and I are seated along one side of the table, waiting while a trim man in a blue-checked sweater flips open ink pads and lays out stacks of fingerprint cards.

"Is this really necessary?" Gavin asks, eyeing the supplies.

"What," Nick says, "you've never guest-starred on *CSI*?"

Gavin arches an eyebrow. "Just how old do you think I am?"

Nick sighs. "It *shouldn't* be necessary, but since you've been mucking about in my crime scenes, I need elimination prints. At this rate, I'm going to have to fingerprint the whole goddamn hotel, because apparently none of you assholes knows how to listen to directions. An hour ago I caught two *teenagers* trying to go through one of our computers—can you believe that? And apparently no one gives a damn about telling me anything, either." He takes a ragged breath and ticks the items off on his fingers. "Your producer has lied to me twice, your cinematographer has lied to me once, your script supervisor keeps waving around her NDA, and your line producer—whatever the hell that is—is pretending she doesn't speak English. And now *you* tell me that not only was Billy Lyle on set the day of both an assault and a serious accident, but also that the stolen computer was found in the cave where Billy Lyle's boat was docked just last night?"

Nick's gaze settles on Isaiah. "Guys like *you*—guys like you, I get—"

"Tread *very* carefully," Isaiah murmurs.

"—I get that you're fucking James Bond or whatever, and that I'm just some dipshit local cop. And you know what? If we were in Iraq or Afghanistan right now, I wouldn't give me the time of day, either. Because I'm not a soldier. But I *am* a detective, and you have got to let me do my job. I'm trying to catch a murderer here—and I'm trying to do it the *right* way, the way it wasn't done twenty-five years ago. Which is hard enough with fucking TMZ up my *asshole*, but this rogue secret agent shit is not helping."

Nick turns on me. "And as for *you*—"

I slink down in my chair.

"—have I heard some *stories*, let me tell you."

I blink. "What? I've only been here for two days. I hardly know anyone."

He pulls out his notebook and flips past the first few pages.

"'Marissa Dahl,'" he reads, "'is a pain in the ass.'"

My eyes go wide. "Who said that?"

"'No boundaries. Know-it-all. Will ask questions until you want to die.'"

"That's clearly hyperbole—"

"'Never shuts up.'"

A suspicion crystallizes in my mind. "You've been talking to the electricians, haven't you?"

"'Constitutionally incapable of minding her own business.'"

He snaps the notebook shut and stuffs it into his pocket. "Look, I don't want any more trouble from any of you, okay? We have our suspect in custody—"

I jolt upright. "You found Billy?"

"—and if all goes well, this will be wrapped up and you'll be back in Los Angeles in a matter of *days*. Then you can go back to doing whatever the fuck it is you do while I very happily never watch another movie ever again. How does that sound?"

We nod, wordlessly.

"Now: Is there any other crucial information any of you might like to share with the one person on this island who is in possession of an advanced degree in criminology? You know—for kicks?"

The room is silent.

"Finally," he says, "an answer that doesn't piss me off."

The moment I'm back in my room, my phone is out and in my hand.

It's lunchtime in Los Angeles, but the son of a bitch picks up anyway.

"This is Josh."

"You *actual* piece of shit."

"Marissa?"

"You've been going around telling people on this movie that I'm a pain in the ass? That I'm a know-it-all? What is *wrong* with you?"

"Hold on, let's be calm about this—"

"Fuck you, Josh, I can lose *jobs* over stuff like that. I can't have that kind of reputation—I can't have *any* kind of reputation. Except as someone who quietly gets her shit done on time and under budget, which I do. Always."

"Oh, don't be ridiculous. Nothing I said was that bad."

"That doesn't make it okay! I'm not hot, Josh. I'm not charming.

I'm not *cool*. I don't get leeway—I don't get a pass. *Not that bad is still bad.*"

"Jesus, do you always have to be so fucking dramatic?"

"When it comes to my career—yeah. It's one of the reasons *I* actually have one."

He laughs in a way that's depressingly familiar. "You and I both know your career isn't what you're upset about."

My mouth opens, but nothing comes out.

"Look, Marissa, I know this sort of thing is hard for you. I know you have trouble seeing the romantic connections between people. Real people, anyway. Someone could fuck right under your nose and you still wouldn't pick up on it—I mean, you probably thought Tony and Liza May were *just good friends*, right? So please, take some advice. Don't make the first move. Let them come to you. Otherwise, you're just going to keep embarrassing yourself with people who obviously aren't—"

I hang up and toss the phone on the nightstand.

Then I topple forward onto the bed, press my face into the pillow, and scream.

I've never in my life spoken to someone like that. I expected to feel triumphant. Fierce. Powerful. But I don't. I just feel small and helpless and shitty, and I know, deep down, that I've probably just made things much worse.

My best friend is probably going to *marry* this man.

It hits me a second later.

Did he just suggest that Tony *was sleeping with Liza?*

That can't be possible, can it? How would Josh know something like that? He isn't nearly as connected as he thinks he is—is he? No, he's probably just messing with me. Setting me up for failure. Trying to sabotage my career—again.

Or maybe—

Maybe he just gave me information that changes everything.

I crawl across the bed and fish my script out of my backpack. I rifle through the pages until I find it: the Post-it Paul left behind.

It's time to find out once and for all if my best friend's awful boyfriend is full of shit.

"I don't know how you got this number, but I suggest you forget it."

The smoky, faintly accented voice is unmistakable. It's Annemieke. Guess that 1 in 17.3 million longshot paid off.

"Please don't hang up," I say.

"Who is this?"

I take a deep breath and adjust the pillow behind my back.

Don't screw this up.

"My name's Marissa Dahl," I say. "I'm the editor on Tony's new movie. I got your number from Paul Collins?"

There's a pause—a pause just long enough, just loaded enough that I want to put my fist through a wall. *Actors.*

"Yes," she says, finally. "I know Paul. What did you say your name was again?"

"Marissa Dahl. Dahl as in Roald, not as in—"

"Dear God, you're the girl from Venice."

"No, actually, I'm on the east side. Well, I'm between apartments at the moment. But I *was* in Echo Park."

A hesitation that can only be called delicate. "Italy," she says. "Venice, Italy."

"Ah."

"You fell into the fountain and pulled Tony down with you."

I wince. "Yes, well—"

"Oh, no, don't apologize. It was, truly, one of the highlights of the festival."

"You know he's never brought it up once?"

She laughs, a sound so bright and musical I almost forget what we're talking about. "Don't worry, I'm sure he's just saving it for the most painful possible moment."

"If he's so awful, why'd you marry him?"

I belatedly register the deep inappropriateness of the question. With a regular person I would promptly walk it back and probably never speak to them again. But I know I don't need to worry about that with Annemieke. She's been answering inappropriate questions her entire professional life.

"I married him because he's very good at what he does," she says. "And I was very tired of men who aren't."

I straighten the edge of the duvet and trace the stitching along the border. "So what changed?"

"Did you see his last movie?" she asks, breezily. "It was dreadful."

"Annemieke," I say, gently. "That film won the Palme d'Or."

"There may have been one or two other reasons."

I scoot forward and loosen my ponytail so I can lie back on the bed. "Was one of them Liza May?"

"Oh, that's the least of his offenses—but yes, I suppose that's part of it."

"Was Paul the one who told you Tony was sleeping with her? Is that why Tony fired him?"

She makes a sound I can't identify at first.

Did Annemieke Janssen just blow a raspberry at me?

"I didn't need *Paul* to point out the obvious," she says. "As soon as I saw Liza's headshot, I knew he was going to fuck her. He's nothing if not consistent."

"Then why did Paul need your number?"

She doesn't respond.

"Please," I say. "I'm just trying to understand."

She sighs. "He contacted me because he was convinced Tony was orchestrating a series of on-set accidents so he could keep Liza in a state of constant distress. Paul thought I might be able to stop him."

I stare up at the ceiling, feeling faint.

The lights. The roller coaster. *It wasn't the 2nd AD after all. It was Tony.*

"But *why?*"

A low laugh; this one isn't musical at all. "There are no limits to what he'll do to get the performance he wants. And for this film, what he wanted was fear—it's a favorite of his, really. I'm sure he told Liza he would never put her in any real physical danger. He wouldn't let anything hurt her. And if it did, it wouldn't take more than two or three days to heal. I'm sure he told her that she should be grateful, really—because without his help, she could never realize her full potential. Only *he* could help her find the best version of who she is."

I'm shaking my head. "I had no idea."

"Didn't you?"

"Of course not. You think I would—"

"But you've heard the stories, haven't you? You've seen his movies. You've laughed, maybe, about his fastidiousness. Read essays, probably, about his exquisite attention to detail, about his deep, unmatched psychological insights, about the tremendous, heroic lengths he goes through to prepare his actresses—and they're always 'his' actresses, aren't they? I can't count the hours I've spent sitting silently beside him while he answers question after question from the press about how it is he understands women so well, no matter that he's only ever made movies about one incredibly specific sort of woman." The silence that follows is, somehow, more pointed than anything anyone's ever said out loud to me. "You knew, even if you didn't know the particulars. You chose to work with him anyway."

"It's not that simple," I say, shaking my head. "I'm just below-the-line talent. And a woman. I can't be picky about my projects."

"At the beginning of your career, maybe." She takes a deliberate beat, and I picture her as she was in Venice, admiring the toe of her shoe, brushing her bangs back with the tip of her pinky. "But you're not at the beginning of your career, are you?"

The truth snaps out of me. "Fine, you're right, I took the job because I wanted it. I wanted the credibility. The prestige. I figured this could get me a guild nomination. Maybe change my career. I didn't care if he was an asshole so long as he was a *great* asshole."

Annemieke makes a sympathetic noise. "I know. That's how they get you."

"Do you think he could have killed Liza?"

"No," she says after a moment. "I don't think so. He was desperate to make this movie, and he was very clear from the beginning that she was the only actress he would consider for the part. But perhaps I'm only saying that because I was married to the man. I'm not sure I would like to think about what his guilt would mean for me." A pause. "In any case, if you're really worried, you should talk to Anjali. She knows him better than anyone."

"Can I trust her? They're so close."

She mutters something in Dutch I suspect I don't want to know the translation for. "You really don't know anything, do you? He'd be twenty times worse if it weren't for her. Find her. She'll tell you everything."

"Wait, wouldn't it be easier if *you*—"

The line goes dead.

Actors!

But then the phone rings again, almost immediately, thank God. It wasn't a dramatic flourish after all—we were just cut off.

"Annemieke—"

"Why didn't you tell me?"

Oh. *Not* Annemieke.

It's Amy. And she knows.

I press a knuckle between my eyebrows. "I really can't do this right now."

"You *kissed* him?"

I've tried very hard not to imagine how this particular conversation would go, but I don't think I've ever responded faster to anyone, to anything. The words spill out, messy, barely distinguishable.

"It was a misunderstanding. I misunderstood."

"You misunderstood what? The distance between two faces?"

"Don't blame him," I try instead. "Blame me."

A second passes. Ten. Twenty. I press the phone to my ear so hard it's going to leave a mark—but I don't hear anything. Not a click. Not a huff. Not a flutter.

I don't hear anything at all.

When she finally speaks, I suppose it's only what I deserve.

"Oh, I definitely blame you."

I close my eyes. Josh. *Fucking* Josh.

"Do I also have to explain why this is fucked up?" she asks.

"No, I know—I know. I let you down."

"Dammit, Marissa, that's not what I'm saying at all, will you just—"

I block out whatever she says next, because, Jesus Christ, I just can't. I know I deserve everything she has to say to me, but I simply don't have the psychological wherewithal at the moment to navigate a love triangle, lopsided though it may be—much less face the realization that I might have lost my best, closest friend over a guy named *Josh*.

I search my mind frantically for a way out of this hell.

It's Nell's face that flashes behind my eyes.

"Amy," I say. "I'm hanging up now."

"Wait, are you even listening? It's—"

I snap the phone shut.

Then I open it back up, power it all the way off, and pitch it against the wall.

There's a noise in the room, a low, rhythmic sound, and it takes me a moment to realize it's coming from me. I pull my knees up to my chest and wrap my arms around them, squeezing so hard my shoulder blades dig into my ribs, but better to focus on that than the hot shimmer in my throat, the panic that will take over if I let it.

When I can breathe again, when my thoughts have settled and my ears have cleared and my skin feels like skin again and not some conductive oxide, I remember something a therapist once told me.

"You can only worry about what's in your circle of control, Marissa," she said, drawing a narrow circle around her even narrower waist.

At the time, I thought, *That seems about right. I have mastery over my belts and not much else.*

But I understand now. There's nothing I can do about Amy. Honestly, there was probably nothing I could ever do about Amy. We were always going to end up this way. With me as a main character, there's only one way that story ends.

I pull myself to my feet. Tony, though—maybe I can do something about that.

SUZY KOH: Today we're very pleased to welcome Annemieke Janssen, who's calling in from her home in Amsterdam.

ANNEMIEKE JANSSEN: Hello, ladies, it's such a pleasure, I'm a huge fan of your work.

GRACE PORTILLO: Thank you so much for being here. I'm not allowed to see most of your movies, but they look really impressive and smart.

ANNEMIEKE JANSSEN: Thank you, that's quite the endorsement.

SUZY KOH: Annemieke, I was hoping you could tell us—what went through your mind when you received that phone call from Marissa?

ANNEMIEKE JANSSEN: I assumed it was a reporter calling, of course. Our divorce had just been announced, and of course the news was all Liza, Liza, Liza. Tony was very prominent at that moment, very big again all of a sudden.

SUZY KOH: And when you heard the news, what did you think? Knowing what you did, did you wonder if Tony might have had something to do with Liza's murder?

ANNEMIEKE JANSSEN: Of course I did. Anyone with any sense could tell that her death would do amazing things for his career.

head down to the lobby in search of Anjali. Now that Billy's been arrested, the hotel's starting to come back to life: A steady stream of housekeepers moves from room to room, replacing towels and soaps and collecting trash. Wade's back behind the reception desk. There's a line at the vending machine. Somehow, though, the place is even gloomier than before. When Billy was still at large, there was a tension in the air—a welcome tension, really, because we could all focus on the chase instead of the murder. It was a solid, finite fear, sturdy enough to buttress back the weight of more burdensome realizations. Now it's impossible to focus on anything but the fact that someone *died*, and decisions we made might have played a part in it.

A gray-faced PA carrying a tray of empty coffee cups directs me to the conference room. "They're *all* in there," she says, glumly.

I blink at her retreating figure. What does she mean by *all*?

When I open the door to the conference room I could be forgiven, I think, for assuming I had somehow stumbled into an emergency room in the midst of a mass casualty incident or the commodities trading floor at the Chicago mercantile exchange. The room is packed with cast and crew alike, and everybody is yelling at everybody else. It takes me five minutes just to elbow my way inside the door.

I go up on my toes, searching the crowd. I spot Anjali over by the printers, surrounded by PAs.

I wave both arms in the air and call her name.

She looks over, and her eyebrows go up.

"I need to talk to you!" I shout.

She shakes her head and puts her hand behind her ear. Then she yells something back that gets lost in the roar.

I start to push my way toward her, but there are too many people, and I'm smaller than all of them. I've barely managed to make it three feet when a hand grabs my sleeve and tugs me forward.

I look up into Anjali's face.

"You're late," she says with exaggerated care.

"I beg your pardon?"

"Come on, you'll be working over here." She drags me across the room to one of the computer carrels. Here, someone with clearly no experience setting up an editing bay has arranged the remaining equipment from the projection room. I note with genuine regret that only one video monitor appears to have survived, and it's the shitty one.

The paper doll taped to the screen has lost an arm.

"Why isn't this in the projection room?" I ask.

Anjali lifts an eyebrow. "We figured you shouldn't be up there."

"Why not?"

She makes an impatient gesture. "The police are in there right now, so you'd be in the way. Or they'd be in the way, I guess, depending how you look at it. Anyway, that's the good news."

I feel myself edging away. "How is that good news?"

"It isn't. I was just trying to make you feel better about the bad news."

"It gets *worse?*"

She nods. "The raw footage is all backed up, that's not a problem, but we can't find any of the drives with Paul's rough cuts, and it doesn't look like they're stored online."

"*Rough cuts?* What are you talking about?" I peer at her face—is she sweating? "Anjali, are you okay?"

She waves a hand at the computer. "We'll have a better workstation back up and running for you by this evening—tomorrow morning at the latest. As soon as we get the go-ahead, we'll send someone to Dover to pick up a new computer, but just FYI, it'll probably take a while to get the software loaded. Our broadband is garbage. Until then, you can work on this laptop." She points to a dented silver MacBook connected to an external hard drive.

I rub my arms against a sudden chill. "*Anjali.*"

She huffs out a breath. "What?"

"Are you telling me we're going to salvage this?"

A frown worries at the corners of her mouth. "Of course we are."

I guess I said it myself: When you stumble on a story like this one, you don't just walk away from it. Creatively speaking, Liza's death was fantastically lucky. Like lightning striking a kite attached to a key that opens a chest full of Oscars.

"You can't possibly have cleared this with Liza's family," I say.

Anjali's jaw tightens. "They'll want her to be remembered."

Something shimmers in the corner of my vision—

Sam Shepard calls off the speedometer readings of the Bell X-1. "Point nine-seven . . . point nine-eight . . ."

"A movie's not a memory, Anjali." My fingers rub against the fabric of my pants. "And it can't take the place of one."

"Well, someone needs to bear witness," she insists, her volume rising. "And why not Tony? Why not us? Who better than the people who loved Liza to hold the police accountable, to interrogate the social structures that, ultimately, targeted and victimized her, to examine the politics of the criminal justice system—" .

"And also you probably can't afford to call it off, right?"

Her eyes narrow. "Forty-eight hours sure can change a girl, huh? You weren't this cynical when we hired you."

I swallow. "You have no idea. Is Tony here?"

"No—now that they've reopened the island, he went to New York for the day."

"Leaving you to handle all this?"

She clears her throat. "Yes, well."

"Look, never mind that. Just—come with me, okay? I want you to look at something." I drag over a second chair. "Sit."

I open the laptop and boot it up. In a matter of moments, we're watching the footage I'm hoping holds the key to all this.

The scene proceeds just as the script described. Liza and a young brown-haired actor—the man playing Tom, Caitlyn's boyfriend—are on a date at an amusement park. Everything is drawn in bold, kindergarten colors: a green bench, an orange roller coaster, pink cotton candy; Liza's sunglasses are very yellow, her lips are very red, the sky is very blue.

Two possible interpretations leap to mind. First, that this scene is a sentimental grace note, an idyllic, Kodachrome moment made piercing and poignant by dramatic irony. Look how beautiful life is; look how quickly it can be taken away.

Or it might be making fun of the trope, laughing at the idea that there's anything novel or profound to be found in an acknowledgment that, yes, life is far less predictable than any of us would like. Deep thoughts for shallow minds.

"It's funny," I say, my eyes trained on the screen. "I've never gone into a movie knowing in advance what the most important scene is going to be. I always figure it out in the editing room."

"And you think it's going to be this one?" Anjali says, a hint of condescension in her tone. "I hate to tell you, but Tony already decided to cut this. He deleted it from the workflow. The only reason it's on here is because we restored from an old backup."

"We'll see about that."

I skip forward; the roller coaster moves to the left, the crowd moves to the right. I rewind; the roller coaster moves to the right, and the crowd to the left.

"I read an interview with Tony in the *New Yorker* a couple months back," I say as I click back and forth. "He claimed that his artistic process is superior to any other subjective interpretation. That what he puts onscreen is as authentic as any artistic creation possibly can be. Does he really believe that or is he just trying to sound smart?"

"If you assume the world is what you make it, then of course what you make will look like the world."

I glance at Anjali. "Are *you* just trying to sound smart?"

"I just mean that Tony has all the confidence of man who's always been able to get things done." She lets out a breath. "Agency's a hell of a drug."

I scroll forward again, but I'm still not seeing it.

"Wasn't the derailment caught on film?" I ask.

"*That's* what you're looking for?" She shifts on her stool. "The camera was rolling, so it has to be in there."

I skip all the way to the end, but I still don't see it. "Maybe it's out of frame?"

"Hold on, I think I remember when it was." She reaches for the laptop and flicks her fingers across the touchpad. "It has to be the last take, right?"

She presses play.

I turn up the sound.

Liza's flirting around her cotton candy, smiling up into the sunlight. Behind her, the roller coaster rattles up the track. The actor playing Caitlyn's boyfriend leans in, his eyes bouncing between her chest and her lips, his face animated by the twitchy enthusiasm of an overcoached actor.

Then, for some reason, the camera goes in close on Liza's face. *Really* close. An extreme close-up, like nothing we've seen in any of the other takes—the stuff of makeup artists' nightmares. Liza's *just* young enough to be able to bear up under the magnification.

"Are you trying to tell me I'm something?" she murmurs.

Her scene partner's response is drowned out by an earsplitting shriek: The roller coaster's breaks must have engaged. There's a scream, then a series of shouts as the crew bursts into motion—or that's what I assume, anyway. The camera never moves from Liza's face.

"Oh, that *fucker*," Anjali breathes.

I pause the footage. Liza's face is half turned toward the roller coaster; her eyes are wide with terror.

"He knew the coaster was going to derail, didn't he?" Anjali asks.

"I think so, yeah."

Anjali shoves her hair out of her face. "*Shit*. I knew something was up with Liza—I *knew* it. But I couldn't get her to tell me what it was. I was trying to *help* her."

"Did you know he was sleeping with her, too?"

Her mouth twists. "What?"

I hesitate, then put my hand on her arm. "It's not your fault. She wouldn't have been able to confide in you. You're too close to Tony."

"I'm really not," she murmurs, still staring at the screen. "Just because I work for him doesn't mean we share a brain—*fuck*. I didn't even agree with him about Billy."

I turn to her in surprise. "What do you mean?"

"Everything I've seen tells me he's not guilty—but Tony, he's so certain, and he has all this *research*—"

"Did he ever tell you why this movie is so important to him?"

"Tony never explains himself. It's one of his 'things.'"

"Do you have any ideas, though? It's never made sense to me. His subject matter tends to be . . . *bigger*."

"Death isn't big?"

"You know what I mean. History and politics and philosophy. That sort of stuff. But this—this is just another movie about some dead white girl. We could make it in literally any town in America, we'd just have to change a couple names. Why *this* one?"

"Well, the tax incentives, for one thing."

I shake my head. "There's some other reason. Has to be."

I grab the mouse and restart the footage. The answer's in here, I know.

It always is.

I scroll back until I come to an image of the actor playing Caitlyn's boyfriend.

"Who is this actor?" I ask. "I don't recognize him."

Anjali laughs. "God, right? I'm always getting him confused with like eight other white TV actors. Is he the third lead from that teen drama on Netflix or the recurring guest star on that quirky comedy on Hulu? No one knows! I'm not actually convinced we didn't cast him thinking he was someone else."

That's when it happens.

If I'd looked at this yesterday—if I hadn't just talked to Annemieke, and if she hadn't just mentioned Venice—I probably wouldn't have seen it. But I'm looking at it today, now, and this time the story doesn't unspool in my mind. Instead it sparks bright and sharp and short behind my eyes, like the lights exploding in the theater, one by one.

The actor on the screen in front of me is an average, inconspicuous white boy in most respects—neither tall nor short nor fat nor thin. His hair isn't mousy or mahogany or sun-streaked or whiskey-colored. It's just brown. He has no visible scars, moles, or birthmarks. His eyes are bright, shining. Green.

And around his neck is a St. Christopher medal.

I can't help it: I laugh. I laugh the way you laugh when you finally get a joke after thinking about it for far too long. With no pleasure, only relief.

Tony's so committed to getting it right, he has no idea he just gave himself away.

grab Anjali's arm, urgently. "Whatever you do, don't be alone with Tony, okay?"

She draws back. "What?"

"I'll explain later."

I fight my way through the conference room, throwing elbows and at least one knee, not caring who I hit. I tumble out into the lobby and run to the dining room, dodging servers and busboys as I race down the back hallway, duck under a passing tray, and throw open the double silver doors.

A man in chef's whites looks up from a dish he's plating with a pair of tweezers. He lowers his reading glasses.

"Get out of my kitchen," he says.

"I'm a friend of Grace and Suzy's," I gasp out.

His forehead puckers. "But you're a grown-up."

"Yes?"

He straightens and wipes his hand on a towel. "You're the one who likes peanut butter sandwiches?"

I nod sharply. "I have the palate of a five-year-old. Do you know where they are?"

He turns to a dark-haired woman bent low over a counter. "Esther—what'd you do with the girls?"

She points her pastry bag at the pantry. "I stuck them on garde manger."

The chef looks at me. "They're on salad duty."

"So—can I borrow them?"

He cocks his head. "Do you know how many salads these people eat?"

I grind down on my molars. "It is *incredibly* important."

He shrugs. "As long as there aren't boys involved."

He settles his glasses back on his nose and returns to his work.

I find Suzy and Grace working diligently, their hair tied back, white plastic gloves on their hands, bodies half-hidden behind a mountain of leafy greens. They look up when I enter.

"How would you two like to help me break into a police station?"

Their smiles could put the sun to shame.

I fly down the driveway, across the lawn and through the trees, the girls thundering behind me. I haven't run this fast or this far in months—in years—and each time my heels strike the ground, the impact rattles my bones, the ache in my hips so acute I barely even notice the pain in my knees or the throbbing of my arm.

We burst out from behind the trees and into the parking lot. Chuck and Tim look up from behind the Smokey Joe.

"Countess Dracula!" Tim calls out.

"Thank God," I say.

Chuck hikes up his pants and hurries over. "Kid, you okay?"

"We need to get to the police station," I say between breaths. "Quickly, please."

Suzy grabs my sleeve and tugs me toward her. "Wait, Marissa—why don't we get a ride from Isaiah?"

I shake my head. "Can't. I have to make sure I'm right first. I have to be *logical* about it."

"Breaking into a police station is *logical*?"

I nod firmly. "Absolutely."

Suzy blinks. "I think maybe you've been spending too much time with us."

I turn back to Chuck. "Can you take us?"

He's frowning at the girls. "I'm not sure I have the authority—"

I put my hand on his shoulder. "Are you telling me the illustrious and august International Brotherhood of Teamsters doesn't have the *authority* to assist the lead editor—who by the way is a member of IATSE Local 700 in good standing—in a time of desperate need?"

Chuck sighs, puts two fingers in his mouth, and whistles. "Little Bob! We're gonna need the Destroyer."

No more than thirty seconds later, the black Escalade emerges from behind one of the trailers.

"'Destroyer?'" I ask.

Chuck nods absently. "'Of worlds.'"

The Escalade pulls up, and the girls clamber into the back seat. I strap myself in on the passenger side and stow my backpack at my feet. Little Bob looks over at me and lifts his eyebrows. "Where to, boss?"

"The police station. And we sort of need to sneak up on them."

He shifts the car out of park. I can feel Suzy and Grace behind me, bubbling with anticipation. God, I hope I'm not doing the wrong thing by bringing them with me.

When we get to the end of the driveway, Little Bob turns right.

"Isn't the main road that way?" I ask, pointing in the other direction.

Little Bob pulls over to the shoulder. Then he reaches across the bench seat and adjusts my seat belt, pulling it tight. He revs the engine. Then he looks back at the girls and winks.

"Where we're going," he says, "we don't need roads."

And then he turns the wheel sharply to the left and lays on the gas. The girls squeal as the car goes off-road.

Maybe I do, too.

Little Bob steers the SUV over a hill, between two houses, and around a tree. We drive straight through what looks an awful lot like a stable and emerge into a densely wooded area that Little Bob nevertheless navigates with ease, finding daylight where by all rights there should be none. Then he takes a hard right turn and, somehow, picks up a dirt road that can't have been used in centuries.

It's like he has Google Maps implanted into his soul.

Another two miles or so and we come to the center of a glade; the truck glides smoothly to a stop. A hundred yards ahead, through the trees, I can just make out a square brick building. There are two police cruisers parked out front.

"We may not do much," Little Bob says. "But we do it better than anyone."

I look back at the girls, speechless.

"That was *beautiful*," Suzy says.

Grace nods, wiping a tear from her eye.

We climb out of the truck and creep over to the edge of the forest, concealing ourselves behind the trunk of a silver maple.

"What's the plan?" I ask.

"We're going to go in first," Grace says. "One of us will tell the nice lady at the front desk that we have *extremely* important information relating to the case."

"Except," Suzy says, "we're going to say everything super fast, using as much post-2018 Instagram slang as we can think of—"

"I'm going to have Urban Dictionary open on my phone."

"—and we're going to let our voices go all high and girly at the end of every sentence, like *this*?"

"I might throw in some Spanish just for fun."

"No, don't do that. These are real cops, remember."

Grace swallows. "Oh. Right."

"And then," Suzy continues, "just when they're really confused, that's when I'm going to ask to use the bathroom."

"But I'm going to keep talking—"

"So they won't think to follow me—"

"And while she's in there, she'll open that window." Grace points to an awning window set high on the back wall of the building. "That's your way in. Billy will be in the holding cell on the south side of the building."

Suzy eyes me. "You know, our original plan was that I was going to break into the file room and steal the crime scene photos. But— I'm assuming we're past all that?"

I chew on my thumbnail and stare at the window. "Yeah. Let's just do one deeply ill-advised thing at a time."

When I enter the room, still smarting from the *tiniest* of tumbles through the bathroom window, Billy's sitting on a metal chair in the holding cell, hands tangled together in his lap, staring at a space a few feet in front of him.

I take a faltering step forward. "Hi, Billy."

His expression doesn't change. Doesn't he recognize me?

"It's Marissa," I say. "We met—God, I guess that was just yesterday."

His head comes up. It takes a while for his expression to clear. "I remember. I'm so sorry—I really didn't mean to push you. I hope you're not hurt."

There's a long list of terms I could use to describe what my vision does in that moment. A zido, a zolly, a smash shot, a trombone shot, the Long Pull, reverse tracking, the *Vertigo* effect. Me, I prefer the term "dolly zoom"—since a dolly zoom is, in fact, a dolly shot that zooms. Whimsical nomenclature has always struck me as something of a contradiction in terms.

If you've seen *Vertigo* or *Jaws* or *Goodfellas*—or any horror movie ever, really—you'd probably be able to recognize the shot. Picture a long hallway: At one end, an unassuming doorway. In the foreground, the hero, going about his business. But then, the lights flicker—behind that door, a noise!—and somehow, as we watch, the hallway *lengthens*, the door falling away like it's being sucked into another dimension.

There's something bad *behind that door.*

The language of cinema may be forever changing, but the English-language translation of this particular shot has remained remarkably consistent ever since *Marnie*. So when the windows on the wall opposite me seem to vanish into the distance, I know exactly what my brain's trying to tell me:

Oh *shit*.

"I panicked," he's saying, "and I don't always make the best choices when I panic. Which I suppose is what makes it panic."

Billy *was* the one who stole the footage. *He* was the one who attacked me. That means—

"Dammit, Billy," I say, my voice small. "I came here so you could tell me you *didn't* kill Liza."

His head snaps up, shock slackening the line of his lips. "What? No. I took the movie, but I never touched the girl. I swear."

"Why should I believe you?"

"Because I have a GPS tracker on my skiff. I was only on the island for twenty minutes, and you can place me in the projection room in that time. It would have been impossible for me to kill her, too."

"Oh." I press my hand to my chest, half expecting to find my heart on the outside. "When people ask, that's probably the part you should start with."

He lets out a little puff of breath that skates along the very outside edges of what I'd call a laugh. "Good advice."

I creep over to the edge of his cell. "Why would you go to all that trouble for raw footage?"

He looks back down at his hands. "I don't think it's going to sound so good when I say it out loud."

"Try me."

He lets out a slow, steady breath. "Gavin told me he was quitting, and you said—remember? You said that if Gavin quit, they'd shut the movie down. And that meant I was never going to get to see it."

"You know the movie makes you out to be a deeply troubled murderer, right?"

"Well, I've heard that one before. Doesn't change the fact that those years were some of the best of my life. I—I guess I wanted to see if they looked the same as I remembered."

His hands twist into a new shape, and he loses himself in a thought I can't follow.

I let him come back to me in his own time.

"But then I heard someone coming up those stairs, and I got scared, because, well"—a glance, fleeting, from under his eyelashes—"you sounded much larger than you are."

"Jumping up a metal staircase will do that."

He looks away. "You should be more careful. I chipped a tooth on that staircase when I was running the projector. I caught my toe on the way up, and"—he claps his hands—"*boom*."

"I still don't understand. If you wanted the footage so badly, why'd you dump the computer in the ocean?"

He casts his eyes up to the ceiling. "I did what I imagine most accidental criminals do. I came to my senses, realized I'd made a terrible mistake, and tried to destroy the evidence."

"Thereby creating more evidence."

"Not my finest moment," he agrees. "Say what you will about

our police force, they've got me dead to rights on robbery. On the other hand, it's a heck of an alibi."

I glance back at the door. Through the square glass window I can see Grace gesticulating wildly to three policemen, all of whom are blinking owlishly and rubbing their chins. But the girls won't be able to keep them occupied forever.

"Billy," I say, urgently. "I need to ask you a question."

His forehead creases. "Isn't that what you've been doing?"

"Yeah, I know, but that's a thing you're supposed to say when you're about to ask a really important one."

He gestures at me to go on.

"You said Caitlyn had a few boyfriends that summer—"

"She went out on several dates, yes."

"Right. Do you happen to remember the boys she went out with?"

His eyelids flicker. "Of course I do."

"Can you tell me their names?"

His lips part; he hesitates.

My hands come up and wrap around the bars. "He can't hurt you, you know. It's kind of a neat reversal, really. He finally has you where he wants you—which turns out to be the one place on this island even he can't get to."

Billy gives me a flat look. "*You* got here."

"Yeah, but I have two teenage girls on my side." I time my next words so perfectly not even Gavin Davies could find fault with my delivery. "Tony Rees doesn't."

If I were another person, a regular person, the kind of person who doesn't mind shaking hands or hugging hello or accidentally just-maybe brushing up against someone for a split second in a crowded room, if being this close to somebody were an everyday affair for me and not something that sharpened my senses well past the point of mild discomfort, if I were able to casually look at someone without being painfully, insistently aware that I'm *looking at someone I'm looking at someone oh God I'm looking at someone*, I honestly think I would have missed it.

But I'm not another person. So I don't.

It's fear that flashes across Billy's face.

I take a step back. "I'm right. Tony was here twenty-five years ago. *He* was in love with Caitlyn. Why didn't you tell anybody?"

"He nearly killed me once. I don't doubt he'd try again."

"But surely *now*—"

His hand slices through the air. "You movie people are all the same. You think just because you didn't know something all along it must be a brand-new discovery. But this isn't a twist—you're just the last person to figure it out. Everyone on the island knows who Tony is. They love him—they loved him when he was coming here as a kid, and they love him even more now. Where do you think all the money is coming from? Not tourists—this is *Delaware*."

"How is that possible?"

"They're all friends, don't you get it? He and Nick were drinking buddies; Francie taught Tony to fish. *He* got invited to the Fourth of July party every year. They're working together—just like they worked together then."

"Why? To get justice for Caitlyn?"

He nods.

"But you didn't do it."

He smiles tightly. "Yeah, well, try telling them that."

I look at the door, then to Billy—then back again.

"What?" he asks, warily.

I straighten my shirt and hike up my backpack. "I think for once you might have the right idea."

SUZY KOH: See? We told you he didn't do it.

TWENTY-NINE

W e need to talk about Tony," I say.

Nick studies me over the rim of his coffee mug. "You broke into *my* station, and now you're making demands?"

"Yes, well." I shift, trying to find a comfortable position in the chair Nick directed me to. It's one of those wooden chairs with the seats that are carved to cradle your butt, but I'm clearly the wrong shape. It's like trying to fit a square peg in a round, really uncomfortable wooden chair. "The fact that he was Caitlyn's boyfriend seems like a fairly important detail."

Through the open door, I hear Suzy tell the uniformed policemen that she has a cousin who works at the Justice Department, so they better not try any funny business. Grace, meanwhile, is on the phone to Little Bob, instructing him to call for a lawyer and post something to Twitter if we're not out in half an hour.

How did she even get Little Bob's number?

"So you know," Nick says.

"I'm honestly impressed you managed to keep it a secret for so long."

His smile is cold. "We didn't keep it a secret. None of you thought to ask."

"*You're* judging *me*? I'm not the one here who beat up an innocent man."

Nick sits back in his chair—his has a pillow, I notice—and steeples his fingers in front of his face. "You don't know what you're talking about."

"I'm sorry, were you not there when they put Billy in the hospital? Maybe you just stood by and watched?"

"Look—I was a kid, and I was terrified. Everyone was saying Billy was some sort of deranged stalker, and I didn't know any better. In the movies those guys never stop with just one. How was I to know he wasn't going to come for me next? Then the cops had to go and fuck things up, and since prison time wasn't on the table, yes, I thought we needed to send a message. It was wrong—I can admit that now. But that's why I'm doing all this. I want to get it right this time."

"You really think he killed Caitlyn?"

He scrubs a hand over his face. "You don't know him. He's a rude little prick—always was. And facts are facts: He's the only viable suspect in Caitlyn's murder. He's the only person who knew her, who had access to a boat to move the body, and whose whereabouts are unaccounted for that night."

"I'm telling you, Billy didn't do it."

"I hate to tell you, but feeling really, really strongly about something doesn't count as proof."

I look off to the side, thinking hard. I clearly need to try another approach here.

"But you agree he didn't kill Liza May, right?"

"It seems unlikely," he allows.

"Okay"—I lick my lips—"bear with me for a moment, then: Did you also know Tony was sleeping with her?"

Nick straightens, clearly surprised. "Liza?"

I lean forward. "And you see it, right? How much she looks like

Caitlyn? You know who else looks like Caitlyn? His soon-to-be ex-wife." I take a breath. "You have to admit, that's some Hitchcock-level shit right there. Pardon my language."

Nick sets his elbows on the desk. *"Jesus."*

I have him on the ropes. I can't stop now.

"It gets worse," I say. "He'd been tormenting Liza for weeks. Knocking her down, then building her back up—only to knock her down again. At first I was like, 'Oh, that's just how he gives notes,' but it's more than that. He didn't think she was good enough to play Caitlyn."

"And you think he killed her for that?"

"It's as plausible as anything."

He opens his mouth to respond—then shakes his head. "He couldn't have killed Caitlyn, I know that for a fact. I was with him that night—we sailed over to Cape May to meet up with this girl I knew."

I sit back. *Dammit.* I really thought I had him.

There's a sharp rap against the glass of the door. Suzy's face appears. "I hope you don't mind," she says, "but I was blatantly eavesdropping."

I wave her in.

Nick raises an eyebrow. "Yes, please, do invite a child into this discussion."

"Trust me," I say, "she's going to come in anyway."

Suzy pulls a chair up to the desk and plops down. "Have you considered that there might be *two* killers? I'm sorry, let me rephrase, it was two killers *for sure*, and before you say 'How could you know, you're just a wee babe?,' you should probably look at these."

She pulls a file folder out of the waistband of her pants and lays it on Nick's desk.

"While Marissa was in with Billy, I found the original crime scene photos," she says, laying two pictures out in front of me. "For *both* murders."

The first image is of Caitlyn; the second, Liza. Neither looks like I expected.

For one thing, the police photographers made no attempt to strive for artistry or elegance or delicacy. And why would they? They're paid to record the bare facts of the image.

It's just that I never knew: Dead girls aren't actually beautiful.

Liza's body also *isn't* laid out identically to Caitlyn's. Yes, they're both wearing orange swimsuits and they're both sitting in beach chairs, but only Liza is draped artfully across the chair. Caitlyn's slumped forward, her arms flopped to one side, a narrow ridge of fat rolling at her waist.

My finger lands on an even more glaring difference between the two: Caitlyn's mouth. Hers is painted crimson. Liza's is bare.

"He definitely needed to fire that makeup artist," I say faintly.

"Right?" Suzy says, looking over my shoulder. "If it was the same killer, surely he wouldn't have forgotten the *blood-red* lipstick. That's, like, serial murder 101."

"What's this about?" Nick asks.

"Liza wasn't wearing lipstick in the movie, either," I say.

"Why does *that* matter?"

I huff out a laugh. "Because it means I've been wrong all this time."

I've been wrong ever since I first saw that shot of Liza back in Century City, a million years ago. It was too easy to assume I was looking at the truth.

I reach for my backpack and fumble around inside until my thumb brushes across a sharp corner of resin-coated paper.

I pull out the still Isaiah took from the editing bay and place it next to the police photos.

Suzy sucks in a breath.

Nick's forehead creases. "I don't get it."

"Liza's body wasn't arranged to look like Caitlyn's," Suzy says.

She points to Caitlyn's picture, then to the still. "It was arranged to look like *Liza's*."

"But that can't be right," I say. I look up at Nick. "Didn't you give the crime scene photos to Tony?"

He shakes his head, his mouth slack. "I gave them to his assistant."

"Wait—seriously?"

"Tony read all the files, but he refused to look at the photos. He said—" Nick's hand goes to the bridge of his nose "—he said he didn't want to see Caitlyn's body through someone else's lens."

Suzy stiffens. "And you just *went* with that? Like that's *normal*? Has anyone ever said no to this guy?"

"It's part of his process—" I say.

"He said it's his process—" Nick says.

Nick's eyes meet mine. Then he comes to his feet and strides out of the room, calling for his men. They're heading back to the hotel, he tells them. They're going to talk to Tony—that's right, *their* Tony. And they might want to check their weapons.

I register all this only vaguely. I'm still stuck on the photos. Something's pinging at me—but what?

Shirley MacLaine, at Debra Winger's bedside, opening her eyes—

No, before that—

Shirley MacLaine, at Debra Winger's bedside, helping her apply her makeup before she sees her children for the last time.

Maybe it's not a movie—

My grandmother, in the hospital the night she died, an emerald green tube of Revlon in her hands.

Suzy shakes my shoulder. "Marissa, you still with us?"

I blink up at her. "Yeah, sorry—just thinking."

"Terrible habit," she says, seriously. "Come on, they're taking us back to the hotel."

"Don't you worry. As soon as Tony tries to get anywhere near here, they'll get him. It's one of the nice things about life on an island."

Wade's smile is so wide, I'm worried he's going to cause permanent damage.

I'm standing in Wade's private office. While the police continue to search for Tony, this is serving as the hotel's temporary operational epicenter. Opposite Wade's desk are eight CCTVs cycling through the hotel's security feeds; behind it, three LCD flatscreens are showing the news. So far, Liza's death has only made the chyron on Fox and CNN; there's been no mention yet that anyone suspects Tony might be involved.

On the local channel, a reporter barely out of adolescence is doing a stand-up in front of the ferry terminal at Lewes; in the background I can see at least three other news trucks. I wonder if anyone's interviewed Georgia.

To my right, through a wide, columned archway, is Wade and Francie's living room. Francie's at the walnut sideboard, standing over a tea service while the kettle steeps, folding napkins and laying out a plate of cookies. In the middle of the room is a small seating area—a coffee table, an armchair, two turquoise couches. There's another TV, too, tuned to an entertainment news channel I don't recognize. That's where the girls are, delivering a nonstop stream of running commentary to Anjali and Valentina, who wear identical looks of consternation.

Isaiah's standing over them, his arms crossed, fingers tapping absently against his elbows. Every three minutes or so, I've noticed, he checks his phone and scowls.

I haven't said anything to him yet.

He hasn't said anything to me, either.

Gavin, meanwhile, is huddled next to the liquor cabinet with

Violet, who wheeled herself in from the adjoining suite for the occasion. She's wearing gold silk pajamas and a platinum pixie-cut wig. When she catches me looking at her, she waggles her charcoaled eyebrows.

I avert my gaze. It lands on a picture hanging just inside the door: In it, Wade is smiling as usual, standing between two other men who look vaguely familiar.

I wander over to examine it. "Is that—"

"Yup," Wade says from behind me, with relish. "Season 4, episode 28."

"So *that's* why I'd heard of this place."

"You're a fan, too, then?"

"God no. My first job out of grad school was cutting promos for Syfy."

He tugs at his collar. "Ah."

"They never actually *found* any ghosts," I explain.

"Just because they didn't find them doesn't mean they aren't there," he says, genially. "After all, who knows *what* went on here during Prohibition? All those smuggler's coves and secret tunnels—"

"They never mentioned Caitlyn's murder," I say. "On the episode, I mean."

Wade pauses. "No."

"Why not? It would've made for better TV."

He glances at the living room. "Well, we made the decision—as a family. We worried it would be disrespectful."

"What changed your mind?"

Out of the corner of my eye, I see Francie's hand freeze over a piece of shortbread.

Wade laughs nervously. "What do you mean?"

"Ten years ago, you wouldn't even let a basic-cable reality series say a single word about Caitlyn's murder, but now you're making a whole movie about it?"

"Well," he says, "we trusted Tony to do it right."

"And how's that working out for you?"

Francie comes into the room, her hands on her hips. "He won an *Academy Award*."

I shrug. "So did Mel Gibson."

Francie opens her mouth—then closes it abruptly, her attention drawn to one of the TVs. They're showing a picture of Tony.

"Do you think he's going to get away?" she asks after a moment.

"No," Anjali says from the archway, one hand resting against a column. "He has money, but he's too used to having people to do things for him. He'll fuck up in some boneheaded, obvious way, they always do. And then he'll have to live with the knowledge that it was irony that took him down. The visionary director who couldn't see what was right in front of his face." She sips from the cut crystal low-ball in her left hand. "I like the sound of that."

From the living room, Gavin catches my eye. He waves me over.

I shake my head. I don't have the energy for him right now.

Undeterred, he points at the empty stool to his left—then to me.

Next to him, Violet lets out a low, throaty laugh. "Oh don't be shy—come keep an old lady company."

Well, *damn*. I can't exactly say no to that. I give Gavin a poisonous look as I head over to perch on the edge of the horsehair stool.

"So," she says when I'm settled. "I hear you like movies."

It surprises a laugh out of me. "Yeah, I do."

She quirks her lips and holds her glass out to Gavin; he tops it off with whiskey. She draws it close and sweeps her hand briskly back and forth above it, breathing in the scent.

"I can't drink anymore," she explains when she opens her eyes. "All I can do is *smell*. I have to rely on Gavin here to tell me what it actually tastes like."

Gavin inclines his head in acknowledgment and takes a sip of his own drink. He rolls the liquid around in his mouth.

"Charcoal and sticking plasters," he pronounces.

She smells her drink again. "Should've known better than to ask an Englishman."

"I am *Welsh*, madam."

She sniffs and adjusts the angle of her chair, turning her back on Gavin. "You know," she says, "I never wanted them to make this fucking movie."

Gavin's whiskey goes down the wrong way; he sputters and slaps his chest.

I shift on the stool. "Well, between you and me, the script was terrible."

She hums in agreement. "It was Francie who insisted, and of course I couldn't say *no*. Not to my own family. I only tell you this because I heard you asking my granddaughter about it."

I glance at Gavin, lifting my eyebrows a little.

He shrugs.

I turn back to Violet. She's watching me closely over the rim of her glass.

"How did she convince you?" I ask.

"She told me that after all these years, Tony was finally going to bring Caitlyn's killer to justice." Her lips press into a smile. "Imagine that."

"Yes," I say, slowly, my hand going to my mouth. "Imagine that."

"I suppose I wasn't surprised he was stuck on her," she adds, looking at her glass. "Young love isn't built to last forever—but you have to let it run its course. Even as a boy, Tony never could let things go unfinished."

Normally I would never be able to look at someone directly for so long—especially someone I don't know. But with Violet, I find I'm incapable of looking away. There's just something about her. Maybe that's what they call star quality.

But maybe it's something else.

"Were you and Caitlyn close?" I ask.

She nods. "Very. Caitlyn wanted to be an actress—poor thing. We had some fun together, though."

"You ran old movie scenes together, right?"

"How did you—oh yes, I forgot. That awful scene." She glances over her shoulder at Gavin. "Would you believe Tony had me read his first draft? He wanted to be sure his blocking was accurate."

I choke a little. "*Tony* wrote the script?"

"He insisted. Said he was the only one who could do it right—with my help, of course."

"But he *didn't* get everything right. The roller coaster—"

"Oh *that*. I don't know how I forgot to mention it. Just slipped my mind, I suppose. The year before, a little boy lost his leg on that thing. There was a terrible lawsuit—the whole park had to shut down. I couldn't believe Tony hadn't heard about it, but I suppose those are *adult* concerns." She pulls out a white linen handkerchief and dabs her lips. "Nothing a young man need trouble himself with."

She folds the handkerchief into thirds and slips it back in her pocket, and that's when it finally comes to me—what I was trying to think of back in the police station.

Francie, in the theater, her arm extended: "My grandmother has worn bright red lipstick every day of her life since she was thirteen. She says no one should have to face the world without it."

Violet's lips: They're red. Bright, cherry red.

I know this color.

My eyes fly to Violet's face, but I can't make sense of it. Is she happy? Guilty? Sad? Has she been confessing to me this whole time and I just didn't notice? Does she even know what she's telling me?

"It would have been a real shame," I say after a moment, "if you'd had an accident like that at the hotel."

"A disaster," she agrees easily. "My husband, you see, he was a bit of a gambler. Didn't believe in insurance—said it wasn't 'sporting.' But I don't suppose I can complain. After all, if he hadn't had a nose for trouble, he never would have married me."

She waves her hand over her whiskey again and draws in another breath.

"Up to then, we'd had the most wonderful year," she says, eyelids fluttering. "Francie had just fallen in love with Wade, and they were just two peas in a pod. They had so many ideas for the hotel. All the things they wanted to do!"

"The hotel is lovely," I say, the sound of my voice dim even to my own ears.

She drops her chin and opens her eyes, and she may be ninety-seven, but there's still something vital in her gaze. "It is."

"I don't think—" I break off, searching for the words, but then I decide that's all I'm going to say.

At my silence, her shoulders settle, her expression satisfied. Her hand—narrow-boned, blue-veined, liver-spotted—reaches out to curl around my knee. Her grip is incredibly strong.

"See that you don't." Then she cranes her neck around to look at Gavin. "Charcoal and Band-Aids. *Really.*"

tell everyone I'm going to the bathroom, but really I'm going to see if I'm right.

I slip out of Wade and Francie's rooms and hurry down the hall toward the elevators. This time, I find the movie theater on my first try. I jog toward the projection room, grimly saluting the headshot that hangs behind the concession stand as I run past.

The scene is already playing out behind my eyes: Caitlyn and Violet, rehearsing *Rebecca*. The projector craps out, like always. Violet reminds Caitlyn to be careful on those stairs—and in those shoes!— but Caitlyn's young, and she's done this a thousand times before. So what if the lights don't work? She's bubbling up with adrenaline, with all the energy your body makes when you get to do the thing you love, and maybe she's excited, too, thinking about a boy she's going to meet the next day. Or maybe she has something planned with Billy, her best friend. Maybe she's just in a hurry. Whatever the reason, her concentration slips. Her toe catches.

I skid to a stop at the bottom of the stairs. I fumble for my phone and flip it open, aiming the display at the third tread. There it is: the splatter Isaiah and I saw earlier today. It wasn't mine after all.

I wonder how long it took before Violet found her.

My throat clenches; the scene continues.

Violet quickly concludes that no one would be served by the truth. She thinks through her options. She's slender and in her seventies, but she's still strong—she dances every day—so she could move Caitlyn's body all by herself. Maybe to another part of the hotel, to an area where the lighting is up to code. At least then they could make the argument that the accident wasn't strictly due to gross negligence. Or she could take the body to the beach, through the same tunnels the rumrunners used during Prohibition.

Yes, she thinks. *That's it.*

She's nothing if not practical, so she forces herself to consider whether she can bring herself to weigh down Caitlyn's body, to feed it to the ocean, to let the waves carry the evidence away. But she decides she can't. Caitlyn meant too much to her. So instead she settles her friend in her favorite chair, arranging her hair to hide the worst of the head wound. And then, in a last act of—what, love? Affection? Contrition? Vanity? She paints Caitlyn's lips a rich Victory Red.

Because no one should have to face the world without it.

She vows to never breathe a word about it to any other living soul. If there's anything Hollywood has taught her, it's that you can't trust anyone with your secrets but yourself.

I close my phone. And there, in the darkness, I let myself linger on the image one last time: A girl in an orange swimsuit, her hair lifting in the ocean breeze.

Only then do I realize: There's a light on in the projection room.

Before we get too excited, let's be realistic: It's probably just Gary the Projectionist. The police have collected their evidence; the production has collected its equipment. The only things left in that room are the DP70 and the Autowind. Therefore, the only person with a benign reason to be up there is the person charged with maintaining those machines.

But if it's not Gary, then I think there's only one other person it could be, which presents me with a dilemma. Do I, Marissa Dahl, professional film editor and avid cinephile, climb these stairs to satisfy my curiosity and find out who's up in the projection room—even though, if this were a movie, everyone in the audience right now would be thinking, *Don't you fucking do it.*

Or do I do the sensible thing and call for help?

If I go up there now—and if it's Tony who's in there—and if it's Tony who killed Liza—it's entirely possible he'll kill me, too. He'll see me and immediately conclude that, as usual, I've been sticking my nose where it doesn't belong and that, therefore, I am most likely responsible for the fact that he's currently the target of a three-state manhunt.

Again, just to be clear, the person in that room right now is almost definitely Gary the Projectionist, that is absolutely the explanation that makes the most sense.

But if it's *not*—

And if I leave—

It'll take me ten minutes, minimum, to get to a part of the hotel that has cell service. By the time I call the police, Tony could be long gone. And what if he has a Brazilian alias all ready to go? What if he just came back to the hotel for one last sentimental item? What if I'm the only thing that stands between him and a long, fruitful career of light, critically acclaimed misogyny? What if this is our one chance?

What if I really am Obi-Wan Kenobi?

What if I really am their only hope?

And anyway, it's just Gary up there—right? So what am I afraid of?

I sink down to my hands and knees and crawl up the stairs, using the elbow of my left arm for balance. Six steps up, I freeze, alerted by some up-to-now dormant piece of my reptile brain. A second later, the entire staircase shifts an inch to my right. I hold my breath, listening for any movement upstairs.

No one comes.

I keep going.

Ten steps left.

Five stairs.

One.

At the top, I flip over onto my butt and scoot back until I hit the wall. I take a moment to catch my breath. It occurs to me that now would be a great time to change my mind, if I'm so inclined.

But all I can see is Tony boarding a private plane to Rio de Janeiro.

Mothersmucker.

I nod a few times to myself—*It's totally just Gary! You can do this!*—and swallow back the stomach acid that's burning the back of my throat. Then I come up on my haunches and creep forward until I can just barely manage to peek around the edge of the doorway.

It's totally *not* Gary.

Tony is working at the melamine table on the opposite wall, his back to me. He's replaced the hot plate with a task lamp and is using the microwave as a laptop stand. He's wearing a pair of Sennheiser headphones that probably cost more than most high-end divorce attorneys.

I crane my neck a little to try to see what he's doing—is he looking at dailies?

He removes his headphones and turns. I go still.

God, he looks terrible. Pasty skin, stubble, new lines that bracket his lips. But when I steal a quick glance at his eyes behind his spectacles, they're the same bottle-glass green—although, again, what does that even mean? Are we talking Perrier? Heineken? Mountain Dew? Be *specific*, people.

He shakes his head and turns back to the computer. I ease my way back into the hall, holding my breath until I'm safely out of sight.

I exhale.

It is, without a doubt, the loudest sound that has ever been made in the whole history of the world.

My eyelids flutter closed.

A moment later, Tony pops his head out into the hallway. He looks down.

"Marissa, what are you doing on the floor?"

I run, right? Now is when I run. That's what Isaiah said—"Next time maybe crawl somewhere with an escape route. Better yet, run." I pull myself to my feet. If I can just take him by surprise, I think I'd be able to—

"Where have you been?"

"I'm sorry?"

"We have work to do."

"What?"

He squints at me. "Work. You do know what that is, right? It occurs to me that I've yet to see you actually doing it."

My mouth falls open. "Well, I've been—I've just—"

"There is nothing," he says silkily, "less interesting to me than excuses. Now come on."

He turns and disappears back into the projection room, and for some reason my legs decide to follow him.

"Tony—have you been here this whole time?"

He heads to the table and leans over his laptop. "I got back from New York a few hours ago. Why?"

Another person, a better, braver person—Grace or Suzy, or

Anjali—would take this opportunity to come up with a speech. A clever set of lines designed to lull Tony into a false sense of security before, somehow, drawing him out and apprehending him, capturing a taped confession along the way. They would appeal to each of his weaknesses—to his ego, to his pride, to his arrogance—luring him into a trap not even Tony could escape from.

Narrative comeuppance comes for us all.

But the only time I've ever been able to pull off a speech is alone, in bed, long after the fact, when I'm going through the endless list of all the things I wish I'd said.

So in the moment, I just say:

"Yeah, I do *not* know what to do in this situation."

Tony gaze flickers. "I know this has been a hard few days—"

I spin and launch myself through the door, but Tony's too fast. His hand clamps down around my upper arm, and he yanks me back toward him. I spin, and the momentum carries me all the way across the room. I slam into the opposite wall, face-first. I crumple to the ground.

My hand goes to my nose; it comes away bloody.

I look up at Tony. His eyes are wide, nostrils flaring. He takes a step toward me—

I scramble back against the wall. "Please don't."

He shoves a hand through his hair and sucks in a breath.

I hold up a hand. "You know what? Let's talk about this logically."

His lips part. "Logically?"

"Yes—logically. Because the cops already know you killed Liza, so killing me won't actually change anything."

He considers this. "It'll shut you up."

I stare up at him. Blood drips down my lower lip and onto my chin. I swipe it away with the back of my hand.

He pulls off his spectacles and rubs the lenses with the hem of his shirt. "How did they figure it out, do you know?"

"To be honest it was mostly speculation until just now. Motive's still a little murky."

He replaces his glasses and cocks his head to the side. "But I bet you have a few ideas, don't you?"

I swallow. "Do you—want to hear them?"

He huffs out a laugh. "Sure, Marissa, go ahead. *Pitch me.*"

"Well—I figure it could have gone one of two ways. Way one, you killed her because you decided your movie wasn't going to get you the justice you were seeking—maybe because you knew Gavin was going to quit, maybe because you knew Liza wasn't up to it, maybe because you finally realized you wrote a terrible script—so you decided to try to frame Billy for Liza's murder. Send him to jail that way."

"Or?"

I'm shaking so hard I can hear the bones rattling in my skull.

"Or—as part of your twisted little director games, you had been putting Liza in increasingly dangerous situations. The night she died, when I saw you with her in the spa—I didn't know it was you then, of course—you were trying to teach her to access her emotions or whatever. If that was the case, there was probably some upsetting sex element at play, which means I really don't want to know the details. But whatever happened, things went sideways, and when she died, you panicked. You figured you'd make lemons into lemonade, try to pin the murder on Billy."

His expression gives nothing away. "Which story do you believe?"

I wipe my nose again; I clear my throat. "I'm leaning toward the latter? But, you know, I'd really like to think you're only capable of killing a girl by *accident.*"

"Jesus Christ, you're like nails on a chalkboard, aren't you?"

I laugh, the blood gurgling in the back of my throat. "Point of pride, really."

The curl of his lip is like the flick of a whip. "If I'd realized who you were at the interview, I never would have hired you. A strange, sad little girl who brings no pleasure to anyone or anything, who no one with any sense can stand to be around."

"That's not *quite* true."

He reaches down and grabs me by my ponytail, pulling me to my feet. He stretches a hand across my collarbone and shoves me against the wall.

"How about we make a deal?" he suggests, his voice barely more than a shadow of a ghost of a whisper. "I'll let you go—if you can name one person who doesn't laugh at you behind your back."

"Me, for one."

Tony turns toward the sound just in time for Isaiah's fist to plow into his face.

He crumples to the ground.

Isaiah's eyes meet mine. We stand there for a long time, just looking at each other. Then his hand rubs the back of his neck. "I know you're probably the kind of woman who wants to save herself, but I saw you on the CCTV, and—"

"That," I gasp out, "was the nicest thing anyone's ever said about me."

I step into his arms and burst into tears.

SUZY KOH: Oh my God, are you kidding? That's what he said? He didn't come up with anything better before he knocked Tony out?

MARISSA DAHL: Okay, but I actually thought it was really moving because, like, he was addressing my emotional needs and not my—

SUZY KOH: But that was his chance to unleash an *amazing* one-liner.

MARISSA DAHL: I guess you'll have to take that up with Isaiah, I don't really know what to say—

SUZY KOH: "That's a wrap."

GRACE PORTILLO: "I'm ready for my close-up, Mr. DeMille."

SUZY KOH: "I think this is the *end* of a beautiful friendship."

GRACE PORTILLO: "I'll see you on the cutting room floor."

MARISSA DAHL: Oh my God, are we done now? Please can we be done. [*pause*] I'd really like to be done.

wait with the locksmith-slash-paramedic while he packs up his bag, feeling a little sorry I didn't give him more to do. Tony's already been taken by helicopter to a hospital in Lewes where they can treat his concussion. I only have a broken nose—and a busted arm, and a bunch of cuts and bruises, not to mention nightmare fuel for at least ten years.

But other than that, I'm unscathed.

Nick's interviewing Isaiah over by the popcorn machine, twenty feet away. He scrawls in his notebook as Isaiah sketches something in the air with his hands. My gaze catches for a moment on the back of Isaiah's neck.

The paramedic buries his hands in his pockets and rocks on his heels.

"So how's the arm?" he asks.

I glance over at him. "You just examined it."

"I could take another look at it if you'd like."

"No, thank you."

"Okay," he says, nodding. "Okay."

Now Nick's gesticulating with his pen, and Isaiah's nodding in agreement. Isaiah's hand goes to fiddle with his wrist—he's unbuttoning his cuff and rolling up his sleeve. He rolls the other one up, too, before adjusting his stance, planting his hands on his hips.

"So do you often find yourself in situations like this?"

I turn to the paramedic slowly. "Do you mean, like—murder?"

He squeezes shut his eyes and scrubs a hand through his hair. "No, I—"

"Marissa!"

It's Nick, waving at me.

I head over, my feet dragging just a little. I can't help but think about how Nick reacted when he arrived on the scene—how he ran right over to Tony and pressed his fingers against his neck before he even thought to look at me. As I approach, I take in the conventionally attractive white-guy features that—red hair aside—are more or less a Rorschach test for how much you hated high school. I wonder if he was doomed from birth to be just a little douchey.

(Why isn't Isaiah looking at me? Did I embarrass myself that badly?)

"You were a lot nicer to Tony than you were to Billy" is the first thing I say to Nick.

Nick raises his eyebrows and scratches the side of his jaw. "Well—you know."

"That Tony is rich and famous and also your buddy from back in the day? Yes."

"Marissa," Isaiah murmurs.

Nick laughs. "What, so *I'm* the villain here?"

"No," I say. "Villains advance the plot. You're just a second-act complication."

He gives me a blank look, his lips rounded on the start of a question I fear very much starts with "what" and ends with "the fuck."

I guess no one ever made him read Robert McKee.

He shakes his head and flips to a fresh page in his notebook. "I need to get a preliminary statement."

"Can't that wait until tomorrow?" Isaiah asks.

"It's just a few questions for now. We'll get to the good stuff tomorrow."

I look down at my feet. I hate the very thought of sitting in a dimly lit room and going over the events of the past three days again and again, over and over, until it comes out right—no matter that this is precisely what I've done almost every day for the last eleven years. No matter that it's what I intend to do for the next fifty. It's not nearly as fun when the story's your own.

"Caitlyn's death was an accident," I blurt out. "She fell on the stairs back by the projection room. Violet carried her body to the beach because she was worried the hotel would be held liable."

Nick's eyebrows go up. "Or we could get to the good stuff now, I guess."

"How do you know that?" Isaiah asks, turning—finally—to face me.

I peer up at him. Is that disgust I see in the set of his chin? Disapproval in the shape of his mouth? Exasperation in the line of his shoulders? What is he thinking? Did I ruin this, too?

He looks down at his shirt. "Is there something on me?"

Even though my nose hurts and my knees hurt and my arms hurt and my brain hurts, I'm suddenly feeling better than I have in years. His eyes—they're crinkled at the corners.

I didn't ruin anything.

I turn to Nick, ready now.

"About Violet—"

———

Something they never talk about in the movies: loose ends. It takes nearly two weeks for the authorities to tie them up, to conduct the necessary interviews and complete the necessary paperwork and drink the necessary coffee, and until that's done we're all stuck here at the Shack. In no time at all we're cranky and crabby and cramped, and the lobby is littered with the investigators' half-empty blue-and-white Anthora cups, the remaining staff too busy or too indifferent to pick up after them.

They let most of the crew head home that first weekend, but I'm not so lucky. I'm too involved, too central, the lead actor who gets stuck doing a press junket while the supporting cast gets to throw back Jäger bombs at the hotel bar.

But routines are my business, and soon enough I fall into a tolerable one: I spend my days talking to cops from Delaware and lawyers from California, and I spend my nights in my room, staring at the ceiling, the cat curled up on my chest. I wish I could say that I'm in shock, that I'm reeling from everything that's happened, but the truth is, I'm always like this when I have to be out in the world for too many days at a time. I have to take to my bed afterward, like a Regency matron with a case of the nerves.

I suppose it doesn't help that in the past two weeks I discovered a dead body, tracked down a murderer, and made not one but *two* phone calls to strangers.

Each night Suzy and Grace join me as soon as dinner service is over, bringing plates piled high with peanut butter sandwiches—and now orange slices, too, because apparently Suzy's mother is beginning to worry about scurvy. They never ask if they're welcome and I'd never suggest they aren't, because why bother with formalities when we all know they'd just wear me down in the end.

I give the girls permission to respond however they like to the press inquiries I've been receiving since the news of Liza's death broke, and they spend hours huddling over my laptop, cackling over memes I'm already too old to understand.

Gavin, meanwhile, has adopted the habit of swinging by after last call. He likes to stretch out on the couch, his fingers laced behind his head, feet dangling over the arm, needlepoint pillows jammed under his shoulders. He doesn't say much, he just flips on the TV and cycles through the channels, grumbling under his breath about reality television, having apparently forgotten what IMDb will always remember: that he was a guest judge for three episodes of *Britain's Got Talent*.

He didn't ask if he could be here, either, but then I wouldn't expect him to.

I don't see Isaiah much. He's busy with other things. Official things. But he always checks in before he goes to sleep, poking his head through the connecting door and looking directly at me.

"Still awake?" he asks.

"Still awake," we answer.

None of us can sleep, of course.

Which isn't to say I'm not trying. But when I close my eyes, the best I can manage is to drift into something sleep-like, a place where hazy, ghoulish images lunge into view like wild beasts, but I still have the presence of mind to be able to hope—idly, distantly—that I'm just thinking of Buñuel or Dulac or Deren. I would not like to be able to come up with such things on my own.

When I'm awake I keep turning over the facts of the murder in my mind, as if we're still in the middle and haven't yet come to the end—even though we very clearly have—and before long I'm indulging in outlandish, maladaptive daydreams, that there's something else coming, some new development, some last-second twist, a revelation that the four of us aren't even really here, maybe, that we're all dreaming, or dead, killed by Tony in a darker, bloodier timeline where things went even more horribly wrong, and this is our purgatory. Or that Liza was really Caitlyn's daughter, or Tony is actually my father, or Suzy and Grace are spirits or secret twins or figments of my imagination. That Caitlyn's alive and well and living on Long Island. That I was the real killer all along.

Evil plans, long cons, elaborate conspiracies, they're all the same: narrative wish fulfillment. Because if God's playing a long game, there's no such thing as a what-if, right?

Like:

What if I'd called Annemieke earlier.

What if I hadn't gone back to the projection room that night.

What if I'd looked through that curtain and seen Tony with Liza.

What if I'd taken Beverly Glen instead of Coldwater.

What if I'd read a goddamned script.

This would all be so much easier if I only had a criminal mastermind to blame.

When I finally fall asleep for real, it's to the delicious image of Josh begging for forgiveness, tearfully confessing he was behind it all from the start.

On the third night, there's a knock on the door. Grace and Suzy look up; the cat leaps off my chest and scurries under the bed.

"Marissa? Are you there? It's Anjali."

None of us move.

None, that is, except Gavin, who lifts the remote, levels it at the television, and turns up the volume.

"I have Kyle here," Anjali calls out after a moment.

I shoot a quick look at Gavin. *Who?*

Prick, he mouths back.

But Anjali keeps knocking, so Grace drags herself to her feet with an operatic sigh and a magnificent scowl. She flips the security latch, twists the deadbolt, and removes the desk chair one of us must have wedged beneath the knob.

Anjali stops short when she sees who's in the room with me. Standing behind her is the executive who hired me.

That's his name. *Kyle.*

"We were hoping to talk to you alone," Anjali says, her voice high and uncertain.

I twist my hands in my sheets and pull myself upright. "My answer is no," I say.

"It won't take long," Kyle says. "Just a day or two of your time."

Gavin perks up for the first time all night. "Dearest," he drawls, "what is he talking about?"

"They're reworking the film," I say. "Turning it into a documentary. I'm assuming they want to put me on camera."

He falls back against the pillows. "Oh, for fuck's sake."

Kyle adjusts his glasses, clears his throat. "We just found out they're not pressing charges against Violet, and we've finally reached an agreement with the DA to get access to Tony while they're preparing for trial. So everyone else is officially on board—everyone except you."

"Why don't you cast an actor to play me?" I suggest. "It's not like anyone knows what I look like."

I mean this to be helpful, really I do, but the words come out sullen and curdled, and I'm about to apologize—when I abruptly realize I don't owe this person anything. My lips curl into a shape they're not accustomed to and then, the strangest sensation: pins and needles, beneath my fingernails.

Kyle, oblivious, comes over to crouch down in front of me.

"Marissa, this could be something really special," he says, as if that holds any weight in our industry. LA is a town of a thousand billboards for a thousand movies, and somehow, each and every one of them is *captivating, astonishing, revelatory, extraordinary.* Enough exposure to language like that and it changes you. Even the simplest of exchanges becomes an exercise in descriptive pyrotechnics. No one in Hollywood is ever just okay. They're *amazing.* They're *spectacular.* They're *great.* None of it means anything.

Strange—but I miss it terribly.

"I just want to go home," I say.

He claps his hands together. "Great. We'll do it in LA."

Gavin groans. "Read the room, Kyle. She hates your guts. She's not doing it."

Someone sucks in a sharp breath. Suzy, I think. Or maybe me.

Kyle turns to me, a wounded look on his face. "Marissa? Is that true?"

My mouth opens and closes a few times. "Does it matter?"

He straightens and shoves his sleeves up above his elbows. "Why don't I give your agent a call?"

"This isn't a negotiation," I say.

He smiles. "Everything's a negotiation."

"In that case," Gavin says, "what do I have to pay you to get the fuck out of here?"

Kyle's expression hardens. "When you're through acting like children, we'll be in touch."

They turn to leave.

I throw back the covers. "Anjali—wait."

She spins around, blinking in confusion. "What—me?"

Her complexion is dull. Her lips are pale. I'd swear her eyebrows have thinned out.

She looks like shit.

"You don't really want to do this, do you?" I ask.

A frown tugs at the corners of her mouth. "Do what?"

"Work for this *clown*," Gavin supplies.

She glances at Kyle. He's already on his phone, oblivious to everything else around him. "I mean—I have to have a job."

I climb out of bed and stand up. "Anjali, you can do better."

A muscle twitches under her eye. "That's easy for you to say. You're Amy Evans's fucking college roommate."

"Well—actually, it was grad school."

"You think *I* could get a job in this town looking like that?" She waves in the vague direction of my face. "Fuck, no. I don't get to be *weird*."

My mouth falls open. "I'm not—"

"Don't you realize how *lucky* you are? We don't all have a future Oscar winner to fall back on. So—feel free to take your big stand or whatever. I'm going to make sure I can keep paying my rent."

She stalks out of the room, slamming the door behind her.

On the sixth night, while Gavin's glowering at a married couple looking for a vacation home in Barbados, Grace clears her throat.

"Marissa?"

I let my head loll to the left. "Hmm?"

"You have an email. From Amy."

My hand hitches; I catch the cat's spine with the edge of a fingernail. She startles awake, tumbling onto the bed. She shoots me a betrayed look from under her paw.

"Marissa?" Grace asks. "Did you hear me?"

"What does it say?"

She hesitates. "It looks kind of personal."

I pull the cat back up onto my chest and stroke the bridge of her little nose.

"I'll read it later."

On the tenth day Suzy and Grace say they're thinking about making a podcast. It won't be like all those *other* true crime podcasts, they rush to assure me.

I tell them, with great affection, that I'd rather eat my own face.

On the thirteenth day, they let us leave. The girls head out first, around lunchtime, cramming an impressive amount of luggage into the back of a twelve-person van that looks just barely big enough to hold the burly, tattooed line cooks who are milling off to the side, chatting and sucking down last-second smokes. Most of the hotel's employees were excused days ago, but they stuck around to keep an eye on the girls.

Suzy slams her shoulder against the rear door until it latches shut. Then she turns to me, wiping sweat from her brow.

"I would like to give you a hug," she says, "but I also want to respect your bodily integrity."

"Because it's totally okay if you don't like hugs," Grace says, coming over.

Suzy nods. "Never forget you're the boss of your own body."

I should let them. I really should. I should gather them close and reflect on the strength of their skinny arms and the ease of their affection, the astonishing breadth of their compassion, and I should resolve, from this point forward, to set aside my fear and discomfort and displeasure, and embrace, literally and figuratively, mankind's limitless capacity for love. I can almost hear it now: the satisfying *plunk* of a character arc slotting into place.

I actually go so far as to take a small step toward them.

But maybe this arc isn't an arc. Maybe it's a loop, emphatically closed. Maybe I shouldn't have to change: a radical thought.

Too radical for me, I think. Because I don't want them to feel unappreciated or worry they're unlovable or think I'm wrong—or think *they're* wrong.

So I open my arms and beckon them near. When their fingers press against my shoulder blades, I can't help but wish I were a grasshopper or a spider or a snake so I could leave my skin behind, but I push through. I want to give them this.

At long last, they pull away.

Suzy pulls out her phone and taps at the screen. "Are you on Facebook?" she asks.

"No."

"Twitter?"

"God, no."

"Kik?"

"You're making that up."

Suzy and Grace exchange a look.

"Whatever," Suzy says, "we'll find you. We're serious about that podcast."

"And I'm serious about my face."

They're still dimpling at me through the back window when the van takes them away.

I bet I don't even last two weeks before I give in.

Gavin, predictably, gets picked up by helicopter. He doesn't bother saying good-bye. He knows it would ruin the effect.

And then it's just me and Isaiah.

We hitch a ride to the dock with Little Bob, who drops us off with minimal fanfare.

"Just doing my job," he mumbles when I try to thank him, as

if the production hadn't shut down in spectacular, public fashion. Although I suppose if anyone on the crew was somehow still drawing a salary, it would be the teamsters.

I secure my backpack and shoulder the soft-sided traveling case I ordered online. Isaiah is heading for the south end of the dock, toward the sleek cruiser Anjali chartered to transport the remaining crew. It takes me a moment to realize the suitcase rolling behind him is my own.

I run over and tug the rollaboard from his grasp. "I'm not going with you."

"Yeah, I know, you hate water. We've been over this."

"No—I mean I've arranged for an alternate mode of transportation."

He looks over my shoulder—at the other boat that's docked here. "You sure?"

I nod. "Positive."

"So this is it?"

"Yeah. Probably." I look down at my toes and wiggle them a little against the tips of my shoes. "You should probably know that I'm not really good at this."

"*This?*"

"Being in touch, I mean. Maintaining friendships. I, um—I don't really like email and I don't really like the phone. And I don't really like texting. Because whenever I try to reach out to someone I just mess it up, like I'll talk too much about P. T. Anderson or answer too many rhetorical questions or text too many times in a row even though I have a Post-it on my computer that literally says, 'Don't text too many times in a row.' But you should know: That doesn't mean I won't be thinking of you."

I draw a breath and look up at him.

"Not in a creepy way," I add. "I mean I'll be wishing you well. Like—in life."

"Would it make a difference if I said I'd also accept a telegram?"

I shake my head. "How would I send a telegram? I don't even know where you live."

The corner of his mouth kicks up. "Maybe one day that'll change."

I let myself look at the crinkles next to his eyes one last time. "Good-bye, Isaiah."

I take my suitcase and head toward the other end of the dock.

"Hey, Marissa."

I turn. "Yeah?"

"How many Army Rangers does it take to change a lightbulb?"

My lips part. "How many?"

"Five. One to change the lightbulb and four to talk about it on the *Tonight Show*."

I tilt my head to the side and study his expression.

"It's funny because they love publicity," I say eventually.

"That's right."

"And you hate the Rangers."

"Yup."

"Because you're a SEAL."

He closes the distance between us and taps me, one last time, on the nose, like we've been playing charades all this time and we've just figured out the answer together. My smile's so big I think my face is breaking.

"See?" he says. "We'll get there in the end."

SUZY KOH: I'm so sorry, but we read your email.

AMY EVANS: Oh my God, you mean *the* email? The furious, five-page list of all the reasons she's my favorite goddamned person in this whole, cursed world?

SUZY KOH: That's right.

GRACE PORTILLO: It was awesome.

AMY EVANS: Would you believe it took her ten days to respond to that?

SUZY KOH: I definitely would. She looked terrified when it came in.

AMY EVANS: She's such a goober. If she would just tell me what she's worried about, we'd be able to figure it out. But instead she just spins out these wild stories in her head. Did you know she thought I wanted to *marry* Josh? I mean—*what*? I liked the guy, but we were never that serious. I just got mad at her for keeping things from me and for automatically assuming I'd pick a dude over her. What the *hell*.

GRACE PORTILLO: So you've made up?

AMY EVANS: I love Marissa—I'll always love Marissa. And I tell her all the time. Sometimes I just have to squeeze her shoulders until she remembers it's true.

SUZY KOH: I heard you're making a new movie together.

AMY EVANS: Yeah, we start shooting in April, I can't wait. It's going to be fucking unbelievable—and we have the most amazing new producer.

THIRTY-TWO

t's different this time, stepping onto Billy Lyle's boat. I have a cat with me, for one thing.

"Best bring her up to the bridge," Billy says, eyeing the traveling case.

"You think?"

"Well—cats don't like water, right?"

We both look down. The cat's pushing her face against the netting at the front of the bag, purring loudly.

"I don't think she's very good at being a cat," I say. But I hold the carrier out to him all the same.

Billy slings the bag over his shoulder and heads for the ladder. He looks back when he realizes I'm not following. His gaze drops to my hands: They're plucking at the ties on the nearest life preserver.

"It's the highest point on the boat," he says after a moment. "The last to go under, if we sink."

"Not if we're hit side-on by a rogue wave."

"In that case it won't matter where you are."

My brows pinch together. "Is that supposed to make me feel better?"

He shrugs. "Just stating a fact. Whether or not it makes you feel better is up to you."

He heads up to the bridge; I stay where I am. After a moment, the boat pulls away from the dock, and I let myself gaze at Kickout, at the Shack, at a place I know I will never think of with anything like affection or pleasure or nostalgia no matter how lovely and dream-like it appears now, gilded by the late-afternoon light. In just a few minutes the island will be small enough that I'll be able to squish out the sight of it with my finger and thumb.

Good riddance.

I make my way to the front of the boat, and soon Billy comes back down to join me. He braces his forearms on the railing, canting his upper body forward, out over the water—still, after everything that's happened, drawn back to the island.

His hair, I think, is the kind of blond you're supposed to grow out of.

Something unfurls inside me, something slow and warm and gentle, and I decide to do something about it.

"The sun's setting," I say.

Billy gives me an unimpressed look. "It tends to do that."

"You know what they call this—in movies, I mean? They call this 'magic hour.'"

He takes a beat, then makes an encouraging noise in the back of his throat. I go on.

"It's not *really* an hour, though. It's an optically advantageous period during which the sun is approximately ten degrees above the horizon."

I watch Billy very carefully out of the corner of my eye.

"It depends on the season, then," he says.

I let out a breath. "Yes."

"And the weather."

I nod. "Yes."

"And the latitude and the topography."

"*Yes*. Everything has to be exactly right. Perfect."

"So—that's why it's magic."

I scuff my left foot against the deck.

"No," I say. "It's magic because it cuts down on the electric bill."

There's nothing natural about the sound he makes in response: It's the noise you'd make if you taught yourself to laugh by breaking up someone else's delight into bits and pieces and trying to put it back together again. You can hear the cracks.

I pull my ponytail over my shoulder and pick at the ends. "Billy—do you think it's better to be alone?"

He nods, and the motion carries down through his neck and spine, so in the end, his entire body rocks in acknowledgment.

My face must show my disappointment, because he gives me a look of patent disbelief. "What were you expecting? I live on a *boat*."

"Not because you *want* to."

"Marissa, I have family in Rhode Island. An aunt and uncle. They are—unaccountably fond of me. After I got out of the hospital, they offered to set me up in a little place outside Providence. They even found a job for me."

"Why didn't you go? Wouldn't that have been easier than staying here?"

The corner of his mouth twists. Up or down, who knows, and with him I'm not so sure it matters. "Wherever you go," he says, "there you are."

He falls quiet, then, and I suppose I don't have much hope of figuring out what he's thinking, because while there are at least ten kinds of silences that could apply in this particular situation, not a single one would apply to this particular person.

Instead, I curl my fingers around the railing and wait.

The water's calm today, the boat steady, sure, whisper-soft, and when my eyes land on a wedge of unbroken horizon, it's not so hard to believe that we're not moving at all. It's the kind of stillness you'd expect to be broken by a dog barking in the distance.

Billy shifts, finally, a roll of his shoulders as easy and inevitable as the roll of the ocean.

"I suppose," he says, "it's not so terrible if you find the right person."

I blink. "You really think so?"

"I do."

I pry my fingers off the railing.

"Okay. Good." I shake the feeling back into my hands. "Good."

I angle my body to the left; toward him, just a little.

Then, when I realize it doesn't bother me, just a little more.

If I look forward, I know, I'll be able to see the ferry terminal in Lewes. There'll be a car waiting for me there, and a driver. Not Isaiah. Just a regular guy.

My flight doesn't leave until late tonight, but I'll go straight to the airport—Baltimore this time—and even though I'm flying coach, I'll pay to use the premium lounge, because business travelers want nothing to do with *anyone*. I'll sneak the cat cold cuts from the buffet and watch *The Right Stuff* on my computer while I wait. Then I'll sit in a window seat on the flight to Vegas and an aisle seat on the flight to Burbank, and I'll take a Lyft to the pet-friendly apartment I leased over the phone this morning. Tomorrow Nell will send me a list of open assignments, and I'll pick whichever one starts first, even if it's *Transformers*. I'll see if I can't work up the guts to text Isaiah.

Eventually, I'll call Amy.

But right now—

I check my watch.

—right now I have seventeen minutes left. Seventeen minutes in this light, in this air, in this unexpected company. Seventeen minutes moving though the world with someone by my side. Someone who understands me. Not talking, not touching, not looking into each other's eyes, not needing to apologize, not needing to explain why.

If this were a movie, it would make for a terrible ending.

But it's not, and it isn't.

ACKNOWLEDGMENTS

I am supremely grateful to Allison Lorentzen, Norma Barksdale, and the entire team at Viking, not just for shepherding this story to publication with tenderness and skill, but also for the incredible patience they have demonstrated over the past five years. I had to write three hundred pages of a terrible book before I could get to this one, and a lesser publisher would have made me put that terrible book out into the world. Thank you all for your faith in me.

As ever, none of this would be possible—on levels both mundane and profound—were it not for my agent, Kate Garrick.

My first readers—Ellen Amato, Megan Crane, David Lapidus, Robyn Morrison, and Scott Korb—managed to talk me through the mess that was my rough draft without killing my self-esteem, and for that I can't thank them enough.

Sam Chidley at The Karpfinger Agency also read the manuscript in its early stages. I can't imagine what this book would look like without the benefit of his notes, which were unparalleled in their discernment. Ivy McFadden had the unenviable task of copyediting my sentences, which she did with grace and aplomb, nudging plot, characters, and dialogue into place along the way.

Steph Cha, batting cleanup, helped guide me through one last pass, generously allowing me to leech onto her exquisite sense of language and character.

ACKNOWLEDGMENTS

All mistakes are my own. Anything you like is almost certainly due to the hard work and generous spirit of the people listed here; otherwise, it probably comes from *Fleabag* season 2.

My friends and family have put up with so much from me over the past few years—but I have also put up with so much from them, without hesitation, and I will neither thank them here nor require thanks from them in return. I will, instead, continue to love them and support them and make space for them as long as I am lucky enough to be able to do so.

AVAILABLE AND COMING SOON
FROM PUSHKIN VERTIGO

Jonathan Ames

You Were Never Really Here

A Man Named Doll

Olivier Barde-Cabuçon

The Inspector of Strange and Unexplained Deaths

Sarah Blau

The Others

Maxine Mei-Fung Chung

The Eighth Girl

Amy Suiter Clarke

Girl, 11

Candas Jane Dorsey

The Adventures of Isabel

Martin Holmén

Clinch

Down for the Count

Slugger

Elizabeth Little

Pretty as a Picture

Louise Mey

The Second Woman

Joyce Carol Oates (ed.)

Cutting Edge

John Kåre Raake

The Ice

RV Raman

A Will to Kill

Tiffany Tsao

The Majesties

John Vercher

Three-Fifths

Emma Viskic

Resurrection Bay

And Fire Came Down

Darkness for Light

Those Who Perish

Yulia Yakovleva

Punishment of a Hunter